THE
Matchmaker's
Lonely
Heart

OTHER PROPER ROMANCES
BY NANCY CAMPBELL ALLEN

My Fair Gentleman
The Secret of the India Orchid
Beauty and the Clockwork Beast
Kiss of the Spindle
The Lady in the Coppergate Tower
Brass Carriages and Glass Hearts

THE MATCHMAKER'S LONELY HEART

NANCY CAMPBELL ALLEN

SHADOW
MOUNTAIN

*To all of us who survived, struggled,
and perhaps lost loved ones in 2020
and beyond, my love and affection.*

*Somehow, the earth keeps turning,
and the sun comes up again.*

Library of Congress Cataloging-in-Publication Data
Names: Allen, Nancy Campbell, 1969– author.
Title: The matchmaker's lonely heart / Nancy Campbell Allen.
Other titles: Proper romance.
Description: [Salt Lake City] : Shadow Mountain, [2021] | Series: Proper romance | Summary: "Amelie Hampton is a hopeless romantic who offers relationship advice to individuals who place 'lonely hearts' ads in *The Marriage Gazette*. She is swept up in mystery, intrigue, and romance when a handsome detective requests her help to catch a killer who may be using the newspaper to find his next victim"—Provided by publisher.
Identifiers: LCCN 2021009367 | ISBN 9781629729275 (trade paperback)
Subjects: LCSH: Dating services—Fiction. | Nineteenth century, setting. | London (England), setting. | LCGFT: Novels. | Romance fiction. | Detective and mystery fiction. | Thrillers (Fiction)
Classification: LCC PS3551.L39644 M38 2021 | DDC 813/.54—dc23
LC record available at https://lccn.loc.gov/2021009367

Printed in the United States of America
Lake Book Manufacturing, Melrose Park, IL

10 9 8 7 6 5 4 3 2 1

CHAPTER 1

My Dear Miss Franklin,

I can only imagine the despondency you must feel at your mother's insistence that you entertain Mr. B's suit. Of course you may continue writing to me for advice or commiseration! You and I know of your desire to marry for love, but your mother is clearly of the elder generation who prefer to err on the side of practicality. Perhaps you might consider a blunt approach, as the elderly often require direct speaking, whether due to hearing loss or lack of compassion brought on by age, one can only speculate...

—Letter from Miss A. Hampton,
THE MARRIAGE GAZETTE

Amelie Hampton blinked in surprise as her normally unflappable aunt called her to task over a mistake that, frankly, Amelie didn't believe was a mistake at all. Poor judgment, at most.

"Amelie," Sally Hampton said, placing her palms down on the rich mahogany desk in her office. "I am aware of the value you place on a marriage based on love and romance. I will also

1

admit that you have an uncanny ability to match personality traits of our clients and your record of success is impressive."

Amelie opened her mouth to speak, but Sally held up her hand. "However, today's afternoon post delivered the third letter I have received from an irate mother who insists her daughter's head has been filled with 'stuff and nonsense' by a staff member named 'Emily.' As we do not have an EMily, but only an AHmelie, I must presume she is referencing you."

Sally's raised brows met the straight black line of her fashionably cut fringe. Her green eyes fixed Amelie securely to the chair opposite the desk. Sally Hampton had built a business around *The Marriage Gazette*, the floundering publication she'd acquired and then turned into a respectable social entity.

Amelie chewed her lip, feeling both defensive and mortified, before blurting, "I am sorry, Sally, but Miss Franklin is despondent—her mother insists Mr. Brocklehurst would be a good husband for her, but the man is odious and twice her age. I merely suggested she carefully consider her own feelings on the matter, as it will be she, and not her mother, who finds herself wed to the man. All other advice in my letter to her was conventional." She shifted in her chair. "Mostly."

Sally's expression did not change, but she finally released a small sigh and sat in the handsome leather chair she'd purchased a year before on a shopping trip to Morocco. "Dearest, I could not agree more with you, but we must tread carefully with our subscribers, lest the *Gazette's* reputation fall into worse straits than it was when I found it."

She picked up a piece of paper that had been folded into an envelope. She scanned the paper and then tossed it back down, finally cupping her chin in her hand.

"Amelie, I appreciate your zeal and your honest approach

to life. You have always spoken your mind, and I love you for it. You must, however, learn the art of finesse. A sense of polite manipulation, if you will, wherein you carefully choose your words and then craft your advice to young women in such a way that your message folds seamlessly into the practical wisdom our subscribers expect from us."

Amelie's heart sank. Aunt Sally was smooth and polished. Even hailing from the Notorious Branch of the Hampton family, she could charm her way into the most exclusive events of the Season. Amelie was not smooth and polished, and as she hadn't obtained such traits by the advanced age of one-and-twenty, she doubted there was any hope of doing so in the future.

"This is why Deborah and Sophia both were married by the time they were my age," she said. "They have finesse in their bones, whereas I have all the charm of that troll." She nodded at the small Norwegian figurine on Sally's desk.

Sally's expression remained flat. "Self-pity is not your natural gift, of that I assure you. Now, chin up. You have a good brain, and you can learn. Aside from that, this troll has enormous amounts of character. As for your sisters—well, never mind."

Amelie's lips twitched, and she rubbed a finger under her nose to hide the smile. Deborah and Sophia were products of their father's first marriage and were considerably older than Amelie and Stephen. She had always fallen in her elder sisters' shadows, and her brother, Stephen, one year her junior, was insufferably obnoxious. Their parents had died when Amelie was young, leaving Stephen legally under Deborah's care, and Amelie with Aunt Sally. Amelie had been well aware at the time that she was the luckier of the two, and her conviction had only grown stronger through the years.

Sally's expression gentled. "If I did not believe in your ability to do well here, I'd not have hired you. You have successfully matched more couples than the rest of us combined."

Amelie's heart lifted fractionally. "You'll allow me to continue answering correspondence? And writing essays?"

"Of course. I trust you will understand what I expect from this point forward?"

"Yes, Sally. Thank you. I shall be the soul of practicality."

The corner of Sally's mouth lifted in a wry smile. "Not too much, I hope. I should hate to see that spark dimmed."

A soft knock interrupted them, and at Sally's command, the door cracked open. Charlotte and Evangeline, Amelie's cousins and fellow *Gazette* employees, poked their heads through.

"Go on, then," Sally said and waved at Amelie. "The three of you have desks to tidy before we close."

Amelie jumped up and made a dash for the door before remembering she must Walk with Decorum. She slowed marginally, but when she reached the door, she turned back, her long, blue skirt swirling around her ankles. "Thank you again, Sally. Shall we see you at Bloomsbury this weekend?"

"I have business requiring my attention here in Town, but perhaps we'll go to Gunthers for ices when I am finished. With the weather changing, we shan't want cold treats much longer." Sally eyed the three young women with something suspiciously like affection before she straightened and waved them off again. "Go, or I shall never finish this pile of paperwork."

Amelie grinned and exited the office with her cousins, whose curiosity was palpable, and softly closed the office door behind her.

CHAPTER 2

Two souls joined in love and devoted to one another's happiness must be the very embodiment of life's splendid gifts.

—*From "Essays on Eternal Bliss" by Miss A. Hampton,*
THE MARRIAGE GAZETTE

Detective Michael Baker stood on the bank of the Thames and looked out over the dark water. Fog hung thick in patches, and an unseasonably cold summer wind blew. He turned his collar up against the cold and stifled a yawn, wistfully thinking of the warm bed he'd left when the constables had banged on his door.

"What do we know of the victim?" His breath fogged around his mouth before dissipating into the cold air.

"Precious little," one constable said. "No information on her 'cept a locket that says 'To my darling Marie.'"

Michael nodded. From the looks of it, the body hadn't been in the water long. Her face was white, almost blue, and a large gash across her forehead stood out in stark relief. Her sightless eyes were deep green, he noted, even through the thick film that often signified death, and he surmised her wet, tangled hair was dark blonde. He put her age at the early twenties.

Voices to his right heralded the arrival of the coroner from St. Vincent's Mortuary. Dr. Neville was stooped and aged, but he impatiently shook off the pair of constables who were escorting him, leaning instead on a sturdy walking cane that was his signature accessory.

Michael nodded at the doctor, and the constables moved out of his way.

Dr. Neville knelt at the victim's head and, with a light hand, lifted her eyelids, turned her head to the left and the right, and sighed.

"I'll check for missing persons reports at the station," Michael said. "Perhaps someone has already reported her absence."

Dr. Neville grunted his agreement and lifted her left hand. "A wedding band. There's a husband somewhere."

"Do you suppose the head wound is the cause of death?"

The doctor lifted a shoulder and then shoved to his feet with his cane. "Can't know for certain. We'll be wanting an inquest, in any case. If we cannot ascertain her identity, we'll notify the papers of a public viewing following the autopsy. Someone will know her."

Public curiosity in the ghoulish often became an ungainly spectacle, which Michael hoped to avoid.

Detective Nathaniel Winston, Michael's new police partner, approached. "Do we need a sketch?" Winston asked when he reached the scene.

"Not certain. Could be an accident or suicide," Michael told him.

Another gust of wind blew across the water, bringing with it a chill that cut through Michael's coat. "Let's do a sketch," he said to Winston. "You're fast, and we don't want to later regret not having one. She did not die here, so we are not looking at the scene of her death. Not worth bringing out a photographer; we'll settle for that later at the morgue."

Winston took a book and pencil from his pocket and flipped through it, instructing a constable who held a lantern to bring it closer. "Dr. Neville," he said as he began drawing, "pleasure to see you this evening."

Dr. Neville snorted. "This morning, you mean. This is what happens when one comes to rely on an underling. He is 'indisposed' at the moment."

"Ah," Michael said, "I did wonder why you attended this time."

The older man scowled, his thick, white eyebrows nearly touching. "It means my instincts were correct from the beginning. Never rely on the dependability of an assistant—even if he is family."

It was well known among those gathered that Neville's grandson left something to be desired as a professional.

Michael hid a smile and moved to Winston's side. He looked over his partner's shoulder and was again impressed with the man's talent. Winston had captured the scene well and quickly, adding detail and depth with a few expert strokes of his pen.

"She washed ashore?" Winston asked as he continued drawing.

"She surfaced, and a gentleman walking along the promenade notified us. Constable Gundersen pulled her in." Michael nodded to the constable who stood wrapped in a blanket, drinking a hot beverage. "We'll attend the good doctor's inspection at the morgue in a few hours."

Winston beckoned the constable with the lantern to follow

him and moved to the other side, looking closely at the scene and continuing to sketch.

While he did so, Michael leaned down close to the young woman's head and examined her face, wishing her ghost still tarried close enough to offer clues. He almost smiled. His sister, Clarissa, believed in ghosts, but he did not. She would likely laugh at his current train of thought. He swallowed and frowned, realizing that the victim was probably near Clarissa's age.

The dead young woman had a family somewhere. Where was the husband? Her clothing bore evidence of her status as one of the respected upper middle class. Her skin was smooth, and a closer examination of her hands showed a woman who probably did little more than the most basic of household chores, perhaps after the maid had left for the day.

Michael understood all too well the difficulties of a life in Town when the fates had not been kind. There was no more justice in finding a fallen woman dead than one who lived a respectable life; tragedy was tragedy, and he did not differentiate. He did not, however, appreciate an unsolved puzzle, and the woman on the ground was definitely that.

Why on earth had she been in the Thames?

"I believe I'm finished," Winston said. "Shall I see you in a few hours at the Yard?"

"I'm headed there now to look through the missing persons reports. I doubt I'll get much sleep if I go home. Perhaps I'll have something for us to go on when you arrive."

Winston nodded and tore out the paper from his sketchbook. He handed it to Michael, adding, "Better put this in the new file, then."

"I shall send word when I begin the examination," Dr. Neville told them.

Michael nodded and glanced down again at the victim as two constables prepared her for transport to the morgue.

Winston frowned. "Pity we do not even have a name."

"The locket inscription reads 'Marie,'" Michael said as the men covered the woman's face with a sheet. "Someone will be missing her."

CHAPTER 3

When minutes spent apart seem like hours, when even a moment's separation is akin to the worst kind of torture, one may take comfort in the fact that she has found true love.

—From "Essays on Eternal Bliss" by Miss A. Hampton,
THE MARRIAGE GAZETTE

Hours after they pulled the body from the river, Michael donned a fresh shirt he kept hanging in his office at Scotland Yard's Criminal Investigation Division. He finished cleaning himself up as constables arrived to relieve the night shift in the outer office, where desks were lined in two rows. His thoughts were heavy, and he was tired, but good-natured bantering and sounds of the building awakening were a welcome reminder that life moved ever forward.

He glanced at the second desk across his office and for a moment, he imagined Stanley sitting there. Stanley had been his childhood best friend, and they had joined the Metropolitan Police force together as soon as they were of an age.

Stanley, who'd been Michael's partner in the CID.

Stanley, who'd married Michael's sister, Clarissa.

Stanley, who'd been killed six months ago in the line of duty.

The loss still stung, would always sting. He knew it would lessen with time, but he felt his friend's death as keenly as when his own father had passed when Michael was a young child. The loss of his mother ten years ago had been a painful blow, and he still thought of her daily. But losing Stanley had been like losing a part of himself. They had grown into life together, guarded each other through thick and thin, and there was nobody else on earth with whom he'd have trusted his sister's well-being and heart.

But he was gone, and Clarissa was now a young widow with a newborn daughter. Their younger brother, Alexander, was a grown young adult with the mind of a child, and Michael had always known he would bear responsibility for Alexander for the rest of his life. He had never begrudged it.

But Alexander had surprised him and Clarissa both, when, after Stanley's death, Alexander had proclaimed he would move into Clarissa's house to guard her and the baby. Michael had objected initially, until Clarissa had privately expressed to him that Alexander's presence in her too-quiet home would be a blessing.

Michael leaned against his desk as he fastened his cuffs. He looked at the empty desk and hoped he would do his friend proud, that he would reach the end of his life knowing he had carried Stanley's responsibilities to the very last.

Stanley had been the lighter of the two of them, the happier. He'd always teased Michael for being too serious, and he'd been one of the few who made him truly laugh. Michael's serious nature had settled in with a vengeance after Stanley died, and while he was aware of it, he was at a loss about how to fix it. He wasn't sure he wanted it to be fixed. If he kept the lightness at bay, the darkness wasn't nearly so noticeable when it descended.

As he straightened and shrugged into his jacket, he looked at the open file on his desk with Nathaniel Winston's sketch inside. After hours of work, Michael believed the victim's name was Marie Verite Radcliffe; her husband had reported her missing the day before. When Winston arrived, the two of them would go to the address provided and speak with Mr. Radcliffe. They would show him a photograph of the deceased woman that had been taken earlier at the morgue and then quickly developed. He would watch the man's reaction and gauge the showing of shock and grief. He hoped it would be genuine. Everyone grieved differently, but sometimes . . . sometimes it rang false, and Michael simply *knew*.

He heard Winston's chuckle in the outer room and glanced up to see him through the glass in the door. Michael had been irrationally resentful when Winston transferred from another division to fill the vacancy left by Stanley's death. But, while the bond with Winston would never be the same as the one he'd had with Stanley, they got on well, and Winston had been wise enough to ease his way into the department with subtlety.

Winston entered the office and nodded. "Quite the crowd out there today."

"Indeed. Not so strange for a Friday, however."

Winston started to shrug out of his greatcoat but paused, motioning toward the paperwork on Michael's desk. "The new victim's file?"

"Yes. Not much in it, but I believe we might have a name. Have you time for a visit?"

"Absolutely." He settled his greatcoat back on his shoulders with a smile. "Have we received word from the coroner's office?"

"Just the photo of the deceased taken this morning. I believe Neville is beginning his examination. Which gives us time to call on"—Michael consulted the file with the husband's information—"Mr. Harold Radcliffe, solicitor." He donned his coat and hat and gathered the slim file in one hand.

As they crossed through the common area, he glanced over at the division director's office. John Ellis was a shrewd and exacting man in his mid-thirties. He was also the youngest Investigative Director of record and had proven himself worthy of the job, despite the naysayers who'd suggested his position was only because of the far-reaching influence of his titled and prominent father. Behind the glass in his door, Director Ellis was playing host to a pair of minor dignities from Paris.

Winston gave Michael a grin as they passed. "Third consecutive day the director has performed the duties of a diplomat. I see the commissioner has delegated his responsibilities beautifully."

"They arrived for their appointment thirty minutes early." Michael pushed the door open, and they stepped out into a drizzly rain. "We're sure to hear the details later."

"I certainly hope so. I've an aunt who writes romantic novels, and she is ever looking for fresh anecdotes regarding the prestigious and well-to-do."

They hurried through the rain to a CID carriage, which was different than customary cabs only in the discreet lettering on the side of its otherwise bland appearance. Michael gave the driver the address, and he and Winston settled in for the short ride.

"Bloomsbury, is it?" Winston said. "Respectable, upper middle class—one might think such folk are immune to disasters such as this."

"We both know disasters do not favor one over another. Our work might be a sight simpler if death restricted itself to one class."

They rode in silence for a time until Winston spoke again. "I must ask, and hope I do not irritate you with it, but some of the lads at the Yard mentioned your undercover assignment last year. From what I could gather, you played the part of a tailor very well." Winston's lips twitched. "A noble enough profession, to be sure, but I'd have thought a cover as a pugilist, perhaps, might have been more readily convincing."

Michael smiled. "Perhaps my secret personae shall be written in future policing manuals and held up as a shining example." He sighed. "The long and short of it is my mother was a seamstress and my father was a constable. He died when I was young, and although my mother was accomplished, she was often behind on orders and needed help. I learned quickly."

Michael managed a smile despite the heaviness of the memories. Plenty of men were tailors, but when neighborhood bullies had realized Michael was aiding his mother, the seamstress, the beatings and harassment had been harsh. He had known the last laugh, though, as he'd continued growing while the rest of them eventually stopped. He'd grown taller than the others in his early teens and then filled into his broadening frame.

Winston laughed. "I have gone undercover but once, and it was an experience I'd rather not repeat."

"Oh?"

"I was obliged to travel with a circus caravan."

Michael chuckled. "Did you throw knives? Tame lions?"

Winston shook his head, and a smile crept onto the corners of his mouth. "I was a fortune-teller."

Michael's laugh grew as the carriage bumped along the busy road. "You must read my tea leaves soon."

"I was not a very good fortune-teller." Winston's smile broadened, and he added, "I was only just able to stay ahead of angry customers who sought my head on a platter."

"Perhaps you were too specific. Better to stick with generalities, I should think."

"All well and good until the one sitting across the table demands more detail." Winston shook his head, his smile rueful. "I did not pretend to speak to loved ones who had passed, though. My scruples occasionally made their way to the fore."

"I suppose the bigger question is whether or not your ruse was successful overall." Michael settled back into his seat and withdrew from his pocket a fountain pen that had been Stanley's favorite. He absently twirled the pen along his fingers.

"Mostly. Arrests were made, but one criminal escaped. A minor player, but sometimes those resurface."

Michael nodded. "One hopes. There is little joy to be found in a case that is concluded but never fully closed."

They rode in silence, and Michael thought again of Stanley, who had been doing just that when he'd been killed—wrapping up loose ends, chasing the one member of a small thieving operation who had gotten away. Michael rubbed his finger along a stain on the dark green barrel of the pen. If only Michael had accompanied him that night, if only Stanley had waited to be certain Michael had received his message. If only, if only . . . It was a constant litany, and Michael sometimes heard Stanley's voice in his head telling him to stop the self-recrimination and get on with life.

At length, the carriage stopped at the door of a picturesque townhome on a tidy street. Michael braced himself for whatever he and Winston might encounter on the other side of the door. He was still learning the ins and outs of Winston's methods, but the man was both trustworthy and capable, with a good amount of policing experience under his belt.

After instructing the driver to wait, the men approached the door, and Michael firmly struck the door knocker against its metal rest. Before long, a housekeeper answered, and when Michael opened his coat to reveal the detective badge pinned to his vest, her eyes widened. She stood back to let them in.

"Me employer, 'e's a late sleeper, he is. If ya tell me yer business, I'll relay the message."

Michael smiled at the woman, stifling a retort about being unwilling to provide fodder for servant gossip. "We must speak with Mr. Radcliffe. It is a matter of some urgency, and I would ask that you rouse him from his sleep."

"Perhaps, before you retrieve him, you might be of some help, miss?" Winston smiled warmly, and Michael was impressed with the man's ability to charm.

"*Mrs.* Pickleford." The housekeeper straightened her thin shoulders.

"Excellent," Winston continued. "Mrs. Pickleford, what news have you of Mrs. Radcliffe? Is she currently in residence?"

Mrs. Pickleford frowned and shook her head. "I am new 'ere, so I do not know much. Presume she's visiting family in Marseilles. She took nofing with her, though, which is strange. 'Er personal belongings is all still here."

"And what has Mr. Radcliffe to say about this?" Winston continued.

Mrs. Pickleford lifted her shoulders. "She goes to 'er family often, but he wired 'em and they've not seen 'er either. 'E talked to the police yesterday morning."

Michael flipped open the pocketbook he used for note taking. "How long had she been missing by that time?"

Mrs. Pickleford scrunched her forehead. "Mmm, two days?"

"Mrs. Pickleford?" A male voice carried down the front steps. "Who is here?"

"Detectives, Mr. Radcliffe, sir. 'Ere to ask about Mrs. Radcliffe, I s'pect."

"Show them to the parlor immediately. I shall be but another moment."

Mrs. Pickleford nodded toward the open door to their left. "Ye heard 'im."

"Thank you, kind madam," Winston said.

Michael followed Winston into the parlor, where he noted several small pieces of statuary, some broken into multiple pieces, sitting on a mahogany hutch near the small fireplace.

"Fancies himself an archaeologist," Winston murmured as he looked at the collection. "One must have hobbies, I suppose."

"You do not approve?" Michael asked.

"There are certain pieces that do no harm in a private collection, but all too often, greed sets in. Rather than donating extraordinary finds to a museum where all can admire, we are left to imagine."

Michael looked again at the pieces carefully showcased on the hutch. "I admit to having no eye for extraordinary finds, but I am rather taken with the craftsmanship of this mahogany piece that holds them."

Winston lifted a brow and nodded. "Beautiful. I wonder if it is a commissioned piece."

"It was indeed a commissioned piece," a voice said from the doorway.

"Mr. Radcliffe?" Michael asked.

"The very same. Dare I hope you've come with news of my wife?" Radcliffe was classically handsome. He wore his clothing well, and his dark hair was neatly styled. Michael imagined those ice-blue eyes had won—or broken—their fair share of hearts.

"We may come bearing unfortunate news, and I must apologize in advance for it," Michael said. "A woman was found last night in the Thames, and she now lies in the morgue. We are not certain she is your wife, but she bears a gold locket around her neck that is inscribed 'To my dearest Marie.'"

Radcliffe lost all color in his face, and he swayed, bracing himself against a side table.

"Perhaps we should sit?" Winston offered.

Radcliffe swallowed and nodded, settling onto the sofa. The detectives took the two chairs near the hearth.

"You are familiar with the locket, then?" Michael continued.

"I . . . I . . ." Radcliffe cleared his throat. "I gave my wife just such a locket a few months ago on our wedding day." He looked first at Winston, and then at Michael. "Could there be two such lockets in existence? Perhaps . . . perhaps somebody admired Marie's locket and had another made? Surely there are many women named Marie."

Michael felt a twinge of sympathy. The man's shock seemed genuine. "Yet just yesterday you reported your wife missing," he said gently. "I have a post-mortem photo of the woman we found; will you look at it?"

Radcliffe nodded.

Michael handed over the photo, and Radcliffe stared at the image, his mouth slack. A dramatic shudder wracked his whole body, then he closed his eyes and handed back the photo. "That is my Marie."

"Are you comfortable accompanying us to the morgue for formal identification of the body? Or perhaps another family member could perform the task?" Michael asked. His initial feeling of trust toward Radcliffe was beginning to waver.

Radcliffe shook his head. "They are in Marseilles. Marie left them behind in France when we married and returned to London. I had hoped—" He shook his head. "I've held to the hope she had simply decided to return to France for a visit; she has done so twice in recent months. When I realized she'd left behind all of her belongings, everything she normally takes with her in the past, I just knew—" He stood and paced behind the sofa.

"How do you suppose she might have ended up in the river?" Winston asked, and then paused. "Would she have had reason to be walking on the promenade with friends, or perhaps an admirer?"

Radcliffe stopped pacing and glared at Winston. "You're asking if my wife cuckolded me? Most emphatically not." He took a breath and released a sigh, his brows pulling tightly into a frown. "I fear she may have done something . . . illegal."

"What do you suspect?" Michael pressed.

Radcliffe's pause stretched interminably. "I suspect she may have injured herself."

A heavy silence filled the air. "Had she mentioned anything, or acted in a way that supports your theory?" Winston asked.

Radcliffe gripped the back of the sofa, and his head drooped. "I cannot bear to tarnish her good name." He cleared his throat. "She was an angel."

"Perhaps we have put the cart before the horse," Michael

said, his instinct warning him to doubt Radcliffe's performance. "We've still to visit the morgue. Then we will know for certain whether the deceased is your wife or perhaps someone else who coincidentally wears a locket similar to Mrs. Radcliffe's."

Radcliffe looked up. "If that photograph is accurate, I've no doubt the dead woman is my wife. Let us visit the morgue quickly. I've no wish to prolong the suspense."

Michael and Winston both stood, and Winston nodded at Radcliffe. "If the victim is not your wife, we shall double our efforts to locate her."

"'Victim'?" Radcliffe repeated, color returning to his face. "You suspect someone of killing her?"

Winston's brows inched up in surprise. "Certainly not. I only meant that she was the recipient of intentional or unintentional harm—a victim of circumstance."

"Of course, of course." Radcliffe rubbed a shaky hand across his forehead. "It is only . . . I am just so very . . ."

Michael nodded. "We understand, sir. The shock of devastating news is never pleasant. Detective Winston and I are going to St. Vincent's straightaway. Would you prefer to join us in our carriage or take your own?"

Radcliffe shook his head as though having difficulty processing the question. "I'll have my carriage readied. If the unfortunate woman at St. Vincent's is indeed my Marie, I shall have a multitude of details to see to, arrangements to make. Such things will take time."

"Surely you would be forgiven for taking a day to yourself," Winston suggested. "The details will wait."

"No, I am at my best when moving, when I've a plan. I fear if I rest for even a moment, I'll go mad." Radcliffe waited at the door while Mrs. Pickleford fetched his jacket. He shrugged into it and tugged on the crisp cuffs of his sleeves.

The ride to St. Vincent's was quick, and Michael barely had time to confer with Winston. "Everybody grieves differently, reacts to shocking news differently," Michael said. "Even so, my inclination is to believe he is not telling the entire truth."

"I agree." Winston nodded, his gaze fixed on the small window behind Michael where Radcliffe's carriage followed. "He may be perfectly innocent regarding knowledge of his wife's whereabouts, but I am always suspect of crocodile tears."

Michael nodded, pleased that his new partner shared his instincts.

The carriage rocked to a halt, and Michael and Winston waited for Mr. Radcliffe to join them.

The morgue boasted high ceilings and gothic architecture, and Dr. Neville's domain bore all the hallmarks of a well-oiled machine. The ancient stone floor was mopped and scrubbed twice daily, sometimes more, and the white brick walls reflected the light from arched windows.

Dr. Neville waved the three men over to the two gurneys in the center of the room. Michael provided quick introductions, and the doctor nodded gravely at Mr. Radcliffe. "I am sorry you must do this painful thing." He carefully lifted the sheet from the young woman's face, and Radcliffe stared, wide-eyed, first at the dead woman's face, and then to the detectives.

"This is my Marie," he choked out. He looked at Neville and asked, "What happened to her?"

"I've yet to determine cause of death," the doctor told him quietly. "Once the autopsy is concluded—"

"Autopsy?" Radcliffe shook his head quickly. "We mustn't, we cannot. Marie's family is religious, and they will take exception to cutting apart—" He swallowed convulsively. "It would absolutely destroy her mother. I must take Marie to France immediately. They will want to bury her in the family plot, and I can do none other than honor their wishes."

Michael studied the man, whose distress was evident but somehow also excessive. "We understand your concerns, Mr. Radcliffe, but an autopsy is necessary. We do not know how she died."

"What does it matter?" Radcliffe turned angry eyes on him. "She is gone!" He gulped back a sob and leaned over the body. He kissed her cheek, and cried, "Marie, why? Darling, why have you left me?"

Winston caught Michael's eyes, one brow raised, as he subtly took hold of Mr. Radcliffe's arm and tugged him back. "Come along, sir. Let us go somewhere we can discuss the matter."

"You cannot cut her open! I tell you right now, all three of you, that if you do so, you will kill her mother—her demise will be on your heads. I am going to visit the magistrate to see this madness halted immediately."

Winston led the man from the room, and Michael murmured to Dr. Neville, "Examine as thoroughly as you can without conducting the actual autopsy. Photograph extensively. Perhaps we shall have enough to determine whether we need an inquest." He looked at the doorway where Radcliffe and Winston had departed, and frowned. "Something is not right."

CHAPTER 4

When the moment is at hand and one happens upon her perfect mate, would that her heart recognizes him. She might then know it is true love as surely as if the clouds had parted and angelic choirs sang to honor the occasion.

—*From "Essays on Eternal Bliss" by Miss A. Hampton,*
THE MARRIAGE GAZETTE

Four months later

Rain poured and wind gusted; the cold autumn day had been a long one. Evenly spaced gas lamps punctuated the dark streets with flickering shards of light. Michael stood under the awning of a dress shop that had closed for the evening. Near the dress shop was a charming restaurant, and across the street stood a young woman.

The woman shivered in the cold and appeared to be watching a couple seated inside the restaurant near a window. She held a small, ineffectual umbrella with one gloved hand while the other clutched the edges of her coat together at her throat. The hat atop her brown hair was simple in style with few adornments, one of which was a long feather that drooped to the side under the weight of the weather.

A shopgirl, he guessed, or perhaps one of London's many new professional middle-class girls who worked as a typist or in some similar occupation. She was well-dressed, but not extravagantly so, and he suspected she led a moderately sheltered life. There was a wide-eyed look of innocence about her that was evident, even though her eyes were squinting against the wind and rain.

Or she could be very good at affecting such an image. Perhaps acting the innocent while helping a predator lure unsuspecting victims into his trap might be the game she played.

Michael had been watching her for nearly thirty minutes and was certain the object of her attention was the couple seated near the window. She had arrived before they did, had observed the initial meeting between Harold Radcliffe and a young woman, and scrutinized them closely when they entered for dinner. She'd turned away for a moment, but then returned her focus to Radcliffe and his companion. She'd been watching them—and Michael had been watching *her*—ever since.

Two months had passed since Radcliffe had taken the body of his late wife, Marie, home to her family in Marseilles. Dr. Neville had noted several suspicious details during his cursory examination of Marie's body, and Michael had begun gathering paperwork necessary to force an autopsy when the department had been served with cease and desist orders involving the death of Marie Verite Radcliffe.

The judge signing the order was one Michael knew fairly well. But when Michael requested an explanation, Judge Adams had advised the detective to "let this one go." Michael had wanted to press the issue further; but though Adams ostensibly advised caution, his words had come out sounding more threatening than friendly.

And now, Radcliffe had returned to Town, resuming his work as a solicitor at the Chancery. He'd told his clients that he had used the time away to grieve and was now prepared to face life as best as a widowed man could.

To Michael's eyes, there was something about him that brought to mind a salesman of outlandish medical cures. He had known the type both in school as a young man and as an officer, having had apprehended more than a few such men in his career.

Radcliffe was the kind of person who believed himself superior in intellect and was so confident in his own charms and cleverness as to get away with the proverbial murder. Perhaps literal murder. Michael spent his evenings tailing the man, unbeknownst to Director Ellis but with full support from Nathaniel Winston, whose suspicions had also only grown when they had been ordered to stop investigating Mrs. Radcliffe's death.

Which was how Michael came to be standing in the darkening autumn night, quietly observing the young woman who watched Radcliffe with an intensity Michael recognized in himself. It could be that the little spy was an associate of Radcliffe's dinner partner, but the partner had arrived at the restaurant before Radcliffe had, and the spy had not alerted the woman to her presence.

Michael had learned to trust his instincts, and they told him the spy was somehow involved. After a few more moments, she turned to leave, and he decided to follow. No sooner had he taken a step forward than a full omnibus crossed between them, followed by another carriage, and then another.

When the vehicles cleared, the woman was gone. He

muttered a curse under his breath and quickly crossed the street, looking left and right, finally catching a glimpse of her skirt as she disappeared into the thickly wooded park nearby.

He followed her into the darkness of the trees and blinked at the loss of light.

A rustle ahead and to his right betrayed her location, and once his eyes adjusted to the dark, he hurried forward. He caught sight of her skirt again as she made her way quickly toward the park's center. She paused at the edge of a manicured clearing to pop open her umbrella again.

A single lamp offered scant light over the trim green lawn, and as she stepped toward it, he called out to her. "Miss? Detective Baker, Criminal Investigations Division."

She gasped and whirled around, clearly startled, only to stumble and land hard on the ground. As she attempted to stand, she stammered, "Leave me alone! I shall scream!"

He opened his jacket to reveal his badge. "I mean you no harm! I am a detective, and I must ask you a few questions. Here—" He extended his hand and took long strides toward her as she scrambled along the ground. "Stop!"

She finally obeyed, gulping down a breath. "What do you want with me? I've done nothing wrong. Rarely am I alone after dark, I mind my own business, and I . . . I do not walk the streets!"

He blinked. "Miss, I am hardly accusing you of anything, much less of walking the streets. Please, take my hand."

He reached down and clasped her fingers, which were cold through her thin gloves. Her lips were blue, and she'd dropped her umbrella. Her hat had fallen off, and the rain made quick work of her coiffure. He might have known a moment's pity if he didn't suspect her of dubious association with a man he firmly believed was a criminal.

He pulled her to her feet, bracing her elbow as she steadied herself and shook her sodden skirt. She looked at him with dismay in her wide eyes, and then back down at her clothing, which was smeared with mud and dead leaves.

He picked up her umbrella and hat, handing them both to her, wary, as the look in her eyes shifted from fear to indignation.

"What is the meaning of this? I have done absolutely *nothing* wrong!" Even bedraggled, she was a pretty girl. Marie Verite Radcliffe had also been pretty. Radcliffe seemed to gravitate toward a certain type of woman, and Michael suspected the man's handsome face and artificial charm went a long way toward aiding his efforts.

Michael was soaked to the skin. He'd foolishly left his umbrella at the Yard, and his hat shielded him only so much. "Come with me, just back a few steps into the trees." He put one hand under her elbow again and extended the other. "As I said from the beginning, I only want to ask you a few questions."

Her eyes narrowed, and she sniffled, fumbling with the closure on her reticule. She withdrew a lacy handkerchief and wiped her nose.

"Please, miss, I am drenched, it is late, and I am cold."

She met his eyes for another prolonged moment before finally nodding once. "Only just right there," she said as they began walking back to the trees.

"Of course." He dropped his hand once they were better shielded from the rain. He removed his hat and ran a hand through his hair with a sigh, shivering involuntarily at the cold droplets that slipped down his neck and soaked into his collar.

He let his breath out on a short sigh and offered the woman a tight smile. "Again, I am Detective Baker. Might I have the pleasure of your name?"

She shook her umbrella to the side, her eyes darting to his face and then away. "My name is Miss Amelie Hampton." She attempted to place her hat on her head, but it wouldn't stay. She muttered something under her breath.

Michael caught the soggy thing as it fell. "Haven't you a hatpin?" he asked, handing it back to her.

"I forget them." Her brows drew together in a light frown.

"Now, then, Miss Emily Hampton, is it?"

"AHmelie, not EMily." She shook raindrops from her hat, frowning at the broken feather.

"'Hampton'? As in *the* Hamptons?"

Her lips tightened. "I fear ours is the Notorious Branch of *the* Hampton family." She paused, then hastily added, "I am not notorious, however! Quite the opposite. I am the picture of circumspection and obedience to the law."

He frowned. "Miss Hampton, I'll be brief. What is your association with Mr. Harold Radcliffe?"

She stared, mouth dropping open, and then she swallowed. She took the slightest of steps away from him, and he braced himself to pounce should she try again to run. His instincts had been correct; the young woman definitely knew Radcliffe.

She didn't run, but shook her head. "I do not know what you mean." Her eyes dropped from his face to his chest.

"I believe you *do* know what I mean. Perhaps you would be more comfortable continuing this conversation at the Yard."

Her eyes were huge, and even in the dim light, he noted

her additional pallor. He was growing less sympathetic by the moment. She knew Radcliffe, she was reluctant to reveal their relationship, and she was playing him for a fool. The innocent act was truly just that.

"No! No, I did not mean to learn his identity, truly! Or even see him. That is, I did not know beforehand who he would be, but just now I realized he was someone I recognized . . ." She trailed off and swallowed hard. "I wanted only to be sure the couple got on, that their meeting was agreeable. Miss Franklin has high hopes for this dinner, but she was afraid she would faint on the spot when meeting the gentleman. I wanted to be sure she was happy, and I couldn't force myself to wait for her report tomorrow. I assure you, I never intended to learn anything beyond that!" She paused in her ramblings and took a breath. "Are you tailing Miss Franklin? Did her mother retain you?" She frowned. "Would the woman truly hire someone to follow her daughter?"

He looked at her in confusion. What was she babbling on about? "Explain yourself, please. Who is Miss Franklin, the young woman dining with Radcliffe?"

"You do not know who she is?" She blinked. "Then why . . . what is your purpose?"

He held to his patience by a thread. "Come with me." He wrapped his fingers around her arm, deciding to hail a cab and cart her back to the Yard.

"No! Wait." She tugged her arm free and rubbed her forehead. Her hand trembled, and when she looked at him again, an involuntary shudder shook her shoulders. She wrapped her arms, umbrella and all, tightly around herself as her teeth chattered. "What was your question? Who is Miss Franklin?"

"Yes," he said, exasperated.

She licked her lips and slowly exhaled. "I am employed by *The Marriage Gazette* and have supplied some helpful . . . advice . . . to Miss Franklin via written correspondence." She scrunched her face as though frustrated. Possibly irritated. She rubbed her temple and added, "My aunt, Sally Hampton, owns the *Gazette* and oversees the publication of personal ads anonymously mailed in. The paper also offers an advice column for those with questions about courtship, marriage, and matters of the heart, as well as answering personal correspondence for those who do not wish their questions to be published."

People meeting via ads in social newspapers was nothing new; his sister threatened constantly to draft one on his behalf. He studied Miss Hampton carefully. "You say the ads are anonymous, yet you know of Mr. Radcliffe's identity."

She nodded.

"Has he enlisted your help in meeting specific young ladies? Did you introduce Miss Franklin to him?"

Her eyes widened again. "No! Certainly not, I would never be part of such subterfuge." She flushed. "Not that sort of subterfuge."

"Of what sort of subterfuge do you ordinarily take part?"

She shivered again and tightened her jaw. "I meant no harm; I am simply curious. Miss Franklin wrote to the paper some time ago, seeking private advice. She was hesitant to submit her questions into the published advice column for fear her mother would recognize it. I answered her letter in a manner that, as it turned out, was unsatisfactory to her mother. Miss Franklin, however, continued to secretly send personal letters to me as she knew I would answer her honestly. I have been corresponding with her since then, but my aunt—my employer—and Miss Franklin's mother are unaware of it."

He remained silent, encouraging her to continue her quick, rambling explanation.

"My aunt must never know!" There was an urgency to her tone akin to panic. "She employed me in good faith and has also blessed me with a coveted spot at Hampton House, where the waiting list to apply for residence is a mile long, at least. I am living on my own for the first time, and I must maintain her confidence!"

At his continued silence, desperation flashed in her eyes. "My brother, Stephen, and his friends have placed wagers that I'll not last a full year on my own. They say that I live with my head in the clouds and the thought that I can become a Woman of Independent Means is laughable." She lifted her chin a fraction. "I am six months into my adventure and have proven my worth well to my aunt." She flushed again. "With the exception of this side project."

Still, he stayed silent, knowing that as long as he did so, she would continue to explain, rambling and panicked though it was.

"I have become so *invested*, you see, in Miss Franklin's success. If she gets on well with the gentleman I helped her select from the personal ads, then my aunt will trust my intuition and perhaps allow me to take on a . . . a sort of matchmaking role at the *Gazette*." She bit her lip, brows pulling together. "As it happens, I feel we should consider deportment and manners training, as well. I was too far away to be sure, but I believe Miss Franklin may have begun the meal using the wrong utensils."

"Miss Hampton, you've yet to explain how you know Mr. Radcliffe. You claimed to have 'helped' the young woman select him from a personal ad. You've admitted you recognized him, leaving me to wonder if you were aware of his identity when you arranged for them to meet."

31

She frowned. "Certainly not. The ad mailed to the *Gazette* came under the pseudonym 'Mr. Dashing.' I happen to know Mr. Radcliffe from my membership at the Cheery Society Book Group, which he also attends. I had no idea until tonight that they were one and the same man."

She grew pensive, and for a moment Michael wondered if she'd forgotten he was there. Then she murmured, "He's not been widowed long."

"Are you privy to details about his private life?"

She blinked and focused on him again. "Only the few things he has mentioned at the book group. Surely true love cannot be so quickly replaced. Perhaps marriage really is nothing more than a practical alliance." She looked pained at the thought.

Mercy. Miss Hampton was indeed sheltered from life's realities. He did not know anyone who had reached adulthood with such a rosy perspective still intact. Even his sister, as lovely as she was, had never been so naive.

"And yet Mr. Radcliffe sought to meet someone new," he prodded, wondering if he was about to witness the bursting of Miss Hampton's happy bubble.

"It is a mystery." Her frown turned speculative. "I oughtn't to be surprised. He is so handsome and urbane, after all."

Michael refrained from telling her that he suspected her paragon of killing his own wife.

"And you felt justified spying on him this evening?"

She looked startled, as if she'd forgotten the initial point of his questioning. "Well, yes, but surely you see it was innocent curiosity. Besides, I initially went to *observe* Miss Franklin, not Mr. Radcliffe. Please believe me, I'd no idea her dinner companion was someone known to me beforehand." Her eyes left his face and landed again on his chest, which seemed to be her pattern when flustered or nervous. "If my aunt were to discover my—"

"Spying?"

She winced. "—my *investigations*, I fear her trust in me would cease on the spot."

"I suspect you would be correct."

"I wonder if you would be so kind as to keep this information between the two of us? After all, I have answered your questions honestly, even at the risk of losing my employment, and despite the fact that you ran me to ground in the pouring rain." Her teeth chattered, punctuating her statement.

"I did not run you to ground."

"Perhaps unintentionally," she muttered.

He sighed, then continued, "I will refrain from mentioning your clandestine activities to your aunt if you will invite me—as a *family friend*, of course—to the next book club where you expect to see Mr. Radcliffe."

Her expressive eyebrows lifted. "Oh, rather like an undercover operation!"

"Yes, but—"

She nodded. "I am a voracious reader, and I am especially enamored of Mrs. Freeman's mysteries. I shall be honored to aid the police with all the knowledge I possess. The amount of insight to be gained from reading novels is tremendous."

A fissure of unease ran down Michael's spine. "I do not require anything aside from your invitation to the group, Miss Hampton. I shall simply be an old friend of the 'notorious branch' of the Hampton family."

"Why must we have a story to tell if you're not going to disguise yourself?"

Any hope he might have harbored that she would leave the

rest of it to his discretion was dashed when he met her inquisitive eyes that studied him without blinking. Now that she saw herself as his investigative colleague, she fully expected an answer.

"I pushed to have an inquest regarding his wife's death," he finally admitted. "The fact that I would show my face at a society group to which he belongs strains credulity, at best. He'll reason that I'm investigating him again."

He'd never insinuated to Radcliffe that he suspected him of being involved in Marie's demise. Radcliffe wasn't stupid, however, and he seemed to have a network of influential people at his fingertips. Michael would have to tread carefully.

"If I am invited by an old family friend," he continued, "the coincidence will be more palatable. I trust he does not share an acquaintance with your aunt and would not attempt to verify a true connection through her?"

"To my knowledge, they are unacquainted." She paused, then frowned. "You hardly bear the look of one who enjoys poetry or novels." She airily waved a hand. "All detectives of my experience have been either disinterested in fiction or lack any degree of romanticism."

"How many detectives have crossed your path, Miss Hampton?"

She bit the inside of her cheek and again tightened her arms around herself. "Two."

He nodded. "You will introduce me to the others as a . . . a family friend, recently reacquainted."

Her lips moved slightly, but he couldn't discern her words. "I'm sorry?"

She shook her head and cleared her throat. "As it happens, the Cheery Society Book Group is meeting tomorrow evening. Is this too sudden for your schedule?"

"The sooner, the better. Come, Miss Hampton. I shall accompany you to your destination. The hour grows late."

"Thank you, but I do not require an escort." She inclined her head, secured her hat once again, and then shook her umbrella.

"I insist." He gestured toward the clearing, and she fell into step beside him. "You said you do not often walk alone at night, is this true?"

Her umbrella bumped against his shoulder, and she angled it to the side, looking up at his face. "When did I say . . . ? Oh, yes, when you ran me to ground."

He closed his eyes briefly. "I did not run you to—"

"I had assumed you were about to chastise me for being alone after dark."

"Do the constabulary around here usually chastise you for being out alone after dark?"

"I cannot say, but I assume most elder people of some authority are particular about such dangers."

Elder people of some authority? How old did she think he was? "As it happens, I do advise against it. You must take care for your safety, 'woman of independent means' or no. The world is full to bursting with people of ill will."

"Such a painfully pessimistic observation, Detective."

"Undoubtedly." Michael frequently saw people either at their very worst or when they had just experienced the very worst. He couldn't pretend it didn't shape his judgment.

She led the way through the other side of the park and onto the street, where they turned and made their way toward several residential squares. "Of course, chasing down miscreants and apprehending murderous villains must be absolutely exhausting. Tell me, do you know them on sight?"

"Who? Miscreants and murderers?" He was miserably cold, he knew she was also, and could not fathom the reason for her continued conversation. If he didn't believe somewhere in the recesses of his hardened soul that his mother was looking down from above and would be grossly disappointed in him, he'd have told the pretty Miss Hampton he required silence for the remainder of the walk.

"Yes." As they crossed another street, her hat slid from her head, and she smacked the umbrella into his neck in her fumbling attempt to catch it.

"Allow me," he snapped and held out his hand.

Wide-eyed, she handed the hat to him. She fell silent, and rather than relishing the quiet, he felt churlish.

His polite communication skills were rusty. While police procedure was an unlikely topic for drawing room conversation, the innocent young woman at his side seemed genuinely curious. Using her to gain seamless social access to Radcliffe was a boon he hadn't expected, so prudence dictated he foster good will with her.

He took a breath, resigned, and offered, "There are some 'miscreants' I recognize after a short interchange. Others are harder to detect."

She nodded, but remained quiet. She must have decided to forgive him for being curt, however, because she eventually resumed the conversation. "I would do better to hone my skills of discernment. My brother, Stephen, has always said I live in a world of fairy tales. That is laughable, though, because the books I read contain all sorts of murder and mayhem, usually committed with revolvers or knives, and once even a machete. I do not suppose such fiction would suit a police detective; seeing the truth of it in the course of one's profession would spoil any entertainment value."

As they walked, Michael was mildly surprised to find himself caught up in her streams of conversation that trailed off but eventually circled back to her original point. It was a pity, really, that life would eventually dull her bright edge.

Miss Hampton fell quiet, and Michael wondered if he'd been so lost in his own thoughts that he'd missed a cue to respond to a comment or question. He looked at her, and realized she'd stopped in front of a large mansion.

"Your aunt's boardinghouse?" The tidy street and neighborhoods surrounding it had once been home to society's uppermost classes. But when the burgeoning new professional middle classes had started to rise and encroach, many people had sold their enormous homes and moved farther afield. Boardinghouses in rougher parts of Town experienced crime that rarely touched these tidy squares and competitively sought-after residences.

"Hampton House. Aunt Sally acquired it some years ago through means the family chooses not to discuss, and she refuses to waste her time explaining. This leads to nothing but endless speculation on my own part and that of my cousins who also live here. One hopes the story is delightfully scandalous, but in truth, it is likely quite dull." She shrugged and smiled, and he realized it was the first time he'd seen it.

His heart jumped the slightest bit, and he absently rubbed his chest. He realized he still held her hat in his other hand, and he gave it to her with a light bow. "Tomorrow evening, then. I shall contact you for details on the book club gathering."

"Oh, yes. I think we ought to discuss your cover story." Her brow wrinkled. "I would hate to say the wrong thing."

"We shall keep it as simple as possible. I am a friend of your brother—Stephen, is it? From former times. You have been kind enough to introduce me in some of your social circles."

She raised a brow, but said, "Very well. However, be certain to avoid any mention of my parents. They passed away years ago."

"Oh." He blinked. "Please accept my condolences."

"Thank you, Detective."

"Just . . . do not concern yourself with details. I will handle my cover story. All I require is a means of observing Radcliffe without raising his suspicion that I am there in an official capacity."

She nodded and turned toward the front gate, but hesitated. "Detective, might you have misjudged Mr. Radcliffe? He is truly a gentleman of the first order. He recites Byron and even composes verses of his own."

Michael bit back the sarcastic reply that sprang instantly to his lips. In the light of the walkway gas lamp, he noted the subtle color that rose in her cheeks. Was Miss Hampton enamored of Radcliffe? He was torn between happily using her willing cooperation to investigate the man and warning her away from him in no uncertain terms. Surely with Michael present at the book group, he could manage any situation the naive young woman might find herself in.

"Perhaps I am mistaken," he lied. "He might merely be a victim of unfortunate circumstance."

She chewed on the inside of her cheek, apparently lost in her own musings. Her hair hung past her shoulders in a bedraggled mess, and she looked small, cold, and wet. The rain pattered steadily on the fabric of her umbrella, which provided little more protection than her hatpin-less hat.

"What is he to have done?" she finally asked, blinking through the raindrops caught on her lashes.

He could not be honest for more reasons than one, most paramount being that Radcliffe was under investigation— admittedly unsanctioned—for murder, and Miss Hampton's face was an open book. If she knew the details of the case, Michael doubted she would be able to keep from giving something away, even as enamored as she seemed to be about playing a part in an undercover ruse.

"I am not at liberty to disclose details," he told her. "I am hopeful things will progress swiftly, and, if you are correct that he is nothing more than a good man who composes poetry and keeps cheery company, he will be none the wiser of my suspicions, and I shall be on my way."

She studied him for a moment with an expression he couldn't quite read. Perhaps he would need to revise his assessment of her after all. Maybe those expressive eyes—hazel, he noted—were capable of holding something back.

She nodded. "Very well. Until tomorrow. Thank you for seeing me safely home, Detective."

He tipped his hat and a small rivulet of water found its way down his sleeve. "I do hope you will heed the counsel of your elders," he said, "and not venture out after dark alone anymore."

She had turned and entered the house before he realized she'd not agreed to heed his advice.

CHAPTER 5

A woman's greatest duty is to marry well, giving her resources to see to the care of not only her husband and children, but aging mothers and grandmothers.

—*correspondence from Mrs. Franklin to*
THE MARRIAGE GAZETTE

Amelie closed the door behind her, leaning against it to catch her breath. She had been escorted home by an actual detective who had chased her through the park like she was a common criminal! If she hadn't been so painfully cold and wet, she might have squealed in delight. Amelie Hampton read about adventures but was hardly the sort to seek them out beyond the pages of her novels. That an adventure had found her was remarkable. That the detective was handsome—albeit irascible—was a boon.

It was a ridiculous adventure, of course, and would come to naught. Mr. Harold Radcliffe was the last person to ever be involved in anything nefarious, but she was happy to bear the responsibility of helping to clear his good name. It was entirely possible he was unaware his name needed clearing since the grumpy detective was investigating undercover, of course, but a good deed done in secret was even more virtuous.

She lost herself in a delightful daydream where she and Mr. Radcliffe sat at the fireplace of their cozy future home and chuckled together about the reason they had fallen in love. He would touch her cheek tenderly, and tell her for the hundredth—nay, the *thousandth*—time that he was forever grateful for her good judgment of character and solid defense of him, an innocent gentleman, in the face of a police investigation where a brusque detective with very blue eyes, which undoubtedly matched the temperature of the blood coursing through his disagreeable veins—

"Miss Hampton!"

Amelie gasped and jumped, heart thumping, as Mrs. Burnette, the housekeeper, bustled down the wide front staircase with an expression that screamed outrage, even if her words did not. Yet.

"Are you waiting for an engraved invitation to remove that dripping wet coat?" Mrs. Burnette reached the bottom of the stairs and hurried across the front hall to Amelie. "Your aunt may own the home, but does she bear daily responsibility for the care of it? No! You young women coming and going at all hours, soaking the entryway and leaving dirty puddles. I have only just finished mopping behind Miss Duvall and Miss Caldwell."

Amelie opened her mouth to defend herself but was cut short as Mrs. Burnette placed her hands on Amelie's shoulders and spun her around to remove the wet coat. Amelie managed to say over her shoulder, "I would have been home much earlier, but—*oof*!"

Mrs. Burnette tugged with surprising strength at Amelie's

41

coat sleeve, and she was jostled about much like a child in similar circumstances. As her arm came free and Mrs. Burnette began working on the other, she realized that she couldn't tell anyone about her encounter with Detective Baker. His ruse would not last long if she gave up the game before it had even started.

Mrs. Burnette stripped her other sleeve clear, and Amelie curled her fingers tightly and held them to her mouth, blowing to generate some heat. She began tugging off the ruined gloves, but her numb fingers refused to cooperate. She managed to pull one partially off as Mrs. Burnette shook out the coat, muttering a string of what Amelie could only assume were curses under her breath. The housekeeper crossed into the parlor where a fire burned cozily behind the grate and spread Amelie's coat beside two others.

Amelie pinched the tips of the glove where she'd tugged free some fabric, and pulled, popping several knuckles but accomplishing little else. "Ugh," she muttered and shook her hand, stepping away from the front door.

"Halt!" Mrs. Burnette returned, face flushed and lips pinched. "Not another step until we remove your boots."

The housekeeper was sterner than even Amelie's mother had been. Amelie obediently froze in place, hiding her gloved hands behind her back.

With an exasperated huff, Mrs. Burnette held out one hand, and Amelie extended hers, wincing while the woman freed her of both gloves, stripping them inside out and dropping them to the floor near Amelie's umbrella, which had not found its way into the umbrella stand.

"I shall do my best to salvage them, young lady, but I cannot make promises."

"Oh, how kind of you to offer," Amelie hurried to say,

hoping to placate her. "I'd given them up as ruined and lost for good."

Mrs. Burnette looked up sharply. "You would consign a perfectly good pair of gloves to the trash heap, then?"

Amelie's eyes widened. "No! No, I simply . . . I only—"

Muttering something that included the words "frugality" and "the irresponsible young," Mrs. Burnette bent down and examined the hem of Amelie's skirt, which bore evidence of her awkward crab-walk along the ground in the park. "What on *earth*? Were you dragged home by a horse?"

Amelie reminded herself that Mrs. Burnette was *not* her mother and that she, Miss Amelie Hampton, was a Woman of Independent Means. She sniffed and straightened her shoulders. "No, ma'am. Of course I was not. I had the misfortune to slip on a muddy patch in the park and fall down."

Mrs. Burnette narrowed her eyes at Amelie before snatching a buttonhook near the shoe rack and then reaching beneath the skirt hem for her foot. "Was there nobody in the park at the time?"

"No. I was quite alone." Amelie waited for a tuttering of sympathy.

"Good. Such gracelessness will never yield an improved reputation, much less impress the eye of a potential suitor."

Amelie's mouth dropped open, but she quickly closed it, resigned. Mrs. Burnette had long ago earned the position of honorary matron of Hampton House and the five residents within its walls. Even Mr. Frost, who was well into his sixties and extremely ill-tempered, fell prey to her scolding on occasion. Amelie had often thought the scolding did little to improve the man's temper, but Mrs. Burnette's aim never seemed to be focused on lightening spirits.

She was more governess in spirit than housekeeper, but her efficiency was unequalled. Clothing was laundered in record time, meals were punctual and delicious, and apartments remained swept and dusted daily by a pair of maids who valued the excellent pay more than the thought of finding work under more personable superiors.

Mrs. Burnette finished unbuttoning Amelie's boots and removed them briskly. "Davie will be around in the morning. I'll see he cleans and blackens these. Fortunate that you have another two pair to choose from for work tomorrow."

"Indeed. Now, then, might I trouble you—"

"For supper, of course. Sarah has set aside a tray. I'll have her warm it and send it up to your suite. I would invite you into the dining room, but of course, the meal was cleared over an hour ago."

Amelie nodded, eager to be alone. She needed to think. As Mrs. Burnette disappeared down the hallway to the kitchen, Amelie climbed the stairs to her room on the second floor.

There was a common area on the second floor, containing a sofa and two chairs, an end table, a lamp, and a fresh flower arrangement. Straight ahead were two large windows that overlooked the front of the house, and a cozy glow of wall sconces reflected in the glass. Amelie, Charlotte, and Evangeline often lounged in the common area following a long day of work.

Amelie's suite consisted of a large bedroom and a small dressing room, accessed by a door to the right of the common area. To the left were several other doors: two led to the rooms occupied by her cousins and two more led to the girls' shared water closet and bathroom. The room adjoining Amelie's was used for storing furniture, surplus linens, and various curiosities

Aunt Sally brought home from her travels that had yet to be given a permanent home.

Stairs continued up to the third floor, where two older gentlemen, Mr. Frost and Mr. Roy, each occupied a small suite. There was an additional room shared by the Wells sisters, Sarah and Katie, who were the Hampton House maids. Mrs. Burnette occupied a small suite at the back of the house near the kitchen where she was better able to manage deliveries and other household affairs.

Amelie fitted her key into the lock and entered her room where she was greeted by the warm glow of a banked fire in the fireplace. Wall sconces had been turned down low, and Amelie breathed a tired sigh as she dropped her reticule and key on the small table near the door.

She crossed to the small dressing room and stripped away her wet clothing, draping them over a drying rack. After toweling off and dressing for bed, she wrapped herself in a warm housecoat. Tired, she made her way back to her bedroom and sat in the small chair near the fireplace.

It might be only one room, but it was a large room in a large house in a respectable neighborhood, and more to the point, it was all hers. Sally Hampton selected her tenants carefully and was extremely fair in the rent she requested from her nieces. Amelie suspected that she'd have been unable to afford her room if anyone else owned Hampton House. Sally had always encouraged Amelie's initiative and desire for independence—even when she'd resided with her in her manor across town after Amelie's parents died—but being officially on her own was exhilarating. That she'd only moved out from under Sally's roof into another home her aunt owned was beside the point. It was a step toward a truly independent life.

She pulled her fingers through her tangled mass of hair and braided it over her shoulder, her brain finally slowing long enough to consider everything that had happened from the moment she'd left *The Marriage Gazette* that evening.

Charlotte and Eva had parcels to retrieve from "Madame Dubois' Hats and Gloves," so Amelie had parted from them with a promise to tell all when they returned home. She'd known the location for the meeting between "Mr. Dashing" and Miss Franklin and had only wanted to be sure they both arrived and seemed to get on well.

To see Mr. Radcliffe there had caused her heart to pound with a multitude of emotions. She'd been stunned to recognize him from the book club meetings, of course, but she also worried that her aunt would somehow conclude that Amelie had learned the identity of a *Gazette* personals contributor and was now following him about Town.

She also felt a strange pang of jealousy of Miss Franklin. Not malicious jealousy, because Miss Franklin was a sweet young woman whose only goal was to avoid marriage to the ancient and odious Mr. Brocklehurst. No, it was the sort of jealousy Amelie's romantic heart recognized, having felt it many times when she had found herself enamored of a gentleman whose attentions were focused elsewhere.

Amelie had been in Hampton House for six months and had attended the Cheery Society Book Group with her cousins for four of those months. Each time the group met, she had admired Mr. Harold Radcliffe from afar. Though Amelie was a voracious reader of romantic novels, she was painfully shy around men in whom she found an interest. She grew tongue-tied and awkward, and slightly ill, and had long ago decided she would rather admire from afar than disgrace herself up close.

He was so dashing! He was incredibly handsome, well-read, intelligent, and carried himself like a nobleman. His clothing was of the finest cut, his taste in tiepins, cuff links, and hats was first-rate, and he commanded female attention with every poetry-laced word. In truth, she'd never truly considered him a candidate for marriage because he was freshly widowed and spoke in such wistful and glowing terms about his late wife. She'd assumed—erroneously, apparently—that he would not put himself on the marriage mart for some time.

She frowned as she stared at the glowing log in the fire and played with the damp ends of her hair. The detective had seemed most determined about his investigation into Mr. Radcliffe, and Amelie could hardly understand it. That such a gentleman would be facing scrutiny from anyone, let alone the police, was simply too fantastic to believe. Detective Baker must be mistaken.

Amelie realized with an uncomfortable start that she would have to find a reason to introduce the detective to Mr. Radcliffe. The thought of approaching him the next night made her slightly sick. She would need to find someone to perform introductions all around. Her mind immediately went to her cousin Charlotte.

Charlotte Duvall was more assertive and self-assured than Amelie. Charlotte was very much like her mother, who had died when Charlotte was young; the two cousins had that in common. Evangeline Caldwell—Eva, to family—was also Sally's niece via her mother, and, of the three girls who lived at Hampton House, was easily the most diplomatic and gracious. Amelie supposed she was the "dreamer" of the bunch, with little to recommend her save a love of romantic and mystery novels.

When the knock on Amelie's door signaling a tray of food

had finally arrived, she wasn't surprised to see Charlotte on the other side, holding the tray. Amelie leaned past the young woman and called out to Sarah Wells, "Thank you for dinner."

"Yes, miss." The maid paused on her way to the stairs and nodded with a tired smile. She bobbed a quick curtsey and continued on her way.

"Amelie, you must tell all." Charlotte bustled her way into the room and set the tray down on the small table that also doubled as Amelie's writing desk. "Did you catch a glimpse of the couple tonight at the restaurant? Do you believe they will suit?" Charlotte dragged a chair from near the fireplace and plunked it next to the desk. "Eat, you must be starving. Why are you home so late? Eva and I arrived over an hour ago."

Charlotte's thick, riotous auburn curls were free from braids and pins and hung down her back in full abandon. She wore a housecoat similar to Amelie's, and her green eyes were bright with energy. They were always bright with energy. Amelie did not believe she'd ever seen Charlotte fatigued.

Amelie had yet to utter a word, though she smiled. She spread the napkin on her lap and took an appreciative sniff of the beef stew in the bowl before her. She was still chilled to the bone, and she put her hands around the steaming bowl and scooted it closer.

"I am late because I stopped to watch the couple." She sipped the broth, choosing her words carefully. She could not admit, even to her dearest cousins, that she was now part of an undercover investigation with Scotland Yard. "Charlotte, you will not believe who they are. Or rather, who *he* is."

"What?" Charlotte leaned forward in her seat. "Who is he?"

"Mr. Radcliffe."

Charlotte straightened and blinked. "Mr. Radcliffe?"

Amelie nodded.

"From the Cheery Society Book Group?"

Amelie nodded. "I cannot imagine why he would find it necessary to advertise in *The Marriage Gazette* for company." She wrinkled her brow. "I am concerned because if it were to become common knowledge that I spied on the meeting, Sally might fire me, family or no." She paused. "What if he has put in multiple ads? Suppose this is not his first time to advertise for courtship? I did not consider that he could be the sort . . ."

Charlotte sat back in the chair and tapped her fingertip against her lip. "Actually, as the youngest of seven children—six of them boys—I can personally attest to the fickle nature of men."

"Perhaps." Amelie continued eating, then gestured to her dessert. "Would you care for the rice pudding?"

Charlotte's eyes widened. "Bless you." She snatched the small bowl and dessert spoon from the tray with a smile. "A man like Mr. Radcliffe—perhaps he is more of a Casanova than we've realized."

"I assume no such thing." Amelie wiped her mouth with exaggerated delicacy. "I believe he is all that is genteel and proper."

Charlotte ate thoughtfully for a moment, her eyes narrowed. "Heaven knows I am not a jaded sort, but I am a realist. He may not be the paragon you've created in your head."

A quick knock sounded on the door, and Amelie called, "Enter!"

Eva stuck her head in the room. "Oh good, you're home." Her hair was wet as though she'd just stepped from the bath; she also wore comfortable nightclothes and a housecoat. She pulled a small footstool from next to the bed closer to the fireplace and sat down with a sigh. Her long black hair was pulled into a loose braid similar to Amelie's. Her eyes were a deep brown, and she possessed the sort of beauty that stopped people in their tracks.

She was an aficionado of gadgetry, photography in particular. She took photographs for *The Marriage Gazette,* and she had recently branched into a side business of providing pictures for private families and groups. Sally had approved the use of an extra storage room in the cellar as a converted darkroom, and Eva's talent grew daily.

The fact that her cousins knew Amelie so well created a challenge for her. She wasn't certain she could manage the ruse Detective Baker would require of her the next evening. The only factor that might work in her favor was that the three cousins had grown up in separate towns; they spent vacations together, but not daily life. They wouldn't know if the detective had ever actually been a family acquaintance.

She decided to dip her toe into the murky waters of intrigue and see if she could make herself believable. "Oh," she said brightly, "I encountered a family friend today! He was a constable years ago and knew Stephen; my brother constantly found himself in one scrape or another." She laughed and waved a hand. "The constable is now a detective with the Yard, if you can believe it. He doesn't know many people yet, and can be rather bashful. I thought he might enjoy the book club meeting tomorrow night."

The other two nodded, faces open and trusting, and she felt horrible for a moment. Of course they believed her, why wouldn't they? As far as she knew, they didn't ever lie to each other. This lie was necessary for the greater good, she reminded herself. And she would tell them the truth as soon as she could.

"What is his name?" Charlotte asked.

"Baker."

Eva nodded. "Mr. Baker, the detective. We shall make him feel entirely welcome. In fact, after the book club meeting, there is a play on Drury Lane that has just opened, and I thought perhaps some of the others might like to join us in attending. He would be welcome, of course, and while it would make for a late night, I think it sounds like such fun."

"Eva, you daring thing!" Charlotte smiled. "A late night out sounds rather spontaneous for one of your responsible nature."

Eva laughed. "Not so much, I fear. You'll note I've chosen a night preceding a day off of work."

"Even so." Charlotte grinned. "We are young but once, eh, ladies? I suspect our time for only ourselves will not last forever."

Her comment brought to Amelie's mind thoughts of marriage and children and hearth and home. Mr. Radcliffe certainly fit nicely into that picture, but the thought itself was wistful. Someone as accomplished and polished as he was would never find someone like her interesting enough to warrant a second glance. Besides, if all went well for Miss Franklin tonight, such thoughts were irrelevant, and she did not begrudge the other woman.

Conversation flowed happily with her friends, and in the moment, she was content. Life was lovely, she was working hard, earning her own money, and if she could keep her tiny acts of subterfuge from her aunt, all would be well. She smiled. Everything was as close to perfect as she could imagine.

CHAPTER 6

Dear Diary,

I can hardly wait for the book society meeting! Of course, as the time draws closer, I shall likely be ill. My nerves twist and my stomach tumbles every time I am in the company of a gentleman I fancy, so my optimism will undoubtedly be short-lived. I wish I could ask Mr. Radcliffe outright if he enjoyed his dinner with Miss Franklin. As it stands, my only opportunity to speak with him will be when I introduce him to the detective.

I cannot imagine what sort of woman would find herself interested in a detective—he possesses all the charm of a badger. Handsome will take a man only so far.

The work hours passed quickly for Michael the following day, and before leaving for the evening, Winston bid him good luck with his ruse at the book club. Michael had informed Director Ellis of his plans, hopeful his superior would be supportive. He'd had the ironic thought that his situation wasn't so different from Miss Hampton's: they both were pursuing a course unbeknownst to their employers.

Ellis hadn't forbidden Michael's activities, but neither had he sanctioned them. He pointedly mentioned that he was un- concerned with what Michael pursued in his free time, but could not lend official support to an investigation that had been firmly shut down by those in higher authority. He also warned that if Judge Adams were to discover CID detectives were again looking at Harold Radcliffe, Michael would be on his own.

Michael retrieved the jacket and greatcoat he'd brought from home that morning. He replaced the sturdy, serviceable coat he wore for work with the finer ones he kept for special occasions. His aim to appear as a genteel patron of the arts and lover of fine literature must be convincing, employment as a CID operative notwithstanding.

A few constables whistled at him as he passed, and he waved them off as he made his way out the door.

Miss Hampton had sent the address to him earlier, and as he gave it to the cab driver, he wondered if there would be enough time to speak with Miss Hampton alone before they be- gan their charade. He checked his timepiece, noting that would be unlikely.

As the cab drew to a halt, Michael saw Miss Hampton standing in a small group assembled outside the modestly styl- ish gates of Dr. and Mrs. Forrester's home. The young woman was flanked by two other young women, who eyed him with open interest as he approached.

Miss Hampton looked decidedly flushed. Her eyes widened, and she said, "Oh, this is Stephen's friend! Miss Evangeline Caldwell, Miss Charlotte Duvall, may I introduce Detective Baker. Detective, these are my cousins."

Michael was impressed. She'd managed the introduction

naturally. He tipped his hat to the trio and smiled. "Indeed. And how fares Stephen, Miss Hampton?"

"Oh, he is working hard with my brother-in-law in the shop back home. He is to remain with Deborah until he reaches his eighteenth birthday. I am certain when I am home for the holidays, they will all be so glad to know I chanced meeting you here in Town! Deborah will insist you join us again for tea and parlor games the next time you happen through Frockshire."

"Please inform your sister I would be delighted." Michael mentally willed Miss Hampton to stop talking. The fewer false-hoods they told, the better. A complicated backstory was bound to cause trouble in the future.

"Kind of your family to invite the constable to dinner, what with Stephen's indiscretions with the law," Miss Duvall offered as an aside to Miss Hampton. She raised one dubious brow in Michael's direction.

"I do not pretend to understand Deborah's methods," Miss Hampton laughed, perhaps too enthusiastically. "I believe she sought leniency for Stephen by providing entertainment for the constabulary."

Michael sighed inwardly. He had only himself to blame for drawing Miss Hampton into the ruse.

"Shall we enter?" Miss Caldwell gestured toward the front door. "Mrs. Forrester procures sweets from the best bakeries in town. I fear if we linger, we are likely to miss out."

"Yes, come, come," Miss Hampton said and moved forward, taking Michael's arm. "We must introduce you to Dr. and Mrs. Forrester. They are familiar with ever so many people and will be the loveliest of contacts to make." Miss Hampton urged him toward the house, the clutch of her fingers on his sleeve betraying her agitation.

He wanted to reassure her that her part in the scheme was nearly finished and she could relax, but her cousins were directly behind them and within earshot. He settled for patting her fingers and giving them a little squeeze; he noted her quiet exhalation.

They trailed behind the other guests into the home's spacious parlor, which was filled with furniture that looked to have been rearranged to accommodate a large group of people. Across the room was a long table bearing refreshments, and in the far corner, a lone violinist softly played Vivaldi's *Four Seasons*.

Miss Duvall caught their attention and said, "Eva and I shall procure refreshments and seating while you introduce Detective Baker to our hostess."

Miss Hampton nodded. "Good, yes." As the two women left them, she continued in an undertone, "Yes, very good."

Michael squeezed her fingers again, and when she looked up at him, he murmured, "You're doing fine. Try to relax, this will soon be done."

"I am relaxed, it is only . . ." She winced. "I feel horrible lying about all of this, and I am not entirely certain Mr. Rad—"

Michael cut off her comment by subtly steering her toward the room's other entrance and out into the hallway. There were a few people chatting, but no one paid them any heed. He pasted a pleasant smile on his face while leading her a few steps farther down the hall, past another doorway and just to the other side of a large, potted plant. Shielding her from potentially curious eyes, he kept his back to the front door and nudged her close against the wall.

"Do not say his name, if you please," he whispered. "Nobody can know he is the reason I am here, especially not the man himself. This entire charade will be for naught if it is over before it has even begun. This is police business; do you understand the gravity?"

Her large hazel eyes locked with his. She took a deep breath and straightened her spine. If he had unnerved her by carting her into the shadows, it didn't show. "What I was attempting to say, and *quietly*, might I add, was that I cannot believe *that man* is capable of anything that would interest the police. If I have led trouble to his door, I will never forgive myself."

"You ought to leave that to me."

"I cannot simply absolve myself of responsibility!" Her eyes sparked outrage, but to her credit, the whisper was not overly loud.

He felt his eye twitch, and his nostrils flared. "Miss Hampton. Our absence will soon be noted. If Mr. Ra—if *the gentleman* is innocent, I shall drop the matter and he will never be the wiser. If *you* persist on spying as he dines with other women, however, I cannot guarantee his ignorance of your behavior, nor your continued employment."

"Oh!" Her brows drew together in a fierce frown as she leaned closer, her shoulder brushing against his coat. "You would *tattle* on me to my aunt?"

"No, my young friend," he said, his temper spiking. He also leaned closer. "You are as stealthy and secretive as a stampeding bull, and you will give *yourself* away sooner rather than later."

She closed her mouth but fumed. He suddenly realized how closely they stood together when he caught the scent of her perfume, which was quite lovely. Her shoulder pressed warmly against his arm, and he was momentarily distracted. They'd moved from polite distance to extremely close proximity in a matter of minutes. Her brow wrinkled, and her full lips tightened as she gave him what must surely seem to her a very fierce expression.

"Tell me what he's done," she murmured.

"I have told you that I am not at liberty to say," he whispered back. "Now, we must return before your cousins come looking." He straightened slowly and released a deep breath. He grabbed her hand, clamped it to his arm, and moved her out of the shadows.

" . . . wouldn't come looking if someone hadn't decided to shove me from the room . . ." she muttered.

He pursed his lips but refrained from comment. Fortune smiled upon them because the hallway was empty. Conversation still flowed from the parlor. He paused at the door and glanced down at her. "You must trust me."

She sighed and lifted her eyes to his. "Have you a wife, Mr. Baker?"

"Certainly not." He scanned the room for a glimpse of Mr. Radcliffe. He had not yet arrived, and Michael felt a stab of frustration. Perhaps the man wouldn't show, and the entire evening would be for nothing.

Miss Hampton muttered something else, and he frowned. "Pardon?"

"I said"—she spoke quietly through a forced smile—"perhaps *you* ought to consider a matchmaking service. I could help you place an ad in *The Marriage Gazette*. I am not surprised you've been unable to secure suitable companionship through your own devices."

He gave her his full attention, torn between offense and amusement. "Perhaps I am widowed."

Her mouth dropped open, and her eyes softened. "Oh, mercy. I am so sorr—"

"I said 'perhaps.'"

She locked eyes with him for a long moment before narrowing hers slightly and lifting her chin. "I do not know that even a professional service could help you."

His lips twitched at her quick response. "I do not know that I would trust a professional service with such a personal task. Especially now that I am aware some *Gazette* employees spy on people who write to the paper." Why was he baiting her? He couldn't remember the last time he'd allowed anyone to distract him while he was working a case.

She straightened her shoulders and looked into the room. "A pity you do not actually know my brother. I've a feeling you'd get on splendidly."

"Should your sister find herself in need of an amiable lawman to set an example for him, you've one to recommend."

Miss Hampton made a dismissive sound and tugged on his arm. As they reentered the parlor, a woman he assumed must be Mrs. Forrester bore down upon them.

"Miss Hampton! Your friends told me you've brought a companion this evening." She smiled widely, and Michael wondered if she'd have waggled her eyebrows if he hadn't been paying attention.

Miss Hampton, for her part, brightened as though she'd never been cross with him, and made perfect introductions. She had relaxed markedly; her irritation with him seemed to have eclipsed her earlier worry. The nervous chatter that had overtaken her introduction to her cousins was gone.

"A delight to make your acquaintance, Detective Baker, and I do hope you'll be a permanent part of our cheery little society." Mrs. Forrester clasped his hand.

"Mr. Baker is much too modest to ever admit it, but he

writes beautiful poetry." Miss Hampton smiled at him. "He also plays the harp like an angel. Has been known to bring grown men to tears."

He returned her smile, recognizing the challenge.

Mrs. Forrester gasped in delight. "Perhaps you might—"

He held up a hand and tipped his head, giving Mrs. Forrester what his mother had always maintained was a charming smile. Of course, she'd been his mother and was thus obliged to make such observations.

"Ah, but our Miss Hampton exaggerates. My skills were diminished significantly in a mill accident. I have just recently regained partial use of my left hand." He flexed his fingers and allowed a small wince to flicker across his face. "I fear the only man now who cries when I play my beloved harp is I."

Mrs. Forrester looked near tears herself, and Miss Hampton eyed him sidelong with something that might have been reluctant respect.

"Thoughtless of me," she said. "How could I have forgotten the mill accident?" She took his arm again. "We were concerned for your mental faculties as well, what with the head injury," she continued as she moved him away. "I confess, I found it difficult to discern between your behavior before and after the accident. Perhaps the lingering oddities are not new."

He chuckled quietly, charmed. Her hand threaded through his arm and rested comfortably there. He covered her fingers with his, noting the smooth skin beneath his fingertips. With concerted effort, he resisted rubbing his thumb across her knuckles.

She led him around to a few people and gestured to Miss Duvall and Miss Caldwell, who sat in conversation with two older women who were identical in appearance and dressed in extravagant gowns that might indicate a desire to attend more auspicious events.

"A mill accident?" Miss Hampton murmured to him.

"A harp?"

"What would you have been doing at a mill? A carriage accident would have made more sense." She frowned as she looked around the room. "I believe some of our book club members might be absent this evening."

"Perhaps my family owns a mill." He followed her to the sofa where Miss Duvall and Miss Caldwell sat, each holding two small plates of refreshments.

"Does your family own a mill?" She looked over her shoulder at him, a brow raised.

He bit back a smile. "No."

Her eyes were expressive, and there was a lightness in them he hadn't seen in anyone in a long time. Of course, he could barely remember the last time a woman had flirted with him, and he doubted this one intended it as such. She was unguarded and possessed a subtle but quick sense of humor he appreciated. The tight band of stress that usually encircled his head eased.

Miss Hampton took the empty spot on the sofa next to Miss Duvall and gestured to the nearby chair. "Detective Baker, will you join us?"

"Thank you, Miss Hampton, I would be delighted."

She took one of the extra plates of treats from Miss Duvall and handed it to him, then accepted Miss Caldwell's extra plate for herself. He noted with some amusement that Miss Duvall had added an extra cookie and small sandwich to his plate. The offerings were so small he figured he could eat the whole refreshment table, and as he glanced at the other gentlemen in the room, noting their full plates, he knew he wasn't alone. He had never developed a taste for delicate food. He was happiest with a hearty bowl of stew and a large chunk of bread.

Miss Hampton made introductions to the two older women seated nearby, and the Misses Van Horne regarded him with open interest. They were dressed as though expecting a visit with the queen, complete with fur stoles and large jewelry that, if not paste, indicated an immense amount of wealth. The sister on the left eyed him and commented that the Cheery Society Book Group was improving by the week; the other nudged her and quietly said something about occasionally leaving treats for others.

He choked on a crumb, and the three young cousins on the sofa passed along—hand to hand—one of several teacups placed on a side table. He gratefully took a sip and nodded his thanks.

Miss Hampton suddenly straightened in her seat, her cheeks flushing as she looked over his shoulder, and he knew without turning around that Harold Radcliffe had finally arrived.

CHAPTER 7

*A gentleman may assure himself of accelerated success in woo-
ing an impressionable woman if he includes poetry in his retinue
of persuasive tactics.*

    —The Gentleman's Guide to Efficient and
    Profitable Courtship *by Sir Percival Prancey*

Amelie didn't know which flustered her more, the unsettling
detective sitting beside her or the arrival of Mr. Radcliffe. She
tried to control the blush she felt stealing across her face and
looked down at her plate. Her appetite had fled, and she wondered if she might become ill. That would definitely leave a last-
ing impression on Mr. Radcliffe.

She glanced at the detective and noted he had also seen
Radcliffe's arrival. Detective Baker had tensed, and the attention
he'd focused on her pivoted to the newcomer. Oddly, she couldn't
decide if she felt disappointment or relief.

Mrs. Forrester greeted Mr. Radcliffe with smiles and
Continental-style kisses on either side of the cheeks, and Amelie
suppressed a sigh. The words of the poem Mr. Radcliffe had written and recited at the last book club meeting flitted through her
mind.

A single tear drips from my eye,
when thy perfect cheek I spy;
Words, like gems, from thy blissful lips,
Fall soft as kisses on fingertips.

With an engaging smile, Mr. Radcliffe accepted a plate of tea cakes from Miss Trunsteel, a tall, beautiful, single young woman whom Amelie had liked well enough at the last book club gathering but in whom she now found several flaws. Mr. Radcliffe followed Miss Trunsteel to a settee just opposite Amelie.

Dr. Forrester dinged a small knife against his glass and smiled as attention turned to him. "I know we are all delighted to chat together, but we must be about the business of discussing the book lest we be accused of functioning as little more than a social club!"

Everyone laughed, and Dr. Forrester gestured to his wife, who began a summary of *Romeo and Juliet*. Amelie tried to relax, but her hands clutching the small plate on her knees trembled.

Charlotte leaned close and whispered, "Is something amiss?"

Amelie glanced at her with a half-smile. "Tired, I suppose."

Charlotte took the plate from her and passed it to Evangeline. She shifted her eyes to indicate Mr. Radcliffe and whispered, "He is probably simply searching for the best possible match. Do not worry about him."

Amelie wished the only reason she was thinking about Mr. Radcliffe was because she wondered if the man made a habit of soliciting dates. No, she was thinking she had led an overly suspicious and imposing detective to the doorstep of a perfectly lovely, tenderhearted gentleman.

As the evening continued, Amelie's attention was split between Mr. Radcliffe, who was very attentive to the group's conversation, and Detective Baker, who watched Mr. Radcliffe closely without seeming to. She knew what he was about because it was a technique she'd perfected herself. Look at him, look away, look back at him, look away.

She realized Mr. Radcliffe was commenting on a question Mrs. Forrester had asked, and Amelie blinked, focusing.

" . . . quite possibly the most romantic love story in the history of written literature, I should say," Mr. Radcliffe was saying. "Tragic, heart-wrenching, exquisite."

"I quite agree," Miss Trunsteel said with a nod. "No other love story could ever equal it."

Amelie scowled but immediately smoothed her brow. Though she admired Mr. Radcliffe, she disagreed with his opinion. Her personal romantic favorite was *Jane Eyre,* though she could never admit it in mixed company; it was far too radical. Miss Austen's *Sense and Sensibility* was another fine choice, but she wasn't about to contradict Mr. Radcliffe by mentioning Miss Austen, either, although she dearly wanted to contradict Miss Trunsteel.

Mrs. Forrester guided the discussion forward and smiled at the detective. "Mr. Baker, our newcomer! Perhaps you'll share an opinion on the merits of Romeo and Juliet?"

Amelie looked at the detective cautiously. Had he ever even read the play?

Detective Baker straightened in his seat and took a breath, looking contemplative. Amelie was about to come to his rescue when he finally spoke. "I believe Romeo and Juliet were ridiculous."

His statement drew a round of laughter and a smattering of applause from most of the men present as well as the elder Miss

Van Horne. Charlotte eyed the detective with something akin to approval, and Evangeline's eyes sparkled as she smiled.

Amelie was stunned the detective's opinions matched her own. She glanced at Mr. Radcliffe, who was studying Baker with a light frown. Amelie wondered if Mr. Radcliffe recognized the detective from their prior association.

"Truthfully," the detective continued, "in terms of romantic satisfaction, I prefer *The Count of Monte Cristo*."

Radcliffe laughed. "Mercedes is faithless. It is not romantic at all."

Detective Baker lifted the corner of his mouth in a smile. "Mercedes was tricked, not faithless. But I speak of the ending. Edmond Dantès does well enough for himself."

Radcliffe nodded. "One could certainly do worse than travel the world with unlimited money and in the company of a beautiful young woman."

She looked at the detective, her sense of disquiet buzzing in her ear like an annoying insect invisible to the eye. Her attention continually turned toward him. She'd earlier felt—and squashed—a thrill when he'd covered her hand with his, completely enveloping her fingers in delicious warmth. Her heart tripped again at the memory, and she curled her fingers into her palm.

He wasn't at all the sort of gentleman she fancied for herself. He wasn't . . . smooth. He looked fine enough, was even handsome in a grumpy sort of way, but he was a restless panther to Mr. Radcliffe's sleek, sophisticated house cat. That Amelie had freed the panther from the zoo and brought him to the house cat had tied her stomach in knots.

The discussion of *Romeo and Juliet* continued, but Amelie had difficulty following it. She'd developed a sudden desire to reread *The Count of Monte Cristo*. Before long, the time drew to a close, and Dr. Forrester reminded them that their selection for next month was Thomas Hardy's *Return of the Native*. As people stood and began working their way to the door, Mr. Radcliffe approached the detective and offered his hand.

"I thought you looked familiar!" he said.

"Mr. Radcliffe, of course!" Detective Baker said. "What a small world we find ourselves in. When my young friend, Miss Hampton, invited me to attend this evening, I'd no idea I would so much as recognize another book club member."

Amelie made a note to tell the detective later that he could always pursue a career as an actor if he decided he no longer cared for law enforcement. She made an additional mental note to insist he tell her some stories from his incognito personae. He'd clearly done it before.

He paused, his brow wrinkling, and lowered his voice. "I do hope my presence here will not keep you from attending in the future. My face is undoubtedly the last one you'd ever wish to see." The detective looked genuinely concerned, and Amelie was impressed. "In fact, I shall find another society to join. I would never dream of driving you away."

Mr. Radcliffe chuckled. "Nor would I dream of driving *you* away! Please, do attend again, detective. I certainly bear you no ill will. In fact, I am endeavoring to move forward with my life, as I know my late wife would have wished it. Marie cared for nothing but my happiness, and perhaps the sight of you every so often will serve as a lovely, if bittersweet, reminder of her love for me." He didn't bother lowering his voice; he made no apologies for his association with the detective, nor his intentions to court again despite his great love for his late wife.

Amelie told herself that her role in the whole deception was now at an end, but she was curious about how the detective would proceed with his investigation. Would he require further assistance from her? Supposing Mr. Radcliffe asked the detective a personal question that he wouldn't be able to answer?

She had forgotten Eva's suggestion from the day before that they attend a play. Hearing her cousin mention it pulled her out of her fog, and she noted—with a decided thump of the heart—that Mr. Radcliffe was amenable to the idea.

Regrettably, Miss Trunsteel also was amenable. She smiled at Mr. Radcliffe, and Amelie wondered at her own pettiness. She had no claim on Mr. Radcliffe's attentions, let alone his affections—she had never even been formally introduced to the man. Miss Trunsteel turned her attention and equally warm smile to the detective, and Amelie found herself doubly irritated. The detective had work to do, and did not need distractions.

Eva turned to the group, eyes alight, and said, "The Misses Van Horne would like to accompany us!"

Everyone stared, and before the moment could become awkward, Mr. Radcliffe said, "Of course! Ladies, how lovely to enjoy your company even longer this evening. I am certain that the mothers of our dear young women here would be relieved to know their daughters are being responsibly chaperoned."

Amelie felt a moment's sting, firstly because she was a Woman of Independent Means, and secondly, because there was a condescension in Mr. Radcliffe's tone that made her feel young and foolish. She was twenty-one years of age, after all, and eminently suited for both courtship and marriage. Two of her friends in Frockshire were married and had borne babies already.

Her gaze snagged on the detective, who was observing the

group with an unreadable expression. She would never have believed his purpose there was anything other than what he claimed it to be. His attention traveled from Mr. Radcliffe to Miss Trunsteel, who hovered near Mr. Radcliffe's side, to the elderly twins making subtle but ribald remarks about their unsuitability as chaperones, then to Amelie's cousins, and then to her. She had the distinct impression that he'd sized them all up and categorized them neatly in his brain. She wondered where he had put her. Probably somewhere between "socially convenient" and "meddlesome."

"I suggest an omnibus," Mr. Radcliffe said. "We shall all ride together to the theatre."

The detective offered Amelie his arm, and when she saw Mr. Radcliffe do the same for Miss Trunsteel, she accepted Baker's. Mr. Baker's lips twitched, and she narrowed her eyes at him. He didn't say anything, and for that she was grateful. He was a detective, so naturally he would have detected she held a *tendre* for Mr. Radcliffe. She wasn't exactly secretive, and she knew her emotions were usually on full display across her face.

The group thanked their hosts and bid farewell to other book club members as they made their way from the Forresters' residence. When the word spread that a small entourage was headed for Drury Lane, a few more gentlemen joined the group. By the time they had all strolled from the Forresters' neighborhood to the nearest omnibus, they were an impressive gathering.

Amelie felt herself finally beginning to enjoy the evening. She relaxed by degrees, and even her irritation with the detective began to fade. He was simply doing his job, and soon he would learn that Mr. Radcliffe was no criminal. As it was, Mr. Radcliffe now stood between the elderly Van Horne sisters, one on each arm. He had them laughing and blushing like school-girls.

She climbed onto the omnibus and settled toward the rear beside her friends, with the detective finding a seat just behind them, and Mr. Radcliffe and the rest of the group in front of them. The carriage dipped as a few extras climbed atop and settled onto the long seat that ran the length of the conveyance. As they made their way to the theatre district, Mr. Radcliffe finally did what she'd been hoping for those last two months—he engaged them in conversation. She was tongue-tied and wished she hadn't eaten even the couple bites of tea cake she'd managed to choke down.

"This is Miss Amelie Hampton," Charlotte said with a smile and held her hand out to Amelie. "We reside at Hampton House in Bloomsbury."

"Ah, lovely!" Mr. Radcliffe's expressive eyebrows rose as his attention lingered on Amelie before turning to the others. "I am to understand you are all 'working women,' is this correct?"

A feeling of unease found its way to the base of Amelie's spine. She did not want to admit they worked for the very publication he'd solicited.

"Indeed," Charlotte told him. "We are each employed at—"

The detective sneezed behind them, close enough to Amelie and Charlotte that they both jumped reflexively. He pulled a handkerchief from his pocket and offered a wry smile. "Apologies, ladies, to be sure."

Charlotte's mouth had gone lax, and now she closed it, raising one brow. Amelie was aware of his motives, however. He'd stopped Charlotte from revealing their place of employment. She knew a moment's frustration, thinking it would have been better to have taken Charlotte and Eva into their confidence.

"Hay fever again, is it, Mr. Baker?" Amelie asked politely. "I do remember you suffering from it when you visited last year."

He nodded and wiped carefully at his nose. "I do beg your pardon, Miss Hampton, Miss Duvall. Absolutely inexcusable."

"How, again, are you acquainted with one another?" Mr. Radcliffe asked.

Amelie swallowed as Radcliffe turned his ice-blue eyes on her. She tried to speak but was unable to form a response. Heat rose to her cheeks, just as the detective answered the question.

"I tutored Miss Hampton's brother, Stephen. I was fortunate to spend time with the family, as well."

"A jack-of-all-trades, then! What subject did you tutor?"

"Humanities."

Mr. Radcliffe smiled. "That accounts for your deeply held convictions regarding Juliet and her Romeo."

Detective Baker chuckled. "Indeed. But once I realized my true calling was in police service, my path became clear."

One of the Misses Van Horne said something in an undertone that sounded to Amelie like a commentary on the benefits of placing a man under arrest, and she exchanged a wide-eyed glance with her cousins; Charlotte choked back a horrified laugh. To the elderly women's credit, they'd not lied—to refer to them as suitable chaperones was true only in the loosest of terms.

When the omnibus turned a corner and the theatre came into view, Amelie felt a moment of genuine delight. She loved the theatre, which was no surprise, given her affection for stories.

Mr. Radcliffe turned around and said, "Now, Miss Hampton, what is it that occupies your daylight hours?" His expression suggested he knew of her bashfulness with him, and he kindly paid her attention.

She swallowed again, and when the conveyance lurched to a rather jerky stop, gave a silent prayer of thanks. In the general ruckus of passengers rising and exiting the bus, she breathed a shaky sigh.

She needed time to collect her thoughts about admitting to her work for *The Marriage Gazette*. It might be that he would think nothing of it, but what were the odds that she would work for one of the hundreds of weekly periodicals published in London where he happened to send his personal ads?

It truly had been only a coincidence, but bringing the detective into the mix was another thread tying them all together in a way that could become suspect if they weren't careful. Mr. Radcliffe was intelligent, and were he to discover that the detective was not actually a longtime friend of Amelie's family, he would smell the deception.

Charlotte caught Amelie's eye as they exited, her gaze both confused and suspicious. She flicked a look from Amelie to the detective and back again.

Amelie's heart thumped. Charlotte, she knew, was also intelligent.

CHAPTER 8

Witty conversation may be helpful in establishing rapport with a debutante, but do not expect the same depth of discourse with her as you would with a male friend or fellow gentleman. The female brain is delicate and must not be overtaxed. Women who pursue education or read excessively develop male characteristics in their facial features. Reserve your complex debates for other men.

—The Gentleman's Guide to Efficient and
Profitable Courtship *by Sir Percival Prancey*

Michael caught Amelie's arm as they followed the rest of the Cheery Society Book Group members into the theatre. He held her back from the others and whispered, "You cannot reveal to him your place of employment!"

Her eyes flashed. "I *know* that, thank you very much, *Mr. Baker!*"

"Inform your cousins—"

"*They* also know that," she hissed. Her nostrils flared, and she yanked her arm free.

"You told them about this though I expressly swore you to secrecy?"

"Of course not!" She exhaled through her nose. "They know that he is the man who wrote to the paper. *I* swore *them* to secrecy that we all happen to work at the very place he contacted. Entirely coincidental, but suspicious on the face of it."

He paused. "Well . . . Miss Duvall seemed ready to divulge—"

"Miss Duvall is the cleverest person I know and would have told him an outright lie before betraying a confidence. Your 'sneezing' act was completely wasted. And quite unpleasant, I might add."

He cleared his throat, poised to apologize, but then was irritated that he felt chastised for simply making certain the charade continued without a hitch. His brows knit together. "What will you say when he asks again where you work?"

"I shall tell him as much of the truth as possible—was that not your counsel?" She glanced down the aisle and waved at her cousins with a smile. "Come, we are causing more curiosity than is wise. I cannot begin to imagine what sort of tale I shall be forced to spin for them later."

He followed her down the aisle, bemused to see that her cousins had arranged the seating so Amelie would be next to Radcliffe. Her step faltered, and he touched her elbow, nudging her forward. He took the seat on the other side of her, and the lights went down.

Radcliffe murmured something to her, and Amelie nodded with a quick smile.

Tension fairly radiated from her, and he couldn't for the life of him imagine what it was about Radcliffe that had women in such knots. Actually conversing with the man and spending time in close proximity to him served only to solidify Michael's prior opinion. The man was as slippery as an eel.

He noted the moment when Miss Hampton relaxed and lost herself in the play. She was an enigma to him, an odd combination of visible emotion and common sense. He'd underestimated her and, apparently, her family. He wished that newfound knowledge would put him at ease. From the moment he'd involved Miss Hampton in his scheme, he'd felt things subtly shift from his control.

The play was a light romantic comedy of errors and might be one his sister, Clarissa, would enjoy. He would have to make arrangements to accompany her for a night away from the baby for a time. He wondered if she would be comfortable leaving her baby with their brother, Alexander, who, although responsible and earnest, had the mind of a child. The familiar stab of worry about his family hit like clockwork, and he reminded himself he was doing everything in his power to see to their support and safety.

As the actors on stage wove their story, his mind drifted to the year before, when Stanley and Clarissa had married, and he'd first begun to feel tendrils of contentment replacing his constant worry. With Stanley to see to Clarissa's well-being, he had removed one responsibility; although Clarissa would have harsh words for him if she knew he'd ever considered her as such. Michael and Alexander had stayed in Michael's small flat, and Clarissa and Stanley had moved a short distance away to a quiet street and had begun establishing a family of their own.

Seeing his sister's grief had altered the way Michael viewed his own future. He could never imagine juggling the responsibilities of both his siblings and a wife of his own, to say nothing of the irresponsibility he felt it would be to expose a woman to such potential heartache. His job involved a high amount of risk, and he wouldn't make a widow of someone he cared for.

Miss Hampton chuckled softly at the antics playing out on-stage, and he glanced to his left. Radcliffe was sharing a smile with her, and when she focused again on the play, Radcliffe's eyes lingered on her face. He then made eye contact with Michael, raised one brow and cocked the side of his mouth upward.

Michael returned the smile and sat back, the false gesture feeling distasteful. He glanced again at Miss Hampton, taking note of how the delicate line of her neck disappeared beneath a lace collar of pale blue. She blinked, the long sweep of her lashes visible in profile. His jaw tightened at the thought of Radcliffe, seated on her other side and leering at her.

He wondered if he'd led Miss Hampton into a lion's den. But then he remembered how she had spied on Radcliffe outside the restaurant. She was clearly smitten with the man, and certainly with Miss Duvall's clever help, she'd have found herself associating with Radcliffe sooner or later.

At intermission, the lights went up, and the audience shifted, conversations began, and people left their seats for refreshments or to use the necessary. He heard Radcliffe's voice and turned his attention to him.

"I still have not learned of your vocation, Miss Hampton, and I am most curious. But wait, allow me to guess. Perhaps with your trim frame and lovely complexion you pose as a model for artists or photographers? Clothing designers?"

Michael fought to keep his expression neutral. Surely she would not fall prey to such ridiculous flattery.

Miss Hampton's cheeks blushed a lovely pink, and she smiled. "No, nothing of that sort."

"Ah. Hmm, as a member of our book club, you are clearly

well-read. Perhaps you have joined the ranks of intrepid females who work for daily newspapers?"

"No." Her smile slipped, but then righted itself. "That does sound exciting, however."

Michael realized he was watching Radcliffe disarm the young woman before his eyes. Gradually fading away was the girl incapable of speaking to Radcliffe without stammering or looking faint. Only a light blush remained, and it served to enhance her appearance, rather than detract.

"A shopgirl, then? You are employed in a respectable boutique where you sell women of quality the finest gloves and linens, and you exhibit long-suffering patience for the haughtiest of customers."

"No." Still the smile remained in place. "Shall I tell you?"

"Please, you must. My curiosity is unbearable." Radcliffe winked at her, his attention completely focused on Miss Hampton, as if she were the only person in the world.

"I am simply an office worker for a small business that provides social services."

Michael tipped his head. All things considered, she'd handled herself well. Miss Hampton was probably free of further scrutiny as long as Radcliffe never asked what kinds of services were provided.

"What kinds of services does the company provide?"

Michael sighed.

"Oh, many things," Miss Hampton said, her fingers clenched in her lap. "Courtship advice, and such. I mostly answer correspondence." She smiled, and Michael wondered if Radcliffe noted the strain in it.

"I cannot help but assume you are the loveliest part of the establishment. One hopes you sit near the entrance as the company's face. Business would certainly become very brisk with you drawing in the customers."

"You're very kind." Her strained smile nearly cracked, but she saved it. Michael did not know much about Miss Hampton's moral compass, but he suspected she was pushing it to its limit.

Miss Hampton's friends rose from their seats, and Radcliffe stood to let them pass.

"We thought to go for some punch, Amelie," Miss Caldwell said.

"I'll join you," Miss Hampton said quickly, and the three of them left the row and made their way up the aisle to the lobby.

Michael stood and watched them leave, hands in his pockets and leaning on the seat back of the chair in front of him. Once they had disappeared, he turned his attention back to Radcliffe, who was watching him with a grin.

"Which one has caught your fancy? You seem particularly familiar with Miss Hampton," Radcliffe said, stretching.

Michael nodded. "I imagine long hours at the Chancery must grow monotonous."

"Not at all. I like to vary my routine, keep busy." He smiled again. "You've sidestepped the question about our three little cousins."

Michael shrugged. "All three are beautiful. I know Miss Hampton well enough, but not her cousins. I do not suppose I have designs on any of them. You have been a member of the Cheery Society Book Group for some months, yes? I suppose you must have a preference."

Radcliffe chuckled. "Miss Trunsteel is a bit more willing to engage," he said, gesturing over his shoulder with his thumb to where Miss Trunsteel was in animated conversation with the elderly twin sisters and the two other gentlemen who had joined the party at the last minute. "I am afraid Miss Hampton and her friends are more skittish than colts. This evening marks the first time any of us have actually conversed about anything personal. The younger ones always require more coaxing."

"I should hate to believe that one of those young ladies will end up with a broken heart."

"Ah, a sentimentalist! No doubt you are concerned for the delicate feelings of your Miss Hampton. It is good to know, however, that should my interests fall in her direction, I would have the blessing of a family friend. I mean, you do not carry a torch for her yourself, correct?"

The words suddenly stuck in his throat, and Michael had to force them out. "I do not," Michael said. "You've no cause for concern on my account. I should hope your intentions are honorable, though; I do have a sense of responsibility for her well-being."

"Of course. You of all people are aware that I am a widower, and I never believed I would find an interest in courting someone new. As I said before, I cannot help but feel that my angel wife is encouraging me to live life to its fullest." Radcliffe smiled, the expression a mixture of sadness and self-deprecation.

Michael wished he could ask if Radcliffe had perhaps hastened his angel wife prematurely into the eternities. "Having never married, I can only imagine the difficulty."

"Painful." Radcliffe nodded. "Loneliness, however, is its own kind of hell. As the Lord said, 'It is not good for the man to be alone.'"

"Indeed."

"Do you have no intention to marry? I would imagine the company of a compassionate wife would be a comfort at the end of a long day chasing criminals."

"I find the prospect of creating a widow out of a good woman to be unappealing. The wife of an officer of the law does not have an easy life."

Radcliffe nodded, and his brow wrinkled in sympathy. "Ah, of course. You've lost a friend and partner to the dangers of the career. Your sister's husband, was he not? Of course you would see her pain more keenly than others. Little wonder you seek to avoid that predicament for yourself."

Michael stilled. He kept his expression smooth, open, despite his rising temper and thumping heart. "How do you know of my circumstances?"

"Oh, I must sound horribly invasive. I happened across an old newspaper article a colleague had in a stack of rubbish to be hauled away. Imagine my surprise when I read about the unfortunate turn of events that befell the very detective who later crossed my path. A shame it is, truly a shame, to lose loved ones. So very painful. Perhaps the human animal would benefit substantially from an absence of emotion. What would our friend Darwin think of such a principle?"

Michael kept his tone even and his expression light. "I do not know that absence of emotion holds any sway in a debate on human evolution. I should think Darwin's observations prove the opposite, in fact. The more man evolves, the higher his plane of morality, the greater his depth of compassion, wouldn't you say?"

Radcliffe nodded sagely. "Of course, you're right." He smiled, and added, "What a boon you bring to our little Cheery Society. I welcome a contemporary with intellect that matches my own."

Michael raised one brow before he could stop himself. "You find the book group to be lacking in intellectual talent?"

Radcliffe opened his hands and gestured to the elderly women, the young men who sat with them, and then the three women who were making their way down the theatre aisle. "You see with whom we are surrounded."

Michael forced a chuckle he didn't feel. "Why attend, then?"

Radcliffe smiled broadly and repeated, "You see with whom we are surrounded. There are more unattached young women joining book groups and societies of every size and shape these days. For a man seeking a wife to mind hearth and home, it is like a garden where every flower is lovelier than the last. The garden, though, must be carefully cultivated. One must take the time necessary to find just the right blossom."

"As a never-married man, I confess uncertainty as to what constitutes 'just the right blossom.'"

"The best sort of garden flower is one who brings substance to the crystal vase, would you not agree? A fullness of beauty to grace a man's home, and a wealth of good breeding and re-sources to bring a boon to the union. A good, strong family name is always the *coup de grâce*."

The lights blinked and an announcement came from the lobby that intermission was nearing its end. The crowd jostled and resumed their seats, and Miss Hampton and her friends navigated the aisle, dodging and skipping to avoid being stepped on. Miss Hampton's hat was lost in the shuffle, and she turned around to retrieve it. Would she never remember her hatpin?

Michael and Radcliffe both stepped aside, Miss Duvall and Miss Caldwell entered the row, and Miss Hampton, crushed hat in hand, paused just enough that Radcliffe smoothly entered next so the seating arrangement was as it had been before.

As the lights dimmed, Michael stole a glance at his partner. She looked at him quickly and took a breath as though calming herself. He thought she might say something, but instead she shook her head and turned her attention to the stage. The lights reflected back on her profile, and Michael felt a sense of unease.

Radcliffe seemed intrigued by Miss Hampton, whether because he found her attractive or easy prey—or both—Michael was unsure. Radcliffe's subtle mention of a potential bride bringing a "boon to the union" also spoke of the man's appreciation of a healthy dowry. Her name might indicate status and wealth, but Michael doubted Radcliffe knew Miss Hampton was associated with the "notorious family branch."

If the man proved to be genuine, and nothing more than a widower, so be it. But Michael's instincts knew there was something more. He needed to find proof soon, however. The Chief Inspector wouldn't allow the investigation to continue if Michael couldn't find something to support his theory. Miss Hampton could be the key.

CHAPTER 9

One must use caution in sharing secrets or
drawing others into a confidence. Be certain a friend
possesses the skills necessary to remain silent.
—THE MARRIAGE GAZETTE *advice column*

Amelie had just arrived home following a long day of attempting to teach a young woman named Barbara the finer points
of drawing room manners. The young woman had been unceremoniously dumped at the *Gazette* that morning by an impatient
father who seemed to expect miracles. Sally had explained that
the paper did not offer decorum training, but when he forked out
an outrageous sum of money, Sally decided the girls could benefit
from the experience of tutoring. Barbara had stubbornly dug in
her heels, and Amelie couldn't say she blamed her.

She shook the rain from her umbrella, pleased that this time
she remembered to place it in the umbrella stand. She had just
removed her coat when Mrs. Burnette appeared, handing her a
calling card.

"This gentleman stopped by an hour ago," the housekeeper
told her.

Amelie examined the thick ivory card that bore a name embossed in gold and impressive in design.

MR. HAROLD RADCLIFFE, *solicitor*

She looked up at the housekeeper, stunned, and said, "What do you suppose he wants?"

Mrs. Burnette took Amelie's coat. "I suppose he wants to sit in the parlor and socialize as civilized people do."

Amelie's heart pounded. Mr. Radcliffe had called on *her*? It was too fantastic to believe.

"Get yourself upstairs and freshen up. He said he would return this evening."

She moved toward the stairs in a fog. "He's . . . he is returning *tonight*?" She was torn between excitement and terror. What if he knew she had spied on his date with Miss Franklin? His intended visit might have more to do with that and less to do with "socializing as civilized people do."

Her foot was on the bottom stair when a knock sounded at the door. She turned as Mrs. Burnette opened it to reveal Mr. Radcliffe. His hat glistened in the lamplight and rain dappled the shoulders of his handsome black jacket. He looked past Mrs. Burnette and smiled when his eyes landed on Amelie.

"I hope I've not come at an inconvenient time?" he asked.

"Miss Hampton has only just returned home and has yet to freshen—"

"Not an inconvenient time at all," Amelie interrupted Mrs. Burnette. She stepped back down and joined the housekeeper at the door. "Please, Mr. Radcliffe, do come out of the rain. Mrs. Burnette, perhaps you'll instruct one of the Wells sisters to prepare a light tea?"

Mrs. Burnette pursed her lips, but she stepped back from the door.

Amelie forced herself to stop twisting her fingers together and reminded herself she had no reason to feel guilty for requesting the tea. As part of the rents, Hampton House provided tea services from the tenants' own purchased stock of food stuffs in the pantry.

"We shall take the tea in the parlor, thank you. Mr. Radcliffe?" Amelie smiled at Mrs. Burnette, who finally took Mr. Radcliffe's hat and coat.

Amelie's legs trembled slightly as she led the way to the parlor on the right. She feared she was much too nervous to enjoy tea and biscuits, so she imagined how Sally might handle the situation. Perhaps she could pretend to borrow some of her aunt's confidence.

Mr. Radcliffe waited until she was seated on a small sofa and then settled across from her in one of Sally's delicate medallion-backed chairs. It was an elegant piece of furniture, and he looked every inch a polished gentleman. She was proud of herself for holding in a dramatic sigh.

Katie Wells entered with a tea tray, which led Amelie to suspect that Mrs. Burnette had sent the girl in with tea that had already been steeping, rather than using tea from Amelie's stash. That way, Amelie's reputation would be preserved, because she would not have spent more than a scant few moments alone with a gentleman, even in a common room with the door wide open. When Katie set the tray at Amelie's elbow and then took a seat with her embroidery in the corner of the room, she knew her suspicions had been correct.

"Miss Hampton," Mr. Radcliffe said while she poured him a cup of tea, "I hope you will forgive my impetuous nature. It is only that I so enjoyed our conversation at the play last week I simply had to call on you. I find your company refreshing and delightful, and, as Miss Duvall mentioned that you live here at Hampton House, I took it upon myself to locate the address."

"Sugar?"

"One, please."

Amelie smiled and handed him the beverage, and then poured some for herself, gratified when the cup did not rattle against the saucer. "I am flattered, of course, and glad you found the house without trouble. That is, I presume you found it without trouble?"

"Quite, quite." He took a sip of his tea.

Amelie tipped her cup to her lips but couldn't make herself actually drink anything. Hoping he didn't notice, she pretended to swallow and then carefully held her cup and saucer on her knees. Her stomach was a mass of knots, and in the back of her mind, she whispered a prayer that she would remain calm.

For all the advice she offered through the pages of the *Gazette*, her mind was frustratingly blank as to how to handle conversation with "Mr. Dashing." Unless she found her tongue and an engaging line of dialogue soon, her opportunity would be lost. Miss Franklin had informed her that, while her date with Mr. Radcliffe had been pleasant, she did not expect further contact from him. Amelie was relieved that she was not stabbing a fellow husband-seeker in the back.

"Tell me, Miss Hampton, about your family. You hail from Frockshire, I understand? How are you related to Miss Sally Hampton, who owns this beautiful home?"

Amelie breathed a small sigh of relief. Mr. Radcliffe was extending a helping hand, and she gratefully took it. "I am indeed from Frockshire, and I am the third of four children. My elder two sisters are married—well, Sophia is widowed—and my younger brother, Stephen, is finishing at university. My parents, sadly, have already passed."

Mr. Radcliffe paused, and although it was a fraction of a moment, Amelie felt a subtle shift. He took a sip of his tea and then smiled. "Of course. Your family is the other—"

Amelie inwardly winced. She nodded, flushing. "The other side of the Hampton family, yes." Her family tree held itinerant gamblers, gentlemen three generations back who lost land and titles in games of chance. Bold, adventurous types who seemed to have passed their colorful love of life to her aunt. Where they were reckless, though, Sally possessed extraordinarily sound judgment.

"And your aunt?" Mr. Radcliffe prompted.

"Aunt Sally is my father's sister. She is truly a woman of independent means." Amelie smiled. "Sally Hampton is a force of nature, and although I would never be so bold as she is, I quite admire her." Amelie ignored the pang of guilt she felt at telling a small untruth. She would dearly love to be as bold as her aunt, but to admit it to a potential suitor—if Mr. Radcliffe was indeed such—would be a nail in the marital coffin. A gentleman did not seek out bold women when searching for a wife.

"I have heard tales of your aunt, all good, of course." Mr. Radcliffe stilled again, but the smile remained in place. "She is the powerful force behind the *Marriage Gazette,* is she not?"

Amelie felt like a rabbit caught in a snare. She should have foreseen the conversation's direction. "She is." She swallowed, but lifted her chin. "She rescued the *Gazette* from bankruptcy and has built a veritable empire from the ashes using her own good business sense and resources."

Mr. Radcliffe chuckled, his handsome face relaxing into ease. "You do well to champion your aunt." He nodded definitively. "She is unconventional, but admirable."

Amelie was certain she only imagined Mr. Radcliffe's patronizing tone. Sitting with him in her parlor was a singularly surreal experience, and that would account for her inability to think clearly. And she certainly did not want to give Mr. Radcliffe the impression that she was a hostile sort of person. She was demure. Proper. An ideal sort of woman.

Her mind flashed back to the night she had spied on Mr. Radcliffe and Miss Franklin, and she shoved the image aside. True, that had not been at all proper, but the cause had been just.

"I have heard of your aunt's extensive travels. I assume she hasn't much time to slake the wanderlust these days?"

"Indeed. The *Gazette* has kept her homebound for some time. Now and again, though, she does manage a quick escape."

"I find it gracious of her to have opened this delightful home." Mr. Radcliffe finished his tea and set the cup and saucer on the tray. "What a remarkable family you have."

Amelie smiled. "I am certain my aunt would be delighted to meet you." She hoped that was not too forward, too bold. Rather, she hoped it was a subtle indication that she appreciated Mr. Radcliffe's attention and would welcome more.

"As I would be, as well." His expression turned serious, and he looked at her earnestly. "Miss Hampton, I suppose you are aware that I am recently widowed. In fact, were it not for a pardon from my former vicar, I would still find myself officially in mourning. He has approved my use of the black armband you must have seen on my jacket."

Amelie nodded, although she had not noticed the armband

at all. She had also never heard of a vicar excusing a person's mourning period.

"I feel, though," he sighed, "that my late wife is most anxious for me to . . . to *move forward* with the life we had hoped and planned for together. She was gone so soon." His brow wrinkled with emotion, and Amelie's heart melted. "I am still here, though, and wish desperately for a full and happy home with children and a mother to love and cherish them. And me." He cleared his throat and looked down at his folded hands. "A home that mirrors the heaven our dear Queen Victoria would have us all enjoy."

Amelie placed her hand on her heart. "Oh, Mr. Radcliffe, of course you would still yearn for such things. I am so sorry for the untimely loss of your dear wife."

The man seemed so broken in that moment, and the memory of his sweet wife was only that. He was alone in the world, his dreams of love having been cruelly cut short. He was a man with the soul of a poet whose sadness and loss cut deeply. He suddenly seemed more approachable, more real. The fact that he still clearly loved his first wife did much to restore her faith in marriages based on love. He wasn't looking to replace her, but to continue forward. She felt herself relax.

"Have you siblings, other family with whom you visit?" she asked.

"Ah, I do not have the same fortune as do you. I hope you relish your kinship and take joy in each visit, each holiday spent together. My parents and brothers were involved in a carriage accident while I was away at school." His brow creased again. "They did not survive. The worst of it is that the last words I spoke to my father were those of anger."

"How tragic," Amelie said, a lump forming in her throat.

She forced herself not to ask what words of anger he had spoken and the reason for them, although her curiosity had climbed several notches. "I would be lost without my cousins and aunt."

"You are a wise woman to recognize the gift of a loving family." Mr. Radcliffe nodded sagely and offered a sad, handsome smile. He sat up straighter as if to shake off his melancholy. "But here I have gone off into the weeds while we are having a lovely tea. The hour grows late. It has been a delight to be with you, Miss Hampton, and again I do hope you will forgive the suddenness of my call, and the fact that I did not even spare you the time to freshen from your day." Mr. Radcliffe tipped his head with a smile. "Not that it was even necessary, if I might be so bold."

"It has been my pleasure, Mr. Radcliffe, and I hope you will feel free to call again. My days during the week are busy in Town, but my weekends are free for entertainment or social pursuits." Amelie felt a stab of disappointment that the call was at an end, but relieved she'd managed to reclaim some of her social graces.

She stood and waited for Mr. Radcliffe to rise also, and then saw him to the door where he gathered his coat and hat. She spotted Katie Wells leaving the parlor with the tea tray, her chaperoning tasks at an end, and from the corner of her eye, spied movement from the dining room, accompanied by the quiet rustle of fabric.

She fought a wry smile and bid Mr. Radcliffe a pleasant evening. Her heart skipped a beat when he bowed over her fingers, and again when he brushed the lightest of kisses on her knuckles. He smiled, and she closed the door quietly behind him.

"Amelie!" Evangeline whispered loudly as she and Charlotte ventured from the dining room. She clasped Amelie's hands and squeezed. "You had tea with Mr. Radcliffe!"

Amelie's head spun, and she laughed. "I did! How long were you listening at the keyhole?"

Charlotte looked at the closed front door and chewed on her lip. "What do you think of him?" she asked Amelie, propelling her back into the parlor.

"He seems lovely, mourning for his wife, lonely." Amelie sank down on the sofa with her cousins. "I know that expression, Miss Charlotte Duvall, and it means you are skeptical of something."

Charlotte sighed. "He seems lovely, I suppose." She paused, "It's only that . . ."

"Out with it, if you please." Amelie folded her arms.

"I once heard my brother, Nicholas, plying a local girl with fine words and deep emotion, but I knew he was fibbing—exaggerating, at least—to win her favor. Mr. Radcliffe sounded much that way to me tonight." She lifted her shoulder. "You know I would love nothing more than for you to find the charming prince of your dreams, and I would love for it to be this man. You've eyed him from a quiet distance for a while, and he seems interested."

Eva squeezed Amelie's hand again. "You've time to ascertain his character, yes? He seems intent on calling again, and he was conscientious of asking about your life and family. Some gentlemen talk so much of themselves there is room for nobody else in the conversation."

"He did seem interested in your family," Charlotte agreed, nodding slowly. "Especially Aunt Sally."

Amelie sighed. "He was merely being polite. I was so tongue-tied in the beginning it was incumbent upon him to carry the conversation."

Charlotte held up her hands, palms out. "You mustn't be

irritated with me for injecting a note of caution into your happy glow. I do not mean to dampen it, but merely urge you to exercise care. I love you dearly and do not wish to see you hurt."

"Oh, Charlotte." Amelie smiled at her cousin. "I know, and I am grateful. I am confused, though—until now you've seemed to like Mr. Radcliffe well enough."

"That was before I heard him speak at length about his life. He seemed . . ." She sighed. "He seemed as though he wanted to leave you with a good impression, though perhaps that's all he intended. I am cynical; my brothers have ruined me." She smiled and stretched, a small yawn escaping.

"I'm for bed," Eva said through a yawn of her own. "Tomorrow will be busy—"

She was interrupted by a brisk knock at the front door. Firm footsteps soon sounded on the hallway from the back of the house, and Mrs. Burnette appeared, eyeing the three girls in the parlor with a slight frown. "At this hour!" she said, as though they were at fault.

Amelie glanced at the clock on the mantel—ninety minutes remained before Hampton House's doors officially closed for the evening. She hurried to the parlor's door and peeked around the corner.

The housekeeper opened the door, paused, and then exchanged a few words before stepping back to reveal the tall form of Detective Baker. Curiously, Amelie felt her heart jump. As he came in from the rain, he removed his hat and subtly shook fine droplets from his coat.

Mrs. Burnette glared at the new spots on the floor, but held out her hand for his things. "Miss Hampton is already in the parlor," she said crisply, gesturing to the room.

Amelie gasped and hurried back to the sofa. Her cousins looked at her curiously.

Appearing in the doorway of the parlor, Mrs. Burnette addressed Amelie. "Mr. Baker to see you, Miss Hampton. Shall I have Katie prepare another tea?"

Anxiety churned in her chest. How on earth would she fool her cousins again about the detective's charade? She'd already lied to them while explaining away the tension that had clearly been visible between her and Mr. Baker the night of the play. "He is as aggravating as my brother," she had finally told Charlotte, whose suspicion over the whole relationship had been apparent.

"Yes, Mrs. Burnette," Amelie said, "please send Katie with a fresh pot of tea."

Mr. Baker waited patiently behind Mrs. Burnette, but having just spent a lovely time with Mr. Radcliffe, Amelie felt her hackles raise in preparation for Mr. Baker's inevitable criticisms.

The housekeeper nodded and left.

Detective Baker entered the parlor, nodded to the three women, and prepared to sit in the medallion-backed chair Mr. Radcliffe had occupied. At the last moment, he moved instead to a settee, and Amelie decided it was a good choice. Mr. Baker was taller than Mr. Radcliffe, and broader. The slim chair did not appear equal to the task of holding the detective for an extended length of time.

"Detective," Amelie said, determined to be professional, "what brings you by this evening?"

Charlotte and Eva exchanged a glance.

"Should we . . . ?" Eva gestured to the door, and they both moved to stand.

Detective Baker shook his head. "No, please stay." He ran

a hand through his hair and then leaned forward, resting his elbows on his knees. "Miss Hampton, the other night, you assured me that Miss Caldwell and Miss Duvall are mature women, capable of keeping confidences." He paused and looked at Amelie's cousins expectantly. "Am I correct in this assumption?"

Charlotte and Eva looked at Amelie and then the detective, the silence lengthening.

"Well?" the detective asked.

Amelie frowned, her irritation and uneasiness growing. "You doubt my word? What is this about?"

Her friends looked at her again, and then Charlotte turned to Mr. Baker. "We are indeed trustworthy, Detective. Please say what you need to say."

Detective Baker focused his attention on Amelie. "Miss Hampton, I know Mr. Radcliffe visited this evening, and I need to know exactly what he said."

CHAPTER 10

*Avoid involving civilians in investigative matters. They will
only impede matters and cause problems to address in the future.*

—Detective Handbook for Investigative Procedure

Michael looked at the three women who eyed him with equal
parts curiosity and suspicion and hoped his instincts were correct.
Director Ellis had informed him that unless he found compelling
evidence to continue surveilling Mr. Radcliffe, he would be wise
to turn his attention to other matters. Michael still felt unsettled
about the whole affair, and his suspicion had only grown after his
conversation with Radcliffe the night of the play.

He looked at Miss Hampton. He was unable to read her expression, other than she seemed exceptionally perturbed. Knowing
that she had just spent what was likely a delightful time with the
man of her dreams, her irritation was to be expected. With some
effort, he shook aside a growing sense of disappointment.

He cleared his throat. "Miss Hampton, would you please inform your friends about the true nature of our association?"

The ladies looked at Miss Hampton, gazes still curious
but now suspicious, and Miss Hampton rolled her eyes. "For

heaven's sake, Detective, you needn't imply anything untoward. Charlotte, Eva, I met Detective Baker for the first time last week after I"—she straightened in her seat—"*supervised from a distance* the meeting between Miss Franklin and Mr. Radcliffe. Unbeknownst to me, the detective"—she indicated Michael—"was following Mr. Radcliffe, and when I left the restaurant, he ran me to ground in the park, demanding to know whether I was in some sort of criminal liaison with Mr. Radcliffe."

Michael closed his eyes. "I did not 'run you to ground,' Miss Hampton, I—" He shook his head. "Never mind."

Miss Duvall took in the scene for a moment and then rose. Michael wondered if she might call for the housekeeper, but instead she closed the parlor doors with a quiet click. She returned to her seat and said, "Detective, why on earth would you have assumed Amelie might be criminally involved with Mr. Radcliffe?"

Miss Hampton spoke up. "And why on earth did you commit me to such subterfuge and secrecy if you had planned all along to include everybody in the investigation?" She seemed offended.

Michael realized how completely at sea he was with a room of young women. He'd spent every hour of his adult life working or caring for his family, which had left little time for socializing with the fairer gender.

He took a breath. "Miss Hampton, I never intended to divulge our subterfuge to anyone, but I have come to realize that opportunities to speak with you alone will be difficult to find. As you assured me your family are trustworthy, I saw few other options. As it stands, this may be irrelevant before long."

She frowned. "Irrelevant, why?"

He held up a hand. "Allow me to explain—"

A knock at the door interrupted him, and he looked at it in exasperation.

"That would be tea," Miss Caldwell stated and answered the door. She took a tray from a young maid and then nudged the door closed with her toe. He waited as she poured tea as efficiently as one might for the Queen. She was lovely, with dark hair and eyes, and was the sort of girl that would have had Michael tongue-tied in his youth.

Miss Duvall accepted the tea from her cousin with a murmur of thanks and watched Michael over the rim of her cup. Her dark-red hair seemed a match for her personality. She was self-assured and assertive; he didn't imagine one would have an easy time trying to deceive her.

Which led him to Miss Hampton. The one who had borne the task of trying to deceive Miss Duvall. Her cheeks were lightly flushed. Her hazel eyes locked on his, and he felt an odd sense of camaraderie with her. As long as she was the only person outside the CID who knew of his suspicions, the situation felt manageable. He felt he could trust her. After all, he knew she'd kept details from her cousins with whom she probably typically shared every confidence. He also knew how enamored of Radcliffe she was, and the man had just spent a good thirty minutes in her company.

"Detective," Miss Hampton said as Miss Caldwell finished serving the tea, "if you are here to ask if I am willing to continue gathering intelligence for you, then you should know that I have conditions."

He eyed her warily. "What are your conditions?"

"I insist you communicate with me regarding any information you gather that would prove Mr. Radcliffe to be the criminal you believe him to be."

He sighed. "I cannot offer you a blanket commitment. I am limited with what I'm able to share."

She straightened in her seat and took a sip of her tea. "Well, then, I suppose I shall be limited with what *I* am able to share."

He was aware in the periphery that the other two women were looking back and forth between them as though observing a match of lawn tennis. "Miss Hampton, please be reasonable."

"I am being perfectly reasonable. If I am to assist you in this investigation, I think it more than fair that I be kept abreast of any developments."

He searched for his patience. Trustworthy or no, he had been on shaky ground with her from the first moment. She took the things he said and twisted them, and then she restated everything in a way that made sense but was entirely opposite of his own ends.

Miss Caldwell delicately cleared her throat. "If we are to be included in this matter, might we be advised as to Mr. Radcliffe's alleged indiscretions?"

Miss Hampton turned expectantly to Michael. "Yes, please. We would all like to be advised of your suspicions." A hint of a smile played at the corner of her mouth. The liveliness behind her eyes reminded him of their time together at the book group gathering. She was quick, and he suddenly felt he ought to be on his guard.

He folded his arms across his chest. "I am not asking Miss Hampton to play a part or engage in any way with Mr. Radcliffe."

Miss Duvall arched a brow. "Yet you arranged for her to introduce you to him under false pretenses at the book group, and you encouraged her to continue her association with him by attending the play afterwards. Do you still refuse to divulge your suspicions to her? That seems unfair, not to mention potentially dangerous." Her green eyes bored holes into his head.

He put a finger beneath his collar and loosened it. The air in the parlor had suddenly grown warmer. The problem was, Miss Duvall was correct. Miss Hampton was now in Radcliffe's line of fire, in part because Michael had put her there. From the man's demeanor, his cavalier attitude about women and requirements for a potential wife, Michael didn't imagine Radcliffe's intentions were admirable.

He knew when he had lost his advantage. "Very well. I regrettably must inform you that I suspect Mr. Radcliffe had a hand in his late wife's death."

The three regarded him with identically blank expressions.

Amelie slowly lowered her teacup to the saucer. "You . . . you cannot *possibly*—" She paused and cleared her throat. "Detective, you met Mr. Radcliffe under pleasant social circumstances. Surely that must have made some positive impression upon you. I am quite certain you're mistaken."

Miss Duvall lifted her chin. "What are the reasons for your suspicions?"

"Charlotte," Miss Hampton said. "You mustn't allow your own recent impressions to color your judgment."

"Amelie," Miss Duvall said patiently, "what better way to color my judgment than with my own impressions? Detective?"

Michael's ears perked up. "What 'recent impressions,' Miss Duvall?"

Miss Duvall glanced at Miss Hampton as if in apology. "Amelie, as I told you, there *was* an edge of insincerity to Mr. Radcliffe's conversation."

"In what sense, Miss Duvall?" Michael leaned forward.

"It seemed to me that he spoke as one who was acting.

Putting on a show of excessive sorrow but without the emotion behind it."

"His wife died!" Amelie lifted her hands. "Of course he feels sorrow when discussing her." She turned to Michael and sighed. "Very well, since I insisted on being informed, it seems I must hear you out. What leads you to believe he may have been involved in her death?"

Michael hesitated, knowing she would be dissatisfied with his answer. "Instinct," he finally admitted. "I have no proof, no leads. The matter will not let me rest, however. When we took him to confirm her identity, I felt something that did not resonate with me. And he behaved in what I considered a suspicious manner immediately following."

The frown in Miss Hampton's brow deepened. "What did he do?"

Michael knew he wasn't sharing secrets that compromised the investigation, but even so, he was not accustomed to conversing with civilians about his cases. He made himself speak. "He refused an autopsy and then took her body immediately to France for burial in her family plot."

Miss Hampton tapped her fingertip against her lip, clearly she had more questions but was willing to wait.

But Miss Duvall nodded decisively. "I am not surprised."

Miss Caldwell shook her head. "Why would he not bury his wife here, close to him? Did he not have a plot for the two of them?"

"A question I also asked myself, Miss Caldwell," Michael said. "Radcliffe talked of her family's strong religious beliefs and the bond she shared with her mother and brother. He said she would want to be in Marseilles."

"Had Mr. Radcliffe purchased a life insurance policy for his wife?" Miss Hampton asked suddenly.

He tipped his head, impressed with the insight. "That very thing is on my list of items to continue investigating. I've been unable to uncover information about a policy to this point."

She nodded. "I believe I mentioned to you that I read detective novels extensively. I have noticed that the motive for the crime almost always leads back to a money source."

Her cousins glanced at her, nodding their agreement of her assessment.

"It is a sound theory," he said, wondering if Miss Hampton truly believed her detective novels were a match for actual professional experience. On the other hand, her affinity for the subject matter seemed to be distracting her from her defense of Radcliffe, so he wasn't about to discourage it.

Miss Caldwell gathered the empty teacups and placed them on the tray. "It is horrifically indelicate to ask," she said to Michael, "but how did Mrs. Radcliffe perish?"

The other two women waited for his answer, leaning forward slightly as if the question were the farthest thing from indelicate.

"I am afraid she was found in the Thames. A constable dragged her ashore."

"She drowned, then?" Miss Hampton asked.

"That was the coroner's official cause of death."

Miss Hampton frowned, and her lips pursed. "I simply cannot believe Mr. Radcliffe would harm anyone."

"Amelie," Miss Caldwell said, her tone gentle, "could it be possible that your judgment is perhaps the *slightest* bit tinged by affection? I agree with you that he seems unlikely to hurt anyone, especially a loved one, but people are sometimes deceptive." She placed her hand over Miss Hampton's.

"You know of my feelings on the matter," Miss Duvall said firmly. "Any man who brings to mind my cad of a brother is not one to trust."

Miss Hampton smiled. "I know you both have my best interests at heart." She sighed and looked at Michael. "I shall continue to encourage Mr. Radcliffe's attentions, if for no other reason than to prove to you his innocence. Should I discover anything untoward or the least bit suspicious, I will relay it straight to you. If you wish, we shall continue the ruse of former friendship with the book society and you may observe Mr. Radcliffe to your heart's content. Perhaps you'll develop a friendship with him! You might have common interests."

"I doubt that very much," he said. "I accept the details of your proposal. I would add that you should take care to avoid situations where you might find yourself alone with Radcliffe."

Miss Duvall nodded. "One of us will always be with her, or the housekeeper or maid if they are here and we are not."

"And you will send word of any new developments?" Miss Hampton said.

He inclined his head. "I will send word if it does not harm the investigation."

She huffed a sigh. "I suppose that will suffice, as I am unlikely to receive any further concessions."

"Very good," he said. "I give you my word I shall endeavor to be as forthcoming as possible."

"Oh!" Miss Caldwell said. "I nearly forgot to mention it, but the Misses Van Horne have planned a rather last-minute Evening of Entertainment at their home this Friday evening, and they are sending invitations to all members of the Cheery Society Book Group."

Miss Duvall laughed. "That is an evening I would not miss for the world. Those women are more diverting than the funniest play. I hear their home is a tribute to all things Egyptian."

Miss Hampton turned to Michael. "There is another reason for you to spend time with Mr. Radcliffe, assuming he will attend. You'll see, in no time at all, you will learn there is nothing nefarious about the gentleman."

She smiled, but it wasn't the full, engaging kind he'd come to expect from her. The woman was trying to convince herself as much as him, he would wager on it. Perhaps some part of her had noted Radcliffe's insincerity, or perhaps she trusted Charlotte's judgment. Either way, he did not wish to see her come to harm.

"I will be glad if you are correct," he told her. It was the best he could offer.

Michael spent a sleepless night, tossing and turning and doubting he would find anything of significance to tie Radcliffe to his wife's death before Director Ellis put a halt to his investigation. When he reached the Yard early the next morning, he was surprised to find a young man in fine clothing seated outside the door to his office.

"Are you Detective Baker?" The man's accent was French.

"I am. And you are?" Michael unlocked his door as the young man stood and gathered his coat and hat.

"My name is Antoine Verite. I have some concerns about a

recent death in my family, and I believe you were the investigator of note."

Michael's heart skipped a beat. "Mr. Verite. Is your sister, Mrs. Marie Radcliffe, the family you speak of?"

Mr. Verite's eyes clouded, but he firmed his chin and nodded. "I am hopeful for your help."

"Please, come in." Michael turned on the wall sconces and shivered. "Allow me to adjust the heater; it will take but a moment. Have a seat." He indicated the chair across from his desk. After adding coal to the heater, he removed his coat and hat and then took a seat. "That should chase away some of the chill."

He studied the young man—mid-twenties at most—and saw a familial resemblance between him and his late sister. "Tell me about your sister, Mr. Verite."

Mr. Verite took a deep breath. "Detective Baker, I do not believe my sister's death was an accident, nor did she take her own life." His voice trembled, but he shook his head firmly. "She was happy, so happy with her husband and her new home. Here—I have the last letter she wrote to me and *Maman*, only two days before her death." He reached inside his coat pocket and pulled out a folded missive.

"May I?" Michael took the letter, opening it along folds that showed wear from continual folding and unfolding. The script was in a lovely feminine hand, and although Michael's French was not excellent, he deciphered enough to realize Marie had indeed expressed happiness in her life, mentioned her husband by name, and promised to visit within a week with exciting news.

"Do you know the nature of the news she planned to share with you, Mr. Verite?" Michael carefully folded the paper and returned it to him.

He shook his head. "Marie was an excellent lace maker, and she had been searching for a quality boutique to sell some of her pieces. We wondered if that was her news."

Michael disliked the next question he was compelled to ask. "Forgive the intrusiveness of the question, but you never heard your sister express a desire to end her life? She did not confide such a thing to you or to your mother?"

"*Mais non.* Detective, my sister was full of life. She had married a man of means who doted on her, fulfilled her every need. He made certain she always had pin money and resources to visit us in Marseilles as often as she wished. She wanted for nothing. She had found 'a man for the fairy tales,' she said. That she would meet such a horrible end . . . It is awful, and I cannot rest without imploring you to investigate, please."

"How does your mother feel about your visit here?"

"Ah, but she does not know. I mean to spare her the pain should my efforts come to nothing."

"A personal question for you, Mr. Verite. Do you or your family hold religious beliefs that would forbid an autopsy of the body?"

Mr. Verite's brow wrinkled. "*Non*, we do not. Why would you ask? Mr. Radcliffe told us the police had found it unnecessary."

"I am afraid Mr. Radcliffe told you an untruth. We wanted very much to perform an autopsy but refrained for the sake of your mother and her 'religious convictions.' Mr. Radcliffe claimed it would distress her to an uncomfortable degree."

The young man's face reddened. "This is a lie!" He shook his head. "Maman, she never trusted him, but I believed he was good for my sister. I supported Marie's decision to marry Mr. Radcliffe, and I convinced my mother that her reservations about him were silly. That she was too protective." He closed his eyes briefly and paused. "Is it too late to perform an autopsy? Perhaps Mr. Radcliffe will not allow it, but she is buried in our family plot. Does that mean"—he swallowed—"that she is again in our care?"

Michael was reluctant to answer. "The husband is still the one to govern her affairs, but if he were to voice protest, especially now that we are aware he lied about family objections to the procedure, he would look suspicious, indeed. I've a feeling he would avoid such a thing at all costs."

"I have a room in town, at an inn. Shall I give you the address?"

Michael studied the man, thinking. "I think it best if Mr. Radcliffe is unaware of your visit. Return home, Mr. Verite, and I give you my word I shall contact you directly with any new information. Feel free to wire here with any questions you might have, in the meantime."

Mr. Verite paused, his brows knit.

"I realize I am asking you to do something difficult. Please know my word is not given lightly or to placate. I will see this investigation through to its conclusion; in fact, I have never stopped. I have a scenario already in motion that I believe will reveal some crucial information."

"You will discover the truth of my sister's fate?"

He smiled grimly and stood, motioning his guest to the door. "My partner and I are of a similar mind concerning the fate of your sister, sir. Again, I ask for your trust. Do I have it?"

Mr. Verite stood and shook Michael's hand. "You do. Mr. Radcliffe killed her, Detective. I know he did."

CHAPTER 11

What a glorious situation in life to hold the attention of more than one gentleman; in such an instance, however, a woman must manage her response to the attention by striking a balance between proper encouragement and behavior best described as "coy."

—The Care and Keeping of Girls and
Young Women *by Miss Hortence Strongberry*

My Dearest Miss Hampton,

It is with every ounce of my heart that I hope to see you in attendance at the Misses Van Hornes' social event this Friday evening. I did so enjoy our tea two days ago, and I hope I am not inappropriately bold when I repeat that I should love to further our acquaintance. At some point in the near future, perhaps I might meet your aunt, Miss Sally Hampton, to express my interest in calling regularly upon you, if indeed you would welcome such a thing.

Until Friday, I sincerely hope,

Yours ever,

Mr. Harold Radcliffe, solicitor

Dear Mr. Radcliffe,

 I am thrilled to receive your correspondence, and I am planning to attend the ladies' social event this Friday evening. I shall be accompanied by my cousins, Miss Duvall and Miss Caldwell. I have also extended the invitation on behalf of the Misses Van Horne to Detective Baker, whom I am hoping will also attend. I do believe the detective spends an inordinate amount of time and energy on his vocation, and he would benefit from healthy diversions. I was pleased with the outcome of his efforts at our society book group meeting and appreciate greatly your overtures of friendship.

 In reference to my aunt, Miss Sally Hampton, I am certain she would be happy to make your acquaintance and extend the best wishes of our family.

 Until Friday,
 Most sincerely,
 Miss Amelie Hampton

Amelie arrived at the Misses Van Hornes' residence with Charlotte and Eva for the much anticipated Evening of Entertainment. All three had rushed to return home from work, freshen, and change clothing for the evening. Amelie had been looking forward to the event all week as a delightful opportunity to see Mr. Radcliffe again, and had been happy to exchange correspondence with him. She was uncertain as to the level of his intent, and as such had avoided offering an official introduction to Sally until Mr. Radcliffe's intentions became more serious. *If* they became more serious.

The thought of such a thing sent a nervous thrill through her. She still had not quite reconciled her heart between hoping Mr. Radcliffe was a true gentleman and knowing Mr. Baker was investigating him for a horrible crime.

She had looked forward with equally as much anticipation to Detective Baker's presence at the event. She couldn't account for it, as she certainly was not as interested in him as she was in Mr. Radcliffe. Perhaps her growing affection for the detective was simply a burgeoning friendship, a natural consequence borne of time spent on a common task.

As she and her friends stepped from the cab and took in the grand facade of the elderly ladies' home, she spied Mr. Radcliffe, who was speaking to Detective Baker just outside the front door.

"Who is that with the detective?" Eva asked. "The third man?"

Amelie frowned. "I do not know. A friend?"

"Does he have any of those?" Charlotte eyed the detective with a frown. "He's rather . . . unfriendly."

Amelie lifted her shoulder, feeling oddly defensive of Mr. Baker. "I doubt he has much time for friend sorts of things." She had deliberately mentioned the detective in her letter to Mr. Radcliffe, hoping to further an association between them that would convince Mr. Baker of Mr. Radcliffe's harmlessness. Regrettably, the detective's insidious suspicion lurked in the back of her mind like an unwelcome guest.

The three gentlemen at the door turned at their approach and smiled.

"Ladies, how beautiful you all are this evening." Mr. Radcliffe lightly kissed each young woman's fingers, lingering over Amelie's, which had her blushing.

She glanced at Detective Baker, whose face remained impassive, but a muscle worked in his jaw.

"Detective Baker," Eva said, "would you introduce us to your companion?"

Amelie took a closer look at the man who stood next to the detective. He was tall with blonde hair, brown eyes, and he sported a neatly trimmed moustache. He seemed, like Detective Baker, to likely have been better suited to other, more exciting activities than enjoying an evening of unspecified entertainment at the home of two eccentric octogenarians.

"Ladies, my partner, Detective Nathaniel Winston. These are Miss Duvall, Miss Caldwell, and Miss Hampton."

"How lovely," Amelie said, smiling but darting a glance from Detective Baker to Detective Winston. "You are also an aficionado of the arts?"

Detective Winston returned the smile, but it was tight. "Indeed. And when Baker described the company he keeps these days, I insisted he bring me along."

Mr. Radcliffe chuckled. "I certainly understand the motivation."

The very air around them felt strained, and Amelie was relieved when Detective Baker held out his hand and indicated for the women to proceed through the door. The awkwardness of the conversation faded when Amelie caught sight of the impressive front hall.

The home looked as though someone had picked up a grand building in Cairo and plunked it down in the middle of Mayfair. Egyptology had been all the rage for nearly a century, with fads coming and going depending on the decade, but this was something else altogether.

"Is that a sarcophagus?" Charlotte murmured at Amelie's elbow.

There was indeed a large sarcophagus standing nearby, guarding the foyer, complete with gold inlay and crossed arms. "My goodness," Amelie began.

"Oh, my," Eva breathed as she entered behind Amelie. "Do you suppose there's still a mummy inside?"

They drifted slowly farther into the hall, joining others who stared, mouths agape, at the lavish decor. Amelie's eyes traveled from the ornate coffin to the high ceiling, where the walls were painted in an exact replica of Shepheard's Hotel in Cairo.

"I wouldn't be surprised if they had hosted a mummy unwrapping decades ago. They are quite the event, I've heard. My former school instructor attended one ages ago hosted by Dr. Pettigrew, himself." She secretly wished to be invited to one—she'd never seen an actual mummy, not up close, anyway. The odd traveling exhibit that crossed through Frockshire years ago hardly counted.

"I have never understood the reasoning. I'd not like people gaping at my remains," Eva murmured. "Would it not be better to give the poor deceased a proper burial afterward, at least?"

A lady next to them laughed. "Now, what fun is that? We would never be able to look at it again! It is still in there, you know." Amelie recognized Mrs. Blakestone, who sporadically attended the Cheery Society Book Group. "Besides, it isn't as though the dead require a Christian burial, after all." She waved impatiently at the girls. "Come along, you must see the spectacular parlor. I am a frequent visitor of the Misses Van Horne, so I know the house quite well."

Amelie looked over her shoulder at the gentlemen, who all watched Mrs. Blakestone with blank expressions. Mr. Radcliffe recovered himself first and smiled grandly, offering his arm to the lady. She heard Detective Winston mutter something to Mr. Baker, but it was lost as the group was whisked along with the tide of people entering an enormous room.

Adjoining the front hall, in equal splendor, was the parlor. Amelie could scarcely believe they were still in London. Tall palms graced the corners, lavish sofas and settees of colorful and intricate designs provided multiple seating groups, and a string quartet sat near the hearth.

Miss Trunsteel joined the group and smiled broadly at them all, her gaze finally resting on Mr. Radcliffe. "Is it not amazing?" she said, eyes sparkling. "We needn't dream of traveling to Egypt anymore—the Van Horne sisters seem to have brought the whole of it to us!"

"It is remarkable," Charlotte agreed. "One wonders where to look first."

"What are we to expect at this Evening of Entertainment?" Detective Winston asked.

"Dear assembled guests," a voice called, and Amelie saw the Van Horne sisters at the front of the room. One of the sisters— Ethel? Margaret?—was dressed in silks and satins of red and gold. "My sister, Margaret, and I welcome you to our humble home, and pray you will enjoy this evening's entertainment."

Margaret wore equally resplendent silks and satins colored in purple and silver. She picked up the introduction as smoothly as if it had come from the same person. "Please find a plate of refreshments and a glass of something that sparkles from one of the servants now circulating with trays. Or find a seat and they will come to you. We'll begin our program in a few minutes' time."

"We've a special guest from Budapest who will soon join us," Ethel finished with a smile.

Amelie took stock of the small gathering around her and wondered where they would sit, and whether she could discreetly elbow Miss Trunsteel aside to claim a spot near Mr. Radcliffe.

Charlotte threaded her arm through Amelie's, and they moved toward the hearth where two large sofas sat at right angles with a settee and other chairs completing the ensemble. It was the largest grouping in the room, and the best to accommodate their growing number. Amelie was unsure how Charlotte managed it, but she soon found herself on the inside corner of one of the sofas, seated next to Mr. Radcliffe. Detective Baker sat on the inside corner of the other sofa, bumping Amelie's knees with his own as he sat.

"Apologies," he mumbled, but loudly enough that Amelie was certain Mr. Radcliffe heard it. She glanced at the detective, her eyes narrowing. He was not the clumsy sort—far from it. And for all that he looked out of place in formal settings, he seemed particularly out of sorts this evening. She wondered if his odd demeanor was a consequence of his companion, who sat beside him and barely managed a tight smile for the others as the refreshment trays circulated.

Charlotte had neatly insinuated herself on Mr. Radcliffe's other side, leaving a frowning Miss Trunsteel to choose a settee with Eva. Mr. Radcliffe handed Amelie a small plate of treats, which she took with a murmur of thanks even as her stomach turned over. She would never be able to eat a morsel of food seated so close to the man with only scant inches separating them!

She swallowed and turned her head away, suddenly unable to bear the sight of the fois gras and crackers on her plate. She gritted her teeth in frustration as much as discomfort; she'd not had such appetite aversion since childhood when Stephen had brought 'round his friend, Bertram Grassley, who had quite captured her heart. She'd not been able to manage a meal in his presence until he'd laughed at something odious Stephen had said about her, at which point her appetite had returned with a vengeance.

The detective caught her eye. "Are you unwell, Miss Hampton?"

"Oh," she said, trying to chuckle, "I ate a quick dinner earlier and find myself quite full."

He looked at her face, and he must have seen her discomfort because he subtly took the plate from her fingers. He quickly slid most of her refreshments to his plate and returned hers with one small cookie and some crumbs. Mr. Radcliffe was conversing with Charlotte, and Amelie offered Detective Baker a smile.

He winked at her, something she would have ordinarily found outrageous, but instead took comfort in the strange sense of friendship she felt. He made quick work of the extra food on his plate, and Detective Winston looked at him with an unspoken question before shaking his head and turning his attention to Mr. Radcliffe.

"It is good to see you out in society so soon, Mr. Radcliffe," Detective Winston said, and Amelie noted the sudden tension in Mr. Radcliffe's demeanor.

"Thank you," Mr. Radcliffe said, tipping his head in acknowledgment. Amelie looked at his face, which was lightly flushed.

Amelie eyed the detective with a surge of anger. What was the man implying? That Mr. Radcliffe was socializing too soon after the death of his wife? Was the black armband he wore around his coat sleeve—admittedly invisible against the black fabric of the sleeve—not enough?

Detective Baker glanced at his partner and lightly cleared his throat. Detective Winston did not seem deterred. "Where is your family, Mr. Radcliffe? Remind me where you spent your youth before coming to London."

Amelie swallowed a gasp and leaned forward to catch Mr. Winston's eye. She whispered, "Mr. Radcliffe's family died in a horrible accident when he was young, and I am certain he does not wish to discuss it." What had Detective Baker been thinking to bring the man along?

Mr. Radcliffe patted Amelie's hand and said, "Thank you, dear Miss Hampton, for your valiant defense. I am certain the detective bears me no ill will."

"Certainly not," Mr. Winston said. "Merely making conversation."

They were interrupted by another announcement from Ethel Van Horne, but Amelie missed it as she glared at the two detectives. They were not paying her attention, however; in fact, Detective Baker was saying in an undertone to his partner, "What are you doing?"

"Nothing," came the terse reply. "I only—"

"These are my friends," Mr. Baker hissed back. "I would never have brought you along had I thought—" He cut himself off as Miss Van Horne's monologue continued.

Mr. Radcliffe radiated tension, and Amelie knew he also had heard the exchange. With a fair amount of dismay, she wondered if Detective Winston was about to muddle up Detective Baker's entire operation. Did the man not know what was happening? Amelie decided she did not like him. Aside from being obtuse, he was extraordinarily rude. Detective Winston might be better referred to as "Detective Witless."

Amelie's mouth twitched at her own humor, and she bit the inside of her cheek, trying to focus on Miss Ethel, who was still addressing the room.

"Our guest hails from Budapest, and he bears the blood of exotic ancestors. He is a psychic of the first order, and Margaret and I have witnessed firsthand his brilliant prognostications. May I present, the Great Prospero!"

An anticipatory ripple of excitement traveled the room as a man appeared in the doorway. He was dressed in austere black from head to toe, and his moustache and top hat gave him the look of an actor in a melodramatic play. Amelie bit her other cheek this time to keep from giggling and joined in the smattering of applause.

"'Prospero'?" Detective Baker murmured.

Amelie thought she heard a low chuckle coming from Detective Winston, but surely that was a mistake. When she stole a glance at the man, she saw nothing but seriousness.

Mr. Radcliffe's swift intake of breath distracted her, and she glanced at him. He was unnaturally pale, although his features themselves suggested polite interest as the Great Prospero made his way farther into the room. Did he know the man?

Prospero paused before a gentleman whom Amelie had seen a few times at the book group gathering. His name was Mr. Groot, and Prospero eyed him with great seriousness before pronouncing, "You, dear sir, are a saint among men. You work tirelessly to care for your ailing mother. I see a bright future in store for you as you reap the reward of such selfless efforts."

A smattering of applause followed the pronouncement, but Amelie was underwhelmed. The Great Prospero could have learned such basic information about Mr. Groot from anyone, most likely from their illustrious hostesses. She bit back a sigh. Would the man provide no more excitement than simple parlor tricks?

Prospero continued to work the room, circling about and bestowing random premonitions on the gathered guests. He stopped at Mrs. Blakestone, who sat straight in anticipation. "Ah, I see a keen woman before me. Bold and brave! Madam, I see delightfully harrowing adventures in your future!"

Mrs. Blakestone's cheeks flushed, and she smiled broadly. "How splendid! I do believe our hostesses have discovered a true soothsayer!"

Prospero chuckled and moved on, and as he approached Amelie's group near the hearth, his eyes locked on Mr. Radcliffe's face and his step hitched the smallest bit before he slowed and finally stopped just behind Miss Trunsteel and Eva, who twisted around on the settee to look at him.

"Ahh," Prospero murmured. "A fine gathering of souls, to be sure. A gentleman who has known his share of loss." He smiled sadly at Mr. Radcliffe, who sat stiffly next to Amelie.

"Orphaned, ostracized, and then widowed." Prospero winced. "I must consult the spirits, sir, and insist they offer something lovely for you! Surely your fortunes will turn, and your heart will find its just reward."

"You needn't bother consulting anything on my account," Mr. Radcliffe said. "I put little faith in such things."

Prospero nodded. "Coming of age under the watchful eye of suspicious villagers has a way of dimming one's faith."

"I would not know; my townsfolk were warm and loving."

Prospero flashed a small smile. "I speak of myself, of course. But as you can see, good sir, I have been—what is the English word?—converted. Perhaps you shall rediscover your faith in the unexplainable."

"Regardless, I choose to create my own fate." Mr. Radcliffe's coloring had returned to normal, and he gave the man a polite smile.

Prospero placed his palms together and nodded once in a light bow before turning his attention to Miss Trunsteel. "Such a lovely young woman! I see a family in your future, my dear."

Amelie's attention was still on Mr. Radcliffe, and she heard Charlotte whisper to him, "Mr. Radcliffe, do you know him?"

It was a good question, and one Amelie had wanted to ask. Uncomfortable tension had passed between the two men, leaving her feeling as though the men had shared secrets to which nobody else in the room was privy. As Prospero finished flattering Miss Trunsteel, he continued making his way through the room.

"I have never seen him before in my life," Mr. Radcliffe whispered to Charlotte. "What an odd question, Miss Duvall. Are you a suspicious sort of person?"

Amelie saw his smile in profile as he quietly addressed her cousin, but it was tight, and the tone fell just shy of hostile. She knew a moment's dismay for her cousin. Had Amelie asked Mr. Radcliffe a question—especially a perfectly polite and reasonable one—and he responded to her in an unpleasant manner, she would have been mortified and embarrassed.

Charlotte was not easily bruised, and Amelie watched uneasily as her cousin straightened her spine and met Mr. Radcliffe's eyes. "Only when circumstances warrant it," she whispered back. She began clapping with the rest of the room, but still held his gaze.

Amelie was torn between relief that Charlotte had defended

herself and worry that her cousin's distrust of Mr. Radcliffe had grown.

Mr. Radcliffe finally broke eye contact with Charlotte and clapped at something Prospero had said. But as he turned his head, Amelie caught the clear expression of dislike on his face. It was fleeting, and as she blinked, Mr. Radcliffe bestowed a smile on her.

"A charlatan," Mr. Radcliffe said with a shoulder shrug. "A nuisance, but entertaining."

Was his dislike aimed at Charlotte or at the Great Prospero? His expression left Amelie with heightened suspicions that a future where Mr. Radcliffe and her cousins regarded one another fondly was unlikely. That thought was troubling, because Charlotte and Eva were important to Amelie. Perhaps all would smooth over. In reality, it was an insignificant exchange, and Amelie knew she tended to put greater weight on people's emotions and intentions than was probably necessary. She often saw catastrophe where others saw misunderstandings.

She leaned toward Mr. Radcliffe and murmured, "I am so sorry that man said such blunt, personal things to you." She frowned and continued, "Perhaps we might inform the Misses Van Horne that it was highly insensitive for them to have shared such things with Prospero beforehand."

Mr. Radcliffe took the liberty of patting her hand. "Think nothing of it, dear Miss Hampton. I know I shall not entertain it any further. Such nonsense is not worth one moment of distress for your lovely head." The difference between the way he regarded Amelie and the expression she'd seen on his face after his exchange with Charlotte was marked. Rather than feel flattered, she was uneasy.

CHAPTER 12

When hosting a house party, bear in mind that the entertainment must exceed your neighbors' efforts if you wish to remain relevant in the eyes of your competing peers.

—The Elegant Lady's Guide to Memorable Hostessing
by Miss Minerva Cross

The performance continued for a time, but Amelie was distracted and lost in her own troubling thoughts. Finally, general laughter filled the room at something Margaret Van Horne said. Applause followed as the Great Prospero thanked the audience for their participation and wished everyone well. As Amelie clapped with the rest, she stole a glance at Detective Baker, whose eye was on Mr. Radcliffe. Then he studied the performer who took one final bow, and Amelie knew the detective would be speaking to the Great Prospero soon.

"And now, Margaret and I have decided to open our home to a most diverting game—a scavenger hunt!" Ethel Van Horne took charge again as Margaret spoke quietly with Prospero and gestured toward the back of the house. With a nod, he took his leave.

Detective Baker shifted in his seat, but did not follow him.

"The rules of the hunt are simple," Ethel continued. "We have prepared a list of clues for you to investigate in a few select rooms in our home. Write the answer next to the clue, and when you are finished, return here with the list. To make the game more interesting, our rules are that you form small teams of no more than three or four. Also, both sexes must be represented on each team. None of this 'ladies against gentlemen' nonsense."

Amelie's heart jumped in anticipation. She had enjoyed games of all sorts as a child at home, but this would mark her first participation in something of this nature here in Town.

A week ago, a few *days* ago, she would have been giddy with the thought of sharing such casual and diverting activities with Mr. Radcliffe, but she still felt the strain in the air following the exchange between him and Prospero.

As the guests arose and chatter filled the room, Miss Trunsteel approached them. "Mr. Radcliffe, I do hope it is not too forward of me, but—" she began.

He held up a hand with a gentle smile. "Miss Trunsteel, I must stop you, for I am unfortunately obliged to leave this gathering early. I have an appointment, regrettably, and was unaware our gracious hosts had arranged such thorough and continued entertainment."

Miss Trunsteel's face fell, and Amelie wondered if it was a mirror of her own. The disappointment at his departure stung, but Amelie was determined to refrain from asking him when they might meet again. Firstly, she was not the forward sort, and secondly, it would never do to appear so desperate.

She fixed a smile on her face. "It has been delightful to see you, Mr. Radcliffe, if even for a short time."

"Likewise, dear Miss Hampton, and I do regret that it was short." He put his hand on his heart and tipped his head to her, and to Miss Trunsteel and Eva, but pointedly excluded Charlotte and the two detectives.

The group made their way toward the hostesses, who were distributing the scavenger hunt lists. Margaret Van Horne handed a piece of paper and small pencil to Amelie, Eva, and Charlotte, each. "The ladies possess a much neater hand, much more legible," she said to the gentlemen with a practical nod. "Now. How are we dividing you? Mr. Radcliffe, Miss Hampton, and Miss Duvall?"

"My dear lady, I must take my leave early, I fear." Mr. Radcliffe bowed over her hand and placed a kiss on her fingers. "Your hospitality and entertainment have been exceptional, and I am glad to have been invited."

Margaret Van Horne did not simper or giggle or make an innuendo-filled aside, as Amelie might have assumed she would. Instead, she arched a brow at Mr. Radcliffe and replied, "A pity, sir. Perhaps another time."

Detective Baker stepped forward. "Suppose Miss Hampton, Miss Duvall, and I form a team? Detective Winston could accompany Miss Trunsteel and Miss Caldwell."

The parties nodded in agreement, and Amelie was grimly satisfied with the arrangement. She intended to demand answers from Mr. Baker regarding Detective Winston's presence at the event.

Loud chatter and laughter continued, and as the group made their way into the foyer, Amelie glanced down at the scavenger hunt list.

Library:

> *A creature small and deadly_____*
> *A companion into the afterlife_____*
> *Comfort on a warm day_____*

Conservatory:

> *Keys that fit no locks____*
> *An angel's dream____*
> *A courtly bow____*

Ballroom:

> *Exotic flora_____*
> *Winged bliss_____*
> *Rebellious love_____*

The list continued, and Amelie studied it as they slowly moved with the crowd. "I believe I can guess some of these answers without seeing the clues," she began, but a small commotion in the foyer made her look up.

"I can prove there is still a mummy inside," Mrs. Blakestone was saying to Mrs. Groot. "See?"

Through gaps between the people, Amelie saw Mrs. Blakestone trying to open the sarcophagus. She shoved against it harder, and in her attempt to prize open the seam along the side, nudged the massive thing against the wall. A grinding noise sounded, and Amelie winced for the condition of the finish. The Misses Van Horne would need to hire out for repairs, unless they kept a plaster mason on retainer.

Ghoulishly curious, she strained to see if the woman would manage to open the sarcophagus, but Mrs. Blakestone's efforts merely succeeded in tipping the huge, standing coffin enough that when it teetered away from her, the momentum it gained tipping back was greater.

Mrs. Blakestone looked at Mrs. Groot over her shoulder, explaining that she'd seen it opened a dozen times. She wasn't paying attention, and when she shoved impatiently at it again with more force, it tipped away again. A collective gasp rippled through the guests, and a gentleman standing on the other side shouted and put up a hand to right it.

He succeeded in sending it back toward Mrs. Blakestone, who finally seemed to realize the peril she caused. She squealed as it rocked dangerously toward her, and as the crowd scampered back, her shawl caught on a wall sconce and held tight.

Amelie's hand flew to her mouth, and she stared in horror, wondering if the woman were about to be flattened.

To Mrs. Blakestone's side stood Mr. Radcliffe, who watched the spectacle with an oddly fascinated expression. Amelie expected him to step forward and free the shawl, but he only stared as if the whole of it were staged for his entertainment.

Detective Baker brushed past her and jostled her hard into Charlotte, whose breath exhaled in an *oof*. He rushed at Mrs. Blakestone and wrapped both arms around her, pulling her to the side and freeing the shawl. Detective Winston grabbed the sarcophagus and, with another gentleman's help, steadied it back into place.

Amelie exhaled a huge breath, along with the rest of the guests, who then filled the foyer with laughter and exclamations of disbelief and a smattering of applause. Mrs. Blakestone shoved at her hair, which had lost a few pins in the melee, and clutched at Detective Baker with her other hand, her fingers visibly digging into his arm.

"Sir," the woman gasped, "you've saved me!"

Detective Baker steadied Mrs. Blakestone for a moment before releasing her. He managed a half smile, but it seemed hard-won. "Perhaps, madam, you'll refrain from such pursuits in the future."

She laughed breathlessly and put a hand to her throat. "Of course," she said, swallowing. "It is only that I wanted to show—"

"What in the name of Ramses is happening in here?" Ethel Van Horne made her way to the foyer, the crowd parting before her like the Red Sea. "Bertha?"

Mrs. Blakestone blinked at Ethel and then burst into tears. "I only wanted to show them the mummy!"

"Bertha! The mummy was removed years ago and donated to the museum." Ethel was the picture of exasperation, and, when her sister joined them, the effect doubled.

"Well, I did not know that, did I?" Mrs. Blakestone said, sniffling.

Detective Winston handed her a folded handkerchief, which she took with mumbled thanks.

Amelie blinked as the chatter continued, and Margaret Van Horne called out, "Disaster has been averted by two dashing gentlemen, dare I say, the Yard's finest!" The small crowd cheered and applauded, and as people shuffled in and out of her line of sight, she caught a glimpse of Detective Baker looking briefly heavenward before nodding and smiling.

Eva had become separated from them and now sidestepped her way back to Amelie and Charlotte, her eyes wide as saucers.

"What . . . what was that?" Eva managed.

"That might have been absolutely horrifying," Charlotte added.

Eva looked over her shoulder and then back. "It might have been awful for Mrs. Blakestone, certainly, but the way the sarcophagus began to pivot—did you see? I think it might have tilted forward and hurt several people. If not for the detectives . . ."

The three women looked again at the scene, where the two detectives were attempting to extricate themselves from admiring partygoers. Mrs. Blakestone was awash in tears, and, at Margaret Van Horne's direction, was escorted away by a maid for fresh tea.

Miss Van Horne continued, "Impromptu excitement is now finished; onward with your teammates to scavenge!"

As people moved forward, the crowd in the hall thinned. Eva's last comment rang quietly in Amelie's ear, and she wasn't certain why until she remembered Mr. Radcliffe's odd response to the impending mishap. He hadn't moved a finger to help. If not for the detectives, indeed.

She looked right and left, and then out the windows that flanked the front door. Night had fallen, but the front garden was lit with gas lamps. She squinted and studied the few people who were outside, but Mr. Radcliffe was not among them.

The odd light in his eyes as he had watched Mrs. Blakestone lingered in her mind as the detectives made their way over to begin the scavenger hunt. Perhaps she'd misunderstood the moment. Perhaps Mr. Radcliffe had not realized there was any danger—sarcophagi were exceptionally heavy, after all, and even without a mummy inside would be difficult to move. He probably thought the woman would never be able to cause actual harm and enjoyed the odd spectacle for what it was.

Even as she formulated the thoughts, they did not sit well with her, and she was afraid they never would. She might not go so far as to suggest the man had murdered his wife, but she was certain in that moment she and Mr. Radcliffe would not suit. He had treated Charlotte with disdain, which had bothered her, and then he hadn't lifted a finger to halt a ridiculous display of something potentially dangerous, no matter how unlikely it seemed. Not only had he missed an opportunity to be a hero by saving Mrs. Blakestone, he'd seemed perversely entertained by her peril.

She was not about to admit as much to the detective, however, or even to her cousins. She needed some time to consider the matter, to let it settle in after having allowed her heart to think that Mr. Radcliffe, a man with manners that could illicit swooning and an appearance to rival the handsomest of princes, might court her, Amelie Hampton. The disappointment was heavy.

Detective Baker straightened his jacket as he reached her side. "Ladies," he said, "shall we go exploring, then?"

Amelie looked down at the scavenger hunt list in her hand, surprised to see it crumpled. She quickly tried to smooth it flat.

"Well done, detectives," she said, grudgingly including Detective Winston in her compliment. "We are fortunate indeed you are in attendance tonight." She did manage a genuine smile for Detective Baker as he glanced over her shoulder to look at the list.

"Any man would have done the same thing," he mumbled, his glance flicking to her face. She knew in that moment that he'd seen Mr. Radcliffe's lack of response.

"I do not believe that is true, Detective," Charlotte commented. "There were many men between you and Mrs. Blakestone who did not lift a finger." She tilted the corner of her mouth in a smile, which signified to Amelie that the detectives had earned her cousin's respect.

Amelie sighed and frowned, again looking at the list but this time not seeing the words on it. Charlotte would certainly side with Detective Baker in overt criticism of Mr. Radcliffe and his potential criminal acts. She realized her pride might be her downfall; it certainly wouldn't be the first time she'd been stubborn because her heart didn't want to admit she might have been wrong. She matched couples for the *Gazette* regularly; how on earth had she so badly mismatched her own?

"Detective Winston," Miss Trunsteel interjected, "suppose you and Miss Caldwell and I begin our search? I do not mind admitting I am a competitive sort." She smiled, and Amelie reluctantly admitted she was free to like the woman again now that she no longer desired Mr. Radcliffe's attention.

Detective Winston smiled, and it quite transformed his face. Amelie blinked; he looked downright pleasant. "In that case, Miss Trunsteel, is it? Miss Caldwell? I suppose we had better be about the business of winning this challenge." He glanced at Detective Baker, who lifted a shoulder in response, but nodded.

Charlotte looked at her copy of the list. "I propose we begin in the conservatory. On the back of the paper is a map of the house, and I believe that is just down the hall this way." She gestured to the right.

"We shall begin in the library, then," Eva said. "To the victor go the spoils!"

Charlotte dashed away, and Eva bolted for the stairs. Amelie couldn't help but smile as the front hall cleared and she and Detective Baker followed Charlotte down a wide hallway that was lit with gas sconces that cast a low glow.

Detective Baker chuckled. "Do you share your cousins' competitive spirit?" he asked Amelie as they rounded a corner.

"Probably not so much against them, specifically. Eva and Charlotte grew up together in the same town and were raised more as sisters than cousins. Such circumstances are likely to foster an element of playful competition, I suppose." She smiled. "I would pity anyone who crossed either of them, however; retribution from the other would be swift and painful."

They followed Charlotte through a wide, arched doorway and entered a large room with a domed glass ceiling through which the dark sky was visible.

"Oh, my," Amelie said, taking in the splendid room. "This is lovely." She turned to the detective, who was also looking up at the beautifully shaped iron supports that gave structure and form to the glass-paneled ceiling. "I find myself increasingly curious about the Misses Van Horne. Their story is likely a fascinating one."

"We shall inquire about it later," Charlotte said, scanning her list. "We've a game to win."

"Charlotte," Amelie laughed. "There is time enough."

"You saw Eva! She took to that staircase at a dead run." She glanced at Detective Baker. "How clever would you say your partner is? Well versed in riddles or games with clues?" Charlotte waved the paper.

The detective frowned as he considered the question, which to his credit, he appeared to take seriously. "He is quite clever, I would say. Quick-witted, talented with pen and paper."

Amelie made a sound of disbelief. "I'd decided to refer to him as 'Detective Witless.'"

Detective Baker looked at her in surprise. "Whatever for?"

She frowned and hoped she didn't look as impetuous as she felt. "As it happens, I wondered why you brought him here. I assumed from his blunt questions to Mr. Radcliffe that he was either unaware of your investigation and desire to foster good will, or he knew and did not care." She sniffed. "Seemed rather daft to me."

Detective Baker laughed, and Amelie found herself surprised a second time that evening at how one simple expression could so transform a face. "Detective Winston is quite an amiable fellow. In fact, most would proclaim him the friendlier of the two of us."

"Certainly hid it well, did he not?" Charlotte commented as she examined the room. "To what end?"

The detective glanced at the door and lowered his voice. "I asked him to join us here this evening. The intent was to provide a foil to my burgeoning 'friendship' with the gentleman."

Amelie nodded. "Of course. Sound investigative technique. Convince the subject to confide in the one who is friendly by applying pressure from the surlier party. Very well, I am obliged to reform my opinion of Detective Winston. I wipe the slate clean as it concerns him."

Detective Baker's mouth twitched. "He will be relieved to hear it."

She scowled. "You needn't be patronizing, sir. I am well aware he has no need of my good opinion, even though I am part of your investigative efforts. I do not suppose you mentioned that to him?"

"I have shared all pertinent information with him."

"Hmm. An evasive answer, but I shall retreat. Charlotte, the clue about keys that fit no lock must refer to either a pianoforte or a piece of written music. I see both." Amelie wrote her answer next to the clue, as did Charlotte.

"An angel's dream is most likely the harp," the detective added.

"Good, good," Charlotte nodded. "And a 'courtly bow.'"

Amelie wandered toward the glass walls, looking out into the large back garden. The world outside was dark, and rain began to patter on the ceiling. The garden was full of thick, tall foliage through which she saw glimpses of lantern light. She folded her arms tightly against a sudden chill. The darkness outside, while lending a certain cozy charm to the room, felt foreboding.

"I wonder if 'a courtly bow,' could be this violin *bow*," Charlotte commented. "Not the same, but neither are pianoforte keys the same . . ."

As Amelie was about to turn away from the window, a shadow caught her eye. She frowned and looked closer, and when her breath fogged the glass, she wiped it away with her sleeve.

"What is it?" Detective Baker asked, joining her at the window.

"A movement against the light, a shadow—I am not certain. Perhaps nothing." Amelie blinked, straining to see into the night.

Charlotte joined them and looked in the same direction. "Perhaps the wind?"

Detective Baker pointed at a grassy plant that shifted slightly under a small gust of wind. "The wind is not blowing too much at the moment; was the movement more significant than that? Do you think it was a person?"

"It could be," Amelie said, but was beginning to doubt herself. "This evening has been such an odd one, my brain is likely playing all sorts of tricks on me." She shrugged. "Either way, there's certainly nothing wrong with a person taking a stroll in the garden."

"In the dark?" Charlotte said just as Detective Baker said, "In the rain?"

Amelie looked again at the spot where a small path disappeared into the trees. It had been a long day, and her eyes were tired.

"A servants' entrance off the kitchen, perhaps? Someone leaving for the day." Detective Baker stood close behind Amelie and peered into the garden again.

She looked up at him, noting the stubble along his jaw and the subtle scent of freshly laundered clothing. It was not, she realized, unpleasant. He placed an arm on the glass, encircling her on one side, and she felt his warmth. At first, she resisted leaning back against him, but as he leaned closer to peer through the glass, she gave into the urge, allowing herself to rest lightly against him. She thought she heard him catch his breath, but when she glanced up at him, his attention was focused on the garden.

He slid his arm from the window, but rather than pulling away entirely, he placed a hand on her shoulder, warming the chill that seeped in from the cold glass.

"We must hurry," Charlotte finally said, turning away from the window. "Eva will be through her second room by now." She didn't look at Amelie or the detective, but a smile twitched at the corner of her mouth. "I am marking the third clue as a violin bow," Charlotte called, scribbling on her paper as she hurried from the room.

"Are you cold?" Detective Baker asked, his voice little more than a whisper against Amelie's ear.

"A bit."

He moved his hand down from her shoulder and rubbed her arm. "Let's move away from the windows."

She remained in place, looking again at the garden, which by now was completely blurred by the rain. "I truly believe I saw something. Someone." She shook her head. "I may be losing my mind."

She felt his chuckle against her back. "If so, you're in good company, Miss Hampton. I fear we're all a bit mad."

The rain increased and fell from the roof and down the sides of the windows in long rivulets. "We should join Charlotte," Amelie said, but remained in place.

"After you."

She looked up at him and turned, and his hand finally fell away from her arm. "Detective," she started. She suddenly wanted him to know that her feelings for Mr. Radcliffe had changed. Would he find her fickle, though?

"Yes?" He swayed toward her but then shoved his hands in his pockets and took a half step back.

She frowned, feeling as though the moment was heavy with something she couldn't define. "I—nothing," she finally finished. Her cheeks warmed, and she began making her way from the room. He matched her stride, and Amelie felt herself blush.

In the corridor, Charlotte was some distance ahead, and Amelie called for her to wait. "Detective," Amelie said, "I could not help but notice the odd exchange between Mr. Radcliffe and the Great Prospero." She glanced around, confirming that they were the only three in the vicinity. "I am quite convinced they know one another."

Charlotte looked over her shoulder. "I am certain of it. He nearly snarled at me when I asked him."

Amelie nodded.

"Miss Hampton, does this mean you are in agreement with the reasons for this whole"—Detective Baker waved his hand and encompassed their surroundings—"exercise?"

Amelie sighed, conflicted. Did she truly believe Radcliffe capable of murder? "I am not convinced of *that*, necessarily, only that he claimed to not know the man when clearly he does."

The detective nodded. "The only reason I can think to deny their association would be to help the entertainer maintain his ruse. Their exchange, however, seemed much more a taunt on Prospero's part than any sort of support from Radcliffe." He spoke the last in an undertone as they reached the double doors leading to a spacious ballroom.

"Why the need for such quiet?" Charlotte asked. "Both men in question have left already."

"I'd rather the others not hear me discussing them."

Charlotte shook her head as she consulted the list of clues. "I would be more surprised if nobody else has discussed them. The entirety of Prospero's performance and their exchange, in particular, was strange."

They entered the ballroom where a few other groups were already searching for answers to the clues.

The detective again looked at the paper Amelie held and scanned the room before the corner of his mouth tilted up in a smile. "'Rebellious love.' That balcony." He pointed to the second floor entrance, where a staircase traveled from the doorway down to the floor. To the right was a small balcony.

"Oh!" Amelie laughed. "Of course! It's a Juliet balcony. That is very clever of you, Detective."

He modestly tipped his head, smile remaining, when Amelie heard a faint sound that she couldn't quite place. She held up her finger and went back to the entrance, listening.

Now, the sound was unmistakable. She turned back to the others in the room, many of whom were watching her curiously. "Someone is screaming," she said, and ran from the room.

CHAPTER 13

*We hardly need mention the importance of sheltering your fair
daughters from life's uglier circumstances. Limit their social en-
gagements to properly chaperoned visits to the theatre or to house
parties hosted by People of Consequence.*

—The Care and Keeping of Girls and Young Women
by Miss Hortence Strongberry

Michael rushed to follow Miss Hampton through the ballroom entrance and down the length of the hallway. She'd not
been wrong—someone was screaming. Though, given their hostesses' eccentricities, he'd not have been surprised to find it part of
the evening's entertainment.

He neared Miss Hampton as she ran toward the front hall,
just as Winston and the others came running down the stairs. The
screams were followed by sobs, and Miss Hampton stood at the
threshold of the large foyer, eyes wide. She'd stopped as if afraid
to take one more step.

She looked back at him and held out her hand. "Detective?"
she whispered.

He reached her side, anxiety growing, and placed a hand under her elbow.

"Look!" Miss Hampton said.

A pool of blood was spreading on the floor at the feet of the sarcophagus. The thing itself was cracked open, and someone had clearly been placed inside. An arm was visible, from which blood dripped steadily off the fingertips. Michael approached it cautiously, still unable to see who was inside. He felt the wrist for a pulse. There was none, but given the amount of blood on the floor, he hadn't expected to find the victim alive.

Mrs. Groot, the screamer, had fainted into her husband's arms. He also looked like he might drop to the floor, but Miss Caldwell swiftly helped him take her into the parlor. Winston regarded the scene, along with Miss Duvall, who stood next to Miss Hampton in shock.

Michael had a sneaking suspicion of who might be inside the sarcophagus. He glanced at Winston. "I hope you brought your sketchbook."

Winston patted his jacket pocket, still looking at the large coffin.

Michael motioned to a maid and the butler, indicating they should come close to help if necessary. He took a breath and cleared his throat, addressing the group gathered in the foyer. "Ladies and gentlemen, where are the Misses Van Horne?"

The crowd rustled, offering up the women in question, who hurried forward with identical expressions of concern that turned quickly to shock. To their credit, they did not so much as sway or faint.

"Am I to understand this is not part of the evening's entertainment?" Michael asked the women.

"Certainly not," Ethel Van Horne replied. "We never stage this sort of thing until much closer to All Hallows' Eve."

Michael opened his mouth to reply but thought better of it and instead cleared his throat again. "Ladies, please gather all of the remaining guests into the parlor, and instruct everyone to remain in the house until we know exactly what has happened."

The small crowd shuffled through the hall, passing by Winston, who stood next to the puddle of blood so nobody would walk in it. Michael approached the sarcophagus, noting Miss Hampton hovering nearby and watching, her hazel eyes a mixture of shock and interest.

"Do you wish to join the others in the parlor?" he asked her quietly.

She swallowed, but responded, "I wish to remain here, but I'll not get in your way."

"Very well." He turned to Winston. "Let us open the thing enough to see who it is."

Winston nodded and went to the opposite side. Together, they slowly widened the gap between the two halves of the coffin. It was a feat easier said than done, however, because the amount of blood spreading on the floor still grew. The sarcophagus was heavy and awkward, and Michael had visions of the whole thing tipping forward.

"A bit more," Michael murmured to Winston. "Just a bit more . . . Stop!"

The victim's head fell forward and rested on interior of the sarcophagus lid. Michael exhaled. His earlier presumption had been correct, and the victim was one of the two he'd suspected they'd find.

He heard Winston's low whistle from the other side. "The Great Prospero has met an untimely end, it would seem."

A butcher knife protruded from Prospero's chest, and although Michael still did not have a clear view of the body, when he moved the man's jacket to the side, he spied two more spots of blood on the shirt. He'd been stabbed at least three times, possibly more.

"I oughtn't jump to conclusions," Winston said, "but if we do find fingermarks on the knife handle, I think I know to whom they'd belong."

"I suspect the same," Michael said. He sighed and stepped back. The sarcophagus remained standing, its deceased inhabitant held eerily upright.

Winston glanced at the group in the parlor as Michael took a handkerchief Miss Hampton handed to him. He wiped his fingers, noting the bright red smudge left behind on the fabric.

"Suppose you begin questioning the guests in the parlor," Michael said to Winston, "and I'll send a messenger to the Yard and to Dr. Neville.

"Does St. Vincent's cover Mayfair?"

"It is irrelevant, thankfully. I trust his skill more than any other." Michael stopped himself from returning Miss Hampton's stained handkerchief, instead folding it and awkwardly putting it in his pocket. He lifted a shoulder in apology, but she waved it off.

He finally took a longer look at her face and noted the pallor. He should have insisted she join the other guests; as much as she claimed she was his "colleague," she was not, and it was his duty to protect the public, not indulge them in playacting.

"Join your cousins in the parlor," he told her. "It is unseemly for you to be witness to this."

Color slowly returned to her cheeks, and she lifted her chin. "I am certain it is, however I am not my aunt's niece for nothing. I . . ." She swallowed. "I want to know who did this." Her eyes darted to the sarcophagus and back to him.

In his periphery, Michael noted Winston turning toward the parlor. He called to him over his shoulder, "Send me one of the Van Hornes, please."

Winston nodded and left.

"Miss Hampton, I do not yet know exactly what we have before us. I have much to do, but I do wish to speak with you later. Earlier, you thought you saw a person outside the conservatory. You may have witnessed the killer making his escape."

She frowned. "I am more than a witness, though; I can help you. You ought to deputize me."

He blinked. "*Deputize* you?"

She nodded. "Then I shall be able to assist you in an official capacity. Temporarily, of course."

"Miss Hampton, I do not have the authority to deputize you, nor would I, even if I could."

"Whyever not? Think of the benefit of someone walking behind you and taking notes."

Michael noted the surreal absurdity of the situation. To his back was a parlor full of anxious citizens, most of whom identified themselves collectively as a "cheery society," while before him was a murder victim stuffed inside a sarcophagus. Next to him stood a lovely young woman whose rosy vision of life would unwittingly come to an ugly end if she pursued her current line of intent. He did not wish to see the spark leave her eyes.

He stepped closer. "This is no business for you," he said. "I appreciate your energy and your desire to help, but it would . . . it would change you, and I should hate to see that happen." He touched her arm again, unable to keep from reaching for her. At the contact, he felt a sudden rush of desire to kiss her, but given the circumstances, the notion was foolish. He lowered his hand reluctantly.

Her lips tightened. "Life changes everyone, Detective. If you do not require assistance, perhaps I shall offer my secretarial services to Detective Winston. Or . . . or I shall investigate this issue as a member of the press. I am a journalist."

"You write correspondence for the *Marriage Gazette*!"

A large clock in the hall chimed the hour, as if reminding him time was ticking away while his victim continued to bleed out onto the parquet floor. Exasperated, he put his hand into his pocket, pulled out his small black notebook and pen, and thrust them at her.

"Fine." He lowered his voice. "Stay out from underfoot, do not say one word unless I ask it of you, and keep everything you learn in the strictest confidence." He'd been on the brink of ordering her to remain naive and sweet, but that was a ridiculous command. Besides, he realized as he looked at her determined expression, naive and sweet as she was, she was also, in her own way, fierce.

She nodded and firmly pinched her lips together, flipping open his notebook and uncapping the pen.

He would never have admitted it aloud, but the thought of Miss Hampton at his side, taking notes in a hand that was guaranteed to be more legible than his was not a bad idea. He would be free to interview, and he trusted she could write quickly.

Miss Ethel Van Horne appeared. "Detective Baker, your colleague informed me of your discovery. I insist you find the miscreant who stabbed our friend and buried him in our front hall." Her eyes were red-rimmed but clear.

He nodded. "I intend to, Miss Van Horne. Firstly, I must send word to my superior and the coroner."

"That has been arranged. Detective Winston sent two of our groomsmen on their way."

He nodded. "Where did you meet the man we know as 'The Great Prospero'?"

Miss Hampton began writing in his book, and when Miss Van Horne looked at her, she smiled but remained silent.

"Miss Hampton is my scribe," Michael said. "You may speak freely."

She arched a brow at Miss Hampton. "His scribe, are you?"

"Miss Van Horne," Michael interrupted before she could make an inappropriate innuendo. "Prospero?"

The elderly woman sighed, clearly disappointed to be robbed of an opportunity for either gossip or matchmaking. "Margaret and I met the man two months ago. He was performing in a vaudeville act on Drury Lane and was quite impressive." Her brows drew together, and she glanced at the puddle of blood on the floor. "He was a good lad. True, he was not Hungarian or a soothsayer or even a credible Medium. He has entertained our guests on multiple occasions, however, to great success because he possesses charm and humor. Tonight, he performed half as long as he customarily does, and he seemed . . . rattled. I have never seen him in such a state."

"Did he say why he was out of sorts?"

Miss Van Horne shook her head. "I sent him for refreshments in the kitchen with the staff and told him I would speak to him later when Margaret and I paid him for his time. He was not there when the scavenger hunt began; we assumed he had left."

"Aside from being shortened, did his performance this evening seem different than others in the past?"

"We had given him basic information on several of the guests—he had the memory of an elephant—but he used not even half of it. Also, his exchange with Mr. Radcliffe was odd. Cryptic, wouldn't you say?"

Miss Hampton nodded, but remained quiet.

"Did he ever say where he was from? Where he had family?"

"A little village called Wickelston, near the coast. I remember because my family vacationed there when Margaret and I were younger. It was smaller, then, and few people knew of it. It has only now begun attracting attention because a new rail line was installed last year."

Miss Hampton shifted her weight to one foot and then the other, catching his attention. Her eyes widened, but she still remained silent.

"Yes?" he finally said.

"I have a question," she murmured.

"By all means." It took some effort not to sound sarcastic, and he was unsure of his success.

"Miss Van Horne, please accept my sincerest condolences for the loss of your friend," Miss Hampton began.

"Thank you, my dear."

"I wonder if Mr. Prospero's family was well respected? Something he said to Mr. Radcliffe caused me to wonder."

Michael reluctantly admitted it was a good question, one he'd planned to ask.

Miss Van Horne frowned. "He did not divulge much of his early history to us, but I was always under the impression that he had struggled. I do not know anything of his family. When he is not using the alias 'Prospero,' he goes by the name of Jacob Stern." She paused and bit her lip. "*Went* by the name of Jacob Stern."

"Thank you." Miss Hampton nodded at Miss Van Horne and then at Michael. She put pen to paper and began writing quickly in his notebook.

Michael escorted Miss Van Horne back to the parlor, where she joined her sister, who was overseeing tea service. When Miss Duvall and Miss Caldwell approached the doorway, Michael realized Miss Hampton had followed close on his heels.

At her cousin's expectant expressions, Miss Hampton whispered, "I've been deputized."

"You have not been deputized!" His frustration with her was reaching new heights.

Winston, who had joined the small group, regarded him with confusion.

"I have not 'deputized' anyone," Michael repeated. "Miss Hampton offered to take notes while I conduct interviews, and I consented." He glared at her. "A moment of weakness I am coming to regret."

She made a motion of locking her lips closed with a pretend key and then throwing it over her shoulder.

Nostrils flaring, he turned back to Winston. "What have you learned?"

"Regrettably, not much, although Miss Caldwell finally managed to calm Mrs. Groot enough to learn that she saw the victim shortly after he finished his performance, and that he looked 'very much concerned.'"

Miss Hampton uncapped the pen and added to her notes. At her current pace, she'd have the thing filled up before the night was out.

She must have read his thoughts, because she held up a hand and said to him, "Never fear, I have a dozen such notebooks at home. Would you find it useful for me to ask Miss Van Horne if they have a residential address for one 'Jacob Stern,' also known as 'The Great Prospero'?"

"Actually," he conceded, "yes, that would save me the trouble."

Winston scratched his chin. "We have constables arriving soon who will gather such information."

"Miss Hampton desires to be useful, and I am happy for the assistance." He was willing to admit, if only to himself, that he wanted her to stay with him.

"You needn't be patronizing." Miss Hampton sniffed and looked up at him as she capped the pen. "I am well aware that you are happy to have me out from underfoot. Perhaps I shall undergo training to become a constable."

"Women aren't employed as constables," Detective Winston said, looking out the front windows. "Too dangerous."

"There was once a day when common opinion said a woman would never be a secretary or work in businesses or in factories." Miss Hampton turned her nose away from Winston and made her way into the parlor. Her cousins still lingered at the door.

"One wonders if she will continue to think of you as 'Detective Witless.'" Michael watched as Miss Hampton approached the Van Horne sisters.

"'Witless'?" Winston's lips rose in a surprised half-smile. "She calls me 'witless'?"

"It is certainly a good thing the American Pinkertons do not share your view of women and appropriate work." Miss Caldwell eyed Winston with arms folded.

"I . . . Miss Caldwell, I did not use the word 'inappropriate.' I said 'dangerous.'" Winston looked at Miss Caldwell, confusion tightening his brow.

"Apparently, that is irrelevant as it seems one can just as easily be murdered during a house party as anywhere else."

"Miss Caldwell, I meant no offense. I confess, I am baffled that my comment has been misconstrued as an insult."

Miss Duvall chuckled. "And Eva is the reserved cousin."

Michael rubbed the back of his neck and turned around to examine the crime scene again. He checked his timepiece and shook his head. "The constables will hopefully arrive soon—you did send word to the department?"

"I did." Winston nodded. "I also sent word to the photographer, but do not know if he will be available. He's unpredictable with his schedule, that one."

"I am a photographer," Miss Caldwell said. "I can fetch my equipment and be set up here in less than thirty minutes."

Winston studied her for a moment and then looked at Michael. "We may as well use available resources; after all, you've deputized that one."

Michael didn't bother to repeat that he hadn't deputized anyone. He looked at the two young women who eyed him expectantly. "Very well. I cannot guarantee what kind of scene you'll be stepping into upon your return, however. The lighting is questionable, and the place will be full of police by then. Are you accustomed to working amidst chaos?"

"Incidentally, I am," Miss Caldwell said. "I do commissioned work for families, which often includes unruly children and sometimes pets." She turned to Miss Duvall. "Will you help me with the equipment?"

"Of course." Miss Duvall looked at Michael. "We shall discuss payment for Eva's services with your superior tomorrow, as tonight is much too fraught with chaos, and I would hate for there to be any miscommunication."

Michael's mouth slackened, and as the two women turned

to the cloakroom for their wraps, he looked at Winston. "What is happening?"

Winston watched Miss Duvall and Miss Caldwell leave the house, and his widening grin became a chuckle. "The department pays our photographer for his services, on the odd occasion we can actually engage him, so it stands to reason another photographer would be equally compensated."

"I highly doubt Director Ellis would ever agree to the same amount. Miss Caldwell is not a man supporting a family."

"Seems rather inequitable, wouldn't you agree?"

Michael gave Winston a half-smile. "Detective, do I hear suffrage leanings despite your assertion about the dangers of police work for women?"

Winston tucked his hands comfortably in his pockets. Sometimes Michael envied him his air of ease. "I may have a family member or two who are known to lead a charge. After a while, one cannot deny that reason is reason, and what's fair is logical."

"But highly unpopular."

Winston smiled again. "That all depends on who is asked." He looked over Michael's shoulder at the grim reminder of why they still stood guard in the front hall. His smile faded, and he sighed. "Do you believe Radcliffe is responsible for this?"

"Don't you?"

Winston nodded. "If we can find proof, perhaps that would be reason enough to force the exhumation of the late Mrs. Radcliffe."

Michael looked at the sarcophagus and the pool of red at the base, which was no longer growing in size. He hoped the crime was connected to Radcliffe, if for no other reason than he wouldn't be forced to abandon his theory about the man's wife. He feared his time justifying the effort was nearing an end.

CHAPTER 14

The danger of allowing women to enter a world better left to men cannot be overstated. The natural order of things will crumble, leaving naught but despair and ruin behind. The family will find itself reduced to ashes, children will run shoeless in the streets, and the evening meal will no longer find itself promptly served when the husband and father returns from his labors at the end of a tiring day.

—*"Evils of the Modern Era," by Sir Joseph Chauvertier*
from THE GENTLEMAN'S JOURNAL

Amelie and her cousins returned home in the wee hours of the morning and dispersed immediately with different tasks. Amelie took Detective Baker's notebook, typed the contents of the notes she'd taken into five sheets of useful content, organized by interviewee. She topped the whole of it with a timeline of the evening's events, interspersing eyewitness accounts with approximate times and locations of each.

Every moment in the Van Horne house was accounted for, as much as she could manage, from the moment they entered the front door until they left, which had been soon after the coroner's office had bundled away the body. Notably absent from her typewritten analysis were the official comments from Mr. Radcliffe, who had left prior to the scavenger hunt, and from two kitchen staff, who had also left the house earlier than the rest of the servants.

Eva and Charlotte worked in the darkroom, developing the photographic plates of the crime scene. They produced several impressive images showing the aftermath of the Great Prospero's unfortunate demise.

Dr. Neville, the coroner from St. Vincent, had been an irascible fellow at first, but had warmed to the ladies throughout the course of the evening until he was quite taken—especially with Eva and her efficiency with the photographic equipment. He complimented her sense of spatial awareness and directives for better lighting and seemed particularly impressed with her exacting eye and insistence on capturing the smallest of details.

When he'd mentioned to the detectives that his preferred autopsy photographer had taken ill, Eva immediately offered to stand in, and Charlotte, who would have enlisted to help anyway, had perked up at the word "autopsy."

Early the next morning, Amelie delivered the detective's notebook and typed notes, along with several photos Eva had developed, to the Yard. She had written Detective Baker's name clearly on the top of the sealed parcel. She was told he had not yet arrived, but she was welcome to leave the parcel with the constables in his department.

She climbed stairs and followed directions to his office, marveling along the way at the rows of desks, file drawers full of mysteries, bookshelves of reference material, and office after office of lawmen going about their duties. She spied more than a few young constables who pecked at typewriters with two fingers; she wondered why the Yard hadn't thought to employ women who'd been certified in office work and typing and were ten times as efficient. By the time she delivered the package and left, her brain spun with the possibilities.

It was Saturday, and while she planned to join her cousins at St. Vincent's for the autopsy, she wanted to locate an address first.

Ethel Van Horne had supplied her a possible location for Jacob Stern's—alias The Great Prospero's—residence. It was farther east in Town than Amelie usually traveled. She had toyed with the idea of telling the detective about her mission, even wished for a moment that he was seated beside her. He would never have allowed it, however, and she did not wish to be forbidden from investigating on her own.

As her cab carried her through the streets and away from everything familiar, her eyes gradually widened in horrified fascination and then dismay. Buildings in the area were stacked high and close together, and most were in a state of disrepair. Children with ragged clothing and filthy faces hovered in doorways or trotted alongside rented hacks and carriages, begging for coin or offering to run errands. She saw a young woman in a thin housedress run barefoot into one of the decrepit buildings and dodge the large man in the doorway, his fist raised.

"Whitechapel," she murmured. She pulled her cloak tighter with fingers that were chilled, even in her gloves, as the cab turned a corner, swerving to avoid three children, a feral-looking dog, and a chicken.

She'd heard stories, of course, and Charlotte had read every periodical or serial by Charles Dickens she could find and then told Amelie what she learned about life in the East End. To see it, to smell it, was entirely different. It was like a living, breathing entity that chewed its residents whole and spat them back out again.

Rolling carts bore the sad remains of the season's fruits and vegetables, and there was a long line of people waiting at both the bread vendor's stall and the fisherman's cart. The smell of refuse hung heavily in the air, and when the cab rocked to a stop, Amelie wondered if she would disgrace herself and embarrass the residents by gagging.

She climbed carefully from the conveyance, stepping gingerly around a puddle of something that did not look like residual rain. She paid the driver and offered him twice as much to wait for her.

She wasn't sure what she hoped to accomplish by searching out Jacob Stern's rooms. She had been largely teasing the night before about being deputized, but there was something about the act of piecing together bits of information to gain a full picture that fascinated her. She wanted to know exactly who had killed Mr. Stern, and why.

She felt the same surge of anticipation at the thought of solving the mystery as she did when reading letters sent to the *Marriage Gazette*. She loved reading what the letter writers said, and did not say, and then finding possible matches that often resulted in a walk to the altar. Although solving murders and matchmaking ought to be as different as night and day, the thump of excitement in her heart was the same.

She pondered over the conflict that had hung in the air the night before between the victim and Mr. Radcliffe, and she knew in the pit of her stomach that there was a correlation. Regrettably, she couldn't simply approach Mr. Radcliffe and demand to know if he had plunged a knife into the Great Prospero.

Three men stood in the doorway of a pub, looking as though they'd been there for hours. One elbowed the other two, and all three leered at her. She tried to ignore the ensuing comments that she wasn't sure she understood, but surmised their meaning from the tone.

A woman passed by and looked at her from hat to boot. "Ye lost, missy?" She kept walking without waiting for a response. Amelie couldn't blame her—the woman probably had mouths to feed and work to attend to without being distracted by a young woman who was clearly out of her element. A tiny bit of help might be nice, however.

A young boy approached her, wearing shoes that seemed too big for his feet, pants that were a shade too short, and a jacket that was so threadbare it was practically transparent. He shoved his hat back on his head and gave her a toothy grin. "For a coin, I'm happy t'help, milady. What'er ye lookin' ta find?"

She cleared her throat and smiled at the boy. He looked no more than six or seven, but looks were often deceiving. "What is your name, young sir?"

"Sammy White. Ye won' find a better guide roun' here than Sammy. I can git whatever ye want. Fancy jewels, ribbons, even glubs."

"Glubs?" She blinked.

"Glubs!" He pointed at her gloved hands.

"Oh, oh yes! Yes, of course." She paused, charmed despite herself. "Sammy, where you do acquire all of these items?"

He grinned again, but shook a finger at her. "A gennleman don' reveal his sources."

He was so little; for a moment her heart ached, a physical ache inside her chest. He looked like he could have walked straight from one of Mr. Dickens's stories himself.

She stepped closer and handed him a coin. "As it happens, today I am looking for information."

The coin disappeared into his pocket before she could even blink. "What kind?"

"I have an address, right here." She rummaged in her reticule and finally pulled out a piece of paper. She read the address to Sammy, and he pointed at the building just next to them.

"Just as I said," she heard the cab driver mutter.

"Door number six, ye say?" Sammy moved to the building's entrance and turned back, expectantly. "Come 'long, then."

Amelie hesitated, and then with as deep a breath as she could manage, followed the lad over the threshold. The hallway was narrow and dim, and sounds of crying children and arguing adults filled the air. The sense of despair hung heavy. They climbed a staircase and were nearly bowled over by children running down, and continued up to the next floor before stopping at a nondescript door labeled "6."

Amelie hesitated. Now that she was there, what was she planning to do, really?

Sammy cleared his throat, and she looked down at him. "Thank you, Sir Samuel," she said with a nod and reached into her reticule for another coin.

He took it with a grin and touched the brim of his hat. She caught him as he turned to go.

"Do you live in this building, Sammy?"

"Nay, some nights I sleep at the workhouse, but I sneaks in and out so they don' keep me there."

She swallowed. "And the other nights?"

He lifted a thin shoulder. "'Ere and there."

She reached back into her reticule for one of her calling cards and handed it to him. "If you have need of anything—possible employment, even—please find me here, or send word." It was an impulsive gesture, and she could only imagine what Mrs. Burnette would say if the little boy showed up at Hampton House. She wasn't naive enough to believe he was as angelic as he appeared, but he was a child. The orphanage in Frockshire where her mother had volunteered years earlier when Amelie had been very young was clean and tidy and provided food and schooling for the children. It was a far cry from the squalor surrounding this little boy.

He took the card with his grubby hands and scrunched up his nose as he studied it. "I can't read these words," he admitted.

"This is my name—Miss Amelie Hampton," she said, tracing her finger beneath the words. "And this is my address in Bloomsbury. I live at a place called Hampton House, which you'll remember because it is the same as my name." She smiled, and as he smiled back, she wondered if she was making a huge mistake. She'd just provided a probable thief who likely worked for an older probable thief with her name and address.

"You keep this to yourself, yes?" she told him. "I should love to hear from you, but nobody else."

He nodded and tucked the card into the small front pocket at his hip. He looked around them as if seeing the hallway for the first time and shook his head. "Best not linger here, miss. 'Tisn't safe for ladies and children. Some men, even."

"Do you worry for your own safety?"

He puffed up his chest. "I run faster than any of 'em."

"See that you continue to do so. You are a smart boy, and I should hate to see you come to harm." She extended her hand. He stared at it for a moment and then shuffled his feet.

"Wouldn't wanna soil yer glubs," he mumbled.

"Nonsense." She reached down and took his thin hand.

"Come now, give us a nice grip. My father always said one can tell a man's integrity by the firmness of his handshake."

He nodded, and she wasn't certain in the dim light, but she thought he may have blushed beneath the layers of dirt and grime. He put his fingers again to the brim of his large hat and turned and ran down the hall and out of sight.

Amelie watched the empty space he left behind and knew there were dozens upon dozens of children just like him. She'd always known it academically, but seeing the conditions first-hand was overwhelming.

She turned back to the battered door, hesitated, then raised her hand and knocked softly. It might be that Jacob Stern had relatives or flatmates who could tell her something about the man. Several moments passed, and she knocked again, this time more loudly.

Nobody came to the door, and she sighed. She tried the door handle, not expecting it to open, but gasped lightly when it did. She looked around the hallway, which was still blissfully empty. Without giving herself time to consider her actions, she opened the door wider and peeked inside.

The room was surprisingly tidy, with a bed that was made, a plush, upholstered chair in fairly decent repair, and a table and wash area adjacent to a cupboard and small stove. There were two envelopes on the ground just inside the door, and looking over her shoulder one more time, she stepped over them, into the room, and closed the door without latching it.

There were few personal touches in the room. On the table was a small stack of papers, the top being a playbill from a performance that had run six weeks earlier on which was scrawled, "What a lovely evening with a true gentleman." It was signed by Ethel Van Horne. Amelie smiled and touched the edge of it with her fingertip. The elderly ladies had truly taken the man under their combined wing.

She walked slowly around the room, feeling melancholy that the man who had left this space a day ago would never return. A small travel trunk sat at the foot of the bed, but she couldn't bring herself to open it. She'd intruded enough as it was. She would confess her deed to Detective Baker, but tell him that officers should quickly examine the room and the trunk's contents before others in the area also realized the door was unlocked. She was surprised the detectives weren't already there, but it was still early.

She walked slowly back to the door, stooping to pick up the two letters on the floor, thinking she would place them on the table with the other papers. A return address caught her eye, and she paused.

Reverend Flannery, Wickelston Boys' Home.

Boys' home? She frowned. The Van Hornes had said Mr. Stern was from Wickelston, but what business did he have with a boys' home? Had he lived there for a time?

She heard a footfall in the hallway, the slightest of creaks just outside the door, and starting guiltily, she shoved the two pieces of mail inside her jacket and waistcoat. She was just turning to see who was there when a flash in her periphery warned her that someone had silently entered.

A hand roughly clamped down on her shoulder, and a thumb shoved hard into her back, turning her away from him.

She cried out in pain and tried to spin away, lifting up her arm as something came toward her. She felt a blinding pain in her arm and the side of her head. She didn't see a face, only shadows.

As she hit the floor, she grunted in pain and sucked in a

deep breath, trying to blink through blurred vision. A huge shadow loomed over her, blocking the muted light from the curtained window. She felt the prick of the corner of one of the envelopes she'd tucked inside her waistcoat now against her neck; it must have shifted as she fell. The shadow moved closer, a hand reaching toward her. She protected her head as her vision began to fade.

A cacophony of sensations struck at once—noise in the stairwell, shouting, a growl of frustration, movement, fading footsteps, the crash of glass, voices blending together, deep voices, a higher register, shadows . . .

Then a hand against her face, her temple, a muttered curse, the pleasant scent of fresh laundry.

And then, nothing.

CHAPTER 15

Police responded to an attack in Whitechapel upon a young woman of genteel breeding and manner. The perpetrator is an unknown assailant who fled the scene. Any witnesses to the event are encouraged to offer official statements at Division H.

–THE DAILY JOURNAL, *afternoon edition*

Michael sat at Miss Hampton's side in the hospital after the doctors had examined her, put her badly bruised arm in a splint, and cleaned up the blood from her head wound. She was still asleep, and he was beside himself, sick with worry. When he'd entered Jacob Stern's rented rooms in Whitechapel and found Miss Hampton wounded and unconscious, his legs had nearly buckled beneath him.

The night before, he and Winston had gone to Stern's flat after leaving the Van Horne residence. There had been nothing of note except a few items of memorabilia from the Misses Van Horne and some playbills from Stern's own performances. The bulk of Mr. Stern's possessions had been located in the trunk at the foot of the bed, along with a few items of clothing and personal toiletries. Michael had collected those while on the scene. He'd intended to return in the morning to ask questions of the neighbors and locals familiar with the comings and go-ings of the area.

He'd arrived with two constables, only to find a young boy screaming that a lady was hurt and directing a constable from Division H to the room. They'd followed quickly, and it hadn't taken Michael long to realize the identity of the "hurt lady." He'd fired off instructions for the constables to secure the scene and then question witnesses about the man who had report-edly escaped through the window. He'd later learned that the attacker had apparently landed on three men who had gathered to watch the activity unfolding, injuring one but breaking his own fall enough to escape.

Michael had carried Miss Hampton down to the carriage, noting after the fact that she was either very light or he'd been so afraid for her life that he hadn't noticed the burden. The ride out of the narrow streets seemed an eternity, and he'd begged her the whole way to awaken.

Now he sat at her side in the hospital, having sent word to her aunt, and still waited for her to wake.

He gathered her limp hand between his. He noted the ink stains on her fingers and smiled despite his worry and frustra-tion. He had seen the parcel she'd left for him at the Yard, and her quick, thorough assessment and compilation of the infor-mation they'd learned the night before had been impressive. The photos were exceptional, and he was forced to admit that the three cousins possessed considerable talent.

He'd handed the parcel over to Winston to study at greater length while he waited for Miss Amelie Hampton to open her pretty eyes. As soon as she did, he was going to deliver a blistering lecture on the folly of wandering the East End alone and the trouble she'd clearly become embroiled in by "deputizing" herself.

Her long, chestnut-colored hair was free of pins and ribbons and curled on the pillow and down over her shoulder. Her lashes lay like fans against her wan cheeks, hiding the eyes that usually sparked with life and humor.

He took the ends of a thick lock of hair between his fingers and rubbed it softly. "Miss Hampton," he murmured, "you must awaken, because I am quite cross with you, and we have much to discuss." He paused as a nurse approached.

"Detective," the nurse said, "Miss Sally Hampton has been located at her townhome and should arrive shortly. Would you like to send for Miss Amelie's cousins?"

"I'll speak with the aunt first, and we'll decide. Thank you."

He'd been the one to provide the hospital with information on Miss Hampton's next of kin and what he knew of her personal life, which was precious little. "She enjoys reading novels, solving puzzles, and helping couples find true love" was hardly useful information. Equally useless was "She has a delightful smile, and while she often drives me mad, I find myself growing quite fond of her. I wanted very much last night to kiss her." He'd not shared that last part, especially.

"Your aunt is on her way," he told Miss Hampton's sleeping form, "and I suspect she will also be quite cross with you. You must awaken and face the consequences."

As if his words had been a spell, her chest lifted in a shallow breath, and a wince crossed her features. Her eyelids flickered, and she blinked against the light in the room.

"Miss Hampton," the nurse said and angled the lamp away from her eyes, "how are you feeling?"

She licked her lips, and the nurse grasped a cup of tea from the bedside table. Helping Miss Hampton take a few careful sips, the nurse then settled her back against the pillows.

Miss Hampton groaned and lifted a hand to her head. She moved her splinted arm and winced again. "What has happened?" she whispered. "Why am I . . ." She looked at Michael and recognition registered on her face. "Detective?"

"I found you in Whitechapel, just after you'd been accosted. Do you remember anything?" He was so relieved to see her hazel eyes open, he quite forgot about the blistering lecture he had planned.

"I do not remem—Oh. I remember parts of it. I was looking for clues." She flushed and dropped her gaze. "I ought to have waited for you, or at least obtained permission. I hadn't planned to enter the place, of course, but the door was unlocked and quite beckoned me in."

The nurse quietly left the room, and Michael leaned close and picked up her hand again. "I suspect you will be the death of me, one way or another. Miss Hampton, you do realize you've not actually been deputized?"

She sighed and closed her eyes. "I was hoping to learn something that might indicate a tie to . . . to . . . a certain someone." Perhaps she assumed the nurse was still within earshot. "It was truly my hope to find a flatmate or friend who could answer some questions."

He traced his fingertips softly across her knuckles. "I understand your hope of finding exonerating evidence for your . . . friend. You must realize now, however, the dangers associated—"

"No," she interrupted, "I find my motives are, that is . . . they are shifting." She cleared her throat and winced again. "My head hurts abominably."

"I am not surprised. The doctor presumes you were hit with something akin to a police truncheon." He touched her arm splint. "Both here and on the side of your head. Do you remember it?"

She frowned and then closed her eyes. "The last thing I remember was picking up the envelopes on the floor."

Michael stilled. "What envelopes on the floor? There were none last night."

She opened her eyes. "Probably delivered by the morning post just before I arrived. Slid under the door is my assumption." Aside from the obvious trauma, she looked exhausted.

For the moment, he set aside the matter of the envelopes. "Have you had any decent sleep?"

"A few hours. I suspect I'll be right as rain after a quick rest."

"Just a quick rest?" He smiled. "The doctor will likely insist you remain abed for at least a week."

She managed an eye roll before closing them altogether with a grunt of pain. "I have no time for such laziness. I am due back at the *Gazette* the day after tomorrow."

"I am certain your aunt will allow you time away from the office. She should be here any minute, in fact."

Miss Hampton's eyes flew open, and she gasped, whether in pain or dismay, he was unsure. "For goodness sake, we needn't bother Sally! She is much, much too busy, and I have no need of mollycoddling." She tried to sit up straight but made pitiful work of it. "Detective, perhaps you might be of assistance—if I could find my way out of here, I will rent a cab to take me home. I still have some coins in my reticule. Where is my reticule?"

"Miss Hampton, you are not leaving this bed until a doctor declares you fit to do so. Be still, or you'll only make things

160

worse." He knew Miss Hampton was stubborn, but not to the point of ignoring an injury. "I will not be of assistance, other than to assure the nurse that you will remain in this bed." He paused. "Why are you so concerned about bothering your aunt?"

She sighed, and for the first time since meeting her, he saw her eyes glisten with tears. "She is . . . my aunt is . . ." She muttered something and turned her head, wiping her eye against her shoulder because he still held her free hand. He released it, and she brushed a fingertip across her cheek.

She sniffled and continued, "My aunt is the most important person in the world to me, aside from Charlotte and Eva. I love my sisters and brother, but Sally is the only one in my life who ever encouraged me to do brave things, extraordinary things. She has never tried to put a muzzle on me, so to speak. Well"— she flushed—"except as it concerns my written responses to some of the *Gazette's* subscribers. But that was for the good of the business, not because she felt I was somehow lacking. I believe she feels a responsibility to steer my cousins and me in a traditional direction, and I wish I dared tell her that we only wish to emulate her free spirit."

"She must be an amazing woman."

"She is." Miss Hampton nodded. "She is strong and has worked so hard. She took a small inheritance and, with what my father called 'a gentleman's business sense,' doubled her money more than once. I want to be like she is, and I do not imagine she has ever been so foolish as to get herself conked on the head and tied up in a hospital."

"Come now, you are hardly tied up." He smiled.

She looked at him, tears drying, and her eyes lingered on his face. After a moment, she bit her lip and put her good hand to her hair, looking down at the long strands as though just realizing it was no longer pinned up. He wondered what she was thinking and figured if he waited long enough, she'd blurt it out. It was her usual mode of communication with him, so he was surprised when the nature of her thoughts came through in a cryptic comment.

"I am feeling unwell." She glanced at the teacup on the bedside table and grimaced.

He took in her sudden state of self-consciousness, flushed cheeks, and refusal to meet his eyes. He'd seen such behavior from her before—she grew ill when overcome by nerves in the company of a gentleman she fancied. He bit the inside of his cheek to keep from smiling, feeling ridiculously and unexpectedly happy.

"The nurse spoke of bringing some dry biscuits to settle your stomach, should that happen." He watched her carefully, feeling like a cad but curious enough to try to confirm his suspicions.

She puffed air into her cheeks and shook her head infinitesimally. He held her gaze for a long moment before she dropped her eyes and blushed.

"It is only natural that you would feel ill following a head injury."

She bit her lip. "I do not believe that to be the source of my discomfort." She cleared her throat and scratched a spot behind her ear.

He forced himself not to grin at her, instead nodding in sympathy. "Of course. I'll tell the nurse you are not hungry at the moment."

"Thank you," she murmured. "I shall be fine, I'm certain." Her gaze flicked up at him again and back down to her hands. She picked at a thread on the blanket.

Absurdly pleased, he took pity on her and tried to direct her attention elsewhere. "You mentioned finding envelopes on the floor in Mr. Stern's room. Do you know what became of them?"

She looked at him again, this time her eyes widening. "Oh, yes! I tucked them into my waistcoat." She looked in confusion around the small room. "Do you know where they have placed my belongings?"

He gestured to a corner where a bag containing her clothing and possessions had been placed. "Shall I get them for you?"

"Please."

He retrieved the bag and placed it next to her on the bed. She peered inside, and with her one good hand, rummaged for a moment before producing two missives. She handed them to him and tapped the one on top with her fingertip. "See the return address? Why is he corresponding with a boys' home in Wickelston?"

"Why, indeed." Michael looked at the postmark, which was two days old. The other letter bore a return address from a theatre on Drury Lane. "Perhaps he is a patron of the boys' home? Sends money to support a just cause?"

"Or perhaps he was raised there."

Michael agreed and thought back to the man's odd conversation with Radcliffe the evening before. "What did he say when he was 'prognosticating' for Mr. Radcliffe?"

"Something about being orphaned, about judgment from small-minded villagers. Mr. Radcliffe claimed to be unfamiliar with such circumstances, and then Mr. Stern claimed to be speaking for himself."

Michael placed his fingertip under the seal and unfolded the letter. He scanned the contents, wondering if several puzzle pieces were already falling into place. Miss Hampton watched him intently, and as she'd already become part of the case's details, he figured there was no harm in sharing the contents of the letter with her. After all, if not for her, they would not have known about the letter at all, let alone be in possession of it. As justifications went, it was as good as any.

"Reverend Flannery, the headmaster of the boys' home, wishes Mr. Stern well, is glad to hear from him after such an extended amount of time, says he was not aware Mr. Stern had returned to the country. He says that he has not spoken with Harold Smith in over a year and cannot verify that it was Harold Smith that Mr. Stern saw in a London coffee shop." Michael scanned the letter, adding, "He concludes by stating he is unable to be of assistance with Mr. Stern's request, but does wish him well, etcetera, etcetera."

"Hmm." Miss Hampton's eyes remained on the paper, but unfocused. "Who is this 'Harold Smith'?"

"I do not know, but it is interesting that Mr. Radcliffe's first name is Harold."

She blinked. "So it is! Was he raised in a boys' home after his parents were killed? The impression he gave me was that he'd been older when they died. Could he have adopted a pseudonym upon leaving? Why would he have done so?"

He nodded. "All questions needing answers. Or it could be that Mr. Radcliffe is not Mr. Smith at all. Harold is a common name."

She nodded. "Which means it could be that Mr. Radcliffe is nothing more than what he appears to be—a man grieving the loss of a young wife." She paused. "A man in search of another wife with whom to share his life."

He watched her, fairly certain he knew where her opinions of Harold Radcliffe now lay, but there remained the smallest doubt. Why it should concern him, other than a general regard for her safety, he couldn't imagine. What did it matter to him how Miss Amelie Hampton felt about another man? As her eyes met his, he found himself perversely wishing she was again feeling nauseated.

"Are you ill?" He heard the hopeful note in his voice and almost clapped his palm to his forehead.

She frowned. "I'm not certain."

"Amelie!" A cry at the door filled the room, and they both turned to see Miss Sally Hampton, looking flushed and formidable. "Amelie Hampton, what on *earth* has happened?"

CHAPTER 16

*Witnesses in an investigation should be questioned objectively,
and the officer conducting such is advised to maintain a professional distance to avoid becoming unduly sympathetic to said
witness.*

—Detective Handbook for Investigative Procedure

Michael stood as the elder Miss Hampton entered, struck at
the similarity between herself and her niece. He imagined he was
seeing Miss Amelie a handful of years into the future. He offered
his hand to Miss Sally, who took it in a surprisingly strong grip.
She looked from her niece to him and breathed deliberately out
of her nose.

"Amelie, why is the nurse telling me you are in the company
of a detective?" She looked at Michael as she asked the question.

He glanced at Amelie, who opened her mouth, but no sound
came out.

"If I may, Miss Hampton?" He indicated the chair he'd va-
cated, and as she sat, he retrieved the spare one from the corner. "I am Detective Baker," he said, opening his jacket to show
the badge pinned to his waistcoat. "Your niece has been assisting

me in an investigation and, I fear, met with an accident this morning."

The woman's hazel eyes studied him unflinchingly from beneath dark hair that had been cut and styled most fashionably. "Fringe," his sister called it, and only the boldest of women were brave enough to sport the look. The rest of her hair was styled in a sleek twist that Winston, with his artistic eye, would say showcased her lean cheekbones. That Michael even knew such phrases these days was a testament to life's strange twists and turns.

"Detective Baker, I am confused as to the Yard's sudden need to employ young women to assist with investigations."

My, but the woman was direct. He opened his mouth to respond, but Amelie held up her hand.

"Detective, many thanks to you for attempting to shield me from the consequences of my own folly. Sally, this is a tale with a wide variety of details, many of which I am certain would bore you to tears. Suffice it to say, I embarked on my own this morning in an attempt to gain information about a murder last evening that Eva, Charlotte, and I were witness to."

Miss Hampton's eyes narrowed. "I can guarantee you, dearest, that I am highly unlikely to be bored by any details you clearly wish to avoid. And how is it that you and your cousins were witness to a murder and I am only now hearing of it?"

Amelie lifted her chin, a gesture Michael was coming to recognize as an infusion of steel. "You are an extraordinarily busy woman, Sally, and we hardly thought it necessary to burden you with trifles."

Miss Hampton looked at Michael, her expression flat. "At what point is murder a trifle?" She shook her head. "Never mind. Explain, if you please. Immediately." As brusque as Miss

Hampton's tone was, it covered a softening in her expression. She placed her hand over Amelie's restless fingers that were toying with a stray loose thread in the blanket.

"I am not angry, dearest. I was terrified. What has happened to you? Are you in pain?"

Amelie took a breath and rubbed her temple with the hand hampered by the splint. She gave her aunt the barest of details about the unfortunate demise of Prospero the Great the night before. She briefly mentioned Eva taking photographs and the fact that she and Charlotte were likely photographing an autopsy at that very moment at St. Vincent's morgue. At the end, she tacked on a quick, "I do believe Charlotte has developed an interest in anatomy and dissection."

Sally Hampton closed her eyes. "Ironic, considering her father is going to have me drawn and quartered."

"I hardly think so, Sally. After all, we are becoming Women of—"

"Independent means, yes, I know." Miss Hampton sighed. "I know you are not children, and I am aware any one of you could have been married with babies by now. I promised your parents that I would shepherd you in that direction to the best of my abilities, yet it is clear that I am doing a poor job as shepherdess."

Amelie lowered her voice. "You would have us avoid the very sorts of things that have shaped you into the person you are?"

"I have never witnessed a murder."

"We didn't actually witness the act itself," Amelie admitted. "That was partly what led me to White—well, the part of town I was in."

Miss Hampton looked at Michael, who forced himself to meet her direct gaze. "She was in Whitechapel?"

He cleared his throat. "She was, but I should like to firmly reiterate that she was not there at my directive." He glanced at Amelie. "Her involvement in the beginning of our association was at my behest, I admit, but it was in a limited capacity. I asked only for an introduction to her book group as a former friend of the family."

"When I absolved you of all responsibility, Detective, I did not intend for you to abandon my cause entirely." Amelie's eyes narrowed as she spoke, and he felt a surge of guilt he immediately resented.

Miss Hampton looked at him. "Detective, I shall be certain my niece is sufficiently occupied for the near future. Perhaps you will then be allowed to conduct your investigation in peace."

He scratched his neck. "I do not mean to suggest she has not proven her worth immeasurably."

"Truly?" Amelie's eyebrows raised sky high. "Truly." She nodded. "I provided administrative support after the murder. I had hoped it would prove beneficial to the Yard."

"From my preliminary review, I should say it is the most comprehensive analysis I've seen produced so quickly after a series of interviews."

Amelie gave a small exclamation of delight, quickly followed by a wince and another temple massage.

Miss Hampton studied him quietly for a moment. "I am certain it's unnecessary for me to explain that my desire for my nieces' safety is paramount. That said, however, I have no wish to stifle any opportunities they may have for education and enrichment. I expect that Amelie would be safely protected in the company of a police detective. I would ask that any further 'help' you may require of her be something she can do at home, or at least in your presence."

"I give you my word, I shall do everything in my power to assure that your nieces are kept safe. It was never my intention to place them in harm's way. As it happens, I do not anticipate requiring further assistance from them." He was strangely disappointed, even as he said it.

"I thought you said Amelie's administrative help was among the best you've seen," Miss Hampton said. She held her niece's hand, and the two regarded him as though they were fighting for a cause he had unceremoniously quashed.

"Miss Hampton, I am confused. I presumed you wished your niece's activity with the Yard to come to an end."

"Well, I would classify 'to an end' to be an extreme, Detective. I only want her kept safe." Miss Hampton gave him an almost-smile. "If Amelie can be of assistance to your efforts, or that of the Yard's in general, she has my full support." She looked at her niece. "I simply insist she not go about investigating potentially dangerous situations on her own."

Amelie nodded. "You needn't worry. After this morning, I am quite cured of the urge."

The point was irrelevant, anyway. Though she had been useful in documenting Michael's interviews, Director Ellis was unlikely to approve of her presence with him at crime scenes and while questioning witnesses.

"Miss Sally Hampton, Miss Amelie Hampton, I must take my leave now. You both have my humblest apologies for any part in today's misadventures that I may have inadvertently caused." He looked at Amelie. "I am relieved that you are on the road to recovery. I was quite . . . I was concerned."

She smiled, a small one, but it reached her tired eyes. "I am grateful for your timely arrival, Detective. I suspect I owe you my life."

Miss Sally Hampton also smiled, and it seemed genuine. "My thanks to you also, Detective Baker." She rose, and when he stood, she shook his hand. "If there is ever anything I can do to show my gratitude, please do not hesitate to call. I do not reside at Hampton House, but I can usually be reached at the *Marriage Gazette*."

He touched his fingertips to his hat and looked one final time at Amelie, who was watching his exit with large eyes and her lip caught between her teeth. She lifted her fingers in a small wave, and he caught himself just before walking into the doorframe.

Wondering when he'd become as affected as a schoolboy by the attention of a pretty girl, he quickened his stride and headed for the hospital lobby. Winston was entering the front door as Michael jogged down the stairs, and Michael wasn't sure if the urgency in Winston's face was a good omen or bad.

"Congratulations, partner," Winston said as Michael joined him at the door. "We're needed in Marseilles. The local officials have decided to disinter a body."

CHAPTER 17

Many a matron throughout the centuries has advised her charges to be vigilant of the proverbial wolf in sheep's clothing. Such advice is certainly welcome, of course, but this writer cannot imagine being so easily deceived. Surely a pretender could never truly be mistaken for a gentleman.

—From "Essays on Eternal Bliss" by Miss A. Hampton,
THE MARRIAGE GAZETTE

Amelie, no. I am striking this paragraph.
See me in my office.
—Editorial notes in the margins by Miss Sally Hampton

Amelie watched the detective leave with a sense of disappointment. She'd not had the chance to ask how he'd managed to get her from Mr. Stern's rented rooms, to a carriage, and then into the hospital. Her appetite for story and detail were unquenchable, and yet she'd been unconscious for all of it. Perhaps she would write a card to him, thanking him for his gallantry—assuming he had shown some.

She wondered if he'd nearly run himself into the doorframe just then because he had been affected by her goodbye wave, or by something else. Could be one of dozens of things, really, because the man had a full schedule, and—

"Amelie," Sally said firmly.

Amelie blinked and realized Sally had been trying to capture her attention. "Yes, sorry?"

Sally studied her, eyes narrowing, and Amelie wondered if she would always squirm under her aunt's close regard.

"He is handsome. Detective Michael Baker."

Amelie lifted her shoulder. "One might say so. I do not suppose I see him in such a light as we have been working together as colleagues."

"Of course, of course. Tell me, dearest, if you were to describe him to a potential *Gazette* subscriber who was looking for a good match, what would you say?"

"Oh. Well, I do not presume to know much about his life aside from the professional."

"Come now, at the *Gazette* you've worked with less information than you must have by now on the detective."

Amelie sighed and frowned, and then frowned some more because the action exacerbated the pain from her head wound. "I would describe the detective as professional, serious, and dedicated to his duties."

"I see. What else?"

"I did not realize it at first, but he does possess a sense of humor, which is a delightful surprise. He also notices details about one's character and is very intuitive. He senses things without being told."

Amelie thought of the night before when Detective Baker

had slid the food from her plate because he saw she was too nervous to eat while seated beside Mr. Radcliffe.

"There are few things more refreshing than an intuitive man." Sally sat back in her chair.

"I suspect most officers of the law possess a great intuition, wouldn't you think?"

"You believe Detective Baker's positive traits are a result of his professional training and not inherent."

"Not at all, I . . ." She paused, troubled. "I suppose I . . ." She huffed a sigh. "He does not believe that *Romeo and Juliet* is the greatest classic work of romantic literature."

Sally chuckled. "You do not care for *Romeo and Juliet* either, my dear, and you are a supporter of romance in any fashion."

"Hmm. Well, be that as it may, he is . . . he is rough around the edges. I do not believe he possesses the soul of a poet. Gentle traits are those that identify a man as truly a gentleman."

Sally smiled and folded her hands comfortably in her lap. "What sort of literature does Detective Baker feel constitutes 'romantic,' then?"

Amelie felt her face growing warm. "*The Count of Monte Cristo,* if you can believe."

Sally laughed.

Amelie scowled. "Why does that amuse you?"

"Only because I have heard you profess the very same thing." Sally's laugh faded, but the smile remained. "I do not mean to tease. I thought I sensed an affection between the two of you, that is all."

Amelie's face grew warmer still. "Surely not," she said, trying to laugh but managing only an awkward cough. "We are colleagues who've not spent much time together. Why, I do not even know if he has a sweetheart." The thought stopped her cold. "He did say once he is not married, nor has he been. He did not mention any other sort of attachment, however."

"As it happens, I've met another gentleman who is interested in calling upon you in a rather more serious vein. He visited two days ago at the *Gazette*. It was late in the evening after you had already left for the day. Said he had visited Hampton House once, unofficially, but sought to introduce himself to family."

Amelie's heart beat faster, and she licked her lips. "Mr. Radcliffe?"

"The very one. Now there is a man who seems to have the soul of a poet, would you agree?" Sally watched her closely.

Amelie cleared her throat. "I believed so, once. I do wonder if his gentlemanly exterior extends into his heart. There are instances that, upon reflection, could be best described as 'put on.' I do not know if that even sounds sensible."

"As a matter of fact, it does sound perfectly reasonable, and I trust your judgment. He certainly knows his way around home decoration trends. He made a point to tell me how much he likes the décor at Hampton House. He appreciates the new-old approach to the Arts and Crafts movement."

Amelie nodded. "He was complimentary about the house, and he seemed quite keen to meet you."

"Yes. He was effusive in his praise of you, and his developing affection for you."

Confusion washed over Amelie, and she suddenly felt exhausted and dejected. What would have once been the most exciting news of the year for her was now fraught with doubt and worry.

She still was not convinced Mr. Radcliffe had killed his wife, but she also no longer believed he was the paragon of gentlemanly virtue she'd ascribed to him at first.

Had the Misses Van Horne's Evening of Entertainment ended only a handful of hours ago? It felt like an eternity.

"You rest, dearest, while I speak with the doctor. We shall sort out this suitor-and-detective business later. If you wish it."

Amelie tried for a smile. "I do not know that there is much to sort, really. It appears one wishes to work with me, and the other wishes to court me."

She considered telling her aunt about the connection between Detective Baker and Mr. Radcliffe, but she decided it could wait. It was enough for now that Charlotte and Eva shared that confidence. Besides, it wasn't as though Mr. Radcliffe was going to ask to marry her tomorrow. She didn't even imagine she'd see him for several days. Her doctor would probably prescribe bedrest for a while.

The nurse returned with Sally and administered a dose of laudanum to help with the pain and ensure she rested. Amelie was certain she was tired enough to sleep without the sedative, but the stabbing pain in her head was relentless. Perhaps she would benefit from a short—*very* short—sleep.

She settled back into the pillow and wished she was in her comfortable bed in her room at Hampton House. She began to think she would never fall asleep, even with the laudanum, but slowly she began to feel as though she were floating. Aunt Sally whispered in her ear that she was to remain overnight in the hospital, but there was a constable stationed just outside the room as a precaution. There was no need for worry.

Sally smoothed her hair gently and whispered, "I love you, dearest."

"I love you, Aunt Sally," Amelie mumbled, reaching up to touch her aunt's soft cheek.

Amelie vaguely registered Charlotte and Eva's visit later

in the day, but the next truly conscious thought she had was confusion. The room was dark, and she couldn't say what had awoken her. A scent? A rustle of fabric? Perhaps simply a feeling that she was not alone in the room. She tried to remember what Sally had said—something about a constable keeping watch—and figured perhaps he had made a noise just outside the door.

She squinted, her eyes adjusting to the darkness, and reached over to the bedside table where a small kerosene lamp burned a low, blue flame. She turned the knob, and the flame danced higher inside the glass. It hurt her eyes, and she squeezed them shut, shielding them with her hand. The pain in her head still throbbed, and she wondered if she'd be able to return to sleep without another dose of laudanum.

Another sound near the door startled her, and she squinted around her fingers, trying to sit up in the bed. There was something off about the room, as though a door had been opened then closed, a puzzle she couldn't put together. The more she grasped at the wispy thought, the quicker it blew away.

But something was clear: someone was in her room. She sucked in her breath, trying to still her racing heart.

"Oh dear, Miss Hampton, how wretchedly clumsy of me." Mr. Radcliffe stood just inside the doorway with a bouquet of flowers and a chagrined expression. "I am so sorry to have startled you! When I learned from your aunt that you'd been injured, I was sick with worry. I've been caught up at the Chancery all day and was unable to visit sooner." He paused. "I'll leave these flowers for you at the nurse's desk and visit again tomorrow. Forgive me."

"No," Amelie said, gasping as she shoved herself fully upright. She winced as she bumped her arm against the side table. "Please, I should hate for you to make a return trip."

Mr. Radcliffe's face darkened. "Miss Hampton, when the police find the fiend who did this to you, I shall have a go at him, myself." He indicated the chair next to the bed. "May I?"

"Of course," she mumbled, her world finally beginning to come into focus. The edges of her reasoning were hazy, but for the first time in what must have been hours, she felt more like herself. "What is the time?" She squinted at the clock on the opposite wall.

Mr. Radcliffe pulled his watch from his waistcoat pocket. "It is half past eight in the evening." He smiled apologetically. "Dreadfully early for a regular Saturday evening, but dreadfully late if one is laid up, I imagine."

Amelie looked at the side table for the teacup, only to find it empty. She was thirsty and frustrated at her inability to move freely and without pain. She'd never been a patient sick person, even as a child.

She managed a half smile for Mr. Radcliffe, who still held the bouquet of flowers. "I presume those are for me?" It was funny on some level, she supposed, that having moved past her short-lived infatuation with the man, she was no longer worried about saying the wrong thing. He was still as handsome as ever, still saying the right things and bearing flowers, for heaven's sake, but something subtle had shifted. Changed.

As he chuckled and made a self-deprecating remark, she tried to reason through her disquiet.

"I'll set the flowers here," he said as he laid them carefully on the side table.

She looked at the door, and realized it had everything to do with her confused brain. A click, a quiet whisper, the door opening, the door closing—she closed her eyes and tried to figure out why it was important. At any rate, it was closed now, which was highly improper.

"Mr. Radcliffe, I wonder if you would open the door and summon the nurse? I'm sure the flowers would appreciate some water. I, too, am quite parched." She nibbled on the inside of her cheek despite her attempt to appear calm.

Even though he had spoken with Aunt Sally about calling upon her with more regularity, for him to assume such familiarity was presumptuous in the extreme. Perhaps she possessed more of the scandalous Hampton family traits than she'd realized, because her anger surged. Even had her aunt, or her mother, or the Queen herself given him permission to sit in her hospital room with the door closed, *she* didn't want it.

He hesitated for a moment, but it was enough of a delay to send her pulse racing again. "Of course, of course, my apologies, again." He rose and quietly opened the door, peering out into the hallway before opening it more and returning to his chair. He perched on the edge of it, however, indicating a clear intention to leave sooner rather than later.

Amelie looked out into the hallway where an empty chair sat just outside her door. "Did you see a constable when you arrived?" she asked Mr. Radcliffe. "It's silly, but my friend, Detective Baker, is quite protective, and he insisted someone sit guard through the night." She smiled, hoping she looked pathetic enough to elicit continued sympathy. The last impression she wanted to leave with him was one of accusation.

"I did not see anyone at all," Mr. Radcliffe said, his brow creasing in a frown. "I shall speak with the nurses at the front desk. If someone is derelict in his duties to protect you, the constabulary will hear from me about it." He leaned forward. "All

I have heard of your accident is that you were accosted. Dear Miss Hampton, whatever happened?"

She weighed her options. She could maintain a sense of honest innocence and gauge his reaction, or she could lie and he would know she was keeping something from him. She was all but certain that someone would have told him by now exactly where she'd been attacked that morning.

"The truth is somewhat mortifying," she said with a delicate frown. "I suppose you have heard about the awful happenings last night at the Van Horne residence after you left?"

He nodded. "Indeed. Ghastly business. I wish I'd have remained to help quell the fear you and your cousins must have experienced."

"We learned the man's true name, and I took it upon myself to visit his rented rooms this morning. I had hoped to meet family, or friends, or someone who might have known him. I felt . . ." She shrugged, looking down at her hands. "I felt so horrible that he had died and possibly left behind loved ones. I wanted them to know he was charming and had spent his last night on earth entertaining people who enjoyed his talents."

She remembered Mr. Radcliffe's stiff reaction to the Great Prospero and hoped he thought her naive or stupid enough to have missed it. After all, it had been Charlotte who asked him about a possible connection to the man, not Amelie.

She looked up to see an image of perfect compassion on his face. It was mixed with something else, though. Relief?

He exhaled slowly. "Of course, you were seeking to comfort others in a time of loss. I would expect nothing less from a woman with such a generous heart. I do hope you have learned that you mustn't do such things alone, however. A hard-learned lesson it is, to be sure."

She managed a flicker of a smile as she nodded, resenting his didactic tone. He was not her father, or her uncle, or her grandfather, or even an official suitor. He was not even a police detective charged with public safety.

Knowing she'd flown from enamored to irritated in the space of mere hours made her feel fickle and ridiculous. Her sister, Deborah, used to yammer on incessantly about kissing enough frogs to find a prince, and Amelie had thought it not only disgusting, but silly. When two people destined to be together finally met, the stars would align and both parties would know in the deep recesses of their individual souls that theirs was a love fated for all time. No amount of frog-kissing should have figured into that equation at all.

And yet, she'd been convinced that Mr. Radcliffe was perfection itself. True, she hadn't felt as though they were fated to spend eternity together, but she had certainly nurtured a hope. Believing now that he might be nothing more than a frog was discouraging. Worse, she was forced to admit Deborah might have been right.

A voice in the distance drew her attention, and Mr. Radcliffe abruptly stood. "You must rest, Miss Hampton. I shall immediately see about your missing constable and arrange for a vase for your flowers." He extended his hand, and she placed hers in it, marveling that this time when he kissed it, she felt nothing but an urge to wipe it clean on the bedclothes.

"Thank you for the visit and the lovely flowers," she said. "Perhaps I shall press one of the blossoms into my book of remembrance."

He smiled grandly and put his hand on his heart. "To know you would do such a thing would be an honor." He nodded to her in a light bow and left the room.

She leaned forward in the bed to watch him walk down the hallway. He quickly crossed the length of it and turned left at the end. If she wasn't mistaken, the nurse's desk was to the right.

She sat back against the pillow with a frown and chewed on her lower lip, deep in thought. She heard voices coming closer, and she was relieved to recognize one as the nurse. As she looked toward the door again, her eye fell to her reticule. She had a hazy recollection of Charlotte telling her she would place it on the side table, but the reticule was now on the floor, and to her knowledge, nobody had visited since her cousins. Perhaps the nurse moved it? But she'd certainly not have put it on the floor.

Had Mr. Radcliffe gone through her reticule? Again, she felt the flash of irritation with a heavier dose of fear. What had he been doing in her room, in the dark, while she slept?

CHAPTER 18

You may find as you continue searching for information that solving the mysteries of a case is not unlike fitting together pieces of a jigsaw puzzle.

—Detective Handbook for Investigative Procedure

Rain pattered against Michael's umbrella as he stood in a small, quiet cemetery in Marseilles. The crew were digging out the coffin of the late Mrs. Marie Radcliffe, and as much as he was not given to dramatics, the cold darkness and eerie stillness seemed to fit the moment.

Winston stood next to him, and Mr. Antoine Verite held an umbrella over his mother, Mrs. Verite, who watched solemnly as her daughter's coffin was again exposed to air. Mr. Verite had returned home to France and informed the local authorities of his visit with Michael and the details surrounding Marie's death. They agreed with him that Marie's death seemed odd, given that she had no suicidal tendencies, and they had informed the Yard that the local law enforcement would be performing an examination of their own. London officers were welcome to observe.

Michael made a point not to mention it to Harold Radcliffe, and he was hopeful they could catch the man by surprise with the news that his late wife had been disinterred as part of a possible investigation into her death. He felt a sense of urgency about confirming something—anything—about the deceased's final moments. Michael and Winston had visited Radcliffe to ask about his whereabouts when Jacob Stern had met his end, and Radcliffe's alibis were confirmed by people at the Van Horne residence who had seen him leave.

They had found no indication of Radcliffe's involvement in Stern's death anywhere in the house. He had, of course, denied any knowledge of the crime and said that night in the parlor was the first time he'd ever met "The Great Prospero." The name "Jacob Stern" meant nothing to him.

As the coffin continued its rise from the earth, Mrs. Verite let out a quiet sob, and Michael regretted the necessity of the somber task. The morgue's waiting carriage maneuvered closer to the deep opening, and Mrs. Radcliffe's remains were placed carefully inside.

The ride back to the morgue was quiet, and Michael appreciated the comfortable silence between himself and Winston. He was a good partner, smart and easy to get on with. He was also private in a strangely subtle way. Although Michael felt he was getting to know the man better, deeper reflection showed he actually knew little about his personal life.

The Verites went home after leaving the graveyard, and Michael and Winston were invited to observe the autopsy. The atmosphere was professional, and the doctors worked in silence for a long time. Michael maintained enough of a distance from the table to avoid seeing more than he wanted to. Winston stood even further back, and paced, not looking at the proceedings once. Michael took note; it seems he was learning bits and pieces about his new partner after all.

Michael motioned to Winston, and the two of them left the room. "Suppose we speak with the Verites while the doctors finish their work?"

Winston was pale, and he cleared his throat. "Splendid."

Mrs. Verite's home was stylishly classic, with a neatly trimmed garden and a parlor filled with leather-bound books and paintings of family and landscapes. She welcomed them in, summoned Antoine, and served them tea.

"We would like to ask some questions about your daughter," Michael said in French to the matriarch. "I deeply regret the circumstances."

The woman nodded, sniffling into a lacy handkerchief. Her eyes were tired, and her thin shoulders drooped. "She was lovely, and a devoted daughter. She played the violin beautifully. She wanted to be a mother." Mrs. Verite smiled. "She said she could not wait until the day I became a grandmother."

Winston nodded. "She sounds like a delightful daughter. And a wonderful sister."

Antoine smiled sadly. "She was a wonderful sister. Others at school complained about their siblings, but I never could, because Marie was my friend. I feel responsible; I told her that marriage to Mr. Radcliffe seemed perfect. He was charming and amusing, and he showered her with love."

Michael nodded. Radcliffe's penchant for charm was, it seemed, his crowning jewel. "And when we spoke earlier, Mr. Verite, you told me that Marie had been looking forward to visiting soon, and that she had exciting news to share?"

"Yes. I only wish now she had written it down in the letter. We will never know."

Winston frowned. "Forgive the indelicacy of my question,

Mr. Vertie, but did your sister ever express any thoughts to you about her husband?"

Mrs. Verite's face darkened, and Antoine looked down at his clasped hands. "She said he was so wonderful to her that she could scarcely believe it, but there was something that bothered me from the first time I laid eyes on him."

Mrs. Verite placed her hand on Antoine's. "This one, he tortures himself for encouraging the suit."

"How would you describe his behavior when he arrived with her for the burial?" Winston asked.

"He shed tears, but they seemed like false tears. He said all of the correct things and wept for our loss, but I learned afterward from our family solicitor that Mr. Radcliffe had approached him concerning the remainder of Marie's dowry that had yet to fund. She was not even cold in the ground, and he was thinking of her money."

"He would have had the entirety of it at once had he been patient," Antoine muttered. "He said he could not wait another moment to become Marie's husband, and so they wed after only two months of betrothal. Marie was much sought-after. She was being courted by three other gentlemen of good standing when she met Mr. Radcliffe at a dinner party held by a mutual friend. After that, she had eyes for nobody else."

Michael frowned. So rather than risk losing Marie to another suitor, Radcliffe had forfeited the opportunity of collecting Marie's entire dowry at the outset.

Winston glanced at him, and the two shared an unspoken thought. Winston had done some digging in London and had located two insurance companies that had provided Mr. Radcliffe with hefty payouts after the untimely death of his young wife. When Winston had asked the insurance agents whether the purchase of two policies on such a young, healthy wife was common, they had both commented that, while it had seemed odd, it was not unheard of.

Added to that was Radcliffe's behavior upon settling the transactions; he had been brusque to the point of rude, condescending, and insistent that the insurance money be applied to his bank accounts immediately. Michael and Winston hadn't found evidence of excessive debt on the part of Mr. Radcliffe, but that didn't mean there wasn't any hidden somewhere.

They finished tea with little more conversation, and Michael and Winston left with promises to share whatever information they received from the coroner.

Once back at the morgue, Michael and Winston slipped into the autopsy room in time to hear one of the doctors exclaim in surprise.

The man stood at a microscope, eye fixed to it, one hand arranging a slide and the other scribbling notes on a piece of paper. He mumbled something Michael couldn't discern, something about the Thames.

"What is it? What did you find?" Michael asked.

The doctor tapped his papers and looked up at them wearily. "I will not have the official report ready until tomorrow, you understand. It must be typed and copied before I can give it to you. I can tell you our findings, however. I found distinct bruising patterns on her neck." He demonstrated by placing his hands around his own throat, thumbs at the front. "Also lacerations to her arms, bruising on her torso, and evidence of burst blood vessels in her eyes. Perhaps most distressing is the fact that the victim was with child. Approximately three months, by my best estimate."

Michael took in a deep breath. That must have been Marie's

"good news." He wondered how he was going to relay the news to the family.

The doctor continued, "You said she drowned in the Thames?"

"We presumed drowning, but were uncertain."

"My official cause of death would be drowning, as her lungs were full of fluid. She did not die in the river, however. The water was fresh with traces of lavender and oil. Detectives, Marie Verite Radcliffe died in her bathwater."

CHAPTER 19

As told by Aesop all those years ago,
"Be careful what you wish for, lest it come true."

—Miss Torrence's Guide to Raising
Well-Mannered Children

Amelie had never been proficient at remaining still for long periods of time, let alone a whole week, and she missed being out and about in Town. Eva and Charlotte resumed their work schedules Monday morning, but Amelie remained in bed, under doctor's orders, which Sally enforced to the letter. When Amelie so much as tried to move around on her own, Mrs. Burnette appeared as though she'd been waiting just outside the room.

Eva and Charlotte spent every possible moment with her in the evenings, spoiling her with attention and little gifts. Her first night home, they snuggled up next to her until she fell asleep; she didn't even remember hearing them leave.

She informed Mrs. Burnette that if a small, grubby visitor going by the name of "Sammy White" arrived, she was to be told immediately. Amelie thought of the boy daily and wondered if his vigilance had saved her life. He'd hailed a constable, she learned, and raised a hue and cry so desperate that her attacker had fled.

The brightest spot of the week was when Eva informed Amelie that Sammy had indeed shown up at the servants' door. Having been warned, Mrs. Burnette had allowed the boy entrance but made him stand just inside the door. She sent Katie Wells to find him some new clothing, then Mrs. Burnette fed the boy and forced him into the washroom where she instructed him to fill the copper tub and wash from hair to toes.

She'd sent him back twice to finish scrubbing behind his ears and at the ring of dirt around his neck. When Katie returned with clothing borrowed from a neighbor whose stable boy had grown too big, Sammy's face had been one of shock and delight. He'd been quite proud of his "respectable shirt, trousers, and suspenders." A new pair of shoes procured from Davie, the houseboy-of-all-trade, completed Sammy's new ensemble, and the difference in his carriage was marked.

Eva immediately took the boy under her wing and proclaimed him her new photography assistant. "He is quite smart," Eva confided in Amelie after he had been with them for two days. "My intention was purely to be kind, but I'm finding his help truly useful!"

When Amelie asked where he was sleeping, she learned he'd been given the tiny bedroom in Mrs. Burnette's suite. She was determined to keep tabs on the boy to prevent "thievery or shenanigans." For Amelie's part, she was relieved that one thing seemed to be going well.

At times, she wondered if the bump on her head had knocked aside her ability to remember where she placed items in her room. She occasionally found things on her dresser knocked askew or items in her clothing drawers slightly mussed.

For all that she was absentminded, she was particular about the state of her clothing, especially stockings, which had a penchant for snagging. When she asked Katie Wells if the schedule for laundry day had changed, Katie had frowned as though Amelie were daft.

Meanwhile, Mr. Radcliffe called on her each day, and each day left flowers for her with Mrs. Burnette, who stood sentry at the front door and refused to let him in.

One evening, after Mr. Radcliffe's latest delivery, Eva joined Amelie by the fire and took her hand.

"Are you well?" she asked.

"I am feeling much better," Amelie said with a smile. "Why do you ask?"

"I feel as though something has been weighing on your mind. Something, perhaps, to do with Mr. Radcliffe." Eva nodded at the flowers Mrs. Burnette had placed in the foyer.

Amelie took a breath, unsure if she felt prepared to talk about what had happened that night in the hospital. But Eva had always offered a listening ear in the past.

Amelie slowly recounted the events she remembered—the sound of someone opening and closing the door, the feeling of someone watching her while she slept, the reticule that had been moved to the floor.

"And you think Mr. Radcliffe deliberately entered your room? While you were sleeping?" Eva shuddered.

Amelie felt cold at the memory. "As soon as he left, I asked the nurse about the constable at the door. She said he had received a message from Detective Baker to meet him on the front steps immediately. He was gone for about five minutes before returning, claiming that the detective was nowhere to be seen."

"The same five minutes that Mr. Radcliffe was speaking to you, I imagine," Eva noted.

"The constable telegrammed the Yard to verify the message, only to learn it had not been sent by them. Detective Baker was not even at the office at that hour. I learned later that he was not even in London." He hadn't told her he was leaving for his work, and while she may not have been an actual colleague, her feelings were bruised.

Eva gasped. "I am so grateful that Mr. Radcliffe did not return, and that you were safe in your room."

"As am I," Amelie said. She was unsure if she could lay the blame for the constable's disappearance on Mr. Radcliffe, but it did seem the only likely solution. "And to think I had encouraged Miss Franklin to accept a dinner invitation with him." She pressed her hand to her forehead, sick with the thought that she might have led Miss Franklin into danger.

"Not to mention the unusual circumstances surrounding his wife's death." Eva shook her head. "I hope you can rest tonight. I am sure Detective Baker will find the answers that can put your mind at ease."

Eva patted Amelie's hand, then rose and made her way to her bedroom. Amelie returned to her room as well, but instead of resting, she picked up her diary and a pen.

She felt as if her mind was filled with puzzle pieces, and if she could write them down, perhaps she could make sense of everything.

She tried to pinpoint exactly what it had been that had sparked her frustration with Mr. Radcliffe—other than the fact that she suspected him of spying on her in her sleep. As she reflected back on conversations with him, she realized that he had always been condescending, more veiled mockery than anything.

In contrast, Detective Baker always spoke to her as an adult. She never was left with the impression that he would just as soon have patted her head than shake her hand, and regrettably, that was the entirety of her impression of Mr. Radcliffe.

The detective hadn't hesitated to step in when silly Mrs. Blakestone was in danger of the heavy sarcophagus, while Mr. Radcliffe had only watched with arrogant amusement. The detective asked Amelie for her opinions about things, while Mr. Radcliffe seemed more interested in Aunt Sally's ownership of Hampton House than anything else.

The question remained: what was Amelie to do? She dearly wanted to continue helping the detective with his investigation, but if she rejected Mr. Radcliffe's interest now, she would lose any opportunity to glean information that might be pertinent.

I must encourage his suit, she wrote in her diary, *to learn once and for all if he . . .*

She paused and tapped the pen against her lip. To put it into words—true words on the page in ink—was frightening.

If he killed his wife. Even though I no longer wish to be courted by him, I desperately hope he is not a murderer. I do not want it to be true that he has done such an awful thing.

She suspected Detective Baker believed Radcliffe killed Jacob Stern at the Van Hornes' Evening of Entertainment, and she understood the reasoning, but the truth was, Mr. Radcliffe had seemed to have already left for the evening. Nobody saw him after the scavenger hunt began, not even staff. She knew from the interviews she had recorded that night that the murderer could have been anyone, *including* staff.

Her thoughts swirled, and she frowned. Such scenarios were

much simpler in the novels she read. She knew that by the last page, she would have learned the identity of the killer, and the endangered heroine would ride into the sunset—or to a church altar—with the deserving hero. What if she never learned who killed Mr. Stern? What if Mrs. Radcliffe's death was never fully investigated? She would be forced to live out her days not having the answers, and that was absolutely unthinkable.

Her resolve hardened, she nodded. She would encourage Mr. Radcliffe's attention as a sort of undercover operation. She would be forced to keep that information from Aunt Sally, who had grown more disillusioned with Mr. Radcliffe since Amelie had been in the hospital.

Perhaps he believed Amelie was wealthy or that Aunt Sally was in some way responsible for Amelie's monetary future. Either way, she was no longer lovestruck by him, and her heart was again safe. The fact that he might be pursuing her solely for a financial interest stung her pride, but not her emotions.

She was learning to accept the reality that true love did not always rule the day, and that many marriages were little more than business transactions. Charlotte had said it for years, but Amelie had believed her cousin was merely jaded. Perhaps Amelie was also becoming jaded with age.

She closed her diary with a sigh. It didn't matter. She, Amelie Hampton, would marry for love or not at all. She would be happy with a man of her choice, or she would travel and work as Aunt Sally did, and she would find fulfillment in supporting herself. She shook her head. That line of thinking was so unconventional as to be downright scandalous. Aunt Sally had braved society's gossipy storms and emerged all the more beautiful for it. Whether or not Amelie was strong enough for such a challenge was a daunting question she did not know how to answer yet.

By the end of the week, Amelie's head pain was nearly gone, and the bruise on her arm, while turning several interesting shades of purple and green, wasn't quite as tender. She informed Mrs. Burnette that she felt well enough to receive any and all callers in the parlor and that she would join the others in the dining room at mealtimes.

Her ability to play a part was put to the test when Katie summoned her at Mrs. Burnette's behest. She went downstairs to see the housekeeper standing in the foyer, faint disapproval on her face.

"I'll not agree that you should be out of the sickroom already," the woman whispered, "but you have a guest, and as you demanded to be allowed to entertain callers, I am abiding by your wishes."

Amelie inclined her head. "Thank you, Mrs. Burnette." She accepted the calling card and saw the familiar raised script she'd seen once before. "Please send tea to the parlor for myself and Mr. Radcliffe." She was proud of her firm, yet pleasant, exchange with the well-meaning but often bossy housekeeper. It was a small feather in her cap.

When she entered the parlor, Mr. Radcliffe, holding flowers, turned from the hearth where he'd been examining a print Aunt Sally had recently commissioned from a talented Arts and Crafts artist.

"Lovely, is it not?" she asked him, gesturing to the print. "My aunt is considering papering the wall with it. She likes the combination of birds and flowers." She smiled. "'Bold, but not overpowering' is her assessment."

Mr. Radcliffe smiled. "You quite admire your aunt, and I should say it is certainly justified. She is an accomplished woman, and the print is exquisite."

"Gauche of me to even think it, of course, but the print alone cost a pretty sum. I can only imagine the cost to paper the entire room." She smiled and took the sofa near the hearth. She indicated the one opposite. "Please, won't you have a seat?"

He handed her the bouquet with a head bow and sat down. "Miss Hampton, you are looking the very picture of health. I trust you are recovering?"

"I am, quite. I'd have been up and about much sooner, if not for my doctor and protective aunt." She lifted a shoulder. "Rather difficult to argue when faced with such formidable foes. Incidentally, sir, I must thank you for the lovely bouquets. They brightened each and every day of my solitary convalescence."

He leaned forward, handsome face earnest and intense. "Miss Hampton, I wonder if you would do me the honor of . . . of addressing me familiarly? By my Christian name?"

She widened her eyes. "Oh, goodness, I . . . I do not know quite—"

He indicated the spot next to her on the sofa. "May I?"

"Yes, certainly."

He moved next to her and held out his hand, which she took.

"Miss Hampton, I find I am quite taken with you, and I believe you share those feelings, if I am not mistaken?"

She nodded but didn't trust herself to verbally confirm it. She felt heat rise unbidden in her cheeks.

"I pray you will understand the sincerity of my intentions

when I say that I never expected to meet another woman who would pique my interest or stir my emotions as did my dear, departed Marie. Imagine my shock to have found such beautiful communion a second time."

She swallowed. "Mr. Radcliffe, I am incredibly honored, but I am not accustomed to rushing into situations. I would ask to progress at a comfortable pace."

"Of course, dear Miss Hampton! I hope I have not shocked you with my ardor. I should dearly love to hear my name on your lips, but if it is too soon, I do understand." He placed his other hand atop hers, and she felt trapped.

She resisted the urge to pull free and said, "Harold, is it?"

He smiled broadly. "It is." He ducked his head in what she assumed was a play at bashfulness. "And when you are comfortable, I welcome the liberty to address you by your Christian name."

She was saved from comment by the arrival of the tea tray, carried in by Mrs. Burnette, herself. She arched a brow at the scene, and Amelie took advantage of the opportunity—as if embarrassed to be caught by the housekeeper—to withdraw her hand from Mr. Radcliffe's.

Mrs. Burnette settled into the corner of the room with her embroidery, and Amelie served Mr. Radcliffe the tea. As she carefully went through the motions, experiencing only minor difficulty with her bruised arm, the man plied her with compliments. Everything from her hair, to her eyes, to her cheeks and lips—nothing escaped his notice, and he paid grand homage to what he described as her "splendid beauty."

She sipped her tea and nodded and smiled, occasionally ducking her head bashfully, as he had done. She was chagrined to realize that less than a month ago, she would have fallen at the man's feet for saying such things to her. She would have felt undeserving, and flattered, and completely overwhelmed. Now that she suspected him of possibly committing crimes, she felt as though blinders had been removed from her eyes, allowing her to see the truth all around her.

He reached into his inner coat pocket and pulled out a folded piece of paper. "I've taken the liberty to write a poem in your honor, if I may be so forward?"

"My goodness, yes, please. It is I who am honored, sir!"

He smiled and leaned closer. "Harold?"

"Harold." She ducked her head again.

"Thy lips are like a red, red rose,

"Thy cheek as soft as dew,

"O, how I wish to ever look

"At you, and only you."

She thought she heard a noise come from the corner, but she covered it by placing a hand over her heart and saying, "Oh, Harold, that was lovely! Simply lovely."

She must have given the reaction he was hoping to see. He beamed and took her hand. She was holding her teacup in the other and felt silly at the awkward pose.

"May I call here again tomorrow? I know you'll be return-ing to your work at the *Gazette* soon, but I shall happily save my evenings for you."

Amelie wondered what he would say if she blurted out that she could probably bring little by way of a dowry to any man.

"I often attend events with my cousins on a moment's no-tice, and therefore cannot guarantee I shall be here every eve-ning for your visits." She did her best to look crestfallen.

"Perhaps you might send word to me if you will be attend-ing an event I may also enjoy?" He smiled, brows raised, and she nodded. "Excellent." He patted her hand and gave it a squeeze. "I must be on my way—very busy afternoon at the Chancery."

"Of course. How fascinating your work must be!"

"Perhaps more tedious than working on criminal cases, but infinitely more lucrative."

She set her teacup aside and stood as he rose, accepting a kiss on the hand. "Thank you again, Harold," she said, placing emphasis on his name, "for all the flowers and cards and notes of well-wishes. I have been overwhelmed with your generosity and your attention."

He smiled broadly. "It was my pleasure, my dear. I only hope to be the one in your life who knows the pleasure of giving you flowers for eternity."

Her smile faltered, but she quickly ducked her head in what she hoped was perceived as modesty. She couldn't help but imagine him at a graveside, placing flowers on his dead wife's headstone. Eternally.

"Until tomorrow," he murmured, and left.

CHAPTER 20

It is highly improper for a woman to accept gifts from a gentleman for whom she holds no affection. He should be graciously thanked, and the gift gently refused, lest the gentleman be led along a primrose path of unrequited affection.

—Miss Wilson's Rules of Etiquette
for Girls and Young Women

Amelie finished her workday, more tired than she'd imagined she would be after spending the day at a typing machine answering letters for the advice column. As she finished tidying her area, Charlotte, whose desk faced hers, let out a sigh.

"Do you remember the carpetbag portmanteau I ordered?" Charlotte asked. "The one best suited for art materials?"

"The one from Poodles and Company?" Amelie rubbed at an ink stain on her finger, wondering if she'd ever be able to keep her hands clean for more than a day at a time.

"Yes. I'm beginning to believe the 'Poodles' are, in fact, little more effective than the canines with whom they share a name." Charlotte frowned.

Amelie set down the handkerchief and looked at her cousin.

"What is it, really? You are not often undone by misplaced or delayed orders. I presume there is another problem?"

"Yes, there is another problem. I have been planning a day trip home to paint the fall colors, and if I must keep postponing it for lack of a decent carrying case, the leaves will be gone."

"Why not simply use your old art case?"

"The handle is broken. Which is why I ordered a new one. I am frustrated because I ordered it ages ago. I planned well in advance, and it has come to naught." Charlotte rested her elbow on the desk and cupped her chin in her hand. "Aggravating, I tell you. To plan on something and have it continually run off the rails."

Amelie's brow knit as she studied Charlotte. "Again, you seem as though something else might be bothering you."

Charlotte's eyes moved from the groove in the desk she traced with her fingertip to Amelie's face. "I am unsettled."

"How so?"

She sighed. "I do not know how to . . . I cannot decide the best course of action for my life. I enjoy working here, but I do not wish to edit personals and society columns forever. What I think I might enjoy seems incredibly far-fetched and out of reach."

"You would like to attend medical school."

Charlotte's eyes widened. "I have never said it aloud."

Amelie smiled. "You've not needed to say it aloud. Eva and I have guessed as much for months."

"You never said a word!"

"You deflect the conversation every time we come near it." Amelie paused. "Probably because you are afraid?"

Charlotte's shoulders drooped, and Amelie found it unsettling. Charlotte was the firebrand, the boldest and bravest of the cousins. "I am afraid," she muttered. "I do not have the luxury of even imagining myself in such a profession."

"It may be difficult, but certainly it is something you could do, if you wanted to."

Charlotte shrugged. "School is so expensive, and I haven't the money to go. Women have been allowed into those hallowed halls for the past three decades; yet I hear tales of poor treatment still. I could never face my family as a failure. My brothers would have no end of teasing at my expense."

"Charlotte, you are one of the smartest people I know," Amelie told her honestly. "I believe that if you want this, you should do it. Can you imagine anything worse than regret?"

"To live with regrets would be horrible." She again traced circles on the desktop. After a moment, she said, "There is a gentleman at home, an old friend of my father's, who has ties to a university. He has offered help and advice to my brothers, and I think he may do the same for me. Even though I am not a boy."

"Ah. This doubles your disappointment at not having the new portmanteau for your trip home. Well," Amelie said, slapping her hands down on her desk, "I suggest you go anyway. See what you can learn from this old friend! And if he refuses to help, well then, the pox take him."

Charlotte's mouth slid into a grin. "You're sounding quite recovered and bold today."

"I suppose I am feeling bold. Staring death in the face has a way of changing one's perspective." She paused. "Dramatic of me. I wasn't truly staring death in the face. But it was frightening."

Charlotte nodded. "It *was* frightening, Amelie. We were terrified for you. You might have been killed. Eva and I couldn't sleep that first night. Do you still have no memory of your attacker's face?"

Amelie shook her head. "None. The local constabulary suspect it might have been a neighbor who knew Mr. Stern had passed and thought to ransack his rooms. I was truly at the wrong place at the wrong time."

"Or it could have been whoever killed Mr. Stern." Charlotte sat back in her seat. "I have stewed about that, I do not mind telling you. I am hopeful your detective is exploring all avenues in the course of his investigation."

"He is hardly *my* detective." Amelie frowned and added, "He left town for work without so much as a by-your-leave."

Charlotte pinched her lips together, clearly trying to hide a smile and failing spectacularly. "One wonders why that should bother you."

"Well," Amelie said, feeling defensive, "we are colleagues, after all." She sighed. "Of a sort. I am wondering about the status of his investigations into both Mrs. Radcliffe's mysterious death and poor Mr. Stern's untimely end. I feel foolish for going to his flat alone in a neighborhood foreign to me. I ought to have known better—I did know better. My curiosity will be the death of me."

Aunt Sally left her office, speaking to her assistant over her shoulder, and then joined Amelie and Charlotte. "Good work today, girls, as always. Eva is still out photographing the wedding?"

Amelie nodded. "She mentioned the wedding party was going to be huge, and we all know how time consuming it can be when there are so many moving parts."

Aunt Sally rolled her eyes. "Mother of the bride wants this, mother of the groom wants that, and we must have at least two photos of grandmother, because she is at death's door. Poor girl is going to need an assistant who has the luxury of time, so not one of you two. We may need to advertise."

Amelie smiled, and as she looked at Charlotte, an idea formed. Sally had been generous with all three nieces and had helped Eva purchase the photography equipment. Eva repaid the advance over time and used the equipment for both *Gazette* and personal use. Often, the two overlapped in the same setting, and Sally, always a generous employer, allowed Eva to do her personal work while on assignment.

Amelie knew her aunt would help Charlotte pay for schooling—she'd offered to fund any sort of training the girls desired—but Charlotte was proud and stubborn. She would never ask it of Sally on her own. Amelie added a mental note to discuss it with Aunt Sally. Her list of things requiring immediate attention was growing.

"I'll check the machinery, and then we shall be off," Sally said.

As Amelie gathered her belongings and put on her coat, hat, and gloves, she wondered if the detective had returned yet and if he was at his office. "I believe I shall stop by the Yard on the way home," she told the others as they exited the building and Sally locked the door. A gust of wind sent her hat flying, and she muttered a curse, hoping nobody overheard.

As she dashed after it, she stopped short when a passerby caught it and handed it to her with a chuckle. "Thank you," she said and crammed the thing onto her head.

"Hatpin," Aunt Sally and Charlotte said simultaneously, and Amelie made a face.

Sally smiled. "If we decide to add deportment lessons to our list of services, I think Eva would be ideal to teach the class on accessories and organization."

"Are you truly considering it?" Charlotte asked as they strolled away from the office.

"When that gentleman brought in his daughter, Barbara, for emergency training, I thought it ridiculous, but then I gave it serious thought . . ."

Amelie's mind wandered as Sally continued speaking, and in her memory, she kept seeing Detective Baker sitting beside her bed in the hospital and holding her hand. His had been the first face she'd seen upon awakening, and as confused and in pain as she'd been, she'd been glad to see him.

Detective Baker. Detective Michael Baker. She wished *he* would ask her to use his Christian name in conversation. Michael Baker. Michael. It was a nice name, a noble name. A strong name for a strong man who had little use for silliness and artifice, but possessed a subtle sense of humor that made her smile. The first night at the book group gathering when he'd fallen directly into step with her, teasing back rather than being affronted when she'd told Mrs. Forrester he composed poetry and played the harp—

"Where are you?" Sally asked Amelie, giving her arm a little shake.

Amelie blinked and looked at her aunt. "I . . ." She smiled feebly. "Woolgathering, I suppose."

Charlotte grinned at her. "Would you care to share the details?"

Amelie wrinkled her nose at her. "No, I would not. Furthermore, I must hail a cab if I'm to arrive at the Yard before the detectives leave for the day."

"Some of them work long hours," Sally said, arching a brow at Amelie. "I suspect the one you're hoping to find will still be there."

Amelie didn't bother to plead ignorance, but she was glad when the walkway became too crowded for them to continue walking three abreast. She felt a raindrop hit her nose, and she looked quickly down the street, hoping to catch a hack before being forced to open her umbrella.

Sally held up her arm and, as she always did, immediately secured a cab for Amelie.

"Are you going this way?" she asked Charlotte and Sally.

"I am stopping by Poodle and Company," Charlotte said and squinted as the rain began to fall steadily. "I'll see you at home!" She dashed behind Amelie's cab and climbed into another one Sally had snagged.

"Be safe, dearest!" Sally called. She shouted directions to the driver, and then to Amelie, added, "Do not walk home alone from any point. Take a cab directly to the house, am I clear?"

"Yes, of course!" Amelie settled back into the cold conveyance and shivered, wishing for the luxury of heated bricks or at least a lap robe. As they drove the busy streets through the rain, her thoughts swirled with the idea that she was on the precipice of *something*. She didn't know what it was, but as surely as she knew anything, she felt change in the air.

The cab reached her destination, which was a hive of activity, even considering the evening hour. She paid the driver and hurried inside, making her way through constables and detectives to the CID department where she knew Detective Baker's office was located. She politely declined offers of help as she went, walking with a purpose that assured she was not stopped by anyone.

Detective Michael Baker, she thought, repeating his name in her mind like a wish as she climbed stairs and walked down the hallway. He might not be there, she cautioned herself, but even still her heart beat a little faster as she approached the large common room where constables and detectives milled about.

The door bearing the names "Detective Baker" and "Detective Winston" was ajar, and light shone from within. Hoping very much she wouldn't find only Winston inside, she knocked lightly and peeked around the corner.

"Yes?" Detective Baker was seated at his desk, and when he saw her, he rose and made his way to the door, his face a combination of surprise and worry. "Are you well?" he asked, bypassing all polite salutation.

She smiled, her heart thumping harder. "I am," she said with a laugh. "And hello to you, Detective."

He smiled, rueful, and ran his hand through hair that looked as though it had received that treatment several times already. His tie was loosened, his jacket slung over the back of his chair, and his shirtsleeves were rolled up to show forearms corded with muscle and definition.

She swallowed, flustered, and lifted her gaze to his face. "I am sorry to arrive unannounced," she began.

"No, not at all." He took her elbow and guided her to a chair opposite his desk. "I am the one to apologize for my shabby appearance." He began to roll down his sleeves, and she held up her hand.

"Please, do not change one thing on my account. I ought to have made an appointment or called in advance." She paused. "I was surprised to learn you had left town."

He nodded as he took his seat. "It was a rather urgent matter." He rubbed his forehead. "I will share the details with you when I am able."

"I shall try to be patient, then." She smiled. "I was hoping to find you here to see if you have made progress on the investigation into Mr. Stern's death."

"Very little," he admitted and braced his elbows on his desk. "I have many suppositions, of course, but until I can tie all of the pieces together, it remains elusive." He sat back and put a hand on the desk as though preparing to stand. "May I offer you tea?"

Her stomach lurched, and she quickly shook her head. "Oh no, no. I am on my way to Hampton House, where dinner awaits." She smiled, but it felt sickly. She'd had tea with him before. Why was she feeling those ridiculous nerves now?

He smiled and settled back into his seat. He looked, if anything, more relaxed. "You are feeling fully recovered, then? No excessive residual effects from last week?"

"I am," she said, grateful for the change of subject. "I have occasional head pain, and my arm is still tender, but otherwise I am almost entirely myself. I must . . . I feel I must apologize to you for my rashness that morning. I can be rather impatient, and I was so anxious to learn as much as I could about Mr. Stern that I wandered into something that was completely beyond appropriate."

"I accept your apology, although it is unnecessary. I understand the motivation to solve the puzzle as soon as possible. Regrettably, much of what I do here does not move quickly." He smiled, but his blue eyes seemed tired.

"Where did you go this week?"

"Marseilles."

She raised her eyebrows high. "Marseilles?"

He nodded, watching her closely.

"Oh. My goodness." Mrs. Radcliffe was from Marseilles,

and she was buried there. "A coincidence, perhaps?" she wondered aloud.

He shrugged. "Perhaps."

She narrowed her eyes. "This is wretched. How long am I to wonder before you are allowed to say anything? You know full well by now that I am completely capable of keeping information to myself."

His lips quirked. "I do know that, quite well. Even with cousins as curious as cats, you kept our business to yourself until I changed my mind."

Our business. It sounded intimate, private, and she felt something warm unfurling in her chest. Had she noticed how handsome he was the first time they'd met? Or had she been too caught up in Mr. Radcliffe's facade to see the detective clearly? He watched her now with those striking eyes that missed nothing, and she wondered if he could read her thoughts.

Her cheeks heated, and she managed a smile but dropped her gaze to escape his regard. It left her examining his shoulders and chest, the white shirt and open collar, the loosened tie and unbuttoned waistcoat. He had the appearance of a man who would return home at the end of a long day and loosen the confines of his professional attire, relaxing with the one person who had the right to see him the way nobody else did—

She blinked. "I'm sorry?" Her face heated more, and she was mortified. If he *could* read her thoughts, he'd find her ridiculously childish. His world was one where hearth and home were probably the last things on his mind.

He smiled, looking suspiciously smug. The scoundrel knew he was distracting her! The expression was enough to have her straighten in her seat, and she welcomed the irritation.

He chuckled. "I said, I am nearly finished here and will see you home, if you wish. Or I can have another constable escort you, the decision is yours."

"I would appreciate your escort," she said, lifting her chin. "The last constable sent to guard me was less than vigilant."

He frowned as he rolled down his sleeves and put his appearance to rights. "How so?"

"He was lured from his post at the hospital, and in his absence, I had an unwelcome nocturnal visitor."

He stilled, all traces of good humor vanishing. "Explain. Please."

"I am surprised you'd not been informed, actually, as it concerned communication with the offices here," she began.

He shook his head. "I've only returned from Marseilles in the last hour. The director has been all day in court, and I'll not receive an update on the week until morning."

"You've not even been home yet? No wonder you look exhausted."

"Do I?" He shrugged into his jacket, and then his greatcoat, retrieving his hat from a hatstand by his desk. "Come along; in the carriage, you'll explain what I've missed."

"Rather high-handed of you to presume what I will and will not do."

"Should you refuse, I'll be forced to revoke your deputy status."

"Ha. I would be thrilled if there were such a thing at stake."

"Oh. I forgot . . ." He looked at a small stack of parcels on the corner of his desk. "I was to drop these by for my sister and brother."

"I can certainly travel home by myself, or with another constable, truly," she hastened to reassure him, even as she felt a stab of disappointment. "Do not alter your plans."

"Not at all," he said, looking up from the parcels. "If you do not mind the inconvenience of stopping along the way to your home?"

She smiled. "It is not an inconvenience in the least."

He gathered the boxes and paused. He lifted the smallest of the three and said, "Actually, this package is for you."

For a moment, she was speechless. "Me?"

His answering smile was sheepish. "It is nothing significant, but as I was collecting treats, I saw this." He handed it to her, and she took it, flabbergasted. "Please, do not be disappointed." He looked at her expectantly. "Open it, you'll understand soon enough."

She pulled the string and unwrapped the thin brown paper to reveal a slender box. She knew better than to believe it was jewelry, and as she opened it, she laughed aloud. "A hatpin! You bought a hatpin for me?"

He chuckled. "I ought to have just handed you the thing outright and avoided this anticlimactic revelation."

She laughed again and looked at the lovely ornament, which was topped with a blue crystal flower. She closed the box, slipping it into her reticule along with the paper and string, wishing she could at least place a kiss of thanks on his cheek.

"You've no idea how timely this is. Aunt Sally and Charlotte were mocking me just this evening as my hat flew off in the wind. I shall keep this pin in my reticule, and then, each morning as I reach my front door having forgotten a pin but cannot be bothered to return *all* the way to my chamber, I'll have this one with me."

He switched off the lights and escorted her from the room. They made their way through the building, and she was acutely aware of him as they descended the stairs and stepped into the cold night. He whistled at a line of waiting hacks, and then, holding the packages in one arm, lent her his other hand to climb inside the cab. He gave the driver an address and then settled in beside her. The cab was small, and she almost sighed in delight at the warmth of his body alongside hers. Sitting next to him was far better than heating bricks or a lap robe.

"Now," he said as the cab lurched forward, "tell me about my errant constable. And who, pray tell, was your unwelcome nocturnal visitor?"

CHAPTER 21

Undercover investigations should be assigned to professional, experienced detectives. Amateurs attempting such exercises may endanger the entire operation with the use of untried skills and methods.

—Detective Handbook for Investigative Procedure

Michael's chest tightened as Miss Hampton explained that Radcliffe had snuck into her hospital room in the dark while she lay sleeping. He now had another reason to wish to pummel the man, but worse was the accompanying fear he felt. Radcliffe, who had drowned his wife in her bathtub and then dumped her into the Thames, now had set his sights on Amelie.

He cleared his throat and shifted slightly to better look into her face. "You mustn't see him, not ever."

Her eyes widened. "But I must! I've encouraged his suit in order to learn more about his involvement with Mr. Stern's murder, and potentially his late wife's. I'll be cautious, but to deny all contact now when he seems determined to pursue a course with me would be foolish."

Heat climbed up under his collar. "Miss Hampton." He fumed, caught between frustration and deep concern. "I beg of you, do not encourage him further. Your aunt must discourage his attentions."

She sighed and closed her eyes. "I am not so naive as to ignore the fact that he is not a good man. I will admit I was completely hoodwinked, but I am no longer enamored of him. If we do not take advantage of this opportunity for me to work undercover, he may slip away!"

"Amelie, he killed his wife!" His words rang through the small carriage and echoed into silence. He wasn't certain which of them was more surprised at his outburst.

She swallowed. "You're sure?"

He nodded and took a deep breath; there was no hope for it now. "We disinterred Mrs. Marie Radcliffe in Marseilles, and the coroner found evidence of murder, likely occurring in a bath."

"Oh!" Her brows drew into a furious frown. "That . . . that . . . oh!" She clamped her lips together and breathed out of her nose for a moment before looking at him in the dim carriage light. "Now more than ever we must lay a trap!"

"No." He closed his eyes. "Ame—Miss Hampton, no. If I am correct in believing he also killed Mr. Stern, Radcliffe may well be the man who attacked you in Whitechapel."

She took in his comment, remaining quiet for a moment. He could see the wheels spinning in her head, and he wasn't certain he'd like what they produced.

"Let us look at what we know," he said, his knee bumping hers as the carriage bounced along the cobblestones. "Apologies," he added.

"None necessary," she muttered. "What is it that we 'know,' Detective?"

"We *know* Mr. Radcliffe and Mr. Stern had a strange

encounter an hour before Mr. Stern's death, in which Mr. Stern made cryptic comments that seemed almost goading in nature, and Mr. Radcliffe's usually unflappable demeanor was shaken. We also *know* it was noticeable enough that nearly everyone in attendance perceived the tension between the two men."

She nodded her agreement.

He continued, "I *believe* Radcliffe located Mr. Stern's address, went to the flat to destroy any evidence of an association between them, but found you there. He may or may not have recognized you, but either way, he struck you from behind, intending to render you unconscious at the very least, but then you turned, and his billy club struck your arm and head, softening the blow to your head."

She bit her lip and looked straight ahead, silent for a moment. "You truly believe he was my assailant?"

He exhaled, hating to put yet another crack in the rose-colored glasses through which she saw the world. "I do believe that," he said as gently as he could. "I am sorry that it is even a possibility. You are a wonderful woman, and even if I didn't suspect him of murdering two people, he does not deserve a moment of your time. He is a rogue, and a cad, and entirely beneath you."

She turned her head, her eyes bright even in the dim light. "That is lovely of you to say." She nodded once and sniffled. "Of course, you probably have the right of it. Everything makes sense."

He handed her a handkerchief, and she wiped her nose.

"Sometimes I do not understand why people are the way they are." She gave him a wobbly smile.

"I admit, I have worried your view of the world would be changed, involved as you've become with me."

She lifted her shoulder. "It is not as though I've been a stranger to sadness; both my parents have passed, and Charlotte's mother died under mysterious circumstances when we were young. I suppose I am always surprised to hear about instances where one person has grievously wronged another." She paused. "I know I must sound like a child to say such things."

"You do not sound like a child, Ame—Miss Hampton. You are a truly good person."

She looked at him beneath her lashes. "I do not mind if you address me by my given name. I feel as if we are friends, and I . . . I do not mind."

It was suddenly insufferably warm in the carriage, and he fought the urge to loosen his collar. "That is kind of you to say so, especially as I have already slipped up."

She smiled. "I am flattered. It suggests a level of comfort that I very much appreciate." She glanced away, but then straightened in her seat and met his eyes. "I enjoy your company, Detective, and hope that when this business with Mr. Radcliffe is at an end, we might at least remain associates."

"Michael. My given name is Michael." The corner of his mouth turned up. She had given away her emotions in the literal stiffening of her spine, which meant it had cost her something to make the admission. His respect for her climbed another notch.

If he wasn't careful, he might develop feelings for her that would give way to hopes and dreams he'd already decided to keep at bay. Feelings that extended beyond a desire to steal a kiss or spend time in her company. The more he respected her, the more his affections grew—these were simply additional reasons to protect her from a life that would inevitably hold more grief. He would not do to her what Stanley's death had done to Clarissa.

The carriage slowed to round a corner, and Michael looked out the window. "We are nearly there," he said. "This is my sister's home, one she shared with her late husband." He swallowed. "Who was also my former partner on the police force."

"Oh, I am sorry," she murmured. "How awful for the both of you."

He nodded stiffly. "Thank you. She has an infant, and also living with Clarissa is our brother, Alexander." He wondered what kind of scenario he was walking them all into by taking a stranger to visit his family, even briefly.

"She has an infant—so her husband's death was recent?"

He nodded again. "Six months ago. Their daughter was born after his death."

"How tragic for you all."

The carriage rolled to a stop, and Michael hesitated with his hand on the door handle. "My brother, Alexander, he is . . . different, and I—"

She leaned forward, raising her eyebrows high, and waited.

"He is just different. That is all."

She looked perplexed, but said, "Different is good. Different is wonderful."

He nodded, but still hesitated.

"Will he hit me over the head with a truncheon?"

His laugh caught him by surprise, and he shook his head, smile lingering. "No. He will definitely not do that."

"Well, then. I am already in better hands." She hesitated. "Would you rather I remain in here? I understand if you prefer to speak with your family alone—"

"No." He opened the door and stepped down, extending

his hand to her. "You are not sitting alone in a carriage." He called up for the driver to wait, and then escorted Amelie to the door of a modest home, tidy and well-kept. He'd not bothered with an umbrella, so they hurried through the drizzling rain, and he knocked quickly.

Michael heard his infant niece, Mae, crying, and the noise grew louder as the door opened. His sister looked weary and near tears.

"Hello, Michael," she said, smiling and opening the door wider. She ushered them inside but glanced in question at Amelie.

"Clarissa, are you mistreating my favorite girl again?" He took the baby from her, and Amelie took the packages from him. He held his niece high against his shoulder, bouncing the way his mother had taught him to do years ago with Alexander. He smiled at his sister as the baby quieted for a moment. "Clarissa Moore, may I introduce my work associate, Miss Amelie Hampton."

Clarissa may have been confused, but she covered it smoothly with a polite smile. Amelie offered her hand. "It is lovely to make your acquaintance, Mrs. Moore."

Clarissa waved toward the parlor across the hall. "Will you join us for tea?"

Michael shifted the baby and moved farther into the front room, but shook his head. "I regret, we cannot stay. The driver is waiting, and I am escorting Miss Hampton to her home, but I brought you and Alexander treats from France."

"Again?" Clarissa smiled and tucked a few wispy strands of blonde hair behind her ear. "You spoil us rotten, Michael."

"Michael?" Alexander emerged from the parlor across the hall, smile wide, and his uniquely almond-shaped eyes happy.

"Hello! I've brought treats." He smiled at his younger brother and put an arm around his shoulders.

"Treats! Are they sweet treats?"

Michael chuckled and looked at Amelie, whose eyes were on Alexander. Her expression was tender and compassionate.

Her eyes glistened, and she said, "Alexander, I am Amelie, and very pleased to meet you!" She turned to Michael and said, "May I?" She held up the boxes.

"Oh, yes. The one on top is for Alexander. The other is for Clarissa and Mae."

Amelie gave Clarissa her gift and then moved to Alexander's side. She handed the box to him. "Do you mind if I watch as you open it? There are few things more delightful than treats." She smiled, and Alexander grinned at her.

As Alexander began removing the paper, Michael glanced at Clarissa, who watched the tableau with interest. She met Michael's eyes with a clear question in her own, and he lifted a shoulder and smiled.

"Open your treat," he said to Clarissa as Amelie folded Alexander's discarded wrapping paper.

Clarissa turned to the parcel and unwrapped the beautiful blue scarf he had chosen from a small boutique. "Ah, it's lovely, Michael. My favorite color. And what's this?" She reached into the box again and pulled out a small, soft toy bunny. "This must be for Mae." She shook her head. "Mae, who has been making her mama *very* irritable today."

"Now Mae," he said to the infant, who rested comfortably against him, "I do hope you will rethink this behavior tonight and behave for your mother tomorrow."

A horse neighed outside, and hoofbeats sounded against the street, reminding Michael of the waiting carriage. "We must be off," Michael said regretfully and handed the baby back to Clarissa.

"I would love one, thank you for sharing!" Amelie accepted a wrapped butterscotch candy from Alexander. "I must agree, the best kind of treats are sweets. I shall put it in my reticule and enjoy it after dinner. It will be my dessert."

"You must have more than one for dessert," Alexander told her.

Michael was certain she would politely refuse, but to Alexander's delight, she said, "Actually, one more would be extra lovely."

Alexander handed her another candy, which she took with a smile. She opened her reticule deliberately so he could watch her deposit them carefully inside. "Thank you, Alexander." She extended her hand. "It has been wonderful meeting you."

"You will come back again?"

"I would love to come back again." She smiled as Alexander shook her hand. She turned to Clarissa, then, and said, "Mrs. Moore, it has been so nice to meet you and your sweet family." She lowered her voice. "I shall send prayers heavenward that wee Mae sleeps through the night. I've done a fair amount of walking the floors with little ones at night so my sister could have a few hours of rest."

Clarissa nodded, looking bewildered, but reluctantly charmed. Michael couldn't blame her; he'd felt much the same way upon meeting Amelie. He kissed Clarissa's cheek and bid both her and Alexander a good evening with a promise to visit again in a few days' time.

He and Amelie hurried out through the rain, and he handed her into the cab before giving the driver the address in

Bloomsbury. He settled in beside Amelie, and as the conveyance moved into the flow of traffic, she smiled at him, misty-eyed.

"My sister has three children, the eldest of whom is like your Alexander. His name is Dennis, and he is quite one of my favorite people. So, you see, different is wonderful." Her brow creased. "I do worry for his future, for how he might be treated or where he will go when he is older and my sister and her husband have passed on. But truthfully, the doctor told her when he was born that he wouldn't live to see his next birthday. He's now seven."

He listened to her tumbling torrent of words and wanted to kiss her soundly. Not because he wanted her to be still, but because she amazed him.

"Honestly, seeing Alexander tonight has made me hopeful for Dennis's future—to know that he might *have* one is a boon. Thank you so, so much for sharing—" Her voice broke, and she cleared her throat. "Your family is lovely."

He found himself needing to clear his own throat. "And thank you for saying so. I do quite like them, but I am hardly an impartial judge."

She looked out the window at the passing streetlamps, distorted through the falling rain. "A wonderful evening. The crowning jewel will be if I arrive home to *not* find Mr. Radcliffe waiting."

Michael felt as though she'd thrown a bucket of cold water directly in his face. "Do you suppose he will be? Did he say he would be?"

"He said he would call every night, time permitting. I feel I should still continue to encourage it in order to solve our mystery, but it has been a long day, and I am weary."

He exhaled, feeling his own fatigue. "You cannot meet him alone."

"I will not be alone. Mrs. Burnette or one of the Wells sisters sit chaperone in the parlor with us. Additionally, Charlotte and Eva should be home soon." She turned to him, eyes big, and if he didn't know her to be a genuinely sincere sort, he'd have thought she was manipulating him. The worrisome part was he wouldn't have minded. Her hazel eyes were beautiful, and looking at them was quite pleasant.

"I'll not condone it. Not even from a professional standpoint."

"Come now, Detective . . . Michael . . . I know from reading extensively on the subject that law enforcement officers regularly employ the use of informants."

"Yes. You, however, are not an informant."

"I am a perfectly placed resource!"

"He tried to kill you."

She scowled. "He did not try to kill me. We aren't *certain* it was him, and even so, he could have done a better job of it, had that been his intention." She exhaled. "I will not be alone with him. I do not desire to ever be alone with him. I do want . . . I want him to slip up. I want him to admit to something, anything, even the slightest detail that I can use. Rather, that we can use."

"You're taking this personally now."

"I suppose so, yes."

"That is the worst motivation for an agent who should remain objective."

"Detective!" Her eyes shot sparks, and she took another deep breath. "Very well. I shall remain objective."

"Amelie—"

She held up her hand. "It is late, and we are both tired. Let us discuss it tomorrow. Or later."

"I am bound to the office all day tomorrow." He sighed and rubbed his eyes. "Suppose I forbid this 'undercover operation' as your superior colleague."

"You did not deputize me. Otherwise that might have worked. My cousins are both occupied tomorrow, and Aunt Sally will be at the *Gazette* all weekend. My time is my own, so perhaps I shall stop by your office with a report."

He eyed her warily. "What report?"

"The report on my brief tea with *Harold*." She grimaced. "I see his carriage there in front of Hampton House."

Michael gaped. "He . . . Did he ask you to address him so casually?" Michael refused to see the hypocrisy. He and Amelie were colleagues, after all.

She nodded. "I did not give him leave to call me by my first name, however. At first, I was feeling peckish, but then I realized it was a wise tactic, on the off chance that men truly do desire more that which they cannot have."

He choked on a laugh. "Who is telling you these things?" Never mind that it was true.

"Sally." She smiled. "Now, please lean back from the windows so he does not see you when I climb down. He may be looking out of the parlor window."

He took immediate offense. "Why may I not be seen?"

"Suppose he were to perceive you as a rival?" She gathered her reticule and straightened her hat.

"But I am only an old family friend, so there is no need for concern."

She paused with her hand on the door. "A very dashing

'old family friend.' Were I he, I would be most concerned." She smiled. "Think of this as an adventure."

"An adventure."

She nodded. "As though we've only just pulled a prank and are hiding from . . ." She frowned. "Hmm. 'Hiding from law enforcement' doesn't much work in this scenario."

"Go, then," he told her, exasperated, "and for heaven's sake, do not encourage him more than you must."

"Conversation," she nodded. "I shall somehow get him talking about his wife."

He opened his mouth to protest, but she had opened the door, climbed down, and said something to the driver. She smiled at him quickly and closed the cab door. He wondered where she'd told the driver to take him as he heard the whistle signaling the horse. He noticed her hat on the floor as the carriage started moving, but followed Amelie's directive to remain hidden. He looked out the back window to see her entering the house.

She was right, he had to admit as he picked up her hat and examined it. Having her still in Radcliffe's good graces was an opportunity that might prove useful. He was not certain, however, that it was worth the risk—even with the housekeeper sitting chaperone in the parlor. He looked again out the back window at the empty street as the carriage turned the corner. A knot formed in the pit of his stomach. He knew they were playing with fire.

CHAPTER 22

Every civilization has its share of secrets. Any time two or more human beings gather to form a community, undercurrents of intrigue or deception inevitably take root.

—Essays on Human Behavior *by Charles Charleton*

Amelie stood in the ticket line at Euston Station and tapped her foot impatiently. The train to Wickelston would depart shortly, and she wanted to be on it, settled, and looking out the window when it did. The woman in front of her was interrogating the ticket master with questions about the train schedule, when she easily could have read the one tacked to the wall. Amelie wondered if the process would hurry along if she began hopping up and down, but for propriety's sake, she refrained.

Just then, she spied a familiar figure approaching her at a quick pace. Her heart thumped in glad anticipation, but she also felt a sudden attack of nerves. He would not approve of her chosen destination for the day, she was sure of it.

"Detective," she said brightly as he dodged a nanny with a small herd of children. "What a coincidence! Are you leaving town for the day?"

He towered over her like an avenging angel, and she blinked. "I am not leaving town for the day, as a matter of fact, nor should you."

"How did you know where to find me?"

"Mrs. Burnette," he ground out.

She glanced in irritation at the woman in front of her. "You have roughly thirty seconds, by my best guess, before it is my turn at the ticket window. Why should I not leave town?"

His nostrils flared. "You know exactly why," he whispered. "You were not to go traipsing about by yourself. We had agreed!"

"Detective," she said evenly, "nobody else is able to accompany me, not even one of the two housemaids. My cousins are not home, my aunt is at work, and upon reflection, I did not see that a law had been passed forbidding one from taking a public train to a public place and wandering about amongst other people. In clear view of other people. Do you see what I mean?"

"Ame—" he began, but was jostled roughly by the woman in front of them who left the ticket window in a huff.

Amelie stepped up to the window, determined in her course. "One ticket to Wickelston," she told the ticket master.

"Two," the detective interrupted. He reached in his pocket and plopped down some money on the counter. He shook his head when she held up her reticule. "Put it back away," he muttered. "For the next time you decide to undertake an ill-advised adventure."

Amelie couldn't deny the thrill that came with knowing Michael was accompanying her to Wickelston. Everything she'd told him was true; she'd tried to find someone to accompany her, but to no avail. When she'd reasoned that she could hardly be accosted in broad daylight, in public, she'd decided to go anyway.

The transaction finished, Michael took the tickets and her elbow, guiding her away from the crowd and toward their platform. They climbed aboard their train, and Michael made note of the compartments as they walked along the narrow corridor. "Here," he said. He opened the door for her, pleased to see the room hadn't yet been filled.

He looked at the receipts and then nodded toward the forward-facing window seat. She took it, and he sat next to her with a sigh. Presumably, if the train was full, they would be joined by four other people, so if she wanted to say something to him, now was the time.

She glanced at him; he had tilted his head back and closed his eyes. Irritation fairly seeped from him, and before long, it spread to wrap itself around her.

Her eyes narrowed, and she straightened in her seat. Voice low, she said, "I did not ask you to accompany me, and furthermore, you are not my father or husband or employer. If you are going to behave like a . . . a sulky child the entire day, then you may as well get off this train and see about getting your money returned."

He cracked one eye open and looked at her, head still resting against the cushion. "Miss Hampton," he said formally, "I do not trust myself to speak with any civility at the moment."

She glared. "You had best find a way to do it, because we shall likely be joined by others and unable to speak freely!"

He sighed and shifted in the seat, giving her his full regard. "Amelie, you are going to Wickelston to investigate Radcliffe's background."

"Yes."

"You are aware a detective made that same journey while Winston and I were in Marseilles and you were on bed rest."

"Yes."

"You promised me that you would not do anything foolish, or be alone at any time with Radcliffe."

She exhaled carefully. "Do you see him here?"

"You are *alone*, Amelie, that is what I see. Should he follow you, no matter whether in the city or elsewhere, you could be at his mercy. He is cunning, and he has set his eyes on you. If he learns you suspect him of crimes, if he thinks you are *investigating* his background, how do you suppose he will respond? We believe he is already responsible for two deaths."

The train whistle sounded, and the people in the corridor hustled to find their seats. Their door opened, and two elderly women and one gentleman entered the compartment and settled across from Amelie and Michael. They gave polite nods, but otherwise did not attempt to converse.

Amelie exhaled quietly and leaned against the side of the train, looking out the window as they began to move. She couldn't explain why she felt compelled to travel to Wickelston. She knew a detective had already made the trip and learned nothing, but perhaps he hadn't turned over the right stones. There was nothing to be lost by her going, and it wasn't as if Mr. Radcliffe was following her movements, for goodness' sake. He had told her during tea last evening that he was occupied all weekend with work and would likely be unable to call.

Memory of the conversation brought to mind something Michael had said about his schedule. She murmured, "I thought you were confined to the office today."

"I was," he said quietly, "but am waiting on several reports —my hands are tied until then, so I decided to make an unscheduled visit to Hampton House."

She frowned. "I told you I would likely be out and about today."

"It is early. I did not imagine you would already be 'out and about.'"

She looked at him, incredulous. "I am a working woman! I rise before the sun each day."

He smiled at the trio across the compartment, who now eyed them over embroidery and newspapers. "Perhaps, dear sister, we shall simply enjoy the scenery."

Dear sister, indeed. She pursed her lips but turned back to the window and watched the world move faster as they gathered speed. The ride to Wickelston would take just over an hour, and she was determined to enjoy herself. The rocking of the train and quiet comfort of the cabin soon relaxed her, and she allowed her eyes to drift closed.

She felt someone touch her shoulder and then lightly shake it. "Amelie, we are arrived." The whisper in her ear pulled her from the depths of her satisfying nap, and she blinked herself awake. Michael's hand was on her shoulder, and the three other passengers were already on their way out of the cabin.

"I slept," she mumbled.

He half smiled. "You did."

She sat up and put a hand to her hair. "You needn't look so smug. I am an early riser; I simply was lulled to sleep by the rhythm of the train."

"Yes. You're a working woman." His smile grew as he stood and stretched. "I can only imagine what our fellow travelers thought of such a statement."

"Hmph." She gathered her reticule and stood, and her hat fell from her lap. She looked at it in surprise. "But I wore my hatpin!"

Michael retrieved the hat and handed it to her. "I removed it for you. It was smashed against the wall." As she secured the hat back into place, he added, "Might I add, the hatpin looks very stylish with that hat. I do not mind admitting I am something of a connoisseur concerning women's accessories. I helped my mother with all manner of projects."

Her lips twitched. "What a good son you were to help your mother. Did she have a business?"

He nodded. "She was a seamstress. My father passed when I was young, and she often required help. Clarissa was too small, and I was there."

Her heart turned over. "Oh, you *were* a good son. And I am so sorry to know you lost your father at a young age. How fares your mother now?"

His mouth quirked in that half-smile, but this time perhaps bittersweet. "She has also passed. Fell ill when I was an older teen."

She stopped fussing with her hat and looked at him for a long moment. "I am doubly sorry for your loss. I understand that pain exquisitely. I imagine the challenge of helping your mother at such a young age was difficult."

"You needn't pity me," he said, not unkindly. "Many others experience worse. I had two loving parents, if only for a short time."

"You were not yet a grown adult, and you took responsibility for your sister and brother." Her heart turned over again. Responsibility for a sister who would have needed a mother's influence as she came into her own, and for a brother who needed special care. She imagined Michael utilizing the skills he learned from his mother to help Clarissa with her adornments.

She cleared her throat. "I do not pity you in the least, my friend. Rather the opposite."

He turned toward the door, but not before she thought she spied a tinge of color on his cheeks. She tamped down the urge to throw her arms around him in a warm embrace.

They left the train, and as she stepped down, Amelie gasped at the sudden gust of cold wind. She turned her collar up and was glad she had worn her warm boots. Michael angled his hat against the wind, and then offered her his arm.

They stopped at a line of carriages and, upon finding an omnibus headed for the center of town, climbed aboard. People chattered and laughed, and Amelie knew that for many, a day away from London's congestion was a treat. As a few more people climbed up, those seated scooted to make room. Michael moved closer to Amelie so that a gentleman could sit beside him, and she gratefully nestled her shoulder behind his, relishing the warmth.

He glanced down at her, but she couldn't read his expression.

"Apologies, dear brother," she whispered, "but I am *cold*."

He raised a brow and whispered, "I am not complaining."

Her cheeks warmed, and she smiled before turning her face to the open-air window.

The omnibus finally began moving, and the mile drive into town proved an interesting one. They passed a section of homes that had clearly seen better days, and several children ran outside in clothing not nearly suitable for the temperature. She frowned and chewed on her lip, feeling the same strands of sympathy and hopelessness she'd encountered in Whitechapel.

As they neared the village center, shops and cafes became visible. On the hillside, stood a large building. It bore the look of a distinguished, if gloomy, mansion, complete with gothic turrets and ornamentation.

Michael pointed at it. "I believe that is the boys' home."

She grimaced. "It looks rather fearsome."

Michael ducked closer to the window for a longer look as the bus continued forward. "Likely considered necessary to encourage discipline," he murmured.

The scent of his cologne was subtle and might have been no more than shaving soap, but it left her with a profound desire to nuzzle his neck with her nose. She closed her eyes, mortified, and patiently waited for him to move away. The gentleman next to Michael said something, and Michael responded, but the exchange was completely lost on Amelie, who wanted to sink through the floor and slither away down the road. What on *earth* would he think of her if he knew what had crossed her mind?

The bus stopped in front of an old inn that boasted a dining room serving the "best tea westward of India." Michael looked at the sign and grinned at Amelie. "We must have a cup of that tea," he said, and she smiled but truly had no idea what he was saying, because he was still close to her.

"Are you ready?" He stood and offered his hand.

She blinked and took it, wishing they could simply remain on the omnibus all day, driving around the village and smelling wonderful.

After the bus pulled away, Michael took a deep breath. "Now, then," he said. "What was the first item on your list of things to do today?"

She looked around at the shops and eateries, each one charming and decorated for the village's autumn celebrations. "I hadn't truly thought so far ahead," she admitted, looking up at him. "The boys' home, I suppose; I wish to speak with Reverend Flannery."

He smiled and offered his arm, and he led her to the sidewalk. "Were you planning to simply march up the front steps and request an audience?"

She lifted her shoulder. "I suppose when verbalized it seems rather absurd." She frowned as they walked. "If he were available, I imagine he would speak with me, if for no other reason than to satisfy his curiosity. Additionally," she said as they walked around a couple who strolled with a dog on a lead, "the tone of his letter to Mr. Stern seemed very pleasant."

The big house on the hill was visible intermittently through trees and buildings placed along the street. "What did the detective say when he returned to London after investigating here?" she asked.

Michael shook his head. "Not much. He said the Father was amiable enough but claimed to have no knowledge of the matter we were investigating or the parties associated with it."

Amelie's reader-brain imagined multiple scenarios. "The detective came here while you were away and I was at home for the week?"

"Yes. Why do you ask?" he said.

"I wonder if a certain *someone* visited the Father before the detective did and warned him to claim ignorance."

"Possible." Michael nodded. "To what end? Hide any connection between himself and Mr. Prospero?"

"Yes. Perhaps threatened him." She wrinkled her forehead. "Threatened him with what, though? Something substantial enough to convince a man of the cloth to lie to a man of the law."

He gave her his half-smile. "Shall we walk up there, or would you rather take a cab?"

"I'd rather walk. It isn't far."

He stepped behind her as the sidewalk became crowded, and followed with his hand under her elbow.

When they'd threaded through the people, he came alongside her again and pulled her hand through his arm. She felt protected, and safe. She'd not realized until that moment how often she'd looked over her shoulder since the attack at Whitechapel. On some level deep inside, she knew she had been trying to prove to herself that she was fine, that she wasn't afraid. The pursuit of that proof had led her to attempt today's journey even though no one had been free to join her.

A few meandering attempts to find the correct road finally led them to the long path to the boys' home. Amelie was a brisk walker, which was to her benefit in matching Michael's longer stride. To his credit, he didn't rush them; but as they neared the big building, her nerves had her wanting to sprint in order to be done with the encounter altogether.

As they neared the wide staircase, Amelie paused, looking at Michael. "You do not believe this is necessary, do you? You're humoring me?"

"I am not humoring you. It crossed my mind yesterday that the detective who visited last week is nearing retirement, and he is, shall we say, eager to be finished. I do not know how intently he pursed his line of inquiry. This is necessary, but I admit I do not like you anywhere near it."

"I'll not interfere," she said, feeling foolish at having pushed her way so aggressively into an investigation that was not hers to pursue. "I'll be silent."

He must have read the embarrassment. He placed a finger

under her chin and tipped her face up to meet his eyes. "The reason I do not want you near this thing has nothing to do with a concern you will 'be in the way.' You are perceptive, and in no way do I feel you are unequal to the task. I believe you could coax a response from almost anybody." He paused. "I simply do not want you hurt again."

She swallowed and nodded as he dropped his hand and nudged her toward the stairs. "In for a penny, in for a pound."

"Yes." She took a deep breath and straightened her shoulders as he lifted the heavy ornamental door knocker.

CHAPTER 23

Simple Christian duty demands an embrace of the orphan and waif. We must care for him as if he were Christ, Himself.
—Thoughts on Care and Keeping of the Unfortunate
by Pastor Ralph Gladston

Michael lifted the monstrous door knocker a third time and let it fall loudly, wondering if either the home's inhabitants were on some sort of educational venture or if they'd simply been instructed to ignore all visitors. He was prepared to turn and take Amelie far from the place; the very air held a threatening element that made him uneasy. The door finally cracked open, and a young man peered out at them.

"We are here to see Reverend Flannery. I am Detective Michael Baker, and this is my associate, Deputy Hampton. Shall we await the reverend here on the porch or inside?"

The boy had a guarded look that Michael recognized. He'd seen it on more orphans and street urchins than he could count.

"Come inside," the boy finally said. He opened the door wider, and Michael kept Amelie close to him as they entered the large foyer. The building consisted of the finest in early Victorian design, but for all its ornate flourishes, it was dark and cold.

"Please have a seat here." The boy indicated a bench beside a door that was probably initially a parlor. "I shall see if the reverend is available."

"What is your name?" Michael asked as the boy turned away.

"Gabriel Grant, sir."

"Thank you, Mr. Grant."

The boy walked down the long front hallway, and Michael indicated the bench for Amelie. She sat, silent, but her eyes were large as she examined the foyer, taking in every detail. As an afterthought, he pulled his notebook and pen from his pocket and handed them to her. "Write down everything," he said. "Deputy."

She smiled, looking equal parts sheepish and delighted, but took the materials and sobered quickly. She flipped open the notebook, uncapped the pen, and stood. She slowly wandered around the room, pen scribbling quickly, its occasional scratching providing the only sound in the cavernous hall aside from the ticking of an enormous grandfather clock. If her last effort as his "scribe" were any indication, he would have a detailed description and account of the experience in his hands by morning.

Before long, the echo of footsteps sounded from down the hall, and a tall man emerged from the shadows wearing the clerical garb of his station. He was of late middle age, with thinning hair and slightly stooped shoulders. As he neared the front hall, he smiled politely and extended his hand.

"Detective Baker, is it? How may I be of assistance today?"

"Reverend Flannery, thank you for meeting with us. I wonder if you might answer some questions about a former resident of the Wickelston Boys' Home. Jacob Stern?"

The reverend tilted his head. "The Yard has already sent a detective with questions about this."

Michael nodded. "We are broadening the investigation and reinterviewing persons who may have knowledge of the case."

Amelie joined him, studying the cleric closely. When the man glanced at her, she smiled politely but remained quiet.

Reverend Flannery nodded somberly. "I remember Jacob Stern," he said. "Would you join me in my office?" He opened the door by the bench and gestured.

They joined him in a room populated with bookshelves that held matched sets of leather-bound volumes, a desk, and three chairs. Michael and Amelie sat opposite the desk, and the reverend sat behind it, folding his hands on the polished surface.

"You are still investigating Jacob's horrible death?" he asked.

"We are." Michael nodded. "He was working as an entertainer in Town, and we attended his last performance. He called himself 'The Great Prospero' and provided fortune-telling to guests at a party."

The reverend smiled faintly. "He was always an entertainer. When he left us for London, he had grand ambitions of the theatre. I fear he did not achieve great heights." He paused. "One can never be certain what life holds for those who suffer ill fortune. I have not communicated with Jacob for years; to hear of his death was a great shock."

There was the man's first lie; Michael had the letter Amelie retrieved from the flat, the letter that Reverend Flannery had written to Jacob Stern.

"We are also seeking information on another former resident. He goes by the name of Harold Radcliffe."

The reverend's forehead wrinkled. "I do not know that name."

Amelie pulled something from her reticule and handed it to Michael. It was a photograph of Radcliffe, posed grandly and taken at a studio. It was the sort of item one might give a woman along with a calling card—a woman who was perhaps more than an object of passing interest. Michael's nostrils flared, but otherwise he kept his expression neutral and slid the photograph across the desk.

The reverend's eyes flickered in recognition.

Before he could deny it, Michael said, "You do recognize him, I see."

The reverend hesitated and then smiled. "I do not usually discuss what I know of past residents; I made an exception with poor Jacob Stern, given the circumstances." He opened his hands. "You are insightful, Detective." He tapped the photograph. "I do know him."

Michael watched for signs of reservation or fear, but realized as the man pulled the photograph closer, he was studying it with pride. He glanced at Amelie, who also watched the reverend carefully, and she flicked her eyes to Michael with a subtle twitch of an eyebrow.

"'Harold Smith' is the name he was given here. I do not know him as 'Radcliffe,' so you understand my confusion."

Amelie stirred, and Michael looked at her. She clearly wanted to ask the man something, and Michael nodded.

"Sir, you said 'Harold Smith is the name he was given here.' Was he raised by this institution from infancy?"

The reverend nodded. "Perhaps because he benefited from a lifetime of tutelage with us from the cradle, he was one of the few who reached a loftier status. He is a solicitor at the Chancery, you know."

"He never knew his parents, siblings?" Amelie persisted.

"Regrettably, no. But perhaps it is for the best; he was abandoned at the hospital with no record of his mother. Better to flourish under God's watchful eye than as a bastard child living in squalor."

Amelie fell silent.

Michael continued. "Do you know if Jacob Stern and Harold Smith had contact in London?"

"I wouldn't know," Reverend Flannery answered. "Once our boys leave home, I rarely hear of them."

There was a second lie. Jacob Stern had apparently written to the man, telling him he'd seen someone in a London coffee shop who might have been "Harold Smith."

Michael nodded but let the silence hang for a moment.

The reverend did not fidget, did not move so much as a finger, until he finally smiled. "Have you any further questions for me?" he asked.

"I do have one," Amelie interrupted. "How were Jacob and Harold and other boys regarded by the local villagers? Were they welcome in town?"

If the reverend thought it an odd question, he didn't show it. "The villagers mostly keep to themselves, as do the boys. Residents of a small town can wield judgment harshly and do not always behave toward the less fortunate with the Christian benevolence one would expect. It does not impact us here at the boys' home unduly; our days here are quite full."

He stood, indicating a clear end to the discussion. He picked up the photograph and returned it to Amelie, saying, "This is yours, my dear? 'Tis a fortunate woman who receives such a boon from an important, educated, and wealthy man."

Amelie smiled tightly and took the photograph. She stood and was on her way to the door before Michael could react.

He thanked the reverend for his time and shook his cold, bony hand once again. "Should you be interested in continued information about Jacob Stern's murder case, I will gladly provide it to you. As you practically raised the young man, I am certain you would appreciate it."

"Oh, we did not raise Jacob so much as provide a place for him to live the last two years before his age of majority. His mother passed, he was in need of a roof overhead, and we were happy to provide it. Short though his tenure was, he was one of ours. I would appreciate any news of the investigation, though, and I am grateful to see such dedication applied to it."

Michael touched the brim of his hat and followed Amelie to the foyer. She clutched his notebook and pen in one hand and tugged on the heavy front door with the other. He reached around her and turned the lock, sliding the bolt back. She looked over her shoulder at him in chagrin as she turned the handle, this time pulling the door open.

"Thank you again for your time," he said to the reverend, who stood at the door and watched them descend the front steps.

"My pleasure, of course," the reverend called after them.

He had an uneasy feeling that the image of the man silhouetted in the doorway of a dark house full of shadows, even before the clock had struck noon, would remain with him for some time.

CHAPTER 24

It has been said that love sometimes catches one by surprise; this writer imagines that someone surprised by such a momentous state of affairs must be abysmally unobservant.

—From *"Essays on Eternal Bliss" by Miss A. Hampton,*
THE MARRIAGE GAZETTE

"Mr. Radcliffe lied about absolutely everything," Amelie fumed as she and Michael neared the road leading back into town. "His name. His past. *Everything*! He played me for a fool, and while I may be naive, I do *not* appreciate that." She had held her composure until they were well out of sight of the house, but then lost her temper completely. "He is a wretched, awful liar who kills people!"

"Not so loud, Deputy, if you please. We are nearing civilization." He guided her into the maze of streets they'd traveled on their way to the boys' home. They reached a secluded stretch of road that was full of trees with leaves turning to rich yellows, oranges, and reds, and she was unable to even appreciate the beauty.

She cursed the emotions that were always so close to the surface. When she was angry, she was teary. When she was afraid, she was teary. When she was touched by a kindness, she was teary. She did not, however, want to shed a tear over Harold Smith. "Michael, he is a bad man."

"I am glad we finally agree." He smiled at her, and she tried to relax.

"When my brother teased me as a child, the worst part of the experience was feeling foolish." She looked away, grateful for the cold gust of wind that gave her eyes a reason to water. "Humiliation is an awful thing to feel, and knowing Mr. Smith perpetrated his lies in order to curry some kind of favor or to use me to gain access to Aunt Sally and her money—I did not see it. Although Charlotte did after eavesdropping on one conversation."

Michael stopped and took her hands. Rather, he took one hand and held the other wrist, because she still clutched his notebook and pen with a death grip. "He has perfected his deception to a fine art. You have done nothing wrong."

"*You* saw him for what he was from the very beginning."

"Cynicism is a requirement for my profession. Had I been a tailor, as my mother advised, I might have become Harold Smith's bosom friend."

She laughed, grateful for the levity. She inhaled slowly and relaxed. "Somehow I cannot envision that."

"Which part? My life as a tailor or as Mr. Smith's confidante?"

She tilted her head as she studied him. "I think you would be a splendid tailor. You may not look the part, but you have a very exacting temperament that would lend itself well to producing lovely things."

His lips turned up in a smile. "How is it I do not 'look the part'?"

"Tailors are thin and stooped, and they wear glasses perched on the end of their noses. Just here." She lifted the pen and used the capped end to tap him softly on the tip of his nose.

He looked at her eyes, her mouth, and then slowly released her hand to cup her cheek. "Miss Hampton, you are quite unraveling everything."

"How so?" she whispered.

"The best-laid plans . . ."

Something in his tone caused her to brace herself. "What are those plans?"

His smile suddenly seemed sad. "My line of work does not lend itself to emotional security for family and . . . loved ones."

She swallowed. "So you have decided to keep yourself free of such entanglements?"

He quietly exhaled. "I have. I had. My father was a constable and died while performing his duty. My brother-in-law and partner died while performing his duty. I saw the effects those deaths had on my mother and sister, and I cannot, in good conscience, do that to a woman I . . ."

Her spirits sank as he trailed off. "What a shame, Detective. I suppose that such a woman would then marry a factory worker, or other laborer, or a man in any one of a number of dangerous professions. Or perhaps a banker, who is accidently trampled in the street by a runaway carriage. Or a farmer who contracts consumption at the village autumn fete and succumbs to it weeks later." She shook her head and pulled back.

He released her, remaining silent, watching her.

She shrugged, stuffing the pen and notebook into her reticule. "We are all going to die someday, and what a pity it would be to lose the possibility for happy opportunities because of fear." She furrowed her brow. "You mentioned the detective who first interviewed Reverend Flannery is nearing retirement, which must indicate he has arrived at a certain advanced age. In fact, I have seen several gentlemen of varying advanced ages in my current comings and goings at the Yard. I am left to believe, therefore, that although an occupation such as yours does carry with it inherent risk, the odds of living a long, full life are not improbable." She paused. "I daresay there are risks associated with hundreds of professions. Yours is not unique, Detective."

She fell silent, deciding she'd delivered enough of a lecture. She tried desperately to swallow disappointment at losing something she hadn't been aware she wanted.

His expression didn't change for a long moment. Then he moved forward and touched her shoulder. He slid his hand along the curve of her neck, up to her jaw and cheek. His strong fingers cupped the back of her head, and he touched her face with his thumb, slowly, as though giving her an opportunity to pull away.

She placed her hand on his jacket and curled her fingers into his lapel. He whispered something—a curse, perhaps, or a plea? She couldn't discern it over the sound of her heart beating in her ears.

He lowered his mouth to hers. He kissed her softly, the warmth of his lips a contrast to the coldness of his nose. She reveled in the contact, marveled at it, at the communion, the intimacy of returning his kiss. He shifted his stance, and she feared he might pull away, but instead, he brought his other hand to her head, deepening the kiss.

As the moment came to a gradual end, her grip on his coat relaxed. He didn't break away, but slowly lifted his head and looked at her with those blue, blue eyes.

"Shall I apologize?" he whispered against her mouth.

"I sincerely hope you do not," she managed.

"Even though we stand in clear view of the world?"

"We are shielded by trees. And we do not know anyone here."

He smiled slowly and kissed her again, soft, small touches that provided a counterpoint to his earlier, more passionate, kiss. He trailed his lips along her cheek and whispered into her ear, "You are the most incredible woman I have ever known, and I love you."

She closed her eyes and exhaled, this time a tear escaping. "I love you," she whispered back, baffled. "I truly do, and it happened without fanfare. How is that possible?"

His breath escaped in a quiet laugh against her hair, and he moved his arms to encircle her and pull her close. He held her quietly, blocking the wind and enveloping her in warmth.

"We shall cause a scandal, and your aunt will have my head," he murmured against her ear. "Or we shall freeze to death in place."

"I am very warm," she murmured into his coat and nuzzled closer. "Also, you smell good."

His laugh rumbled in his chest, and she felt it against her cheek. "As do you, Amelie Hampton." He sighed. "What am I going to do with you?"

"You could kiss me again." She felt her cheeks warm, but she was determined to stay in the moment as long as she could.

He looked at her as though she was the only person on earth, and she lost herself in the depth of his blue eyes. "I could spend a lifetime kissing you, and it would never be enough."

"Good," she whispered. "I do hope you will make an effort."

He spread his fingers around the back of her neck and

threaded them into her hair, pulling her close again. He drew her body up against his with an arm wrapped tightly around her waist, and she reached for his shoulders as he descended, crushing his lips to hers.

She opened herself to him, relishing in each sensation as feelings crashed over her. He was right—it would never be enough. She breathed him in, wanting to stay in his embrace forever. Every practical thought fled, and her only reality was the feel of his lips as he kissed her as though he were starved for air only she could provide.

Her legs were weak, and she again clutched his coat, gasping as he finally released her from the spell he'd woven. He trailed his lips along her neck, his uneven breaths warming her skin as he eventually calmed and loosened his embrace by degrees.

"Wait," she whispered, leaning against him as she tried to catch her breath. "I cannot stand."

She felt his smile against her skin as he placed the softest of kisses just below her ear. "Deputizing you was pure folly," he murmured. "We shall never get any work done." He slowly kissed her cheek, her eyelids, and then finally rested his forehead against hers. "I love you. We must finish this thing so that I know you're safe, and we can move beyond it."

She ducked her head, suddenly feeling shy. What did one say after being kissed senseless in the street?

He lowered his head to catch her eyes and rubbed his thumb across her cheek. "Are you well?" he murmured.

She nodded at him with a small smile. "I am searching for something witty to say."

He grinned. "Lack of wit is not something I would ever associate with you, Amelie Hampton." He kissed her once more, firmly, and then released her, threading her arm through his and pulling her close. "I confess to also feeling rather scattered. There are a dozen things we should probably do here in town, but I can't manage to pin down even one."

She smiled up at him. "Now that you've deputized me, I have an idea."

"Do you, now?"

"We must find the town storyteller. Every village has at least one, and I have questions."

He took a deep breath and released it. "Let us find this worker of magic, then. Where shall we start?"

"The main street leading through town. I'll know her when I see her." She was glad for a purpose to move forward again, preventing any awkward comments she might feel compelled to blurt out. She still felt the touch of his lips on hers, and she forced herself to refrain from tracing her fingertip along them.

She walked closer to him, now, feeling the thrill of it, and their pace was considerably slower than it had been before. She felt giddy, and while Michael hadn't proposed, what had just transpired was a far cry from "I shall never marry and make a woman sad with my passing."

As they neared the village's main street, she scanned the establishments. She remembered Miss Van Horne talking about Wickelston and the increase in tourism with the coming of the railroad. Accordingly, many of the pubs, cafes, and shops looked new. She hoped to find one with some history behind it.

"Smells good," Michael said as they passed the second pub. "We are approaching the noon hour, coincidentally."

"After," Amelie told him, surprised that despite the butterflies in her stomach, she thought she might actually be able to eat something in his presence without suffering from nerves.

"Let me just . . ." She pointed across the street and tugged on his arm. "There!"

Madam Seville's Ribbons and Hats was well-kept, but appeared older than the rest. As they reached the front door, Amelie glanced at Michael and hesitated. "Perhaps you ought to remain here. I may not learn anything with you hovering about."

"I believe I'm insulted."

She patted his arm. "This is my domain. I shall be but a moment."

He didn't argue, but looked inside the large, plate-glass front window and gestured with a head nod. "Stay in sight, if you please."

"Of course," she said, but she couldn't imagine an unseen enemy doing her harm in a shop full of people. She entered the building and was nearly overwhelmed by the sumptuous array of ribbons, lace, and haberdashery brilliance.

"I should like one of everything, please," she whispered to herself and turned in a circle.

A woman's delighted chuckle sounded behind her, and she turned to see the proprietress, who was a middle-aged woman with a pink pinafore atop a lovely gray ensemble. A pencil was held tight through the bun atop her head, and she placed a tape measure in her pocket as she greeted Amelie.

"They are all rather spectacular, no?"

"Most assuredly," Amelie answered honestly. "I am visiting for the day, but I shall bring my cousins back soon just for this shop alone."

"My name is Hallie, and I own this establishment. Are you looking for anything in particular?" The woman's smile seemed genuine and welcoming.

Amelie sighed. "I would dearly love to browse, but I actually am on a quest."

"Oh?"

"You see, a gentleman of recent acquaintance has expressed an interest in courting me, but I have heard unsettling rumors. I should like to determine their truthfulness before I either confront him or agree to his suit."

The woman's brow knit. "How may *I* help you with this?"

"I have been told the gentleman was raised here in Wickelston. I have a photograph," she added, opening her reticule and producing the same picture she had shown the reverend. "It may be that only longtime residents of the village would recognize him, if at all, but perhaps—"

The woman held out her hand. "I have lived in Wickelston all my life. If he is to be recognized, it would be by me."

Amelie held her breath and handed over the photograph. Hallie fished spectacles from her pocket and examined the image.

She looked up at Amelie, her coloring draining from her face. "My dear, I would not let my daughters near this man if he were the King of England."

CHAPTER 25

Michael paced slowly outside the little shop as Amelie spoke at length with a woman inside. His view was partially obstructed, but he kept Amelie in sight as the woman spoke expansively with her arms and hands. He occasionally caught sight of the shopkeeper's face, which was animated, her eyes wide.

His mind kept traveling back to the kiss. He was still reeling from it, from the intensity of it. He'd kissed her in the middle of a civilized country lane as though he was a sailor on shore leave. He wanted to regret it, because surely he should, but he kept envisioning scenarios wherein they might repeat the action. Continually.

He was going to propose to her, and the thought made him happier than he imagined possible, but she was a romantic woman who deserved a grand gesture. He also needed to take up the matter with her aunt.

When he'd left his house that morning, he would never have

guessed that by the lunch hour, he would have changed his entire philosophy on marriage and family. Her impassioned words, summing up her view on life itself, rang truer than anything he'd ever heard. He had seen her obvious feelings for him written clearly across her face, and to know she returned his affections, and after such a relatively short time, was a relief. In recent days, he'd accepted his burgeoning feelings for her but had planned to do nothing about it. Her declarations, spoken and implied, had freed a band around his chest he hadn't realized he'd placed there.

He made another pass by the window and saw Amelie at the counter, purchasing something from the woman. They exchanged a few more words, and the shopkeeper grasped Amelie's hand, speaking earnestly. Amelie finally exited the store, carrying a small paper sack. She was pale and trembling, and Michael couldn't get her away from the store quickly enough.

He guided her to an outdoor cafe that boasted a few firepits, thinking they would sit for a moment and order tea.

She shook her head. "I do not wish to be overheard." She chewed on her lip and looked around. "Let's walk there."

She pointed to a small church and adjoining graveyard. Rain began to fall, misting, and a cold fog crawled in and began settling over the village.

He put his arm around her shoulders, and they hurried down the street, nearly running by the time they reached the old church. She pointed to a small mausoleum on the cemetery grounds, with steps and a protective overhang. The ground was spongy, and they picked their way through the mud, Amelie holding her skirt off the ground.

They reached the small building, on which the family name, Wilmington, was proudly etched.

"Many thanks, Wilmington family," Amelie said as she ran up the steps and rested against the gray stone door. She put a hand to her chest as she breathed, and Michael joined her, bewildered.

"Amelie, what is it?"

"Oh, Michael." She swallowed and took in another breath. "It is worse than we imagined." She closed her eyes. "When he was eighteen years of age, Harold Smith killed a girl here in Wickelston."

Michael exhaled slowly. "Tell me everything you know."

"The shop owner, Hallie, has been well established in town for years, and the family goes back generations. As long as she can remember, the Wickelston Boys' Home has been in operation, but it was not always the fearsome place it is now. Reverend Flannery instituted a strict protocol of behavior and expectations that many in town feel is disproportionately harsh. Rumors have spread, over time, of a series of unmarked graves on the property, but villagers leave the reverend alone, and in turn, he supports businesses in town but otherwise keeps to himself.

"Harold Smith was a charmer, Hallie said, and by the time he was a young man, had all the village girls swooning. The village adults and elders, however, tended to shun the boys from the home and instructed their children to give the place a wide berth. Hallie said that as Harold grew older, he developed an edge that bordered on cruelty, although few people ever saw it.

"He had his eyes set on one young woman in particular. Her name was Vivien, but she lived in that poor area we passed on our drive into town."

He nodded.

"She fell quite in love with him, and he apparently made

empty promises. He was preparing to leave the boys' home and move to London for work the reverend had arranged when Vivien confided in her sister that she was carrying Harold's child."

Amelie shook her head, and her cheeks flushed. "According to Hallie, what followed was never clear, and it is difficult to parse fact from rumor, but the facts are that Vivien disappeared the night before Harold was to leave for London. But rather than London, the reverend sent Harold to school in Paris.

"For the *coup de grace*," Amelie continued, still breathing quickly, "the villagers learned these details and gossip from another boy who had gone to live at the home when his mother passed."

Michael briefly closed his eyes. "Jacob Stern."

She nodded. "He told a few of the village girls that Harold killed Vivien and that he and the reverend 'took care of the rest.' Shortly afterward, the reverend sent Jacob away. Most people believed he'd gone as far as Hungary."

"That would explain where he learned his accent and the Great Prospero routine."

"Harold was the reverend's protege, not someone threatening an old man as we suspected. Reverend Flannery's reaction during the interview certainly makes more sense now. I believe he saw Harold as a son, and he will do anything to protect him. Even as an adult." She thought a moment. "The reverend said he didn't keep track of what his charges did after leaving the home, but he knew that Harold was a solicitor at the Chancery."

Michael nodded, impressed again by Amelie's observations. "We might presume that Harold met and married Marie Verite in France, moved to England, purchased insurance policies on her life, and then killed her in order to collect the money. We know he'd harassed the Verite family's solicitor for the remainder of Marie's dowry, which hadn't funded yet."

"Meanwhile, Jacob Stern also returns to England and tries to establish himself as an actor. The Van Horne sisters become his patrons, and he occasionally entertains their guests as Prospero. One day, Jacob spies Harold in a London cafe but does not confront him. Instead, he writes to Reverend Flannery to ask if Harold Smith has returned to London, and . . . " Amelie paused. "Asks to borrow money?"

Michael shook his head, more pieces clicking into place. "Extortion. He attempted to blackmail Reverend Flannery."

Amelie's mouth dropped open. "Of course! His career is floundering, and he is lacking funds. Perhaps, planning to claim ignorance and deny his own involvement in covering the crime, he threatens to blackmail the reverend about his involvement in Vivien's death and disposal. Meanwhile, Harold sees Jacob at the Van Horne's Evening of Entertainment and realizes he's been recognized. He confronts Jacob, knocks him unconscious, stuffs him in the sarcophagus and stabs him." Amelie shivered. She quietly added, "It is more sobering in reality than reading about it in a book."

Michael looked over the graveyard, which was quickly becoming enveloped in fog now that the rain had stopped. "Let's return to the train station. We've done all we can here for today." He glanced at her askance and smiled. "Good work, Deputy."

"Why, thank you, Detective. You shall have my written report by tomorrow."

He chuckled and grasped her hand. They walked carefully back through the graveyard, avoiding the largest patches of mud.

"Oh, I nearly forgot!" She handed him the small sack from the shop. "This is for Alexander. Hallie had a jar of treats on her counter, and I thought he might enjoy them."

He took the sack from her and cleared his throat around the lump that had formed. "Thank you," he managed. On impulse, he stopped, pulled her close, and kissed her soundly. He then pulled back and said, "I've a feeling things will get messy before they get resolved. Mr. Smith will not go down easily, and now my worry for you has tripled."

She smiled. "I promise I'll not take another trip on a train without you."

"I suppose that is a start."

They wound their way back onto the main street and boarded an omnibus scheduled to return to the train station in ten minutes. Michael's worry that had begun as a tickling irritant was growing into something much bigger. He settled Amelie next to the window and sat next to her, no longer bothering with pretense. He put his arm on the seat back behind her, and she relaxed into his side.

For all his days spent worrying over the pain he would cause his loved ones should he come to a premature end, he had never considered the reverse. He rested his chin against Amelie's hair and closed his eyes.

There was no turning back now.

CHAPTER 26

Dear Diary,

Some time ago, I wrote a piece for the Gazette where I rather ignorantly castigated one who falls in love and is surprised by it. I am forced to eat my words, because I fell in love and have been surprised by it. I am in love with Detective Baker—Michael—and my heart is full of affection for him. Each day I count the moments until I will be with him again.

That I once fancied myself experiencing such emotion for Harold Radcliffe, now revealed to be Harold Smith, is not only laughable, it makes me ill. I feel as though the gauze has been stripped from my eyes, and I see the wolf in sheep's clothing. My challenge now is to continue feigning an interest in him in order to somehow find proof of his crimes.

Amelie was nearing the end of her workday when the front desk receptionist summoned her with the news that she had a visitor.

Charlotte grinned and raised an eyebrow at Amelie, and Eva mimed applause. Amelie rolled her eyes but couldn't stop the smile that quirked at the corners of her mouth. She had told her cousins all about her day trip to Wickelston with the detective, and they had squealed with delight as they all sat in the middle of her bed and ate leftover dessert.

She followed the receptionist to the front of the building, and her step faltered when she saw Harold Radcliffe waiting behind the counter.

Her heart pounded. She'd known this moment would arrive but hadn't decided how best to behave. She had told Michael she wasn't going to discourage Harold entirely, but that she would make excuses to be unavailable when he called at Hampton House.

The coroner in Marseilles was scheduled to deliver their laboratory results on Mrs. Radcliffe's autopsy, but until they did so, the Yard were leery of tipping their hand. Mr. Radcliffe had disappeared before, and they feared he would do so again. She had to make him believe that nothing unusual was occurring until they had evidence enough to place him under arrest.

She pasted a smile on her face to disguise her dislike of him and made sure to keep the counter between them. "Why, Mr. Radcliffe! What a surprise." She extended her hand to him across the wooden surface, and he took it, kissing her knuckles while maintaining eye contact.

"Miss Hampton. Delightful to see your lovely face. I missed you over the weekend. I trust you had an enjoyable time of it?"

She nodded. "I quite enjoyed myself. I bought some accessories, visited my favorite bookshop, and spent leisure time with my cousins. And you?"

"Oh, I was very busy. I spent my time answering correspondence, visiting acquaintances. Each spare moment was spent poring over dull documents." He continued to look at her directly, unblinking, and then smiled. "Are you available for tea this evening?"

She swallowed and cleared her throat. "I am afraid I am otherwise occupied. My cousins and I have a prior obligation."

"Tomorrow, perhaps."

She nodded. "Yes, perhaps. And again, it is lovely to see you and thank you for taking the time to stop by. I know how busy you are."

"Never too busy to visit a cherished acquaintance." He leaned closer and spoke in an undertone as though performing a stage whisper, "Besides, I must restore myself to your aunt's good graces. She seems to have misunderstood my visit to you in the hospital."

Amelie tipped her head. "Oh? She's said nothing to me." That much was true. She had told Sally about Harold's nocturnal visit, and Sally had expressed her displeasure, but then stated she would take care of the matter. Amelie had had no idea what that meant.

"She believes my intentions were less than proper, and nothing could be further from the truth. In fact, she has informed me that you are no longer interested in seeing me socially. Can you imagine why she would claim such a thing?"

Amelie frowned. "I certainly cannot imagine it. I did not express such sentiments to her." That much was also true. Sally knew nothing of Amelie's plan to keep Radcliffe on the hook to gather information from him.

"Such an unfortunate misunderstanding." He smiled again and straightened. "I shall call on her soon to make things right."

Something about his tone sent chills down Amelie's spine. "Allow me to speak with her. I am certain she will understand my wishes when we have had a chance to chat."

"Of course." He turned to go, and then, as if in after-thought, said, "I believe tomorrow evening is the date for our book group, so perhaps I shall see you there."

Amelie nodded. She had forgotten about the meeting.

"You'll bring your detective along, of course?"

Amelie managed a tight smile. She felt like a mouse being deliberately toyed with by a cat. "If he would like to attend, I am certain he shall."

"Excellent. I look forward to another opportunity to cross literary swords." He tipped his head, placed an impeccable-looking hat on his impeccable hair, and left.

Amelie stared at the closed door and breathed slowly, intentionally, in and out. Her heart thumped. How did he know? Had Reverend Flannery contacted him? It had been two days since her trip to Wickelston, and the post could certainly have delivered a letter in that time. Or perhaps the reverend had sent a telegram, warning him that a detective and young woman with a photograph of him were asking questions.

She returned to the back offices and sat woodenly in her chair. "It was Radcliffe," she told her cousins. "He knows we were asking questions about him." She thought of Hallie, the shop owner, and winced. Radcliffe had no reason to suspect the woman of sharing information, but all the same, Amelie was concerned. Would he ask around the village, trace Michael's and her footsteps?

She needed to alert Michael immediately. "I must send a telegram to the Yard," she said to Eva, who was proficient in all gadgetry. "Will you help?"

"Of course." She led the way to the telegraph machine, and they relayed a simple message for Detective Baker: *Smith knows.*

Charlotte put an arm around Amelie's shoulders. "Everything will be fine. Shall we go home?"

Amelie nodded. "Is Aunt Sally in her office?"

Charlotte shook her head. "She hasn't returned yet; she's still in the meeting with a distributor. We'll speak with her at length about all of this in the morning."

Amelie nodded and gathered her things, frustrated that her happy glow had been dimmed by a man she not only was no longer attracted to but by whom she was now repulsed. The girls bid goodnight to the other employees and left for Hampton House.

At dinner than night, Amelie's stomach was in knots, and she barely registered the conversation flowing around her. The house's elderly gentlemen residents, Mr. Frost and Mr. Roy, were in attendance at the meal, which was a rarity and usually provided a fair amount of entertainment as they argued over whose pet had done the most damage to their shared upstairs hallway.

"I am fine," Amelie said as she climbed the stairs with Charlotte and Eva. "I am tired, and my head occasionally aches. I am merely in need of a good, peaceful night's rest."

Eva pulled her close when they reached the common area. "We will stick together like bread and jam. Yes?"

Amelie smiled. "Yes. Raspberry jam, though. Blueberry will turn our teeth purple."

Charlotte hugged her tightly and kissed her cheek. "Sleep well, darling."

The three separated to their own rooms, and Amelie closed her bedroom door with a sigh. She divested herself of jewelry, hairpins, waistcoat and tie, and was turning to enter the dressing room when she spied a bright red paper on her white pillowcase.

Hoping it was something left by either Katie or Sarah after making the bed for the day, she walked forward slowly, her lip caught between her teeth. Her name was scrawled across the red envelope in heavy, black ink.

It was not from one of the housemaids.

Suddenly fuming at the thought someone had violated her personal space, she snatched the envelope from the pillow and turned it over, her heart tripping at the large *R* stamped into the wax seal.

She ripped it open, trembling, and unfolded the ivory paper inside.

Dear Miss Hampton,

Imagine my surprise to learn from an old friend that you paid him a visit with your *old friend. Naturally, I do not appreciate the inconvenience this presented for my friend, and in the future, I would have you address me personally with any questions or concerns.*

I do hope you consider seriously my quest for your hand. I have decided that you and I suit beautifully, and your devoted aunt will be a valuable resource for us in the future. I think, perhaps, you are unaware of her true financial holdings, but I am not. You may not realize that as a solicitor with access to records public and some private, I have a wealth of information at my fingertips. You must convince your good aunt that your interest in me has grown stronger than ever before.

And if you ask your housekeeper if this missive was left at the door, to be delivered to your rooms, she will tell you honestly that it was not. I have delivered it here, to your rooms, myself, because I would have you know I can be anywhere at any time.

And now, my dear Amelie, for I must grow accustomed to addressing you familiarly, I must leave your beautiful bedroom and speak with you at the Gazette, *where I expect you will be finishing your workday. I anticipate the thrill of looking into your eyes and seeing for myself the truth of my old friend's allegations.*

Yours ever,

Harold

Amelie sank down hard on the floor next to her bed and stared at the letter until the words blurred. Suddenly the strange anomalies she'd begun noticing after her return from the hospital made sense. He had been in her bedroom before. He had likely looked through her jewelry boxes and clothing drawers. Had he found and read her diary? Trembling, she reached up and yanked open her nightstand drawer and grabbed the small yellow book inside.

She leaned against the bed, feeling tired. Her head ached, and her bruised arm hurt, but most of all, she was angry. Who did he think he was that he could enter her room, uninvited?

She remembered sneaking into Jacob Stern's rooms not long ago and reassured herself that she had been there searching for clues to his killer, not creeping about and leaving threatening letters on his pillow.

How would she ever sleep soundly again? How had Radcliffe gained access to her room in a house that was always occupied? She wished desperately for Michael to be there, wanted to sit next to him and lay her head on his shoulder. She had to tell him about the letter, but she was afraid to move even though she knew she was alone in the room.

She was uncertain of the amount of influence Radcliffe truly held. Would she have to marry him to keep him from ruining the people she loved? The more her thoughts twisted around, the less she was able to formulate a logical course of action. What could she do?

She heard the distant sound of someone knocking on the front door, and then the heavy tread of Mrs. Burnette's footsteps as she made her way into the foyer. Suppose it was Mr. Radcliffe?

Galvanized into action, she scrambled to her feet and grabbed the fire poker from the hearth. Letter still clutched in her fingers, she dashed out of the room in bare feet, her hair in shambles, and shirtwaist open at the collar.

She flew down the stairs, fingers wrapped painfully around the fire poker, and stopped abruptly when she saw Michael trying to explain to Mrs. Burnette why he should be allowed to cross the threshold.

She cried out and dropped the poker to the floor, where it clattered heavily. Mrs. Burnette turned in surprise, and Amelie launched herself at Michael, a torrent of tears breaking free. She registered walking backward with her arms still locked tight around him as he entered and quietly closed the front door.

Before long, she heard footsteps on the stairs, and she lifted her face to see Charlotte and Eva, with mirrored expressions of shock. Sarah and Katie Wells and even young Sammy White had also run from the back of the house, and soon everyone stood in an uncomfortable silence as Amelie tried to calm herself.

Michael guided her to the parlor, and she heard him ask Mrs. Burnette for some tea. Charlotte and Eva descended the rest of the stairs and followed them into the room. They sat in chairs, leaving the sofa for Michael and Amelie.

Michael kept an arm around her shoulders, and when she realized he was trying to get information quietly from her cousins, she collected herself.

"I do not have a foggiest idea," Charlotte was saying, and Eva shrugged, her worried gaze glued to Amelie.

Amelie thrust the letter into Michael's hand, and he smoothed it on his leg. She felt him tense as his eyes raced over the paper. He quietly exhaled as he finished.

"He was in my room," she murmured.

"Then he visited you at the *Gazette*? When he left, you sent the telegram to me?"

All three nodded, but Charlotte closed her eyes. "Amelie, did you say he was in your room?"

Michael handed the letter to the others, who read it, heads close together. Eva's hand flew to her mouth, and Charlotte's eyes narrowed in outrage. She stood abruptly and paced to the front window.

Amelie leaned forward and rested her elbows on her knees. She buried her face in her hands and softly traced her fingers to the side of her head where the wound throbbed painfully. "I was an idiot," she muttered, "to think I could somehow fool him, to tease out information with clever conversation."

Michael rubbed her back and rested his hand at her neck, under her hair. He gently massaged for a moment, and she closed her eyes.

"I'll send word to my director and Detective Winston immediately," he said. "We'll put together a plan. Two constables will monitor the grounds in shifts, day and night." He took Amelie's hand. "I'll send a telegraph from Euston Station and return straightaway. I'll not be gone longer than twenty minutes."

Amelie nodded and looked at Michael, feeling rather pathetic for having collapsed. "I am sorry for such dramatics."

He shook his head. "No apologies. I am glad you telegraphed from the *Gazette*. I didn't receive the message until a short time ago and came straight here." He gave her fingers a squeeze. "The net is tightening, but try not to fear. We received the evidence packet from the coroner in Marseilles an hour ago. By tomorrow at noon, we shall be prepared to submit it to the crown prosecutor."

Amelie nodded. He raised her hands to his lips and placed a quick kiss there before leaving the room and disappearing into the night.

CHAPTER 27

BODY OF ENGLISHMAN'S
WIFE DISINTERRED

Details shared by one in the coroner's office who has knowledge of the circumstances suggests the autopsy results point to a suspicious death. Surely a thorough investigation is already underway, and many pointed questions shall be put to the husband in question.

–THE DAILY JOURNAL, *London*

Michael jogged the short distance from Hampton House to Euston Station. He was furious and wanted a few moments to clear his head.

Radcliffe had entered Hampton House, had gone into Amelie's *bedroom*. It had taken every ounce of self-possession to remain calm for Amelie's sake, when all he'd wanted to do was find Radcliffe and pound him into the mud. The man was a coward who preyed on women, and Michael's worry was compounded twofold. Radcliffe was determined to marry Amelie, and Michael couldn't rule out the possibility that he would use coercion or force to accomplish his ends.

Still fuming, he reached the telegraph station and paid to send a quick message to the Yard. He knew Director Ellis and Winston were both still there, so they would see it.

Once finished, he paced the platform to try to dampen his rage. Trains would run for another hour, and although it was less crowded than during peak travel times into and out of the city, there were still a fair amount of people at the station. He watched men and women of all ages sitting down in the train cars with visible sighs of relief to be off their feet after a long workday.

He rested a hand on his hip as he massaged tight muscles in the back of his neck. He looked at the train car he and Amelie had occupied only days before, and the thought that he wouldn't be able to keep her safe terrified him. He also wondered how long it would be before Radcliffe targeted him. He'd clearly communicated with Reverend Flannery, and although his end goal seemed to be marriage to Amelie, Michael didn't suppose for a moment that Radcliffe would let Michael's interference in his life simply pass.

Winston had mentioned ownership of a family cottage that was rarely used. It was an hour outside of London, and he'd offered its use to Michael before. Perhaps he would persuade Clarissa to take Alexander and the baby away for a short time. At least until Radcliffe was formally arrested and not in danger of doing anyone harm.

Calmer now, he left the station and began making his way back to Hampton House, this time at a slower pace. The streets were largely quiet, and the fog swirled in tendrils and wisps around lampposts and gardens. The night felt eerie and suddenly sinister. He was not given to flights of fancy, but something significant in his life had shifted. His love and worry for Clarissa and Alexander was ever-present in the back of his mind, but now he was consumed with images of a refreshing young woman who brought light into his day. She had somehow wrapped herself around his heart, and he refused to imagine a life without her.

Before long, Hampton House came into sight, and Michael could see one of the Yard's carriages already making its way to the mews behind the house. Director Ellis and Winston must have dropped everything and run for a carriage upon receiving the telegram. He reached the door just as a bewildered Mrs. Burnette was preparing to close it. He slipped in and joined his colleagues, who had entered the parlor.

He hurried to make introductions, as Amelie and her cousins had not yet met Director Ellis. Winston placed a hand on Michael's shoulder with a quick squeeze.

"Are you well?" Winston asked.

Michael nodded. "Well enough. I appreciate your help. I fear my thinking is muddled at the moment."

"Is this the letter?" Director Ellis asked, picking up the wrinkled paper on the coffee table.

"Yes, sir." Amelie cleared her throat. She had taken to pacing behind the sofa, and he couldn't blame her. Everyone in the room seemed too agitated to be still.

Mrs. Burnette and two housemaids carried in trays and set them on a side table near the door. Eva took up the task of pouring the tea and arranging sandwiches. Winston approached and asked her something, and Michael noted the ease with which the Hampton cousins communicated with all of the police. Of course, their bond had been forged in the fires of Jacob Stern's murder, and all three women had participated to a great degree in studying the aftermath. Director Ellis was probably unused to women working with police, but he hadn't commented on it at any point to Michael. His only question had been whether or not they were proficient with their tasks.

Mrs. Burnett's eyes were wide with worry. Until tonight, Michael had only seen her looking perturbed. She gathered coats and hats to hang in the foyer, and the maids helped Eva distribute the tea.

Director Ellis beckoned Michael closer. "I'll have the packet for the prosecutor's office delivered by special courier tonight. I've alerted him to the possibility that the alleged may take flight, so I am hopeful that we shall know within a day or two if they'll conduct an inquest. We'll place Mr. Radcliffe under twenty-four-hour surveillance as well as station constables here."

"Very good, sir." Michael nodded. "I believe he is guilty of at least three murders, but I do not know if we can find enough evidence to prove it."

"Three? His wife, Mr. Stern, and . . . ?"

"A young woman in Wickelston. The situation there is speculation and rumor at this point, but I'd like to speak with local authorities about any investigations they conducted into her disappearance."

"I'll make contact tomorrow." John Ellis accepted a cup of tea from one of the maids with a nod. "Suppose we all sit for a moment," he said to Michael.

The director was young for his position, but he had worked tirelessly to prove he was equal to the task. His hair was the color of dark coffee, and his eyes were tawny. They resembled those of a lion in the London Zoo, and Ellis's temperament wasn't so different. He was calm, decisive, calculating, and when necessary, fierce. Michael did not know much of his background, other than he was the son of a powerful man and had not followed family expectations.

The others gathered, and Michael joined Amelie on the sofa. She still shivered as if cold, despite the comfortable warmth provided by the fire. Now that the situation had calmed, he knew he couldn't justify putting his arm around her, so he settled for sitting close.

She glanced at him with a small smile. Her eyes were red-rimmed, and she held her tea on her knees as he'd so often seen her do when her appetite had deserted her. "Apologies for assaulting you earlier," she murmured.

He leaned over and whispered in her ear, "I have no objection to an assault of that kind."

Her lips formed a more genuine smile, and he was glad. Her hair was down, and her clothing disheveled, but she was still lovely. She'd had a quick education in life's harsher elements over a short course of time, and she carried a wiser, if more guarded, air about her than the young woman he'd first seen spying on Radcliffe and a dinner date.

Director Ellis relayed the same details he'd just told Michael. "There will be two constables stationed here at the house 'round the clock. I am hopeful this will provide some level of security, although I understand, Miss Hampton, that there was some confusion while you were hospitalized. You may trust my word that no officer will abandon his post."

"Thank you, sir." Amelie finally took a tiny sip of tea.

"Have any of you noticed anything out of place, something obviously different that shouldn't be?" Ellis continued.

They all shook their heads, even the maids and housekeeper. Mrs. Burnette spoke up. "I know every inch of this house, and I would never have believed someone had been in it. Nothing has been disturbed, nothing at all."

Ellis nodded. "Miss Hampton, I presume such is the case with your personal suite?"

"Yes. If I hadn't seen the envelope on the pillow, I might never have realized he'd entered. In recent weeks, however, I've noted things out of place. I believe he must have done so deliberately; he clearly is capable of skulking about without leaving a trace." She shivered involuntarily, and Charlotte crossed the room to retrieve a small blanket that she placed on Amelie's shoulders.

She stood behind her, hands resting on her hips. Miss Duvall had also clearly been settling in for the night; her curly red hair hung down her back in a loose braid, and she wore a housecoat over what must have been nightclothes. Energy fairly radiated from her slight frame.

"What are we to do, then?" Charlotte asked Ellis directly. "We cannot simply wait for him to attack."

"Book group is tomorrow evening," Amelie interjected, sitting straighter in her seat. "He told me he 'might' see me there, and made some reference to the detective." She glanced at Michael, eyes narrowing. "I do not know if *you* are safe from harm, Mich—Detective." She flushed, but looked at Ellis and said, "He shall require protection also, wouldn't you think?"

Michael shook his head and started to respond when Amelie set her teacup down on the coffee table and turned her attention fully to Michael.

"Your family! Does he know where they live? Does he—"

Michael caught her hand. "I have already considered it, and I will make preparations for them to leave Town for a small holiday. Detective Winston has offered property in the past."

Winston nodded. "Of course. We'll discuss the details as soon as we are finished here."

Ellis looked at Charlotte, who still stood sentinel behind Amelie. "Miss Duvall, I understand your frustration. I, also, do not relish inactivity in the face of danger. I must ask, however, that you do not attempt to contact Mr. Radcliffe or do anything that might be construed as taking matters into your own hands. We must proceed carefully and in the proper order so that when the time comes, he will be successfully convicted in court."

Charlotte nodded, but her green eyes narrowed, and her expression tightened. "I appreciate your words, and I understand how the system works. I do not relish the thought of Amelie looking over her shoulder for an indeterminate amount of time." She paused. "How would you advise your loved ones, if it were your family?"

Director Ellis met her eyes without blinking. "I would hide them away, just as Detective Baker is set to do with his. Circumstances require inconvenient measures at times. Perhaps the three of you would be better off vacationing away from Town for a while?"

Michael hid a smile. Ellis was not overtly confrontational, his tone was moderate, and the words perfectly reasonable. He must know, however, that to suggest retreat to someone of Charlotte's personality was akin to waving a red flag before a bull.

Charlotte raised a brow, and Michael wondered if she knew she had been baited.

"I'll not speak for Amelie, but I shall remain here. We support ourselves, thus we have actual responsibilities. We do not have the luxury of packing up on a whim with no consequences."

The director nodded once. "Very well, then. We stay the course and remain vigilant. Incidentally, I am feeling exceptionally rude to be seated while you are standing. If you do not plan to take a seat, I hope you will absolve me of my duties as a gentleman."

Charlotte bit the inside of her cheek and seemed poised to return fire when Amelie interrupted. "Very well, Director, Detectives. We have our marching orders. We shall go about our activities as usual, but with heightened vigilance and caution. I know we are all grateful for your swift arrival here, and unless there is anything left to still discuss, I'm certain you would like to call the day finished."

Michael smiled. "We shall contact you tomorrow at the *Gazette* with any news. Ladies," he said as he stood, nodding to the cousins and household staff collectively. "Please take care."

He knew he would not find a moment alone with Amelie, but he caught her eye amidst the bustle and conversation. He winked, and she smiled. She looked exhausted, and he tamped down another flare of anger at Radcliffe. All plans for a romantic proposal would have to wait, and it was one more in a long list of grievances Michael laid at the man's feet.

From the moment Marie Verite was pulled from the cold, dark river, all their lives had become inextricably linked, and Harold Smith Radcliffe left nothing but death and destruction in his wake.

CHAPTER 28

INQUEST!

The first day of the inquest into the suspicious death of Marie Verite Radcliffe begins today, and although this newspaper has offered, on multiple occasions, to publish a statement from Mr. Harold Radcliffe or his attorney, they have been unavailable.

–THE DAILY JOURNAL, *London*

For the next two days, Amelie felt as though she were waiting for an ax to fall. She, Charlotte, and Eva went about their usual routines, but they were careful to always be together.

Sally had met with Director Ellis to satisfy herself on the details of his course of action, and after a lengthy discussion, he had apparently told her that he saw the family resemblance between her and her nieces, one in particular. He had also ordered constabulary to monitor her home in Town where she currently resided and had been surprised when she'd not argued the point.

"I may relish my independence, but I'm not a fool," she told the girls later.

Michael moved his family to Detective Winston's cottage, and the neighbors were told Clarissa and Alexander were vacationing on the Continent for a time. Amelie worried, but she knew it was the best possible option. Michael had helped them leave quietly, and they could only hope Radcliffe was not having the home watched. Michael was certain they hadn't been followed, but it seemed as if everyone was on edge.

While Radcliffe claimed to have influential friends or people who "owed him favors," one thing he did not have was an endless supply of money. While the prosecutor reviewed evidence in Marie Verite Radcliffe's case, Michael followed a trail of breadcrumbs Radcliffe had left all over London. The trail eventually crossed the channel to France, and Winston had spent the day tracking down information that, combined with Michael's research, showed Harold Radcliffe was a gambler.

His preference was horse racing, having developed a taste for it even before he moved away from the boys' home. He apparently had at least one open account still unpaid in Paris, and one rather large debt owing an organization in London. He represented the organization as their solicitor, but apparently his work-for-trade was not enough.

It made such perfect sense, Amelie thought, the scenario might have come straight from one of her murder mystery novels. The motive was usually money.

Radcliffe had married and then killed Marie Verite for her money. He wanted to marry Amelie for Sally's money, claiming to have knowledge of an impressive financial portfolio. When Sally had read the letter, which was now in the evidence file, she had snorted in disbelief.

"He is correct about one thing," she told the three girls, "I would give anything for your safety. Before he extorted money from me, however, I would introduce him to the business end of the derringer I carry in my reticule."

Late that afternoon, Michael and Detective Winston called on them at the *Gazette*, and they gathered in Sally's office to hear the news. "A formal inquest into Mrs. Radcliffe's death begins tomorrow morning," Michael told them. "The prosecutor feels enough evidence exists to convince a jury to send the matter to trial."

Amelie hoped Michael was right. Just because there would be an inquest did not mean Mr. Radcliffe would stand trial. The inquest was held only to determine if a crime had been committed. Then Mr. Radcliffe would be arrested, charged with murder, and the trial would begin.

The detectives were still at the *Gazette* offices when a message arrived for Amelie. Her heart thumped when she saw the handwriting on the envelope, and she flipped it over to see a familiar wax seal stamped with an *R*.

Michael took a handkerchief from his pocket. "If there are fingermarks on the paper, we can use it as evidence. Please, allow me to open it."

Amelie handed him the letter and he opened it carefully without touching it with his bare hands or wiping off potential evidence.

My dear Amelie,

I invite you to join me tomorrow evening for the play currently being performed at the very theatre where we first sat side-by-side. A carriage will collect you at Hampton House at 7 o'clock p.m.

Until then,
Yours ever,
Harold

Amelie swallowed hard and looked to Michael. "Tomorrow evening? But, doesn't the inquest begin tomorrow *morning*?"

Michael nodded, his eyes concerned. "He must be feeling quite bold to demand to see you while he is under such scrutiny." He folded the letter and frowned. "What is the man planning?"

Early the following morning, Amelie sat with her aunt and cousins in the gallery and watched the proceedings for the inquest into Marie's death.

Michael was testifying, explaining the scene wherein Mrs. Radcliffe's body was pulled from the Thames. The jury were allowed to question the witnesses, and several asked Michael to recount Mr. Radcliffe's reaction upon learning of his wife's death, especially his demeanor and his immediate comments.

The jury then quizzed Detective Winston on his impressions of Mr. Radcliffe at the morgue, his behavior upon seeing his wife's corpse, and his reasons for demanding her body be sent to France without an autopsy performed.

Dr. Neville testified that he had specifically requested to be allowed to perform an autopsy but had been denied, and that they were then forced to settle on photographing the body. He also testified about his recollections of Mr. Radcliffe's behavior that day.

Before long, a recess was called, and Amelie exhaled as though she had held her breath through the whole of it. They exited the building for a quick lunch and were soon joined by Michael, Detective Winston, and Director Ellis.

"Perhaps you should specialize in crime scene photography, Eva," Charlotte told her as they ate meat pies from a street vendor located next to the building. "After seeing those taken for Mrs. Radcliffe's autopsy, I believe they do not compare to those you did for Mr. Stern."

Eva shrugged. "He was certainly less trouble than my live subjects." She paused then lowered her pie instead of taking a bite. "That is to say, the process was much less chaotic, and I do enjoy photographing people who are alive."

Amelie laughed. "Nobody here will judge you for preferring dead subjects to live ones."

"That much is true," Detective Winston said with a nod. "Gruesome as it is, the dead are often much more cooperative."

"At any rate, whether my subjects are in a morgue or in a drawing room, I believe Sammy White is the perfect assistant. I'm pleased with his efforts, and to my surprise, he's quite strong for his size."

Amelie smiled, and Michael drifted to her side as Eva described the first photography sitting in which she'd included Sammy.

The conversation flowed, and Amelie turned to Michael, happy for a private moment.

"I thought you were brilliant in the witness box," she said, and he chuckled.

"That is one of the easier parts of the profession." He moved closer, leaning a shoulder against the wall and creating a private cocoon for the two of them. "How are you faring?" His voice was low, and her fingers itched to touch his lapels, to pull herself into his embrace.

"Well enough," she managed, surprised her voice was unsteady. Though between the heady sensation of his nearness and her continually climbing nerves, it shouldn't have surprised her at all. "I am nervous. I cannot imagine why Radcliffe would have sent that letter. He knows I will not meet him at the theatre."

"You are most definitely *not* going, and I do not care what he believes he has in his arsenal that will compel your compliance otherwise." He frowned, finishing his meat pie in one large bite. Wiping his fingers on a handkerchief, he added, "The inquest will finish today, and hopefully the jury will not be long in rendering a decision."

She frowned. "Was Alexander worried about going away for a time?"

"No. He sees himself as Clarissa's and Mae's protector, and truthfully, I believe he has been a reliable comfort for my sister."

"I feel as though I have brought danger to everybody's front door." She had no appetite for the rest of her pie and handed it to Michael.

He wolfed it down in a few bites and then shook his head, again wiping his fingers clean. "You did not bring danger to anyone. If you'll recall, it was I who ran you to ground in the park and insisted on your involvement."

She smiled. "You did not 'run me to ground.' Well, perhaps a little. You were quite fearsome, you know. Stern expression, stern voice, prepared to haul me downtown to the Yard . . ."

He chuckled. "It had been a long day, and I was running short of options investigating Radcliffe. When I saw you observing him, and then when you admitted to knowing him . . . I suspected the worst."

She shook her head. "I *was* participating in subterfuge, though. My character was not sterling."

"Your character is exceptionally sterling," he said, lowering his voice. "You are a bright spot for me in a frustrating world."

"I . . ." She glanced at the others, who were still in animated conversation. "I wish very much for another day at a seaside town. Perhaps not spent hunting for incriminating information on a potential madman, but just . . . together." When had she become so bold? Had she known a month ago she would be standing much too close to a man who was most definitely not a relative and saying such things . . . the kinds of things one shared with a lover . . .

Her cheeks burned, and she stared at his chest, rather than his face.

"Amelie." His voice was just above a whisper, a rumble she felt resonating clear to her soul. "Look at me."

She lifted her face and caught her breath at the way he studied her. As though she were the most important person in the world. As if he would carry her away on horseback to a magical kingdom.

"I love you," he whispered. "When this business is finished and you are safe, we will be together. Do you trust me?"

Her eyes nearly filled with tears, a combination of anxiety and love and too many feelings to hold inside. "Yes." She nodded. "I do trust you." She sniffled, and he reached in his pocket for his handkerchief, but it was the one he'd used to clean his hands.

She laughed and retrieved her own handkerchief.

They were interrupted by Director Ellis, who called, "Baker, have you seen today's daily edition?"

They turned toward the others, and the director held up a newspaper that bore a bold headline on the first page.

JUDGE ADAMS REMOVED FROM BENCH IN SCANDAL

Michael's mouth slackened, and he took the paper, scanning it as Amelie looked on, confused. She looked at Sally and whispered, "Who is Judge Adams?"

The director motioned to the paper. "He is the judge who blocked the initial investigation into Mr. Radcliffe. We began asking questions just before Radcliffe disappeared to Marseilles to bury his wife, and we were told in no uncertain terms by Judge Adams to leave matters alone."

Michael looked up at Director Ellis, anger in his eyes. "The paper says that the judge was being blackmailed, and when the inquest into Radcliffe went forward anyway, incriminating evidence was placed in a newspaper man's postbox."

Amelie sucked in a breath. She glanced uneasily at the others and said, "This was Mr. Radcliffe's doing?"

"It would seem so," Director Ellis said, "but we've no proof beyond what the paper is reporting. I believe a visit to Judge Adams this evening is in order."

"Perhaps he'll talk more freely, now that he's lost everything," Winston said, looking over Michael's shoulder at the newspaper.

A quiet bell sounded from inside, signaling the end of the recess. They were making their way back inside the building when a young clerk of the court approached Michael with an envelope.

"This was delivered for you here, sir," the boy said.

Michael took the letter, frowning. "Thank you," he said absently as the boy left.

Amelie caught a flash of the envelope as Michael turned it over, and her heart beat into her throat. He grimly broke the wax seal and read the letter's contents. His face reddened, and he strode away from the group, his fist clenching as he removed his hat and drew back as though to throw it.

He took a deep breath, then returned to the group, handing the letter to Winston, who read it and passed it to the director.

"Michael?" Amelie felt numb, frozen to the spot. "What is it?"

Michael looked out over the crowd. "Is he here, even now?"

Director Ellis motioned the group to the side of the hallway so others could pass by, then shook his head. "He would not show his face today. He seems to have a flair for the dramatic, however. He wanted you to receive this here, in the midst of the inquest."

Amelie thought she would go mad before someone finally shared what was written on the paper, but Michael looked so furious and distraught, she fought instead for patience.

Charlotte addressed Director Ellis. "Is this something appropriate for us to know? I'll not be demanding, but if you can share, I wish you would put us out of our misery."

Michael pinched the bridge of his nose. "Apologies," he mumbled, then cleared his throat. "Radcliffe is a solicitor for civil matters that go before the Chancery. That body also hears cases involving institutionalization of those who are infirm, or mad, or—" He swallowed, and Amelie's hand flew to her mouth.

"Or like your brother."

CHAPTER 29

Dearest Miss Hampton,

Thank you so much for the candy! Michael gave it to me yesterday, and I have enjoyed it very much. Clarissa is writing this note because her script is much tidier than mine. I shall sign my own name, however. I hope to see you again soon!

Your friend,

Alexander Baker

Michael was unsure how he managed to sit through the rest of the inquest. He vacillated between fury and fear. Director Ellis dispatched a team of constables to take Radcliffe into custody. He was now making veiled threats against a policeman, and Winston and Ellis planned to question him at length.

Radcliffe had no legal standing to have Alexander institutionalized. Michael's brother had never so much as put a foot out of line. He was always with family, he had never harassed or hurt another person in his life. He was gainfully employed from home, making hat ribbons under Clarissa's watchful eye.

Radcliffe did not play by the rules, though. He did not give heed to decency or feelings of genuine concern for others. He cared only for himself, and from the sounds of it, had been that way for some time. Whether the responsibility for his character lay with Reverend Flannery or was an accident of birth, Michael did not know nor care. He wanted the man permanently behind bars and to face the consequences of murdering his wife.

How many officials had Radcliffe managed to blackmail? Did he truly have a network, or was that part of his grandiose illusion? Was Judge Adams the one man he had in his pocket, or were there others capable of fabricating information that would see Alexander locked away in an asylum? Alexander would die in such a place, after enduring torture and humiliation.

As the group departed from the courthouse, Sally Hampton said she would accompany her nieces back to Hampton House and remain there for the evening. Director Ellis ordered two constables to go with them.

Amelie placed her hand on Michael's arm, her eyes wide with concern. "Do what you must to protect them. I will be fine with my family, and I will not meet Mr. Radcliffe this evening. He will be in custody, and we shall be safe at home."

Michael rubbed his head. His thoughts were so splintered he hardly knew what to think. He finally nodded. "I'll go back to the Yard with the others while they question him. I'll come to you as soon as I can." He paused. "I am so sorry, Amelie. I am sorry to have involved you in any of this."

She shook her head and clasped his hand. "I would not chose to be anywhere else. Now, go."

The women left with the constables, and Michael raced to join Ellis and Winston. The trip back to their offices was quiet, unbroken only when Ellis said, "He may have dirty politicians and corrupt judges, but I have my share of honorable resources, as well. Your brother will be safe and left alone, I give you my word."

Michael nodded his thanks and glanced at the director. It was well known in law enforcement circles that Ellis's father was a high-ranking member of Parliament and that the father and son were not warm with each other.

"Director," Michael began, "I do not mean for you to compromise your own—"

Ellis looked at him askance and smiled. "I made a vow I would never use my father or my birthright or my position in society to further my own career. But it would be irresponsible of me if I did *not* appeal to a member of Parliament over an injustice perpetrated against the family of a distinguished detective and servant of the Crown."

Michael exhaled, feeling a small flicker of hope. He had spent the entirety of Alexander's life protecting him from those who would hurt or mock him. His mother had loved the baby even when others told her there was something wrong with the boy. Anyone who knew Alexander knew the opposite was true. His father had passed shortly before Alexander's birth, so it had fallen to Michael to fill the role. He loved Alexander with his whole soul, and as he stared out of the carriage window at the fading light, he fought back tears of anger and abject fear.

"We will not let anyone take your brother," Winston said, seated across from him and watching his face. "Do you understand? I will stand armed at the door, myself."

Michael realized his partner was serious. "Thank you, Nathaniel." He nodded. "My thanks."

"My family lives less than a thirty-minute drive from the cottage where Clarissa and Alexander are staying. When we get to the office, I'll write a quick message and send it on the mobile post train. They'll receive the message in an hour, at most, and they can go to the cottage to be sure all is well."

Michael swallowed past a lump in his throat. "I hate for them to be in harm's way."

"We have a few servants who are more than equal to the task. When my mother learns of the situation . . ." Winston smiled. "She will raise the hounds of hell. She does not suffer injustices of this sort."

"We've not discussed much about your family, Winston," Ellis said. "What . . . where . . ." He paused, pursing his lips. "What did your father do?"

Winston smiled. "This and that."

CHAPTER 30

You may find that the quickest way to a woman's heart is to take her for short holidays when she least expects it. Women quite adore surprises and the like, and you'll find yourself on the receiving end of her delight and gratitude.
—The Gentleman's Guide to Efficient and Profitable Courtship *by Sir Percival Prancey*

Radcliffe's carriage was not due to arrive for another hour, and the Hampton House residents were restless. Amelie borrowed a dustrag from Katie and had gone to work in the parlor, dusting surfaces that bore not a speck of dirt anywhere. Charlotte was in the kitchen, rolling out dough for a pie, and Eva was in her darkroom, organizing supplies and tidying up. The house was a flurry of quiet activity, save for Sally, who stood at the parlor window and looked out into the fog.

"You love him—Detective Baker?" Sally turned to face her.

Amelie swallowed. She hadn't expected the question yet. She nodded. "I do. I do love him."

"Has he proposed marriage?"

"I suspect he plans to do things in their proper order. He'll speak with you first, most likely." She managed a smile. "I do not know how much of that sort of thing will be on his mind until all of this mess is settled." She clenched the dustrag. "Alexander is like Dennis, Aunt Sally. If he is taken—"

"He will not be taken." Sally's expression hardened. "We have enough clout and money among us to protect him. Enough coins cross the right palms and the world will spin in the other direction, if you wish it."

Amelie nodded. Sally was a force, and Amelie relied on it. "I should like to be that person," she said, more to herself than her aunt. "The one who makes everything right."

Sally crossed the room and took the dustrag from Amelie's hands, setting it on the mantel. "Dearest. Do you not know that you already are? All three of you. You make everything right for me." Sally's eyes misted, and Amelie shook her head.

"Oh, you mustn't do that, Aunt Sally, or I shall become a puddled mess." She kissed Sally's cheek and laughed.

"Has anybody seen Sammy?" Eva asked from the door. She wrinkled her forehead. "He was to have helped clean the dark-room, but Mrs. Burnette said she's not seen him in nearly two hours. I've searched the house top to bottom and even spoken with the gentlemen upstairs."

Amelie swallowed. "He was to remain here all day for his chores." She took a breath. "This is new for him, this routine and responsibility. Perhaps he went to the train station for a treat." *Please, please, Sammy, be at the train station for a treat.*

Eva shook her head. "I do not think so. He was looking for-ward to helping me. He is learning the names of all my different supplies." Eva bit her lip and looked at the front entrance. "He was very excited."

Amelie looked uneasily at Sally. The thick dread that had

knotted in her stomach when she found the note on her pillow tightened again.

Charlotte appeared in the doorway, her apron, hands, and forehead dotted in flour. "Is he here?"

Eva shook her head. "Nobody has seen him."

Charlotte frowned. "Surely the constables would have noticed him leaving."

Amelie felt a spark of hope, and Eva dashed for the front door. She yanked it open and called to the constable who was making a circuit from around the side of the house.

"Yes, miss?"

"Have you seen my assistant, Sammy? So tall, blond hair, respectable shirt, trousers, and suspenders?"

"Not today, miss."

"What time did you arrive for your shift?"

"Two hours ago, miss."

Eva stilled, and Amelie saw her fingers tighten on the door until they were white. "That was the last time he was seen here," Eva said.

Charlotte and Amelie joined Eva at the door.

"When you arrived to change out with the other two constables, did the four of you chat for a time? Talk together, during which time the boy might have slipped by?" Charlotte asked.

The constable scratched his neck. "I s'pose so, miss. I do apologize. I'll ask Constable Russ if he saw the boy."

They waited at the open door as the constable disappeared into the fog again, then heard him calling out to his partner. He returned quickly and said, "Russ did see the boy, ma'am! He was walking that way toward a carriage sitting just outside that door." He pointed two doors over. "A nice, expensive carriage."

"Did he get in the carriage?" Charlotte asked.

By this time, Constable Russ had also come around the corner. "He did, miss. Next I looked, it had driven away."

Amelie stepped back from the door, followed by Charlotte, and then Eva, who closed it quietly. She leaned against it and looked at Amelie and Charlotte, her pretty features tight with worry.

The clock struck half past six, and Amelie reentered the parlor and slowly sat down near the fireplace. "Radcliffe was to have sent a carriage to collect me in thirty minutes. Presumably, he has already been taken into the station for questioning, but . . ." She trailed off, wondering if Sammy's disappearance was connected to Radcliffe's mad plans.

Sally walked the length of the room and back. "I ought to have just installed a carriage here as I'd planned."

"Sally?" Amelie asked.

"When you girls moved here, you said you did not want a carriage, but that you would travel to work and back by omnibus and cab—like others who come to the city." She put her hands on her hips. "After tonight, that changes. You may still travel to work as you wish, but it will be by private carriage for your own safety."

Charlotte tried to find a clean place on her pinafore to wipe her hands. "We must get word to the detectives that Sammy has disappeared, possibly abducted. Given his connection to us, it would not be a surprise in the least. Sammy has become a regular fixture in this house, and anyone observing our comings and goings would know it." She nodded toward Sally. "I do see your point about the convenience of a carriage."

"Thank you, dearest." Sally walked toward the front door and opened it. The constables were waiting just outside. "One of you must take a note to the detectives. The other will remain here on the grounds."

"Yes, ma'am," Constable Russ said.

"Wait here. I will write the message."

Sally disappeared, and Amelie stared at the parlor doors, feeling numb. Charlotte and Eva sat with her.

"I am so sorry, girls." Amelie shook her head. "If I had not been such a ninny about Radcliffe, none of this would have happened."

"All of it would have happened, but perhaps in a different manner," Charlotte told her. "Amelie, you cannot take the blame—it is not yours. Radcliffe was set on a course the moment he returned from France to find a new wife. He joined book groups and attended musicales, and sooner or later, he would have made the connection between the three of us and Sally. With or without the detectives' involvement, we still would have been involved." She shrugged. "We were all enamored of him, at first. He pursued you."

"Because I am the most easily fooled." She waved a hand at their protests. "It doesn't matter, and I mustn't feel sorry for myself when he is wreaking so much havoc with other people." She thought of Alexander, of Sammy, and felt ill. "We may assume Radcliffe will keep Sammy safe because he knows I will not comply with anything if the boy is harmed in any way."

Eva looked at Amelie, stricken. "You truly believe he has the boy?"

Amelie nodded, wincing. "Who else would lure him to a carriage and then whisk him away? I do not believe his associates from his former life either had resources to abduct him, or frankly, reason. Radcliffe has been inside this house; he may have overheard Sammy talking with the Wells girls or Mrs.

Burnette. It would not have taken long for Radcliffe to realize the boy has become someone of importance, especially if he knows I made an effort to rescue Sammy from the East End."

Sally returned to the door, letter in hand, and spoke quickly to the constables. "Take this to Euston Station immediately; the trains into the city run every ten minutes."

She shut the door forcefully and leaned against it, just as Eva had done. She heaved a sigh and eyed the three cousins from the front hall. "Try not to fret," she told them, and then disappeared toward the kitchen.

Charlotte rubbed her forehead with the back of her hand. "She tells us that in an effort to convince herself of the same."

The clock struck the hour, and to Amelie it sounded like a death knell. On the one hand, if the constabulary hadn't found Radcliffe to bring him in for questioning, then the man was still moving around, pulling levers in an effort to make them all jump. If they had found him, however, and he had made arrangements for Sammy to be taken somewhere, the odds were slim that he would give up the location. Either way, the picture did not look good for the young boy.

For Amelie, the guilt would not ease. If only she hadn't taken Sammy from the life he'd known in Whitechapel. If only she hadn't tried so hard to make everything perfect for people. She wound up doing more harm than good. If only . . . if only . . .

The knock at the door was jarring, and Amelie jumped from her chair. She opened the front door wide to reveal a man in pristine footman's garb. "Miss Amelie Hampton, please?"

"I am Miss Hampton."

The man held out an envelope, one with a script that was now unpleasantly familiar. "I am instructed to wait," he said.

Amelie's heart thumped uncomfortably. She tore into the letter and scanned the lines.

Dearest Amelie,

We no longer have time to attend the play, as your detective has sent out an order for my arrest. I am certain you understand that will never do, and I am vexed to an extreme at the level to which the man has disrupted my plan.

Accompany my driver to the carriage, willingly, and the boy will remain unharmed. In fact, I will allow you to personally see the boy back into the carriage for his safe return to Hampton House.

No delays. No constables. And absolutely no detectives. Come immediately or I shall presume you are not committed to our union, thus necessitating the sacrifice of the boy. I should hate for poor decisions on your part to result in additional tragedies, this time of those you would most certainly not forget.

Ever and eternally yours,

Harold

Amelie's hand shook, and she steadied it by clamping her other hand beneath it. Her cousins crowded close and read the letter. Eva gasped, and Charlotte paced away and then shouted, "No! Why is he able to do this?"

The door was still open, and the cold snaked in. Amelie motioned to the carriage driver to wait, and then closed it.

Sally came running from the kitchen, along with Mrs. Burnette and the Wells girls. Amelie silently showed her the letter and tried to objectively view her options, even while she continued to tremble.

She heard the driver conversing with the constable in the front garden. All of her senses swirled, and she felt as if she were caught in the center of a maelstrom, where she was still while the world around her careened.

"I'll do it," she said firmly after Sally finished reading the letter.

"You will not," Sally said. She looked at the others. "She will not. You will not, Amelie."

Amelie shook her head. "I am not playing the martyr. If we are smart about this, we can make it work."

Charlotte's mouth dropped open, and Amelie held up her hand. "Either Detective Baker or Detective Winston will arrive here shortly, along with a handful of constabulary. I will stall the driver by telling him I must change my clothing. While I do that, Charlotte, you go in the back to the mews and borrow the neighbor's mare, the new one you rode last week in the park."

Charlotte nodded, wary.

"You will follow the carriage to see where I am taken. Once you know where I am, you find the nearest telegraph station and send a message to Euston Station. That would be faster than trying to navigate traffic and deliver the details in person. Eva and the guard outside will wait at Euston Station for your instructions."

Eva swallowed and nodded.

"Sally, you remain here to coordinate with the police and await Sammy's safe return. When Eva returns from Euston with the constable, she will relay the message to you and the rest, and . . . and in ride the cavalry. I shall be rescued, and Radcliffe arrested. As he is clearly not in police custody, this is an effective way to track him to his location."

"This is madness. I'll not risk your life," Sally stated. "We shall await the detectives."

"We do not have the luxury of time, Sally!" Amelie shook her head and moved to open the door. She poked her head out and said to the carriage driver, "Please wait one moment; I must change my clothing."

He nodded but glanced at the constable, who watched in confusion. "You see, constable? The young lady accompanies me willingly." To Amelie, he said, "Five minutes, no more."

She closed the door, braced to do battle with her aunt, when Charlotte said, "She is right, Sally. We do not have another choice. This is the best option we have to save the boy and hunt down Radcliffe."

Amelie dashed for the stairs with her cousins close behind. While she ran into her room and grabbed a heavy cloak and gloves, she did not allow herself to think beyond the most basic of notions.

I am going out into the cold. I shall need my cloak, my gloves, a scarf, a hat.

She gathered each item, then snatched up her reticule from the small side table by her door. She threw on the clothing as she ran, noting a flash of Charlotte's coat on the landing below her as her cousin tore down the stairs and ran for the back of the house.

Each step of the plan crystalized in her mind as she thrust her hands into her gloves and ran to the door.

"Wait!" Sally cried.

"I am sorry, Sally. We've no time." She turned to Katie

Wells. "Please go next door and explain why Charlotte is stealing their horse."

Katie nodded, wide eyed, and hurried away.

Amelie grabbed her aunt in a quick, fierce hug before she opened the door and stepped onto the cold porch. She was out of breath and tried to slow her steps long enough to give Charlotte time to saddle the mare or bribe a lingering stablehand. She didn't allow herself to consider that Charlotte might be detained; her cousin was more resourceful than any of them.

She made a show of shaking out her scarf and winding it carefully around her neck as the carriage driver tapped his foot. She slowly descended the steps with him, still holding her hat.

"You may don that inside the carriage," the driver said, motioning to the accessory.

"Have you a name, sir?" Amelie said, her voice a thread of sound.

He hesitated. "Burton."

She nodded. "I am Miss Hampton, as you know. I have a family and a delightful life. Should I require assistance at any point, I trust I shall be able to call upon you."

He looked at her impassively as he opened the door and gave her his hand. She took it, squeezing his fingers tightly as she climbed inside. He frowned as she took her time settling into the plush seat cushion. He finally closed the door and secured the handle. As the conveyance dipped with his weight as he climbed into position, she gently tried the door handle. It was, of course, locked.

It didn't matter. She wasn't going to try to escape. She would see for herself that Sammy was well and unhurt, bundle him into the carriage, and then face Radcliffe. He wouldn't kill her; she doubted he would even harm her. He needed money from Sally, and he wouldn't see so much as a ha'penny if something befell Amelie. She would use the knowledge to her advantage, she decided. She squeezed her eyes tight and uttered a desperate prayer.

Burton signaled the horses, and the carriage moved quickly down the street. Amelie removed her special hatpin from the box inside her reticule. She exhaled slowly, kissed the crystal flower adorning the end, and then anchored her hat securely to her hair.

Only then did she allow herself to think of Michael, and only then did tears gather in her eyes. He would be worried, he would be angry she had acted quickly and rashly, and she could only hope he would understand.

She was unable to see if Charlotte had followed, as there was no window behind her. There were many pieces to the hasty plan that could fail spectacularly, but she forced herself to let it be. She had done all she could. Her nerves were strung tight, and fear clogged her throat as she wondered what Radcliffe had planned for her. She knew enough of his history to hold her own in a match of wits, she hoped. She would keep him talking, appeal to his vanity, and stall long enough to give the others time to find her and arrest him.

She recognized the twists and turns leading them away from Bloomsbury, south and closer to the social center of London. She thought they might stop somewhere on Drury Lane or Covent Garden. Burton whistled and kept the horses pulling forward, and they continued closer to the river, to the businesses and warehouses and factories near the docks.

The pace eventually slowed, and Amelie drew in a breath. Burton drove them down one narrow alley, then another, until she was uncertain where they were. He turned into the drive of a small storage warehouse, whistled, and then stopped. She heard the gear-driven mechanism of an opening door and waited, her hands in tight fists on her lap.

The carriage dipped again, and after a moment, the door opened to reveal Burton, and just behind him, Radcliffe.

"I am not moving until I see Sammy."

Radcliffe smirked, but snapped his fingers to the side. Another man in a uniform matching Burton's appeared, holding Sammy by one arm. The boy snatched it roughly away and lunged at the carriage, and Burton stopped him short by yanking on his shirt collar.

"Sammy." Amelie willed her voice to remain steady. "Are you hurt?"

"No, miss," he mumbled. "I want you to return home. Ye can't go with this bloke." He glared at Radcliffe.

"Now, calm yourself, Mr. White." Radcliffe smiled and held his hand to Amelie. "Exit the carriage and Mr. White will be taken straight to Hampton House."

Amelie looked at him and then at the other two henchmen, her anger and fear making her want to scream. Instead, she imagined Sally and the calm business end of her derringer. Amelie exhaled. She could pretend.

"Mr. Radcliffe, you should know that if Mr. White is not delivered immediately to Hampton House, if any harm befalls him at all, you will never see a penny of my family's money." She looked him in the eyes, feeling her own blaze. "Do you see that I am telling you the truth?"

He finally smiled. "My dear, I believe you are." He nodded to Burton. "Return the boy to the address where you retrieved Miss Hampton."

Amelie pointed at Burton. "I can only assume you will be

paid well for your services, and I can assure you I have access to far more resources than Mr. Radcliffe does. The same condition holds. If that boy"—she thrust her finger at Sammy—"is hurt in any way, you will not receive your money. That will be the least of your worries."

Burton nodded, and to his credit, he did not smile or laugh at her. Perhaps he believed what she said.

Amelie stepped out, taking Radcliffe's hand, and Sammy shouted and began struggling. She grasped his thin shoulders and bent down. "Get into the carriage. Mr. Radcliffe intends me no harm, and before you can blink, I shall be with you at Hampton House." She paused as the boy's eyes filmed over with unshed tears. "Sammy, I cannot be distracted with worry over you. Promise me you will return to the house and remain with Sally. Eva is beside herself with sadness at your absence, not to mention the fact that she desperately needs an assistant." Amelie managed a gentle smile.

He finally nodded, and she released him. To her surprise, he threw his arms around her middle and squeezed. Before she could respond, he climbed into the carriage, and Burton locked the door behind him.

"That was beautifully done, my dear." Radcliffe wrapped his fingers around Amelie's arm and pulled her back as the carriage drove away. "You nearly had me convinced that you will be with him soon."

"What do you want with me?"

"Straight to the point, I see. You're a far cry from the girl who couldn't look me in the eye when we met." He nudged her to a carriage inside the warehouse. Two horses stamped as the second henchman checked the components, securing them to the conveyance.

"You are nothing like the man I thought you were when first we met." She looked at him in the building's dim light. How had she thought him so unbelievably handsome?

As they circled around the carriage, she noted a large trunk secured to the back. She swallowed. "Are we going somewhere?"

CHAPTER 31

Could there be a day more joyful than one's wedding day? Years' worth of dreams made manifest from the flowers to the dresses.

—From "Essays on Eternal Bliss" by Miss A. Hampton,
THE MARRIAGE GAZETTE

Radcliffe held out his hand to help her climb in to the carriage, but when Amelie stalled, he shoved her. She landed hard on her sore arm and grunted. As she climbed fully into the seat and he entered behind her, she rubbed her arm and said, "You've done enough damage to me, don't you think?"

He chuckled. "Fortunately you did not die that day. Had that happened, I should have been forced to use one of the other girls, and you are by far the easiest of the three."

As much as she told herself the comment didn't matter, it stung, because it reinforced what she already believed about herself. The trouble was, Radcliffe was canny, and she suspected he already knew her insecurities. He would have her defeating herself if she wasn't careful, and she steeled herself for battle.

Radcliffe rapped the ceiling with his cane, and the carriage slowly moved forward. As she looked at the cane, a puzzle piece snapped into place. "That! That was what you used to strike me."

He looked at it. "Well, yes. What else should I have used?"

She shook her head. "I had almost believed that as horrible as you are, you were not the one who attacked me that day."

"Silly girl. You'd left me no choice. The flat should have been empty. The police had been there the night before until all hours, and I couldn't risk showing my face."

"What were you looking for?"

"A letter."

"From Reverend Flannery."

He looked at her, expression cold. "Yes. Jacob Stern was brave before he had a knife to his throat. He goaded me before a room of people and thought I would leave it alone?" He shook his head. "The fool was supposed to have remained in Bucharest. The fact that I returned to London should never have been an issue. He saw me one day and wrote to the reverend demanding money in exchange for his silence regarding an . . . incident. Stern was expecting a response any day and said that if I left him alone, he would share the bounty. Of course, it would not do for the police to find correspondence at Stern's flat that connected me to him."

She decided against acknowledging his reference to Vivien. "The letter did arrive, only that morning before I did. I thought you must have known of its existence, because you searched my reticule for it that night in the hospital."

It was an assumption on her part that he neither confirmed nor denied. His expression remained impassive.

"The letter does not refer to you as 'Radcliffe,' only 'Smith.' I doubt Mr. Stern knew you had adopted that name. *None* of us knew you as 'Smith.' The letter was not worth your time."

His face hardened. "I did not know that, did I? Besides, it mattered not—you and your 'old family friend' reasoned enough to travel to Wickelston and ask questions."

She quietly sighed. "After which, the good reverend told you we had been there."

"The good reverend is a father to me. You would do well to treat him with respect."

"He has nothing to do with me."

"He will once we are married." Radcliffe smiled. "Just as we shall maintain close and loving ties with your family, so we shall with mine."

Her heart pounded painfully. "Why do you assume I shall play along cheerfully? I am not a willing participant, and my acting skills are not good enough to fool anyone."

"I suggest you sharpen those skills, my dear, or else I foresee your family succumbing to 'accidents,' one at a time."

"Your accidents leave much to be desired." The element of scorn in her voice was not forced.

He looked at her sharply. "Explain yourself."

"Marie Verite's body was disinterred in Marseilles."

A muscle worked in his jaw.

"Her autopsy showed bathwater in her lungs, not river water. Did you not read the evening paper? The inquest details were laid bare. I suspect the verdict will come in early tomorrow, because the evidence was damning. A trial is looming in your future. If you hadn't been so preoccupied with planning the details of my abduction, you might have heard."

His face turned red enough that she saw it in the passing light of the streetlamps. "She was my wife! They had no right to disinter her or perform an autopsy!" His voice rang in the carriage, and she flinched.

She pressed her advantage, hoping to keep him distracted so that if Michael and the others did manage to track them down, Radcliffe would not notice until it was too late. "I suspect jurisdictional trifles will be sorted in the courts. The French police certainly felt their actions were justified, as she was still officially a French citizen and buried in the family plot on French soil. At your direction."

She nearly smiled. She found it easier to maintain her calm even as he grew increasingly agitated. As unpredictable as it made his behavior, it was a boon to her wounded pride at having ever been so taken in by his false charm. She'd been fooled, and now she was the one stripping back the layers to reveal the corrosion beneath.

"You walk on thin ice, my dear." His nostrils flared.

"If you lay a hand on me, Sally will never believe I am happy in your company."

He smiled. "I know where to strike so that the world is blissfully unaware."

"I do not believe you have the luxury of taking such a risk. From what I have learned in recent days, your need for money is truly desperate. Your life is forfeit should your debts go unpaid."

He sucked in a deep breath, looked out the window, and then exhaled. He smiled again, and this time it chilled her. "You shall remain intact for now, my darling, but there will come a day when I am no longer in need of your services."

"And you will dispatch me with the same efficiency as you did poor Mr. Stern."

He scoffed. "Poor Mr. Stern is in a far better place. He grew to near manhood in a normal home! With a normal family! And still, he was pathetic." He shook his head. "Stammering and begging and attempting to exchange his life for a share of the extortion money. As if I would ever participate in a plan that would endanger the man who thought of me as his son."

The events began playing in Amelie's head as though she was reading it straight from one of the novels she loved so much. "You confronted Mr. Stern that night, exchanged words. You knew if he told the world your secrets, your life was finished." She shook her head. "You couldn't allow him to live; you never planned to. You had to silence him immediately, for if he was willing to taunt you in public, no matter how vague the words, you knew he would cause problems the moment he was free."

She leaned forward in the seat. "You agreed to share the reverend's extortion money. Then you forced him into the sarcophagus, stabbed him, and slammed the door shut."

She was breathless, and her words hung heavy in the silence.

"You should write penny dreadfuls, my dear."

"Which part is fiction?"

"Oh, it's all true. I didn't realize I was gaining such a creative wife." He smiled and crossed his legs as though they were going for a pleasant Sunday drive.

The carriage stopped, and she looked out the window at a nondescript building with no signage. A single light burned in a window near the entrance. The driver climbed down, met someone at the door, and returned with a parcel. She fought despair as she realized Charlotte had probably not picked up their trail after leaving the rendezvous point for the exchange with Sammy. The police would search the area, but what if they didn't find Amelie in time?

Radcliffe watched her closely, eyes narrowed, lips curled in a smirk.

She hated to give him the satisfaction of asking, but she had to know. "What is that?"

The driver climbed back to his seat and clicked the horses forward. They rounded a corner and picked up speed.

"What is that?" she repeated.

"A marriage license, procured through private contacts."

She stared at him, her chest rising and falling in uneven breaths. She knew Radcliffe planned to marry her, but certainly such a thing couldn't happen so quickly, unless . . . "Are you taking me to Gretna Green?"

"Gretna Green?" he repeated. "That is much too far away. No, we are going to visit family."

His words settled around her like a heavy weight. He was taking her to Wickelston, where the reverend would marry them with or without her consent.

"I will not do this."

"You will do this. Come now, Amelie, do not become hysterical. You know how much is at stake for you if you cause problems. Your family is painfully vulnerable, even with a pair of constables patrolling night and day."

Remain calm. Remain calm. Think.

"Not to mention the precarious position of Detective Baker's loved ones, hidden away in their 'secure' cottage."

Her eyes burned with tears she tried desperately to keep at bay. How did he know so much? How was he able to always be one step ahead of them? "You'll be arrested by morning, you know."

"Did I not mention our wedding travels? By tomorrow morning, we shall be far, far away. The reverend is generous in his gifts."

Her vision blurred, and she looked out the window,

desperate for a way to save herself. She noted a bridge, but she was so turned around she did not even know which one it was. Her breath came in shallower gasps, and a ringing in her ears had her wondering if she would faint.

She heard a far-off whistle, so distant she might have imagined it. It stilled her mind enough that she again was in the center of the maelstrom, calm while everything else spun. She closed her eyes, prayed for help, and then lunged at the door.

CHAPTER 32

You must fight, my female friends, and never stop. If under attack, you must endeavor to forget all you have learned about proper behavior and claw your way to freedom. Others in your life may have alternate suggestions, but if they do not involve kicking and biting, clawing and hitting, you may safely disregard them.
—Mrs. Thornburg's Motivational Pamphlet for
Self-Protection Against Nefarious Attack

*(A single print run was made, but a few remaining copies
may be found in the back of the occasional bookshop or
kicked under the shelves at the lending library.)*

Amelie wrenched the handle down and leaned out of the moving carriage as it crossed the threshold of the bridge. Her sudden movement caused the carriage to bounce, throwing her shoulders forward even as Radcliffe shouted and lunged for her. He tore the door from her hand, reaching for her wrist and missing.

Her shoulder hit the cobblestones, but before she could roll free, Radcliffe grabbed her ankle. She was dragged along the ground, stunned, her fingers scrambling for purchase that kept slipping away.

Radcliffe shouted to the driver, who had noticed the mayhem

and tried to halt the horses. They were nearly to the middle of the bridge before he managed it, and Amelie seized the moment to jerk her ankle free.

She crawled, then scrambled, tripping on her skirt as she reached the railing. Using it as a guide, she started running into the dense fog rising from the river.

Radcliffe shouted behind her, and she heard the driver cursing. Was nobody around? Would nobody see them?

She drew in as much of the thick air as she could manage and screamed as she ran, her breath coming in gasps. Her coat was torn and snagged on the bridge. She fumbled with the fastenings as she moved, trying to free herself from it.

She had finally pulled her arm from the confines of the tight sleeve when she was struck on the neck from behind. Clinging desperately to the railing atop the sides, she stayed on her feet and turned in time to see Radcliffe's cane coming down at her again.

"Help!" Her scream echoed down the bridge and along the water. The shout cost her, as she struggled to draw in another decent breath.

She blocked the cane with both arms, protecting her head. He flipped it sideways and shoved it against her shoulders, smashing her back against the hard stones.

She brought up her knee, catching the inside of his thigh, and he grunted, shifting enough that she was able to wrench her arms against the cane and push it back toward him. His face was inches from hers, and he didn't utter a word. The look in his eyes was feral, and she knew she was staring at her own death.

No! Her screams echoed through her head as her vision blurred. She brought her knee up again, this time causing him enough pain that he bent toward her, and she shoved up against the cane.

Using his shoulders to shove her back, he lifted her from the ground, bending her painfully against the railing.

She sucked in a huge breath and managed to gasp "Stop!" even as he lifted her higher. He pushed with such force that she feared her spine would snap over the edge of the rail. Her arm slipped out from under the cane, and he crushed the hard metal into her chest. The world slowed as he moved his hands from the cane to her throat, his eyes bulging as he squeezed. He shook her by the throat, and her feet dangled in the air.

She scrambled for a grip on the railing. Her hat shifted back on her head as her hair began to slide free from its pins. As her arm flailed in one last desperate attempt to grab hold of something, her fingers brushed a crystal flower.

She clasped the hatpin and pulled it out, clutching it in her fist like a dagger. With her remaining strength, she stabbed it into her attacker, not knowing where it would connect.

Radcliffe gave a harsh shout and, shoving her away from him, threw her into the cold night air. She tumbled back, terrified to see the bridge moving farther away from her.

She stretched her arm, watching her fingers grasp at air, in fractions of moments that lasted an eternity. She thought if she could just reach a little higher, she would catch herself.

With a jarring, blindingly painful crash, she connected with the icy water, gasping one last breath before the river pulled her under.

CHAPTER 33

"Aunt Sally?"

"Yes, Amelie?"

"Where shall I find my true love?"

"You are but seven years old, dearest. You needn't fuss about it now."

"Oh, but I am not fussing! I simply want to be sure I shall know him when I see him."

Michael's blood ran cold as a terrified scream tore through the night. Riding horseback, he reached the middle of the bridge just as unmistakable sounds of a faint splash echoed from below. "Amelie!"

He dismounted and ran through the fog, seeing the carriage moments before he would have crashed into it. He dodged to the side and collided with Radcliffe, who staggered and fell against him. He grabbed the man's hair and pulled, shouting, "Where is she?"

Radcliffe turned his head, and Michael saw Amelie's hatpin protruding from the side of his neck.

Michael dropped the man to the ground and dashed to the

side of the bridge. The river appeared through intermittent gaps in the fog, and he saw a white hand break the surface of the water seconds before it went under.

He stripped off his coat and vaulted up and over the side of the bridge, bracing himself for the impact, which was nearly paralyzing in its freezing grip. He kicked back to the surface against the strong current, gulping in air as he scanned the dark waters for any sign of Amelie. He swam a distance, glancing up at the bridge and trying to judge where he had last seen her.

Amelie, please, please fight. Surface just once more . . .

He saw a ripple to his left and lunged for it despite knowing he might have imagined it. He dove beneath the surface, but the water below was an inky, muffled world. He heard only the rushing current and his beating heart.

He forced himself down as far as he could, and his fingers brushed against something. With renewed hope, his lungs burning, he shoved hard against the current one more time and clasped a handful of fabric.

Pulling upward with every last bit of strength, he neared the surface. As he swam, he made contact with an arm. He finally erupted from the water and gasped in a breath. He turned the body over, feeling long strands of hair against his hands, and positioned his arm across Amelie's body, holding her above the river's waves.

He began pulling with his other arm and kicking for the shore as he heard shouts from the bridge, and the long, loud blast of a constable's whistle. Barking dogs sounded from the shore, and he heard Winston's voice as he ran the length of the bridge to the other side.

He struggled for breath, terrified he was too late, when he heard a splash and saw Winston approaching with long, even strokes. When he reached Michael, he breathed, "Here, let me take her, mate. You just swim, I'll be right beside you."

Michael reluctantly lifted his arm, now numb with cold, and took his first look at Amelie's face, which was pale, her lips blue. He let out a sob, a harsh, gasping sound, and tried to touch her face with fingers that shook and tangled in her hair.

"Swim," Winston said firmly. "Michael, go. I've got her. We must get her to shore."

With limbs that struggled to obey, he swam again for the shore, breathing raggedly as his feet touched the riverbed. He staggered out of the water and collapsed, registering a flurry of activity as people rushed toward him. Someone placed a blanket around his shoulders, and as Winston dragged Amelie up beside him, he heard Dr. Neville's gruff voice.

"Turn her on her side, turn her on her side!" The old man approached, cane thumping in the mud and rocks, and bent down next to Michael.

Winston coughed and pulled in a deep breath, and Michael placed his blanket around Amelie as Winston followed the doctor's instructions. He turned Amelie toward Michael, and Michael leaned down next to her face.

"Please, you must awaken, Amelie." His voice caught. "Your aunt will be furious with you if you do not awaken—" He grasped her cold fingers, absently registering the setting, the familiar smells, the very same bank where they had pulled Marie Verite from the cold river months before.

"Pound on her back," Dr. Neville barked at Winston, and as Amelie's limp form moved with each hit, Michael's desperation grew.

He clutched her hand tightly, resting his forehead against it.

Winston continued thumping between her shoulder blades,

and her body rolled toward him each time in a false animation that was especially cruel.

Tears fell from his eyes and flowed onto her hand. "Dearest, please. Amelie, I love you. You mustn't leave, I haven't proposed." He felt a sob crush his chest, a raging emotion that he hadn't felt since he was a young child, hiding alone in his room after his father's funeral.

Anger and frustration surged, and he finally shouted, "Amelie!"

Winston thumped her back again, and this time she coughed.

Michael looked up, daring to hope as she continued to cough and spurt water. He sat up, pulling her over his legs as she gagged and cleared her lungs.

A collective sigh of relief circled through the group gathered at the water's edge. Dr. Neville crossed himself and then whistled for a stretcher. Winston scrambled to his feet and ran to help Dr. Neville.

Amelie shuddered and struggled to breathe, still coughing and gagging. He rubbed circles across her back and murmured nonsensical things that would probably embarrass him later. He didn't care, and as she finally began drawing regular breaths, he allowed himself to believe she might truly be with him.

She pushed back from him with wobbly arms, and in the light of several lanterns, he caught sight of her throat, which was red and bruised. His heart thumped faster. He noticed for the first time her hands were cut, her nails torn. Now that she was warming up, blood began dripping from her fingers and the sides of her hands.

She fell limply against his chest, but she was still breathing. She placed her hand on his arm, barely squeezing, but it was enough.

She whispered something he didn't hear, and he lowered his head next to her lips. "*Now* you propose?" she rasped.

He laughed, stunned that he was even capable of it. She coughed again, and when she subsided, he said, "I was waiting for a good moment. I wanted to make a grand gesture, to flood you with romance." He winced at the choice of words.

"Did you just jump into the Thames to rescue me?" Her voice was scratchy and quiet.

"I did."

"That is grand enough."

He closed his eyes and kissed the top of her head. "Is that a 'yes'?"

She nodded. Her eyes were closed, but the strength in her hands increased. She gave him a squeeze. "I still wish to be officially deputized."

He laughed, and Winston, who had returned to speak with them, grinned. "If he does not deputize you, Miss Hampton, I will, gladly." He put a hand on her shoulder. "Dr. Neville would like to transport you to the hospital now."

"Stay with me, Michael?" she mumbled and coughed again, shivering.

"Of course."

"I have so much to tell you." She stiffened in his arms and lifted her head, squinting through the fog toward the bridge. "Is he dead?" Her voice was flat, and he wondered how long it would be before the shock wore off and her emotions tumbled free. Even the most hardened policemen experienced a level of disruption in the aftermath of violence, and he wished he could spare her.

He looked at Winston, who lifted a shoulder. "He was alive but unconscious when I crossed the bridge. They were loading him into the police wagon, probably for transport to the prison hospital."

She swallowed, frowning, and her brows knit. "He was killing me. I only wanted him to stop."

Michael shook his head and touched her cheek. "You acted in self-defense. I am so proud of you."

Her eyes sharpened their focus, and she looked at him. "He threw me from the bridge." She paused, then said it again, her voice still a whisper but increasing in intensity. *"He threw me from the bridge."*

"I know, dearest. He is going to stand trial on multiple charges, if he lives."

The orderlies brought the stretcher to them, and she shifted, wincing. "Where did I stab him?"

"In the neck." He watched her reaction.

She appeared to take the information in stride, looking at the bridge. "Michael," she said as she shifted over to the stretcher with a pained groan.

"Yes?"

"If you hadn't given me that hatpin, I would be dead."

He smiled and touched her cheek. "Well then, I am very glad I acted on the impulse." The thought that what she'd said was literally true was too much to absorb in the moment.

"I'll ride alongside," he told the orderlies.

The attendants carried Amelie on the stretcher to the ambulance, and Michael followed next to Winston.

"Nathaniel, I—"

Winston held up his hand. "No need. I won't pretend I didn't suffer apoplexy when I saw you jump off the bridge, but you can make it right by paying for my lunch next week."

Michael laughed, then sobered. "Thank you. For everything.

For helping me guard my family, for helping save her life—truly for everything. I am fortunate to have you as a partner and a friend."

Winston blinked and nodded, stepping back. "Likewise. Now get in the wagon before they leave you behind."

Michael touched a finger to forehead in a salute and smiled. He climbed into the ambulance beside Amelie. A medic had covered her with additional blankets and placed a pillow carefully beneath her head. He had also retrieved a roll of bandages and clean cloths, dabbing at the side of her face.

"How did you find me?" she asked Michael as he took her cold hand and warmed it between his. "I told Charlotte to telegraph the address, but then we changed carriages and left."

"She telegraphed from a station not thirty seconds' ride from the first location. When she returned to the address, she realized Radcliffe had taken you away in a different carriage. She searched the nearby streets for any sign of you. By then, we'd deployed the cavalry and dispersed to cover more ground. We heard the commotion, followed the shouting to the bridge, and—"

He pressed his lips to her hand and held it there, closing his eyes. "When I found the carriage and Radcliffe but saw no sign of you . . ." He shuddered involuntarily. "We could be facing a very different outcome now, and I wonder if I shall ever recover."

"We are not facing that outcome though, are we?" Amelie's voice was still thin, and she coughed. "Let's not dwell on something that did not happen."

He pressed another soft kiss on her knuckles. Her advice was sound, but his heart still raced.

"I think Eva should photograph my wounds," Amelie said. She coughed again, and the medic helped her turn to her side.

Michael pulled himself to the present. "Amelie, that seems rather . . . I mean, there are many other times she can memorialize you on film—"

Amelie shook her head. "No, no." She sighed. "If he is not dead, he will stand trial. He said something about fighting the findings from the French autopsy report because he hadn't given permission for it. He would probably be convicted anyway, but if he is not, we will never be safe. The only witness to the events on the bridge was his driver, and I do not know if he could be compelled to testify. If I do not have proof of what happened here, I may not be believed on my word alone. Nobody actually saw me going into the water; he could claim I was hysterical, stabbed him, and then jumped."

Michael felt that they had more than enough evidence of Radcliffe's crimes to see him hanged, but her idea was sound. He nodded. "As soon as we reach the hospital, I'll send a messenger to your family. Eva can bring her camera, and we'll take some photographs. I do not mind telling you it will not be pleasant to open his case file and be confronted daily with reminders of your ordeal."

She half smiled and closed her eyes. "I shall have Eva take a formal picture of me that you can keep on your desk."

"Do you remember our discussion by the water?"

She chuckled. "Your grand gesture?"

"Ah, good. I was concerned you'd think it was part of a nightmare."

"It was the only *good* part of a nightmare." She cracked an eye open. "You've no regrets for said gesture?"

"None. My only question is how long must I wait?"

She lifted her hand and dropped it back down. "No need to

fret on that score. I know a place where we can procure forged legal documents."

He blinked. "I'm sorry?"

She laughed.

CHAPTER 34

Dear Diary,

I have survived to my wedding day! As I reflect on recent events, I find it odd to be grateful to Harold Radcliffe for one thing: If not for him, I'd never have met Michael Baker.

I feel as though I am on the brink of a marvelous adventure. Perhaps, for some, love strikes like lightning, but for me, it crept upon me like a thief in the night. A very handsome thief, who has quite stolen my once-lonely heart.

Amelie and Michael smiled as Eva ducked under the hood attached to her camera. "Perfect," she said, lifting her head back out. "Hold." She triggered the mechanism and finished the last of the wedding photographs.

"Thank you, Eva, for accommodating such a large party." Amelie sighed.

Eva chuckled. "I've known most of these people all my life, silly. I've had years to mentally prepare."

"No, Mae, do not eat that," Charlotte said as she carried Michael's niece away from several sweets that had fallen on the ground in the garden. "Now that this child is mobile, she is an absolute menace." She tickled the baby as she wandered back toward the house. "Your mother is speaking with a very kind gentleman," she whispered to Mae she walked. "We must be on our best behavior as to not frighten him away."

Amelie looked at the Notorious Hamptons who were gathered for Amelie and Michael's wedding celebration. While she was happy to have everyone there to celebrate, and happier still for the reason they celebrated, she was restless.

Michael placed his arm around her waist and pulled her close. "We can leave anytime, you know."

She chuckled. "You mustn't tempt me. We must at least enjoy dessert. Besides, my grandmother has been dying to know all about your tailoring skills. She refused to believe me when I told her."

"And how glad I am that you told her." He looked at her flatly and then shook his head.

"I found it a worthy distraction. She does not understand why I would choose working as a detective's assistant over writing for the *Gazette*." She paused. "Truthfully, she does not understand why I want to continue working at all."

He winked. "She hasn't taken a good look at your esteemed colleague, apparently."

She pushed his arm. "Please go chat with her. I shall eat some petit fours with Alexander and the Van Horne sisters, and then we shall leave."

He sighed, but kissed her quickly and went in search of her grandmother. Amelie gazed fondly at the gardens, the lovely spring blossoms, and was grateful the weather had cooperated for the party to spill outdoors. Naturally the wedding had been held at Hampton House, and as she looked at it now, she knew she would miss it. It had been her first venture into the world away from home, and she regarded it with misty nostalgia.

The new home Michael had purchased for them was lovely, and she had enjoyed setting it up with Charlotte and Eva. She had no regrets, and while it was a bit farther from the center of Town, she had quick access to both Hampton House and the city by rail.

Radcliffe had survived Amelie's attack with the hatpin and now sat in a cell, charged with several crimes. He had dragged the court proceedings on with countersuits about his late wife's autopsy, but Amelie had the comfort of knowing that he was not a free man, nor would he be.

Police detectives in Wickelston were opening an investigation into the rumors about Reverend Flannery's administration of the boys' home. It was early, yet, but there was talk of Detective Nathaniel Winston taking the lead.

Charlotte emerged from the house, still holding Mae, who was happily chewing on her favorite toy bunny. Eva was behind her, followed by Sammy White. He was Eva's shadow, whenever possible, and accompanied her to photography assignments all over town. She directed him to the final piece of equipment that needed to be put away. He said something—probably cheeky—and grinned. Eva tousled his hair and shook her head, smiling as she joined Amelie and Charlotte.

"The dress is splendid, and you will look lovely in the photographs," Eva said to Amelie as she placed an arm around her and Charlotte. "I would call the day a success, wouldn't you?"

Amelie nodded and leaned her head on Eva's shoulder. "Is Clarissa enjoying answering correspondence for the *Gazette*?"

Amelie asked. "I worry my leaving has made too much work for everyone else."

"She is doing very well," Charlotte answered, bouncing Mae. "She does most of it from home, and when she comes to the offices, she brings this little menace!" She nuzzled the baby's cheek with her nose, and Mae laughed. Charlotte glanced at Amelie. "Do not fret, darling. While we certainly miss you, we are managing well."

"Have you spoken with Sally about her offer to pay for school?" Amelie asked Charlotte.

Charlotte frowned. "Not yet. I am still undecided."

Eva gave Charlotte a squeeze. "It is fine, Char. We are all afraid now and again."

"I am not afraid," Charlotte snapped, and Eva winked at Amelie.

"I am merely saying," Eva continued, "that big decisions are overwhelming at times. And even though something that may be perfectly suited to one presents itself—dare I say, is practically handed to one on a silver platter—one often shrugs it aside and doesn't give a fig for the possibility of regrets."

Amelie laughed, and Charlotte scowled at them both. "This baby has eaten far too many sweets today. I am going to hand her straight to you when I see the tell-tale signs of her discomfort."

The back door opened, and Amelie heard Michael saying, "And that is how I would hem a pair of tweed trousers." He poked his head outside and looked at her directly, neither smiling nor frowning.

Amelie laughed again, and Charlotte, smirking, said, "I cannot believe you sent him into the lion's den. Between your grandmother, the siblings, the aunts, uncles, and unruly cousins, it's a wonder he's still here."

Eva hugged Amelie and kissed her cheek. "You'd best rescue the poor man. Enjoy your holiday. We will be here when you return."

"I love you, girls."

"We love you too," Charlotte said, her eyes bright. She waved her hand. "Now go!"

Amelie caught Michael just inside the door, and they headed for the parlor, where Sally was explaining the resurgence of the Arts and Crafts movement to a small crowd of detectives from the Yard, Director Ellis, and Charlotte's six elder brothers, who were surprisingly mellow with age.

She grasped Sally in a warm embrace. "It is time we were off."

"I am so very proud of you," Sally whispered in Amelie's ear.

Amelie's eyes burned. "I love you, Sally. Thank you for always taking care of me. From the very beginning."

Michael waved, Amelie made her goodbyes, and they escaped out of the front entrance where their carriage was waiting, their luggage already secured in place.

They climbed inside, but before Amelie could settle into the seat, Michael pulled her onto his lap. She laughed as he kissed a spot on her neck just behind her ear, but soon relaxed into a sigh as the carriage pulled forward and Michael traced his lips along her jaw.

"I adore you, Mrs. Baker," he whispered.

"I adore you, Detective Baker." She took his face in her hands and softly kissed his lips. "How glad I am you caught me spying all those months ago."

"Fortunately for me, you let me catch you." He smiled

against her mouth and softly nipped. "And now I have the benefit of a wife and a deputy all in one."

She laughed and wrapped her arms around his neck. "One of these days, I do hope you make it official."

"I believe I just did." He smiled, and then he kissed her, and as the carriage traveled the short distance to the train station, she lost all desire for any further conversation.

ACKNOWLEDGMENTS

This book was written during a global pandemic, and while it ought to have been a simple endeavor, I found it very difficult. As always, though, the writing process itself was a familiar comfort. Even while the world was full of chaos, I took refuge in solving Amelie's and Michael's problems. That much, I figured, was under my control.

To my family—my humble and grateful thanks, especially to my little niece, Lucy, who gifted me with her seven-volume series about a flower, complete with illustrations. Along with the stories, she included a note of encouragement that I carry with me all the time.

To Shadow Mountain, specifically Lisa Mangum and Heidi Taylor Gordon, along with Chris Schoebinger, Heather Ward, Rachael Ward, Troy Butcher, and Callie Hansen—thank you all for helping and cheering this process along.

To my agents, Pam Pho and Bob DiForio—gratitude always and forever. I can—and do—email with questions day and night, and the responses are always quick and reassuring.

To my writing community, and especially Jennifer Moore (*Inventing Vivien*), Josi Kilpack (*Rakes and Roses*), Cory Anderson (*What Beauty There Is*), and Margot Hovely (*Time's Dagger*)—this would be a painful and lonely process without you. Every time I have plot problems, a brainstorming session fixes everything.

To readers and reviewers and everyone posting amazing pictures of my books on Instagram—thank you for your support! I am in awe of this community and the support you offer; glowing reviews as well as tactful constructive criticism for books you might not have loved means so much to an author. Your kindness and professionalism is so very much appreciated.

Discussion Questions

1. The "Lonely Hearts" advertisements were essentially the social media dating platform of the Victorian Era. Do you think dating and finding a partner is easier now than it was then? What elements have remained the same? If you were to write a Lonely Hearts ad for yourself or a friend, what would you say?

2. Amelie believes that true love is sudden and inevitable, like fireworks, but comes to realize that it can also be a slow and subtle change, like the warmth of a cozy fireplace. What points in the story helped trace Amelie's changing feelings about love? Do you believe in "love at first sight"?

3. Detective Michael Baker loves his job despite its inherent dangers, and he has sworn to never marry in order to protect those he loves—and himself—from future heartbreak. Do you think he was right to do so? Is love always worth the risk?

4. Amelie and her cousins, Eva and Charlotte, take pride in being "Women of Independent Means." What do you think that phrase meant in Victorian England? What do you think that phrase means in today's society?

5. Both Amelie and Michael have a strong support system with their respective families. Amelie's cousins are always there to cheer her on and consult with her. Michael's sister and nephew

provide him a safe place to relax and leave behind the stress of his job. Who do you have in your support system who are your cheerleaders and your protectors?

6. Ethel and Margaret Van Horne are eccentric sisters who love Egyptian history. What hobbies, pursuits, or collections do you have that might surprise others to learn of?

7. Sally Hampton has traveled the world and brought back many souvenirs and items of interest. If you could travel anywhere in the world, where would you go, what would you see, and what would you bring back home with you?

𝔄BOUT THE 𝔄UTHOR

NANCY CAMPBELL ALLEN is the award-winning author of eighteen published novels and several novellas, which encompass a variety of genres, ranging from contemporary romantic suspense to historical fiction. Her most recent books, which include Regency, Victorian, and steampunk romance, are published under Shadow Mountain's Proper Romance brand, and the What Happens in Venice novella series is part of the Timeless Romance Anthology collection published by Mirror Press. She has presented at numerous conferences and events since her initial publication in 1999.

Her agent is Pamela Pho of D4EO Literary Agency.

Nancy loves to read, write, travel, and research, and enjoys spending time with family and friends. She nurtures a current obsession for true crime podcasts and is a news junkie. She and her husband have three children, and she lives in Ogden, Utah, with her family, one very large Siberian Husky named Thor, and an obnoxious but endearing YorkiePoo named Freya.